About the Novel

Down in Laos is a superbly written war story set in Southeast Asia during the seizure of *USS Pueblo*, the Tet Offensive, and the Battle of Khe Sanh in 1968.

Down in Laos is not a tiny story. It is a classic suspense, action-thriller about a naval ship, an air wing, and a pilot who is shot down and becomes a prisoner of the Pathet Lao.

Mr. Partel entertains his readers in page-turning style, and leaves them a little smarter about the world. His self-described genre—journalistic fiction—brings historical observations and ideas to the attention of the reader. So when downed navy pilot, Lt. Campbell, becomes a prisoner of war brutalized at the hands of the Pathet Lao, his plight parallels the Book of Job and subtly provides a comparison of Western Civilization with totalitarian states that lack a moral compass. Mr. Partel's sense of history does not ignore the social issues of the mid-1960's in military and civilian life, and in the tradition of *South Pacific*, *Down in Laos* touches on these issues briefly but deftly.

This is authentic historical fiction about the naval air war in Southeast Asia for avid military readers. And for readers who want the historical background and the social context reminiscent of Patrick O'Brian's naval novels of the Napoleonic Wars, they will find this tradition carried forward 150 years as *USS Ticonderoga*, Attack Carrier 14, succeeds the frigate in this well-written yarn of modern naval fiction.

— Navy Log Books

What US Navy Pilots Who Flew the Missions are Saying

"...extraordinary, riveting saga....captures the tension of the height of the Cold War, the rising toll of the war in Vietnam....will leave you feeling like you've "been there—done that." A compassionate story of faith and determination, Down in Laos is an important read that tells it like it was."

Jay "Rabbit" Campbell, RADM USN (ret.), fighter pilot, 163 missions in Vietnam and Desert Storm

"I've read nearly every book about aviation in Southeast Asia during the Vietnam War. Frank Partel's book, one of the best, is a page turner...I couldn't put it down....I highly recommend it."

Attack pilot, Paul Galanti, CDR, USN (ret.) Vietnam 11/65 - 2/73, the last 6 years and 8 months as a POW

"An ambitious bite out of the apple of sea going life with a high degree of credibility....the life and times of Tonkin Gulf carrier air operations during the Vietnam War. Military, professional or layman, you will enjoy this book."

Richard "The Beak" Stratton, CAPT, USN (ret.), naval aviator and POW, 1967-73 for 2,251 days

What Others are Saying

"....suspenseful and noteworthy....Mr. Partel has managed to marry the moral and ethical discussion with an action-suspense format....a heightened sense of understanding that Mr. Partel's characters provide about what the hell really happened during Vietnam.

*Jack Shea, **Martha's Vineyard Times***

Down in Laos

NAVY LOG BOOKS

Modern naval fiction for sophisticated readers

Published by Navy Log Books,
a division of Navy Log, LLC,
1905 Bay Road, Suite 210
Vero Beach, FL 32963

ISBN 978-0-9893059-1-4

Printed in the United States of America

Also by

Francis J. Partel, Jr.

A Wound in the Mind,
The Court-Martial of Lance
Corporal Cachora, USMC

The Chess Players,
A Novel of the US Navy's Cold War at Sea

NAVY LOG BOOKS

The scriptures, written long ago, were all written for our instruction, in order, through the encouragement they give us, we may maintain our hope with perseverance.

The Letter of Paul to the ROMANS 15:4

FRANCIS J. PARTEL, JR.

Down in Laos

HEROISM & INSPIRATION
DURING THE VIETNAM WAR

NAVY LOG BOOKS

Dedication

Down in Laos is dedicated to:

- the US military chaplains who serve
  the Armed Forces of the United States, and to,

- the 20 crewmen from crews Two, Five, and Seven
  of Observation Squadron 67 (VO-67) who were
  killed in action in 1968, and to,

- all American servicemen,
  especially US Navy and Air Force pilots,
  who lived the hell on earth of prisoners of war
  during the Vietnam War.

Author's Note and Acknowledgment

I needed the help of several wonderful people to whom I am very grate-
fully indebted while writing *Down in Laos*.

As in my last novel, I have been the beneficiary of Steve Feinberg's
experience as a screenwriter. His advice, encouragement and wisdom have
been particularly welcome and useful throughout the creation of this
novel. I'm not sure that without Steve's words in my ear, "Keep writing!"
and the memories of his words in my mind that I would have completed
Down in Laos without them.

I am also deeply appreciative of the technical assistance and support
that I received from two naval aviators who flew attack aircraft from the
decks of carriers on Yankee Station in the Gulf of Tonkin at various times
during the Vietnam War.

Lt. Colonel Patrick N. Rounds, USAFR, flew military attack aircraft
for over 28 years. Before he flew with the USAF Reserve, he flew 98
combat missions in the A-7E Corsair from the deck of *USS Coral Sea*
CVA-43 while on active duty as a lieutenant with the US Navy. Subsequently he flew the A-7D with the Iowa Air National Guard. Though not
an A-4 Skyhawk pilot, Patrick's general knowledge of strike warfare, pilot
training, especially SERE (survival, escape, resistance and evasion) training, and his combat experience over North Vietnam filled in a lot of the
blanks in my knowledge of naval air operations.

Captain Kenneth "Dutch" Rauch, USN (ret.) has over 150 combat missions over Vietnam in the A-4F Skyhawk. He transitioned to the A-7E and
flew variously from the decks of *Ticonderoga, Oriskany, Enterprise,
Midway, and Kitty Hawk.* After commanding a squadron, Dutch was
commanding officer of Training Air Wing 2. Dutch's specific knowledge
of the A-4 Skyhawk and air operations in 1968 were extremely helpful in
writing this story. Dutch and I have only recently gotten to know each
other despite the fact that we both made the 1968 WestPac deployment
together in *USS Ticonderoga* CVA-14.

Dutch was a junior pilot with Attack Squadron 23 (VA-23) while I was
one of the ship's two strike controllers, and we undoubtedly dined in the
wardroom together and communicated many times on Button 8, Panther
Strike's radio frequency. Neither of us recalls meeting each other in person in 1968. That in itself is a statement about life aboard an aircraft carrier at sea with 3500 officers and men aboard.

Ed Witt was an Aviation Machinist Mate, Petty Officer First Class with Observation Squadron 67 (VO-67) and flew as a crewman. "The Ghost Squadron," its mission, and Operation Igloo White were classified top secret for 25 years. I'm grateful to Ed for providing me with first hand information on VO-67's operations in 1968 and their innovative contribution to the American effort during the Vietnam War.

I am also indebted to many humbling stories of courage that I have read which were told or written by American prisoners of war about their incarcerations during the Korean and Vietnam Wars. I am especially indebted to Dieter Dengler's story who is one of only two US Navy pilots downed in Laos and to have escaped, survived the jungle and to have been recovered. So too, I am indebted to Alice and Dick Stratton who invited me to lunch at Atlantic Beach, FL. I thought I had finished *Down in Laos*, but after meeting "The Beak" and his wife, I made subtle revisions to the story. Captain Richard A. Stratton, USN (ret.) was held as a prisoner of war in North Vietnam for over six years. His capture was the result of a malfunction of his plane's ordnance. As Dick said "one can make choices in life," and after active duty with the navy, Dick became a clinical social worker and put himself at service to others. My character, Lt. Campbell's story is a fictionalized composite of the brutal experiences encountered by many of these American heroes.

In my quest for understanding the *Book of Job*, I read several exegeses of the text, some with multiple, polysyllabic words that had me searching the dictionary frequently with little illumination to me as a lay reader. However I found the *Oxford Study Bible* the most useful Bible in my quest, and I am particularly indebted to Jack Miles, an exceptionally gifted scholar, for his extremely erudite, Pulitzer Prize winning book, *God, a Biography*.

Finally, as in the past, this novel might never have appeared if it weren't for my very able, former administrative assistant, Linda Reese, who always cracks the code on the mysteries of word processors that confound me.

Any errors or omissions are entirely my own.

October 1, 2014
Vero Beach, FL

Foreword

Down in Laos, Heroism and Inspiration during the Vietnam War is not a tiny story. It is a big canvas, cross-genre story about a ship, an air wing, and a pilot who is shot down and captured, and it is a story of inspiration and faith.

As with my prior novels, an earnest effort was made to ensure the historical accuracy of this fictional story, by that, I mean, at the theater level, to the best of my knowledge, the operations, dates, units, call signs, weapons, strategies, tactics and places are accurate. When place names are used, I use the names employed at that time and the slang, names, words, and phrases are those of that day.

With regard to the technologies and implements of war, I have generally referred to them generically and have avoided using the Mark/Mod or other similar jargonistic system to identify them—a criticism that was fairly and commonly made of my prior full-length novel. As a practical concession to story-telling, the radio transmissions by pilots tend to be more frequent and more detailed than in practice. Experienced air wings can form up 30 aircraft over a ship and proceed to the target with extremely frugal use of words.

I am also pleased to tell part of the untold story in Chapter 6 of Observation Squadron 67—a squadron that was itself classified top secret as well as its mission and Operation Igloo White. I have accurately reflected the skepticism aboard *Ticonderoga* about Operation Igloo White and concern for the hazards and risks for these missions, but the courage of the men in the Ghost Squadron was never doubted. VO-67's story was classified top secret for at least 25 years, accordingly its courageous contribution to the war was not widely known. The squadron quite possibly flew the most dangerous missions in the Indo-China theater dropping sensors over the Ho Chi Minh Trail at speeds of 250 knots at levels below 3000 feet—precisely the airspace and airspeeds scrupulously avoided, if at all possible, by carrier-based squadrons. During their six months of combat operations, VO-67 lost three of their 12 unique aircraft and 20 members of their squadron. In 2003, thirty five years later, their remains were returned to the United States and buried at Arlington National Cemetery.

For some readers it may come as a surprise to learn that there were active and intensive air operations over Laos. A quick look at a map (p. 297) will explain why. The Ho Chi Minh Trail was actually a system of multiple, border-agnostic trails from North Vietnam leading south, that crossed back and forth over the Vietnam and Laotian border. Furthermore, missions against Laotian targets were deliberately cloaked in secrecy from the American press and the American public and were conducted under what was referred to as Operation Steel Tiger. Steel Tiger missions were a fraction of the missions and sorties conducted over North Vietnam during Operation Rolling Thunder, however, the Laotian parts of the Ho Chi Minh Trail were neither respected by the US nor by the North Vietnamese and were no less defended than the Vietnamese portions. The losses were generally proportional to the respective frequency of the missions. However, the probability of recovery for a downed pilot or ultimate return from Laos was significantly lower than the abysmal return rates for pilots shot down over North Vietnam.

One of the decisions taken by some men, who witness first hand the human carnage and destruction of combat, is that a few such men choose the clergy and dedicate their lives to facilitating peace among men. My character, The Reverend Ogilvy Osborne, better known as O, makes this decision in the frozen hills of Korea similar to the experience of Major Paul Moore, USMCR at Iwo Jima. Moore later became Episcopal Bishop of New York, and had been awarded the Navy Cross for heroism at Guadalcanal. Osborne returns as a navy chaplain, and he and a young Roman Catholic priest are called to serve at Khe Sanh. During the Vietnam War military chaplains were at the nexus of many moral, ethical, and political conflicts. I took just one of these conflicts and portrayed it to represent the physical courage and moral decisions taken by these chaplains to serve the religious needs of American servicemen.

I have deliberately intended without embarrassment to develop the religious theme of this novel. There are many reasons why some men survived the brutality of being prisoners of war during the Korean and Vietnam conflicts, but a nearly universal testament cited by virtually all POWs was having faith in God. So Campbell's faith, and his occasional doubts, are in every way a truthful and accurate part of the American POW experience during these wars.

Joseph Conrad in *Heart of Darkness* draws our attention to the regression in man's behavior as he moves beyond civilization. Regrettably, not all civilized societies hold a benign view of *all* men. War does not square with the morality, ethics and teachings of God. In fact, what we cherish and celebrate most about Western Civilization—its emphasis on the dignity and the inalienable rights of the individual is derived directly from the notion that a god which is moral and just must by definition appreciate "rights," between himself and among his people. The very notion of justice acknowledges by definition that certain entitlements exist, and that there are legitimate claims which are deserving, and meritorious. Without these God's decisions cannot not be just, but must be viewed as arbitrary. But that is not the case. The Ten Commandments, given to Moses by God, clearly suggest the existence of rights when they enjoin certain behaviors, as for example, when it can be said that one has a right not to be victimized by theft, or one has a right not to have false witness borne against one. So, too, does Jesus teach that there are certain duties and obligations—rights—between master and servant. As my character, Cannon, suggests, the history of Western Civilization may be fairly said to be the History of Christianity, and the Judean-Christian teachings are the moral and ethical compass of Western Civilization, and the notion of the sanctity of the individual, not always complied with by men, distinguishes it historically from all other major civilizations.

Nevertheless, in the main, this is a suspense-action thriller about the American air war over Indo-China, especially about the US Navy and US Air Force over Vietnam and Laos, during the first half of 1968. This was an ominous time in the war. During this period the *USS Pueblo* was seized by the North Koreans in international waters, the Battle of Khe Sanh took place just south of the Demilitarized Zone on the Laotian border, and the Tet Offensive occurred across South Vietnam—all of which may have been coordinated, sequenced events by mutually cooperative communist nations to stretch American resources. It is also the time when American public opinion began to shift significantly against the war, and when Operation Rolling Thunder, the heart of the air war over North Vietnam, was scaled back as the Johnson Administration signaled, with various bombing halts, the American desire for peace negotiations.

Down in Laos is also a novel of its times and does not ignore topical issues nor ideas of the period. Despite the rhetoric and controversy of the anti-war movement, I believe it can be fairly said that the American cause was a just and noble cause to end North Vietnamese subversion and aggression against a fledgling, albeit, a corrupt and imperfect democracy, at a time when there were perhaps no more than two dozen liberal democracies in the world.

It might also have been entitled "Lieutenant Campbell's Story" as it is very much about his suffering at the hands of his Laotian adversary and his sense of injustice about his continuous suffering, and the temptation to doubt his faith in God while a prisoner of the Pathet Lao in Laos. His story is a modern allegory for the Biblical *Book of Job*.

The *Book of Job* is a remarkable book to have been included in the Bible as it tends to contradict the notion that goodness is rewarded and wickedness is punished by God. The notion of reward for living a righteous life is a core belief of Christianity. The Adversary (often translated as Satan) suggests that the blessings given to Job by God might be construed as bribes to induce Job's behavior and to secure his loyalty, and in this sense the Adversary might be said to indirectly introduce the notion of virtue without reward, that is, virtue for the sake of virtue, into Judean-Christian thought. As we learn, Job, a righteous servant of God, suffers unusual trials and tribulations at the hand of the Adversary, to the point, that Job questions the meaning and purpose of suffering, and why God should permit his suffering to occur and to continue. In despair, Job questions the authenticity of God as being a *moral* and *just* god—two critical dimensions of Yahweh/God as generally described throughout the Old Testament without which God is not God. The words *moral,* and *just* are never associated with God throughout the *Book of Job* and do not qualify the notion of God's omnipotence. So, when God answers Job, He puts a series of questions to Job, essentially saying that His power should be self-evident to Job, and His power qua power, alone, is sufficient to prove His authenticity. Moreover, this is the last time that God speaks directly to His people in the Old Testament, and no further statement is made by God to amend or clarify His words, and readers of the Bible are left perplexed without further explanation from God.

This significant departure from the way God is revealed elsewhere in the Old Testament cannot be over-emphasized and challenges a fundamental notion that distinguishes the Judean-Christian religious tradition from other gods, false gods and other religions in the Old Testament, namely, that there is but one God, a moral, just, loving, all-powerful god. Accordingly, the *Book of Job* has vexed theologians through the ages to explain, as Rabbi Kushner asks why "bad things happen to good people." In lieu of a satisfactory answer to that question, one might ask what does a mature person do with one's life as a result of being subjected to unjust suffering, and how does it affect one's search for purpose and meaning in life. *Down in Laos*, in part, explores this problematic question, and, answers it, in part, in the Epilogue.

Francis J. Partel, Jr.

Chapter 1. December 4th, 1950, Toktong Pass, Chosin Reservoir Area, Korea

A cold front of Siberian air remained over the Chosin Reservoir area driving temperatures down to 35 degrees below zero. For six days Fox Company, 2nd Battalion, 7th Marines from the First Marine Division, held the hill in the bitter cold and in the snow that controlled Toktong Pass between Yudam-ni to the north and Hangaru-ri to the south—the avenue of withdrawal for the entrapped First Marine Division. Of the 220 men comprising Fox Company who took up positions on November 28th, 1950, just 82, many of which were wounded, were able to hike off the hill. At least two efforts to relieve Fox Company failed to clear the 59th Regiment of the Peoples Volunteer Army which threatened the way for Fox Company and 3000 fellow marines to move south to the sea. Fox Company was held together by their commanding officer, badly wounded on the second day of the fight, he maintained his lines, checked his positions, and directed their efforts from a stretcher until they were eventually relieved five days later.

Kneeling in the snow, an M1 carbine cradled inside his left elbow, his gloved hands placed together, pointing towards the gray skies in prayer, was 1st Lieutenant Ogilvy Osborne, a veteran platoon leader, who was counted among the walking wounded with shrapnel wounds in his neck and shoulder. He began to recite silently the 23rd Psalm, *The Lord is my shepherd.* A navy corpsman dropped to a knee beside him. Seeing the corpsman beside him and another marine being borne on a litter asking to be brought to him, he waited and he began again aloud, "The Lord is my shepherd, I shall not want. He maketh me to lie down in green pastures..." The sounds of intermittent artillery rolled through the hills and mixed with the wumpf of mortar fire and the crackle of small arms. As he continued he was joined by several other marines whose verbal participation peaked with the words, "Yea, though I walk through the valley of the shadow of death, I will fear no evil: for Thou art with me; Thy rod and Thy staff they comfort me." Lt. Osborne continued on alone with the less well-known words. The stifled sobs of the Fox Company men and "silent tears" could be heard as he recited, "Thou preparest a table before me in the presence of mine enemies: Thou anointest my head with oil; my cup runneth over. Surely goodness and mercy shall follow me all the days of my life: and I will dwell in the house of the Lord forever."

Osborne had led his platoon ashore at Inchon and liberated Seoul with the First Marine Division. The Division and Fox Company re-embarked and were redeployed to the eastern shore of Korea at Wonsan where they began their drive to the North. Well-respected as a fighting man and very well-liked as a man, Lieutenant Osborne was now surrounded by more than a dozen men from Fox Company.

He looked around and what began as a private prayer had become a small congregation of survivors on the side of a snow covered hill. "Lord, we, the living, thank you for the breath of life. And as we are still tens of miles from the safety of the sea, we ask you for the strength to keep faith with You, Heavenly Father, and to keep faith with our fellow Marines, and to guide us through the trials before us and to spare as many of us as will suit Your Divine Plan. We also ask You, Lord, to shed perpetual light upon those who have fallen here, and we ask You, Lord, to make the wounded wh..." Here he stopped and more accurately rephrased, "to heal the wounded," before continuing. "We ask You, Lord, to help us deal with the grief we are feeling and to mourn our friends who gave their lives here so that others with names we do not know, and with names we can scarcely pronounce shall enjoy the benefits of living as free men. Finally, Heavenly Father," Osborne wiped tears from his eyes and cheeks with the back of his right glove before resuming, "I am personally asking You, and Your son, Jesus Christ, please walk with me; give me the courage and strength to do my part and lead these wonderful and brave men with wisdom. For all these things, for one and all, we ask from You, Lord. Amen."

Osborne looked around and into the hollow eyes of the men around him before speaking again. He assessed what he saw and what he experienced before beginning, "Almighty Father, about us lie the corpses, friend and foe, of over a thousand men frozen in the snow who are testament to man's organized inhumanity to man. If I should survive this day, this week, this war, Lord, I shall lay down my sword, and with You, Lord, and through You, Lord, serve You, Lord, and my fellow man. Amen."

Five years later, a letter from Seoul, Korea, 1955

October 7, 1955

The Rev. Dr. Howard L. Hall
Headmaster, Westbridge Christian School
Box 142
Westbridge, Mass.

Dear Howard,

Esther and I are grateful for your personal report on Peter's progress at Westbridge, and it pleases us much that he has been honored as a student deacon and has been elected to lead the International Club on campus. We are also grateful that you have taken a personal interest in him and have received him as a guest in your home during the holidays. Your news of his progress is very welcome as we see him so little since he has been these last four years at your school. To think that he now stands six-feet tall, well, Esther and I can hardly imagine him. We are also delighted that you are encouraging his application to Princeton with its Presbyterian connection and pleased that early discussions with their admissions staff have gone well.

We have decided not to seek a church in the States, but rather have been persuaded by the Mission that we are very needed "Korea Hands" and thereby agreed to remain here in Korea with the Mission for another two years. That will bring us to nearly a decade of bringing the teachings of our Lord, Jesus Christ to the South Koreans and to continue to bring succor to them as they rebuild their country after the Japanese occupation and the most recent conflict. As you know the Presbyterian Church, as it were, is quite ramified here in Korea, and we have agreed to lead the American mission and join with the Scottish mission, in an effort to unify it under a common council.

However, I humbly write now, Howard, for a favor. Our second son, Augustine, is quite unlike Peter. The Koreans have nicknamed Augustine, "Little Tireless One," as he has both enormous energy and stamina and an unusual degree of inner toughness. Despite our efforts he has absorbed much of post-war refugee behavior. A survival-oriented behavior which emphasizes self-preservation and a general disregard for following the rules of civil behavior. He is reserved and smiles little, much in the manner of the Koreans themselves. He has seen the senseless results of war—carnage, vast destruction, pandemic starvation—at far too young an age, and he has been hardened by it. Still he has taken well to soccer and to the martial arts where he has demonstrated remarkable skill, calmness and extraordinarily quick reflexes. He is also extraordinarily fascinated with aviation and regularly builds model airplanes and aspires someday to break free from the ground and fly. He is shorter in stature than Peter, but compact, and likely to be stronger.

Alas he is stubborn, but not entirely rigid, nor much of a scholar. Regrettably, quite unlike the Koreans, he is poorly motivated towards scholarship. Their culture views formal education as an asset that cannot be taken from a person—a lesson learned after 18 years of war over a 22 year period. Fortunately this does not extend to our faith which he practices fervently and is a cause for joy with Esther and me. He is given to petty thievery which his mother and I have overlooked as it is in the cause of snitching food and clothing for members of our refugee congregation who remain weak, famished and sickly.

Howard, we would be most grateful if you and the faculty could find it in your hearts to accept the challenge and work with our boy. He is quite bright, though not apparently on par with Peter's intellect. He was younger during the war and appears to have been scarred by the war and made resentful and is frequently given to anti-communist slogans typical of the reconstruction ethic here in the South. However, he is resourceful. The conditions here have not been conducive to learning, but Esther schooled him when we were refugees, and he remained here with us throughout the duration while Peter was mostly spared living with his grandparents and at Westbridge. There is goodness and righteousness in him, and his thievery may be excused in a Robin Hood sort of way, though he tries Esther and I mightily when it comes to the books, we take comfort that God must have a plan for so rare a combination of flaws and virtues.

Yours in Christ,
Ian
The Presbyterian Mission Seminary,

c/o Embassy of the United States
32 Sejongno, Jongno-gu Seoul 110-710
Republic of Korea

Howard L. Hall, D.D., Headmaster
Westbridge Christian School.

November 12, 1955

The Reverend and Mrs. Ian MacD. Campbell,
Teacher of Ancient History and The Holy Bible
The Presbyterian Mission Seminary,
c/o Embassy of the United States of America
32 Sejongno, Jongno-gu Seoul 110-710
Republic of Korea

Dear Ian and Esther,

I shall write briefly to allay your anxieties.
We have reserved a place for Augustine MacD. Campbell next fall in the Class of 1959. Further, I have spoken with John Clough about the need to provide financial aid; he will be contacting you forthwith about a plan for your second son.
I am certain that you and Esther are doing great, good work in Korea, and it is the very least that we at Westbridge Christian School can do to play our part.
Mary joins me and the faculty in expressing our pleasure in the honor of having your second son entrusted into our custody. We are all most delighted to have the opportunity to assist in God's plan for Augustine.

Yours in Christ, the Lord,
Howard

Four Years Later, April 1959, a Lacrosse Game

It wasn't the weather that you would choose to play a lacrosse game in. But they wanted to play. And they needed to win if they had any chance for a .500 season. And there was no calling the contest off anyway. It was a tough, rebuilding year for the Northfield Academy lacrosse team of 1959 which tested the leadership of its co-captains, Robert Cannon and Dutch Van Vechten, who were also roommates.

It is mid-April in the Berkshire Hills of Western Massachusetts and a moist, large-flake, springtime snow began falling shortly after dawn and continued to fall throughout the morning covering the field with a wet, white blanket before turning to rain around noon. The field lines had been shoveled in preparation for play. And every footprint immediately compacted into a gray slush which was tinged, here and there, green by the grass underneath. But, by the third period, the field was torn up by the players' cleats and was mostly all mud.

The temperature climbed a few degrees above freezing though it continued to rain. A steady light, chilling rain. The kind of rainy day that makes for the most miserable of lacrosse games as the leather and the gut in the wooden sticks are altered by the rain. Accurate passing and clean catches are infrequent and the hard rubber ball spends much of the game on the ground. Even cradling the ball on the run is a challenge. It was a day to score early before the field and the sticks deteriorated and before the leather gloves and the uniforms became thoroughly soaked, heavy and waterlogged. Small clouds of vapor came from the lungs beneath the helmets and cast a ghoulish atmosphere on the field. Here and there patches of fog gathered around the lacrosse field and across the Northfield campus as the warmer air wafted its way over the superficial snow.

"With this weather, more than anything else, we want to score early and play from ahead," Cannon said to his teammates before the game. But they did not.

The visiting opponents from the Westbridge Christian School scored first. Late in the second quarter, just before the first half ended, Northfield tied the score on a man-up, power play. And they scored again with just 1:48 remaining in fourth period when an errant pass was intercepted by a Northfield midfielder who quickly brought the ball down field creating a four-on-three advantage. He feinted towards Cannon as Cannon was crossing in front of the crease. When the defenseman switched to take the midfielder, the midfielder managed to get a soft pass off in the wet to Cannon who took careful aim at the goal. But his shot was off target and hit the top of the crossbar, bouncing in front of the goal and disappearing in the mud. Cannon darted after his own rebound and shoveled the ball, mud and all, behind the goalie. He thought he saw the ball and the mud flying in the right direction, when "smack," he was viciously hit from his blindside, momentarily lifting him off the ground. He was checked, full tilt by a Westbridge midfielder who was madly dashing back to defend his goal. Cannon staggered and fell immediately to the ground, unconscious, not knowing that he had scored the go-ahead goal. His helmet visor and face mask enmeshed in the cold mud as he lay motionless on the field.

The loud clunk of hard leather helmet against leather helmet alerted everyone that this was no normal collision. There was a moment of confusion and cheers erupted from the Northfield side, but they promptly died out when they realized the Westbridge goalie was frantically signaling over Cannon, lying prone in the mud, to the Northfield side for help. That brought the trainer racing onto the field, mud splashing from beneath his feet, while the school's doctor, a tall, elegant, middle-age man in a khaki storm coat, charcoal fedora, and galoshes strode purposefully with his medical bag in hand towards the team's crease attack man and co-captain. Several players from both sides were now gathered around Robert Cannon, the trainer and the doctor. Cannon still had not moved, and bright red blood was flowing freely from a cut above his left eye.

By now Dutch Van Vechten realized that Cannon was seriously injured, and he came stalking after number 23, who had delivered the heavy hit, a clean play, but nevertheless an injurious play. It didn't matter to Dutch whether it was a fair play or a foul play; Van Vechten wanted to avenge the injury to his roommate. Dutch stood in front of 23 bullying him and shoving him backwards, with medium-force, cross-checking with his stick, seeking to provoke a fight. But 23 did not respond as you might expect a competitive teenage male to react, and instead backed away. Dutch, at six feet five inches and two hundred and thirty pounds, a big man for 19 years of age, glowered at his shorter but solidly built opponent. He had heard him called "Augie" and "Ti" once or twice by his teammates in the course of the game. Now he read in black magic marker, the word, "Tireless," obviously his nickname, written above the visor of the white helmet. Coach Haselton, who taught senior English, immediately separated Dutch from 23 and ordered Dutch to the bench.

23 did not appear to be in the least bit intimidated, and he exhibited a strong sense of self-discipline and left immediately for the Westbridge bench while Mr. Haselton herded Dutch off the field with Dutch shouting, "You SOB 23. You come into my half of the field and I'll kill you. I'll kill you 23; you little shit." That drew a two minute penalty for unsportsmanlike behavior, and Northfield's remaining co-captain was ejected from

the game. Both co-captains, first-string, returning lettermen were now out of the game.

The doctor and the trainer now had Cannon sitting up, his helmet removed, and the trainer was holding a clean white towel over his wound. "Couple of stitches, Doc."

"Yup, and I'm afraid Mr. Cannon will have a damn-good headache for several days. 'Fraid he'll miss the Exeter and Dartmouth Frosh games. Could be back for Deerfield." The doctor continued his examination, and then confirmed that Cannon had suffered a concussion. "Yup, I'm sure of the concussion, Red. Judging by his eyes, I'd say behind the upper left occipital lobe. Okay, Red, let's see if we can get him on his feet."

Several minutes later the trainer, Red Walsh, and the assistant coach walked the unsteady Cannon, a white towel over his head, to the field house.

For the remaining minute and forty-eight seconds, Northfield played zone defense and broke up several Westbridge attempts at getting a good shot on goal. Number 23, who ran as eagerly as he did in the first quarter, was a dangerous threat throughout the game. After the teams lined up and shook hands at midfield, 23 ran after Cannon and caught up with him. With helmet under one arm and his stick in the other gloved hand, he bowed to Cannon, saying, "You are a most worthy opponent. Be well. May you return to the field of competition soon. God bless you."

That was all. No apology offered nor required. Simply profound respect from one worthy competitor to another worthy competitor and a blessing.

Chapter 2.

It was November 1967, and Ltjg. Robert F. Cannon, USNR, was anxious to get underway for his last at-sea period aboard the anti-submarine, aircraft carrier *USS Essex*. He was filled with ambiguous and ambivalent feelings.

Many men, like Cannon, develop a love for the sea and hold her in great affection. She floats their dreams, provides them with a means to test their mettle, and nourishes their curiosity. They travel the world upon her richening their lives beyond the rewards offered to sedentary men. The fair price for passage is vigilance and prudence—vigilance for signs of her inconstancy and the dangers represented by her awesome power and prudence with regard to their appropriate assessment. Nevertheless, Cannon loved being at sea, and he enjoyed his bridge watches and carrying the responsibility of Officer of the Deck in an American aircraft carrier with 3000 men aboard and his obligation to a captain who trusted his seamanship and judgment.

Some men avoid responsibility; others seek it. Cannon fell into the latter group, and during this particular period, *Essex* would operate without the carrier division admiral on board. Captain Meehan would be the Officer in Tactical Command, and his responsibilities for running the various task group exercises and maneuvering the formation would devolve to the Operations Officer, the navigator, and to the Officer of the Deck. Cannon loved a challenge, and despite his relatively recent qualification as OOD, he was eagerly looking to prove he was more than up to the test and that the confidence placed in him was deservedly meritorious.

He also had strong nostalgic feelings for this ship and the officers and men who served her—the first duty assignment to which he reported as a raw ensign after officer candidate school and combat information school. He had been mentored by Commander Pebbles, now a four-striper, who had moved on to a career-enhancing billet on the staff of the Chief of Naval Operations in the Pentagon. Pebbles appointed Cannon as his administrative assistant, a position that Cannon initially resented bitterly, until he realized, in the fullness of time, that the position provided him with a far broader perspective of tactical operations, naval strategy, the naval establishment, and the workings and politics of the officer ranks far above those that a young division officer might encounter. As he matured, Pebbles exposed him to the carrier division admiral, his chief of staff, and other aides. Pebbles catalyzed a small coterie of senior officers within the ship, and with the admiral, and his staff, who along with Pebbles, recognized Cannon as a high-potential "comer" and took an early interest in his career.

Cannon was excited by his impending orders to *USS Ticonderoga*, Attack Carrier 14. His next ship was leaving San Diego shortly after Thanksgiving for the Gulf of Tonkin, where he would catch up with her after the first of the year in January, 1968. She would launch her first air strikes against North Vietnam just after Christmas Day in 1967. Technically he was going to be the ASW Officer in the Operations department, but he doubted that there would be serious ASW operations for an attack carrier on Yankee Station, and with no experience in strike warfare, he expected to be assigned to duties which would pose a stiff, on-the-job, learning challenge to himself in a combat environment where he only had book knowledge. He read everything that he could on Operation Rolling Thunder, the air war over North Vietnam, and he stretched his imagination as far as it would take him to anticipate what he might encounter.

The ambivalence was to a very great degree provided by the extended separation that he would suffer from his fiancée. Laetitia Martin and he were engaged just weeks ago after a four month romance that had been substantially constrained by *Essex'* deployment to the North Atlantic and subsequently to the Mediterranean where *Essex* augmented the Sixth Fleet and met the Russian challenge in NATO's lake in the aftermath of the Six-Day, Arab-Israeli War.

Tish Martin was a graduate student at Columbia University in art history. She was intelligent, unusually attractive, awakening to the woman's movement, and among other things, an anti-war protestor who expressed serious moral concerns with war in general and, in particular, with the US involvement in Vietnam which she preferred to view as a civil war. Despite this profoundly central conflict between them, they were immediately, uncontrollably drawn to each other, and passionately in love. They were compatible on several dimensions—intellectually, spiritually, socially, and they were magnetically attracted to each other—so the stress of his going to war appeared unlikely to terminate the engagement. Still the brevity of their courtship was cause for doubting its authenticity and endurance, and the length of their impending separation would do little to foster their relationship; on the contrary, it was likely to jeopardize its continuation.

To a lesser, but, nevertheless to a troubling degree, Pebbles replacement, Commander Knight, treated Cannon with indifference and eventually shunned him. Knight had an unflattering reputation within the ASW aviation community and was generally feared and disliked. Everywhere about the ship, and particularly among Knight's peer department heads, there existed a general anxiety that the friendly and effective working relations around the ship were likely to change, and not for the better.

Some observed an indication of Knight's nastiness when he adroitly arranged for, some might substitute the word banished, Cannon to a billet in the Weapons department until he departed for *Ticonderoga*, allegedly, so that his department might accelerate a request to BuPers for a replacement officer. Knight had been off-putting from Cannon's very first overture of cordiality, perhaps because he was setting a tone for the department that sometimes referred to Cannon as Pebbles' teacher's pet, that he was no longer held in special esteem. Among the middle-grade officers intimidated by Cannon's profound intellect, his reputation for a short temper, and by those who envied his closeness to Pebbles, this was received with a small degree of schadenfreuden. But it also made them wary of Knight as they observed how he so rudely, perhaps disparagingly, expended the talent of a junior officer who had honestly earned the respect of his shipmates. If Knight had been so dismissive of Cannon's abilities, they legitimately wondered if Knight posed a terminal threat to their own careers.

Cannon missed the former Operations officer and the inclusion in the important issues affecting the ship, the task group, and their mission. Now as a short-timer, he reported to the Aviation Ordnance Officer, a mustang, an amiable man, but an officer who could not be reasonably expected to invest in Cannon. Lt. Kovacevich, USN, gave Cannon a red, long-sleeve jersey worn by ordnance personnel on the flight deck, admonished him to try not to get himself killed, and directed Cannon, if he should insist on being on the flight deck during flight quarters, to stick next to the Ordnance Officer like foul odor on pig manure, although as Cannon recalled, Karl Kovacevich used a substantially saltier phrase.

So for the first time in Lieutenant Junior Grade Cannon's career he found himself standing the rail in service dress blues as the ship got underway and stood out from Quonset Point. He stood with the aviation ordnance men on the number two elevator located amidships on the portside of the flight deck. He recalled standing on the number two elevator in the benign Caribbean sunshine during last winter's Operation Springboard with the departmental yeomen and Commander Pebbles during an abandon ship drill so many, many months before. Now, for the first time in his career he was not part of the sea and anchor detail, not on the bridge comparing fixes with the quartermaster and the navigator as a member of the radar navigation team, not applying his skills and abilities to the safe navigation of the ship. He felt diminished and abandoned, perhaps better said, discarded and unimportant. He tried to rationalize it as the inevitable consequence of his orders and shrinking tenure aboard *Essex* rather than the result of a Machiavellian deed. Anyway that was the professional way to present it, and emotionally that is how he masked it to the outside world, but inside him, it wounded him deep-down. The man hadn't the slightest interest in being anything other than an important member of the first team.

Two days later Cannon stopped by CIC to check on the surface picture, and frankly, just to be with the radarmen for a few moments before proceeding to relieve the watch on the bridge and stand the 16 – 20. He expected a full watch. The air wing flew aboard that morning. The ship was presently at flight quarters, and the air wing was engaged in carrier qualifications, a slight misnomer. The pilots were all qualified naval aviators and were routinely training up their landing skills on a moving deck after being on terra firma for several weeks. When the air wing got somewhere around 120 to 130 traps, the plan of the day called for *Essex* and the five ships in company, two destroyers and three destroyer escorts, to refuel from the fleet oiler, *USS Kankakee*.

Cannon ducked into the combat information center, and in the dim light his familiar six foot-two inch frame was immediately recognized by the men manning the surface watch.

"Hello, Mr. Cannon."

"Hello, Ski." Radofsky was a third class petty officer striking for second class. Cannon extended his right hand and shook hands with the petty officer. "Ready for the second class exam, Ski?"

"Pretty soon, sir, pretty soon."

"Good. Good." He was not known for small talk and less so before going on watch. He paused to study the surface status board which was displaying the screening ships in station, the plane guard ship, and two skunks, unidentified radar contacts, which presented no risk of collision while *Essex* was on Foxtrot Corpen, the course that brought the wind directly down the angled deck which was offset by 10 degrees from the longitudinal axis of the ship. The desired wind was 350 degrees relative to the ship's head at 30 knots.

"How they treating you in Weapons, sir?"

"Just fine, Ski. Just fine. Any sign of *Kankakee*, Ski?"

"Not yet, sir. The ECM shack has been looking for an SPS-10 radar from the west, but nothing so far, sir. Sir, do you know Mr. Harvey, sir?" Cannon turned on his heel and saw an unrecognizable ensign getting up from a chair behind a radar repeater. Cannon extended his right hand.

"Cannon. Bob Cannon. Nice to meet you."

Taking Cannon's hand, "Yes, sir. Jeff Harvey, sir."

"Welcome, aboard, Jeff."

"Just my first watch as surface watch officer here in CIC, sir."

"I remember feeling anxious on my very first watch at sea with *Essex*. Ski and these good men will keep you out of trouble. But I found it helpful to stand the watch down here," Cannon was suggesting that the officer stand where he could observe the radarmen's work rather than sit comfortably behind a console, "where you can watch the radar repeater and observe the data being plotted on the DRT, and then see it displayed on the surface status board." That was the little kind of thing the men noted when they sized up a young officer. "Good luck, Jeff."

"Yes, sir. Thank you, sir." Cannon noted Harvey was a shiny new ensign and was too deferential and overly used the word "sir" with a JG.

"Heard from Captain Pebbles, Mr. Cannon?"

"I have. I have, Ski. Planning to visit him in Washington on the way to *Ticonderoga*."

"Tell him we all miss him, sir. I mean the men really miss him. Things are changing in OI, sir." He paused. Radofsky's eyes met Cannon's and then Ski added, "And we'll miss you, too, sir." Cannon was entirely professional as a naval officer and gave no acknowledgement to Radofsky's intimation although he could imagine how things might be changing.

"Tell the men, I'll pass that along to the good Captain Pebbles when next I see him. He always said you were the best OI division in AirLant." Then he turned to leave for the bridge, stopping at the doorway and wished Harvey, who had now moved to the position that Cannon suggested good luck for a second time.

He arrived on the bridge about twenty minutes before the watch, and rather than relieve the watch early, he took a few minutes to observe flight operations. The air wing was practicing with touch-and-goes. It was a way of getting more landings in a limited period of time than taking a full trap which would reel out the arresting wire and require a catapult launch. With a touch-and-go the pilots touched the deck and simulated a number three wire trap, and pushed the throttles of the twin engine Grumman S2F

Tracker forward for full power and flew off the angled deck and re-entered the Charlie pattern. This was a pattern off the portside of the ship used during visual meteorological conditions, where they ascended, turned downwind, and turned left for the base leg, and set themselves up on final approach for another landing.

Cannon noted the sun was low in the autumn sky and that it was covered with a broken level of cumulus clouds which were purple and glowed orange around their edges, sighted the ships in company, and watched half a dozen landings from the bridge on the 03 level which looked down two levels on the flight deck. He scanned the bridge status board and noted the ship's course and speed. She was making 20 knots to produce 30 knots of apparent wind for flight operations on four of the ships eight boilers.

"I'm ready to relieve you, sir." He saluted the Officer of the Deck, who turned towards Cannon and returned the salute. Other members of the bridge team were arriving to relieve their counterparts in the pilothouse—the boatswain mate of the watch, the messenger and helmsman, and the quartermaster at the navigation table, as well as the junior officer of the watch and the junior officer of the deck. The off-going personnel began briefing their reliefs.

"I am ready to be relieved. Just got a message from *Kankakee* giving us her position. Quartermaster is plotting it now."

"Got it. Is the order of refueling out?"

"Negative."

"Okay, I got the surface picture when I passed through CIC on the way up here. I relieve you, sir."

"I stand relieved. Mr. Cannon has the deck and the conn." The bosun answered, "Mr. Cannon has the deck and the conn," and added, "Aye, aye, sir."

"Quartermaster, do you have *Kankakee* plotted yet?"

"Yes, sir. Just checking her range and bearing now, sir."

"Thank you." Turning to his JOOD, "Mr. Lawrence I want you to take the conn."

"Yes, sir."

"Ensign Lawrence has the conn." Again the Boatswain Mate of the Watch acknowledged the change in conning officers.

Few OODs routinely gave up control of the conn to the JOOD, but Cannon had observed that aircraft carriers did not maneuver like destroyers and conning skills were less critical on carriers.

In fact, carriers were normally the formation guide and other ships maneuvered about them except when replenishing. Steering was a matter of controlling the ship's heeling moment to minimize the risk of aircraft breaking loose. Carriers made wide turns so the heeling moment would not exceed 10 degrees. Commercial pilots and tugs were employed to nudge carriers alongside piers and to steer the ship in harbors and narrow channels that destroyers routinely did for themselves, and the destroyer-men needed to have superior shiphandling and conning skills. So Cannon concluded that for carriers, conning was a routinely delegatable function.

Cannon surmised that the tradition of OOD as conning officer was brought over from the pre-carrier navy without regard for the different conning requirements. Furthermore, Cannon reasoned, the commanding officer of a carrier was senior to every destroyer or destroyer escort captain and therefore would be the senior officer present afloat and be the officer in tactical command when an admiral was not aboard. When this occurred the managerial responsibility of the OOD expanded in accordance with the captain's responsibilities, and Cannon figured that the conning role added unnecessary intellectual complexity to the Officer of the Deck's managerial responsibilities when the captain was OTC.

The navigator and assistant navigator were responsible for the training and performance of the bridge watch teams, and while JOOD's frequently conned during transit periods and during flight operations, they were commonly relieved by the OOD during formation maneuvers. They agreed that Cannon's argument had merit, and as aviators they were aware of new notions of cockpit management in multi-engine aircraft which were off-loading certain tasks from the pilot to the co-pilot while the pilot retained command of the aircraft. They recognized the analogy with Cannon's observations, and they continued to allow him to experiment with his watch structure but withheld endorsing it as standard operating procedure.

"Mr. Cannon, *Kankakee* is 285 true at 128 nautical."

"128 nautical miles, ah shoot! Mr. Cahouet, please compute Romeo Corpen," the replenishment course, "quickly for us." Cannon stepped over to the navigator's table and examined the chart with *Essex's* and *Kankakee's* positions at 1600.

"Romeo Corpen will be 240 at 10 knots, sir."

"Very well." Cannon picked up the phone and called the captain in his at-sea cabin. "Captain, Bob Cannon on the bridge, sir. We have Kankakee's 1600 position, sir. She's 128 nautical to the west of us, sir, and we are opening on her on fox corpen."

"Damn. Where the hell has she been all day!"

"Yes, sir. We have four boilers online, Captain, may I suggest we go to six, sir."

"What's your point, Bob?"

"Sir, when we come off fox corpen that will give us a closing rate of 42 knots, sir, at least three hours plus to close her. Given the time to put the boilers on line, we pick up only 20 to 30 minutes depending when we conclude flight ops on all eight boilers at flank speed, sir." Captain Meehan thought for several moments.

"I think we better call for all eight, Bob, so we can make 33 knots. Tell Al, I'm sorry. Know he wants a couple for maintenance, but with this wind, everyone is in for a late night."

"Captain, may I invite your attention to the DEs. Their max speed is 27 knots."

"You mean they can't stay with us?" Captain Meehan paused before continuing, "Okay, but we can take the destroyers with us, and leave the DEs to catch up, and then take a DD as plane guard when we are both done refueling and commence night flight ops. We need the landings before the weather closes in. You see any problems with that, Bob?"

"No, sir."

"Okay. Let's run it by the screen commander before we execute. See if he has any problems with it."

"Aye, aye, sir."

"I'm gonna squeeze in a shower here. I'm getting ripe."

"Sir, I'd like to send *Kankakee* a message and take her under tactical command, give her a rendezvous point, sir."

"Okay. That makes sense. Let's do it. Call the navigator in on that. Also call the Chief Engineer, CAG and the Air Boss and tell 'em I want to review this with 'em on the bridge in 10 minutes."

"Aye, aye, sir." Cannon called the CIC Watch Officer on the telephone, briefed him on the plan, and told him to pass the plan to the screen commander over the CI net, and if there were no issues, request that the screen commander designate the plane guard destroyer.

These were precisely the conditions that Cannon considered when he delegated the conn to Lawrence. Cannon knew that the captain wanted to discuss whether the air wing was getting their traps and in particular how many night landings were required.

Lieutenant Commander Harry Dobbins, the assistant navigator, appeared on the bridge. "Permission to enter the bridge, sir." Harry wore a big grin and was putting on the most recently qualified OOD as the navigator's station was on the bridge and access could not really be denied.

"Granted." Cannon responded with a smile. "Just a minute please, Harry." Cannon went over the 1MC, "Engineering Officer of the Watch, Bridge."

"Engineering, aye."

"This is the OOD. We will need eight boilers online. The oiler is about 130 nautical away."

"130 miles... Engineering, aye." Cannon checked his wrist watch as he turned to Dobbins, an officer with whom he had particularly good relations. They shared a mutual respect for professionalism and found it admirable in each other. Cannon briefed the assistant navigator on the situation including the position of *Kankakee* and the captain's plan.

"Harry, let's assume we conclude flight ops at sunset in 21 minutes. Would you agree?"

"Affirm. I think that is what the captain will decide."

" 'Kay. We turn out of the wind, pick up an intercept course for *Kankakee*, forty minutes later we'll go 33 knots. Can we estimate a rendezvous point with *Kankakee* steaming at 15 knots with those assumptions?" "Yes, ay-firm."

"Okay, good. The captain agrees that we can give her a "KILO ROMEO ONE," and steer her at 15 knots for rendezvous. Please advise her of expected Romeo Corpen at 240 tack 10"

"Yes, sir."

" 'Kay. Let's plot it, and draft an op immediate message to *Kankakee*, info our task group and ServLant, for the captain's signature."

"Aye, aye, sir." Dobbins said it again with a smile. The smile was in part a response to Cannon's sense of authority that went with his deck officer role, and, in part, in admiration for his former student's crispness, clarity, and confidence as *Essex*' newest OOD. There were more experienced OODs who would be more deferential towards the assistant navigator, less self-confident, and would await direction from him. Cannon ran a taut watch, anticipated situations well, and rightfully assumed the authority which was delegated directly by the captain to the Officer of the Deck and by Navy Regulations. Cannon stepped over to the 5MC and notified the Air Operations Officer and the Commander of the Air Wing of the Captain Meehan's desire for a meeting.

"Gonna be a pitch black night for the approach, Bob." He was referring to the approach to come alongside the oiler for replenishment."

"Yes, Harry. Figuring on that, but we have a clear November atmosphere. It *ain't* the approach I'm thinking about, Harry. I'm just trying to get the deck divisions and the air department to bed earlier." He turned to his JOOW, "Mr. Cahouet, when you get *Kankakee* on the radar scope I want you to give us a course to steer with a two thousand yard closest point of approach."

"Why two thousand yards?" Dobbins asked. There are two thousand yards to a nautical mile. Dobbins, of course, knew the answer but he was in the habit of constantly testing his OODs.

"Still breaking my chops, Mr. Dobbins?" He smiled at Harry Dobbins before continuing. "I'm just figuring at our 48 knot closing rate, a safe CPA (closest point of approach) in the dark, and how difficult it is for another ship to judge a carrier's aspect especially when the white hangar bay lights are showing. Given the transfer, I want a pretty safe CPA..." Transfer is the lateral distance and closest point of approach that the ship would take in a U-turn as *Essex* maneuvered to approach *Kankakee* from astern, "as we slow from 33 knots. You have any thoughts, Harry?"

"Sounds reasonable to me."

"How 'bout you, Mr. Lawrence?" asked Dobbins.

"In this sea state, sounds pretty good to me, too, sir, but I have never conned at 33 knots."

"Neither has the assistant navigator," whispered Cannon where Dobbins could hear him.

"Bridge, Combat, the screen commander concurs and designates *Stickell* as our DD, call sign, Red Cross, sir. *Gearing* and the DE screening units will follow in a column astern at best speed, sir."

"Combat, roger on that, please advise the Screen Commander and *Stickell* to prepare to make 33 knots."

The Golf flag making *Kankakee* the formation guide was now flying from her yardarm and she was within 7000 yards of *Essex* in the pitch black night.

Cannon did not know the JOOD well, retook the conn and began slowing *Essex'* speed from 33 to 25 knots. This was not the time with a tricky maneuver in the black of night to test the JOOD. Normally he assigned the signaling to the JOOD when he had the conn, but he retained the responsibility for signaling, too. He grabbed the PriTac handset and spoke clearly, "Red Cross, this is Banknote, YANKEE WHISKEY ONE. TACK, MIKE SPEED 25, over," meaning to *USS Stickell,* DD-888, the lifeguard ship, 'follow in my wake' and informing her of *Essex'* speed. "Break, break, Golf Oscar, immediate execute, SPEED 10. I say again, immediate execute, SPEED 10, standby... execute, over." This was to *Kankakee,* call sign, Golf Oscar, to reduce speed.

"Red Cross, wilco, out."

"This is Golf Oscar, MIKE CORPEN 240, MIKE SPEED 10, out."

Cannon turned towards the Junior Officer of the Watch. "Mr. Cahouet, I want you to feed me the radar range and relative bearing to *Kankakee* every minute, please."

"*Relative* bearing and range every minute. Aye, aye, sir."

Cannon then began a sweeping left turn to bring *Essex* behind *Kanakakee* to begin the approach alongside *Kankakee's* portside. "Very well." Cannon checked the pit log indicator, illuminated by a red light on the dark bridge, which indicated the ship was slowing to 27 knots. There was no risk that he would undershoot his approach and neither was there a risk of collision, a normal concern. Now he considered whether he would overshoot the oiler and have a long distance to make up from behind the oiler. He wanted to keep his speed up until he was directly behind *Kankakee,* then he would bleed his speed off until he was along her portside, a hundred feet apart, at 10 knots with the wind 5 degrees off his port bow.

The ship was now heeling at just over 10 degrees. Captain Meehan and the navigator arrived on the bridge. So had most of the ship's department heads that held the rank of commander. Along with Dobbins, they watched as Cannon brought the ship smartly around. It wasn't a matter of danger now; it was a matter of how neatly they approached *Kankakee.* It was a matter of pride in seamanship, and how long they would take chasing *Kankakee* until they got the first line, a messenger, sent with a line gun, over the side. Cannon was at least double the desired range to begin the approach, but this was appropriate given that it was night, and both ships initially approached each other from opposite headings at a high closure rate. He coolly maintained 25 knots. It was a matter of elegance.

"I'm moving to the conning station on the starboard wing. Helmsman, increase your rudder to left 12 degrees." Cannon was attempting to tighten the turn but at the risk of excessive heel. "Primary, Bridge. We may roll 15 degrees to starboard."

"Primary understands." *Essex* inconsequentially heeled to 12 degrees, but the Air department had the aircraft, oxygen carts, tugs and miscellaneous equipment well-chained to the flight deck and hangar deck per standard operating procedure, and everything remained secure.

"*Kankakee* bears 010 at 4100 yards." *Essex* began to close Kankakee from astern.

"Very well. Mr. Dobbins, we all ready with the stadimeter set for Golf Oscar's truck light?" a more precise and ancient instrument based on the Pythagorean Theorem for calculating close distances.

"Standing by, Bob"

"004 at 3800."

"Thank you, Mr. Cahouet. That will be all that I need from you. Helmsman, steady up on new course 240."

"New course 240, aye, sir."

"Very well." We're going to roll out long but on track, Harry. Might take us six to eight minutes to arrive at the optimal point of approach."

"That'll be good enough, Bob."

Commander Deane, the ship's navigator, announced "Commander Kni," he paused and stammered, "Knight will be first on the conn." Dobbins and Cannon reacted with mild surprise as Deane uttered Knight's name knowing full well that relations were awkward between the young officer and his former department head. Had Deane thought about it more carefully he would have assigned Knight's conning session after Cannon had been relieved and off watch. All of the department heads got conning time during underway replenishments, unreps in navy jargon, in hopes that they would be prepared for selection as commanding officer of a deep-draft command such as an oiler, a pre-requisite to obtaining a carrier command.

"Change speed to 20 knots." When the helmsman acknowledged the engine order, Cannon announced, "Commander Knight has the conn." The helmsman acknowledged that Commander Knight was the conning officer. "Range and bearing, please."

"001 at 3500 yards sir."

"Very well. Now *soto voce*, he spoke to Knight. "I'm here to coach you Commander. I'm here to help." Knight did not respond.

"Bearing 002 at 3300 yards." Three minutes later they were 2300 yards astern the oiler at 20 knots. Knight made no effort to reduce speed.

"Sir, I think we're coming in a little hot. Let's take some speed off." Again, Knight ignored Cannon.

An uncomfortable atmosphere settled over the captain and the officers on the bridge. Everyone sensed *Essex* was approaching too fast. A delicate drama was unfolding between Cannon and Knight. The junior officer as the Officer of the Deck was responsible for getting *Essex* alongside

Kankakee despite the fact that a senior officer held the conn. His former department head, a full commander, was considered spiteful by some and few felt Knight had ever done anyone's career good. The OOD and the captain were charged by Navy Regulations with the safety of the ship.

Dobbins now called out the ranges. "2000 yards... 1900... 1800..."

"Sir, we're too hot. Our closing rate is too high at 20 knots for this distance. Let's make our speed 12 knots now." Knight ignored him. "Sir, we must decelerate."

"Make your speed 14 knots." The helmsman ignored the error in phrasing and responded, "Change speed to 14 knots, aye, sir." The tension rose between Knight and Cannon, and it was felt throughout the bridge. Captain Meehan was reluctant to intercede. Knight was still new on board, and Meehan did not want to appear to overtly criticize Knight in front of the senior officers. He was also keenly interested in seeing how the young officer would handle the situation. Would Cannon have the moxie to assert his position as OOD?

"1500 yards... 1400..."

"Sir, we're too damn hot." Cannon was whispering. "Recommend you make our speed 10 knots... now!"

"Change speed to 12 knots." Cannon's anger was rising but he took a deep breadth. He virtually had an insubordinate senior officer on the conn who was forcing a confrontation with the authority of the deck officer.

"Belay that," ordered Cannon. "Indicate speed 10 knots." Cannon looked Knight in the eye who returned a mean, vengeful look, in the faint, dim red light emanating from the pit log and the gyro compass repeater. Cannon checked the speed on the pit log. It was pegged at 14 knots and slowing. However, there was confusion in the pilot house as to whom was the conning officer and whose orders were meant to be followed as the conflict between the conning officer and the Officer of the Deck played out. "I repeat, indicate speed 10 knots."

"10 knots, aye sir."

"Very well, Commander Knight has the conn."

"Commander Knight has the conn, aye, sir." Cannon clarified and restored the chain of command. He now thought of the consequences if Knight remained insubordinate and forced him, in front of the captain, in front of Knight's peers, to relieve him from the conn. *Commander, don't push, dammit don't push, Commander*, he thought to himself.

"1100 yards... 1000 yards... " The ship was still moving through the water at 14 knots.

"Commander, indicate 9 knots." This speed indicated how wrong the approach was going. Cannon realized they were likely to overshoot *Kankakee.*

Knight ignored the Officer of the Deck. Cannon looked into Knight's face as if to ask why. *Why so damn stubborn? Why create this awkward situation?* A situation so embarrassing to both officers that could only result in the humiliation of one or the other. Perhaps both. Knight stared at the junior officer with contemptuous smugness and threw down the dare to the junior officer. Cannon glanced at *Kankakee's* white sternlight and his seaman's eye knew that an embarrassing overshoot was now unavoidable.

"Sir,' Cannon, spoke very softly and very respectfully but nevertheless very firmly, "I am relieving you, sir. Stand clear of the conn, please, Com..."

"Like hell..."

"Lieutenant J.G. Cannon has the deck and the conn. Change speed to 7 knots," Cannon announced the change with unmistakable authority and confidence.

The level of tension backed down only slightly as Cannon assumed control of the approach. Several officers were aghast at what they had just witnessed. Knight was committing suicide with his career. The navigator shot a look at the captain who did his best to appear unperturbed. The conflict at the conn was now resolved, but the current position of the ship relative to *Kankakee* was extremely poor and the approach might not be salvageable.

A different kind of tension grew palpably. Cannon now focused completely on the problem of a badly flawed approach. He could try to "grease" the carrier into replenishment station or go around again and recommence a second approach, something that would delay refueling by at least another 20 to 25 minutes and the subsequent night carrier qualifications.

"600 yards... "

"Harry, I'm going to try and save it. I think I have enough rudder." The *Essex* class was a four screw, single rudder ship. The rudder was relatively small, deliberately designed to minimize quick darting turns, which were considered undesirable for what was intended to be a stable, floating airfield. The rudder's effectiveness would diminish as the ship's speed through the water diminished to what was the equivalent of stall speed on an airplane. A stalled rudder aptly defined loss of steerage. Cannon considered below five knots to be stall speed. "I'm not taking a wave off."

"Go ahead and try it. Just watch your bank suction." a condition where the deep draft of both ships and the clockwise rotation of Essex's four screws might draw her to starboard and into *Kankakee*. "You okay with this, Captain?"

"You're a pilot, Harry. At this point, fly the airplane."

"Helmsman, come left one half degree to 239 decimal 5 degrees. Steer nothing to the right of 239 decimal 5." Cannon hoped a half degree would offset the bank suction phenomenon. His rudder order sounded certain, but in his mind, he was quite uncertain if he could pull this off.

"Aye, aye sir. Steer nothing to the right of 239 decimal 5 degrees."

"Very well. Mind your helm carefully," Cannon coached.

"Aye, aye, sir."

Cannon noted *Kankakee's* bridge as *Essex* slipped by her. *Essex* was about twice the length of the oiler, proceeded to ease past *Kankakee* by nearly a full a length. Her hurricane bow was now 800 feet ahead of *Kankakee's* bow and the oiler only slightly overlapped *Essex* stern. As *Essex* slowed below 10 knots, she began slowly to fall back, a dangerous and therefore an undesirable, unseamanlike means to get to station. It was an embarrassing act in full view of *Kankakee's* crew. In distinct contrast, *Gearing* had been taking fuel from *Kankakee's* starboard side for several minutes. Cannon had no time for embarrassed feelings and remained focused on the task at hand. Now he was using his seaman's eye, taking the speed up by a half knot, step by step, or better said, fine tuning his ship's speed, turn by turn, by increasing the shaft revolutions carefully, reducing the speed differential between the two ships until he had the replenishment stations aligned and had *Essex* steaming at 10 knots on 240 degrees true, Romeo Corpen.

"The First Lieutenant reports first line across, sir," reported the talker on the 1JV sound-powered circuit.

"Very well."

It was now nearly 2000 hours and Cannon's relief, who prudently avoided interrupting Cannon in the middle of the approach, stepped forward to relieve the deck. When Cannon stood relieved, he stepped to the portside of the bridge and headed for the wardroom below. Knight was waiting for him in the dark, and he grabbed Cannon by the shoulders and whispered. "You smart ass, sonuvabitch, don't you ever countermand my orders again. You bastard. You just flushed your career down the shitter."

"Commander, the Officer of the Deck is the captain's legal representative on the bridge. You should have taken my suggestions as if they were the captain's orders. You embarrassed us both, and the entire ship in front of *Kankakee*."

"You smart ass, Ivy League twerp..." Dobbins noted the ugly scene that was developing and moved swiftly across the bridge and stepped between the two officers, and spoke directly to Cannon.

"You're off watch, Mr. Cannon. Go below. That's an order."

"Aye, aye, sir." He shot a look at Knight, who glared menacingly towards him.

"As for you, Commander Knight, I'm going to recommend that you observe a few unreps before you take the conn again. You cannot intimidate an aircraft carrier alongside a fleet oiler."

Chapter 3.

Ogilvy Osborne sat in the dark of the living room while his wife, Fiona, cleaned and tidied up the kitchen after Thanksgiving weekend. There was a dying fire in the fireplace and the embers glowed softly, providing the only light, a softly flickering, orange light in the room. A slight hiss escaped from the end of a wet log. Over his crossed leg, with a front paw on either side of his knee, was perched the family Cavalier, King Charles Spaniel, his chin resting on his master's knee. Sir Charles, or Charlie, seemed to be aware that the chaplain was about to depart for nearly a year. His son and daughter had left for boarding schools on the East Coast after making a special effort to join him in the rented mission-style, beach house in Coronado before their father deployed with *USS Ticonderoga* on the next day. That Sunday morning Fiona and the children sat in the pews of Christ Church, a traditional, gray stone, Gothic-style church, a style ubiquitously favored by Episcopalians for their churches, as their father celebrated Holy Eucharist.

Despite Ogilvy and Fiona's efforts to keep the mood light, a dark melancholia occasionally crept into the weekend. The chaplain sat alone now, feeling full of grief, and tears began to flow from his eyes and down his cheeks as he allowed himself to recall the scenes of combat in the bitter winter snow of the hills of Korea. Like a slide show, the scenes dissolved one into another. Now, in the pre-dawn morning, descending into the madly bobbing Higgins boat, his arms and legs nearly failing him, numb with anxiety, doing his best as their platoon leader to exude confidence and lead his men ashore at Inchon.

"Are you scared, sir?"

"Scared as hell, Murphy! Scared like a white rabbit in a fox hunt," a literally non-sensical reply that nevertheless communicated everything. "Now, let's give our weapons a final check, men." It helped to do something. He gave them something to do, something useful. "Pass the word on down. No friendly fire. Check the safeties on your weapons again." He reached for his .45 caliber pistol, pointed it in the air and pulled back the slide chambering the first round and reset the safety before replacing it in his shoulder holster. Then he did the same, recalling his hand trembling as he fitted the 15 round ammunition magazine into the M1 carbine that he carried and pulled back the operating rod to chamber the first round in the weapon and pushed the safety on with his thumb. "Watch your thumbs," referring to the nasty manner of the M1 Garand rifle to smash a thumb when being inspected. "Make sure all grenades are secure on your person."

The scene shifted to Toktong Pass. "How're the shrapnel wounds, O."

"I'm okay, sir. A damn sight better than most. How's the leg, sir?"

"Adequate." That was all he said. One simple, stoical word—adequate. "You're second in command, now, O." Captain Samuels looked up from the litter, his eyes sunken, red, and ringed with fatigue. Osborne returned the look, focusing all of his attention on his commanding officer. "We're to hold the pass until relieved." He continued slowly and deliberately. "Until relieved, O. Got it?" He paused and searched Osborne's face to assure himself that Osborne understood the gravity of the situation. Osborne responded with a serious nod. "There's still a regiment of ChiComs over there." His voice was monotonic; the words were matter of fact, staring away in the direction of Toktong Pass.

"Yes, sir."

"Or damn well die trying," handing to Osborne the Morning Report with appended casualties, more than half the company dead, dying or wounded, unable to walk like the commanding officer.

Osborne envisioned Samuels turning his head, fixing his expression upon him, time and time again, saying those words, over and over again, words spoken or taken as words of determination or plight, or words mixed insanely with determination and plight, a seemingly sane appraisal of an absolutely insane set of circumstances. Osborne looked back at Captain Samuels before the face dissolved into the next scene.

A horrific scene of smashed and broken bodies, shredded and separated limbs, decapitated corpses. His men, their men, red blood, frozen red and pink in the snow. Purple blood that had coagulated and dried, bluish white flesh of dead men, frozen men. Sounds...the groaning and agonies of men horribly wounded and dying, some weeping; some crying for their mothers. The lives of healthy young men destroyed, wounded and productive lives impaired, and still others, like Osborne, and everyone else who survived hell at Chosin who would be condemned to suffer a lifetime of nightmares. Nightmares of sheer terror that drive men into silence about the origins of their nightmares and clouded the rest of their lives with a sadness that ebbed and flowed throughout their years. Experiences that they wanted to forget and could not forget, that they could not adequately relate to anyone else unless they had been there. Experiences that became a source of distance between them and other men, and their wives and their children.

"Dear," Fiona's soft, feminine voice interrupted his thoughts, "Dear," she called, "come to bed. It's our last night together, dear."

"In a few minutes, dear." He stroked Sir Charles once or twice, wiped his tears away, and began to carry Charlie upstairs. Ogilvy Osborne had served his time in hell. He might have remained the popular rector of a wealthy parish in Beverly Farms, north of Boston, living safely, playing golf and sailing, watching his children grow up, living comfortably in a large house that his wife had inherited in nearby Manchester. Though he had vowed to serve God in peace, never to take up arms again, God, he believed God had another purpose for him, that God had planned for him to become a Marine officer for some other purpose. God, after all, surely had seen to it that he had escaped from hell to some end, for some greater purpose.

As the Vietnam War heated up, with every filmed report on television, Ogilvy Osborne felt God calling him to minister to those who were going to where he had been, to where he could uniquely serve, to those going into the hell of combat. Ogilvy prayed to God asking God for clarity, asking God if He truly wanted him back at war, until Ogilvy heard the voice of God. Just as Ogilvy Osborne had felt called by God in the hills of Chosin to serve the Lord in the cause for peace, so did he feel called to serve the men who would go to war now. "Go. That is your congregation. That is My plan you." As clear as a church bell on a quiet night he could hear the Lord, "Serve Me by serving those 'who will damn well die trying.' "

Word of the bungled approach spread rapidly around the ship and was not only a matter of discussion among the officers, but was a hot topic down in the chief's quarters, on the mess decks and throughout the berthing compartments around the ship. The story of Knight's insubordination and lack of a seaman's eye were especially poignant within the Deck divisions, part of the Weapons department—the seamen, the boatswain mates, the helmsmen, the men on the deck plates of the sponsons whose pride was wounded by the catcalls and the indignities from their counterparts in *Kankakee*. These were the men who stood watches in the pilot house and knew a proper approach from a poor one, the men who witnessed the ugly approach as they stood ready to receive the lines and hoses from *Kankakee* to begin the refueling evolution.

This event made Cannon's last weeks in *Essex* even more awkward. With the exception of Tish and two officers, Cannon steadfastly refused comment on the incident. The latter only occurred when Cannon was summoned by Captain Meehan to his in-port cabin.

"Bob, you're leaving the ship in a few of days. So the XO and I wanted to speak with you on the record about the unfortunate events with Commander Knight." Cannon swallowed hard.

"Yes, sir."

"I need for you to understand that we are doing some informal fact-finding. This is not a judicial process, but we want you to be on the record with the XO and me, and to be scrupulously honest."

"Yes, sir. Am I under some form of suspicion, Captain?"

"No, Bob. Certainly not."

"Is Commander Knight considering legal action against me?"

"Not that we are aware of," answered the Executive Officer, Commander Spargo.

"I see." He paused, "So, how can I help you, sir?" Spargo began the questioning.

"Take us through your decision process. What factors were you considering when you relieved Commander Knight of the conn?" Cannon looked off at a squadron plaque decorating the white bulkhead while he thought for several seconds to collect his thoughts before turning towards the two senior officers and answering.

"I did not consider the situation dangerous; it was inconvenient. From a safety perspective I figured we still had enough sea room to turn left and initiate a second approach to *Kankakee*. I did consider the inconvenience, the lost time at flight quarters, wasted time and energy that would be absorbed in a second approach by all hands involved in the refueling evolution, and the cascade effects on subsequent ships and crews scheduled to replenish behind us. I gave serious consideration to Commander Knight's rank, that he was in a career-enhancing billet, and that I pretty much figured that I was not making a friend of the Operations Officer in the ship."

"Yes."

"But I considered the conning officer to be insubordinate. I was the deck officer. I was the direct representative of the Commanding Officer, and my suggestions and recommendations should have been taken as if they were yours, Captain." Here he shifted his gaze to the captain from the XO. "If he had been an ensign, I would have relieved him a thousand yards earlier."

"That's a pretty strong statement."

"Yes, sir, it is. And I think, sir, on the record, it's an accurate one. I also considered that the captain would be put in a very delicate position where he might have to choose between backing his Officer of the Deck or his Operations Officer. If it had been an ensign, Dobbins or the navigator could give him a tongue-lashing, and maybe a note in his fitness report, and that would be the end of it. But for Commander Knight...to so visibly...to so explicitly ignore the advice of the deck officer, who along with the captain, is legally responsible for the safety of the ship, to seeing to it that the ship's work is carried out efficiently, to be so blatantly provocative in front of his peers and seniors, it was virtually impossible to ignore."

"Yes, now...well...uh, was there any bad blood between you?" Spargo continued to lead the questioning.

"How do you mean that, sir? If you mean, was there anytime when I was disrespectful towards the commander? The answer is no. Did we ever have a disagreement or harsh words? The answer is no. But I would be less than fully candid with you if I didn't say I was displeased with being transferred to Weapons, although I think I can understand Commander Knight's point of view."

"So you never argued? You were never disobedient? You weren't sullen or insolent?"

"No, sir."

"I see. Now both you and Commander Knight are known to be pretty bright and forceful, and you both have been known to have a temper. But the two of you never had words?" Cannon's face reddened. He knew that Pebbles, his former boss, would have shared the assessment of his fitness report with the XO and CO. He knew that Pebbles had admonished him to control his anger, and that it was an issue, that he was expected to get it under control. To hear it now from Commander Spargo in front of the captain embarrassed him.

"Before the incident in question, that is correct, sir. Entirely correct, sir. Subsequently, we had words on the port wing of the bridge."

"We are aware of that. What do you suppose...how would you explain Commander Knight's behavior?"

"Sir, I cannot. I'm absolutely baffled. Commander Knight had nothing to gain and everything to lose. He might not be the most likable man, but to the best of my knowledge, no one has ever questioned his competency or his decision-making. I can only hypothesize that something else is at issue with the commander. Perhaps, something else is operating somewhere else in his life...displaced hostility."

"Displaced what?"

"You know, sir. Maybe you are angered by one person, and you take it out on another. The scape goat, the whipping boy, sir. But, that is purely, ungrounded speculation on my part, sir."

"Yes, I see." Spargo glanced over at Captain Meehan as he considered the thought. "Thank you, Mister Cannon. That will be all. Please regard this conversation and the very fact of this meeting as strictly confidential."

"Yes, of course, sir." Cannon got up to leave, then addressed the two senior officers. "Sir, may I ask a question?"

"Yes?"

"Captain, if you were in my place, how would you have handled the situation?" Captain Meehan took his time to respond, but his response did not avoid the question.

"Confidentially, Bob, I would have hoped that I had the courage as a junior officer to do exactly as you did. Our problem is not with you."

Professor and Mrs. Cannon, along with their two daughters, visited their son aboard *Essex* for Thanksgiving dinner. Cannon's two younger sisters, Hadley, 20 and Morgan, 22, were very attractive young women and were rarely without male attention. Cannon was the eldest and the well-rounded, scholar-athlete in the family who collected a fair share of the family honors. Partly because he had been off in an all-male boarding school, Cannon had been shy with women. Partly out of a sense of sibling rivalry, as a teenager, his sisters teased him relentlessly and unmercifully about his shyness and insecurity with girls. "You're a nerd…egghead. You were born ugly. You're not handsome." Later he outgrew his shyness, but the teasing left a toll in his mind. His relationship with his fiancée, Laetitia Martin, an unusually good-looking woman, who herself had been some-what of a skinny, late-bloomer, eased that sense of insecurity but at present, had not fully cured it.

He was in the duty section for Thanksgiving Day and the Weapons department duty officer, so his family, fully aware that they would not be seeing him for nearly a year, came for the day on the ship. Cannon asked two young ensigns, Harvey from Operations, and Simms from Communications to join them. Neither Jeff Harvey nor Chuck Simms found this to be a burdensome task; on the contrary, both women were fun, energetic and attractive. Hadley, the younger, looked more womanly and mature than Cannon remembered her. Morgan was the extroverted, independent daredevil while Hadley fit the role of baby in the family. She was the more sensitive of the two girls and had promise as a writer. After dessert was served, Cannon leaned towards the two ensigns.

"Gentlemen, my sisters have never been aboard a naval ship, let alone an aircraft carrier. Would you be so kind as to offer them a tour of the ship?" Morgan looked over at her older brother, as if to say, *you read my mind perfectly. How did you ever get so smooth, so quickly?*

"Girls," said Professor Cannon, "I think we need to be leaving for home by three P.M." He was speaking to his daughters but indirectly to the two young officers.

"We'll have the women back here, in the wardroom lounge, by 1445, sir." Simms looked at the professor. "Would that be okay, Bob?" asked Simms. Cannon checked his watch. It was 1350.

"Yes," he smiled, "that should give you and my sisters ample time for a thorough tour of the ship. It's all in your good hands." He looked at all four of them as he spoke the words and his expression was saying *enjoy yourselves and deport yourselves in accordance with a naval ship.*

Harvey, the more junior of the two ensigns and still overly deferential towards a lieutenant junior grade answered with a snappy, "Yes, sir." Mrs. Cannon watched her son with an approving smile. After the foursome left, Cannon asked his mother and father to join him for another cup of coffee passing an inverted salt shaker briefly over his cup before he took a sip.

"Say, can I get on that tour, too?"

"Of course not, Dad." He winked. "I'm conducting a special chaper-ones' tour for you and Mother in 10 minutes." Then he told them about the incident with Knight without mentioning the meeting with the CO and XO before moving on to mention the details of an engagement party that the Martins were planning for December. Louise Cannon had given Brooke Martin her guest list several weeks earlier, but Cannon and Tish's parents had never met, and Tish and he wanted to take both sets of parents to din-ner in New York as soon as possible so that they all could meet before the party, and he needed to provide some tentative dates to Tish. Then he led his parents on a tour of *Essex*, and along the way pointed out what he ex-pected would be different about *Ticonderoga*, Attack Carrier 14, only 5 hull numbers apart but 100 feet longer.

Bong, bong. "Lieutenant Junior Grade R.F Cannon, United States Naval Reserve, departing," was passed over the 1MC by the bosun mate of the watch as directed by the OOD. Several junior officers came to the quarter-deck to say good bye and to wish Cannon well, thoroughly embarrassing him as they shook his hand and slapped him on the back. Then he picked up his black leather briefcase with his left hand and came to attention facing the OOD and saluted with his right hand.

"I request permission to leave the ship, sir."

"Permission granted," and he returned the ritual salute. The group of officers watched as Cannon walked smartly halfway over the brow, stopped, faced the fantail and snapped off a prolonged, professional salute, his last salute aboard *Essex*, holding it reverently for several seconds in honor of the national ensign, the ship, and the men who served in her. He then descended to the ground and walked with military bearing, his shoulders back, towards his green MGB parked on the carrier pier, opened the right door and placed his briefcase on the floorboard. He walked behind his car, looking back at the ship over his right shoulder. She was no longer his ship.

He took a deep breath and looked over *Essex*, examining every detail with fondness for the old girl, the first of the new fleet carriers that defeated Japan in the Pacific War. Every detail flashed a memory—a storm at sea, the Russian harassment, the Badger crash, the Van Voorhis incident—every detail, every event triggering uncountable lessons in his personal development which in some cases expedited his decision-making and in other cases provided words of caution and tempered his judgment. He felt a heavy sense of responsibility to the Navy which had invested nearly two years in his development, and the Navy was now deadly serious about asking for the return at war.

He had no false notions of glory about war, nor an adolescent sense of patriotism. Nevertheless, he was intending, without reservation, to give the Navy all that he could and his very best to his shipmates. The man who was often known for showing his intellect and hiding his emotions, save anger, breathed heavily as he drove towards the main gate at Quonset Point watching the haze gray hull behind him fade from view in the rear mirror.

Cannon and Tish walked from her apartment on West 114th Street and Riverside Drive across Broadway and entered the Columbia University campus through the 116th Street gate. She was headed for a class at Avery Hall while he had an appointment with Professor John Meaney at nearby Schermerhorn Hall.

Tish was smartly, but casually, dressed for the early December air in stiletto blue jeans, and knee-high brown leather boots which matched a well-cut, brown suede, leather top coat which just covered her hips. Around her neck she wore an Arran Island, off-white, woolen scarf and matching tam o'shanter, and over her shoulder she carried a green canvas book bag. Cannon wore what he knew Meaney would expect of him, a coat and tie, beneath a navy blue, down, ski parka. He carried the morning's *New York Times* and a spiral notebook under one arm while he held her hand with the other.

"I'm going to embarrass you again, Carissimo. I want all of my classmates to know what a lovely man I am going to marry." She placed her left hand around his shoulder and pulled herself up into him, and kissed him with a long, lingering kiss squarely on the lips. Students were scurrying around them. A co-ed smiled at them as she passed by, while they stood there embraced in the middle of the brick walkway. Predictably, Cannon tensed up, still uncomfortable with a public display of affection. "I'm so madly in love with you, nerd," a reference to a mischaracterization given to her about him before she met him on Chappaquiddick Island last May. He wrapped his arms around her, holding the *Times* and notebook with one hand, and kissed her with unenthusiastic reservation in return. "You're getting better at this public affection, Caro." She spoke Italian fluently and sprinkled her English with Italian words, especially the words for dear and dearest, when she referred to him, and they had become proper nouns.

"C'mon, you'll be late for class." He looked at his watch. He also would be late for his half-hour appointment with Meaney.

"Oh, Robbie...."

"Tish, I love you, *and* I like to be punctual. We'll have tonight together."

"Sometimes, I just wonder how much I matter to you. Enjoy your day, nerd." She turned abruptly away from him and walked, or perhaps stomped, quickly towards her class. An artsy young man with Botticelli-like, golden hair greeted her, putting his arms around her and kissing both cheeks. The European style greeting struck Cannon as overly familiar as the artsy man with charm continued to usher his fiancée through the door placing his hand on her waist as she passed through the doorway. Cannon watched her, his steel-gray eyes narrowing, as she entered the doorway of Avery Hall with her square-jawed, blond classmate. Then he checked his watch, pivoted abruptly, and ran for the entrance to Schermerhorn Hall, racing up four flights of stairs to Meaney's office on the top floor.

Associate Professor Meaney is an interesting man. He is a confirmed bachelor who lives on the Upper West Side with his mother. A graduate of the College, he matriculated to Harvard for a Ph.D. and became a senior member of the Government Department. During the war, he served in the Research and Analysis section of the Office of Strategic Services with the naval rank of lieutenant commander and applied his energies to anti-submarine warfare and intelligence. He is also an expert on the life of Saint Augustine and is often consulted by the Archbishop's office in New York on various church matters. It is a matter of speculation on campus whether he confidentially consults for the CIA, and it is presumed, at the very least, that he spots talent at Columbia for subsequent recruitment by the agency.

"Welcome, Robert, welcome. So nice to see you again" and shook Cannon's hand warmly and patted him on the shoulder as he showed Cannon to a chair in front of his desk in his office.

"Likewise, professor. Sorry, I'm late, sir." Meaney ignored his tardiness, and noted a new sense of maturity and self-confidence in the young officer.

"You witnessed some remarkable events last summer with *Essex*, Robert."

"Yes, sir. Your advice about the Soviets proved prophetic. We're damn lucky the Israelis prevailed. The Russians have bought their way into Egypt and Syria with arms. And now we shall see how effectively they have breached NATO's wall of containment on her southern flank."

"Yes, Robert...well, now you are moving from an intense chapter in the Cold War to a hot, shooting war."

"Yes, sir. But before we get to that, I experienced another event. I got engaged to marry, sir, to a wonderful woman who is a graduate student here at Columbia, Laetitia Martin."

"Congratulations, Robert. And what is Miss Martin's area of study?"

"Art history, sir."

"Very good. Very good. I'm sure she must make you very happy."

"I'm a very lucky man, sir." Meaney looked at a clock on the sidewall of the office and uncharacteristically cut him short.

"But that is not the subject of your agenda?" Cannon refocused himself instantly.

"No, sir. I wanted to avail myself of an area of your expertise. Namely your knowledge of Saint Augustine."

"Yes?"

"Sir, I wonder if you might lead me through the concept of a just war."

"Just war… yes, that indeed was codified by St. Augustine…although the application of his concept to rationalize the Crusades is in conflict with our notion of freedom of worship and freedom of choice of religion."

"Yes."

"What context prompts your curiosity, Robert? Is it Vietnam and the anti-war movement?"

"Yes, …and, uh…my fiancée is a war protestor."

"I see. And this is a matter of strife between you?"

"Yes, sir. But I really want to get my own thinking right about it, real politik, aside."

"I understand. I think we both regret Johnson's escalation, and the public mood is critical to the politics of continuing the war's prosecution." He paused and looked directly at Cannon. "Well, we're not at the point of draft riots, but public opinion, although still in the minority, has been growing progressively against the war, and we're entering an election year. I'm sure you are fully aware of all of that."

"I am, sir."

"Well, given our limited time, let me recognize the contribution of the Romans, particularly Cicero, and Augustine, and Aquinas as well, and let me dispense with the intellectual history of the concept, and allow me to acquaint you with two parts of the current notion. The first part addresses when war may be necessary and justifiable, and the second discusses how it may be fought. Of course, all of this is predicated by an injunction necessary for all cultures in order to preserve themselves and survive, namely that thou shall not kill or thou shall not murder. Do you follow me, Robert?"

"Yes, sir."

"Nevertheless, there is a notion that some wars are necessary and are justifiable under certain, qualified conditions."

"Uh, huh." Cannon began taking notes in the spiral notebook.

"First, force is justifiable if all other means have been exhausted, and if it is the last resort...and if the use of force is likely to succeed in correcting a massive evil...against the human rights...of a major population. Further, today many believe a just war needs authorization from a supranational authority such as the UN, but I find that unworkable given the veto power of the states in the Security Council and the significantly disparate cultural differences around the world."

"Yes. That's self-apparent."

"It's a nice thought. But continuing…motive and the intention must be free of self-interest such as waging war to obtain geography or material value such as petroleum. Finally, the benefits of a successful conflict should outweigh the expected degree of evil...and harm caused by war."

"Hmm. That's pretty well-defined."

"Yes, it is quite specific. One can see why some say for the Allies, World War Two was a good war...the war that gave war a good name."

"Yes. Understood."

"Now, with regard to your fiancée, given that Ho Chi Minh liquidated a million of his own people gaining and consolidating power for the questionable benefits of communist socialism, one can reasonably satisfy the moral requirement, but given the uncertainty of the outcome, a real politik thought as well, and the destructive power being unleashed both above and below the DMZ, and the difficulty of separating combatant from non-combatant, the justification is weakening."

"Many say it is a civil war, sir."

"No. I don't think so. I do not believe that the war can be accurately described as a civil war given that these are two independent states. It is still subversion and invasion of the South."

"Yes. It seems to be a proxy war between us, the PRC and the Soviets."

"Yes, I think that is both a fair and correct assessment. But the anti-war movement, fairly in my opinion, is right to ask, are we using the minimum necessary force, whether due regard for civilians can be or is being observed, and whether or not the destruction of property, and the infliction of casualties among the civilian population do not substantially exceed the potential benefits of the war. It's the Truman-atom bomb decision, if you will."

"Unfortunately, our cause is undermined by a corrupt, less than noble, government in the South. All of the above provides the motivation for the strict rules of engagement, which the military dislikes, and the usurpation of their authority by the White House to keep our effort on the right side of the line."

"Unh-huh."

"Finally, with this definition of a just war and guidelines for conduct of a just war in hand, one can well-imagine how one might deviously design a strategy to wage war and develop tactics to exploit some of the more humane values reflected in this Western, Judeo-Christian concept—a religious orientation and culture alien to the majority of the world's population and not universally accepted."

"Yes."

"Robert, I regret to say our time must be up. We must conclude now, Robert. I'm due shortly to teach those who are still paying their tuitions, Robert." Meaney's humor was often subtle.

"Thank you, sir. I have the conceptual framework. Thank you very much. One more time you have been very generous with your time, sir."

"Stay in touch, Robert. I see that your old, chess-playing boss is now on the staff of the Chief of Naval Operations. Flag rank looks particularly promising for him."

"Yes, sir. I'm having lunch with him in Washington on the way to Travis Air Force Base."

"Very good. Please remember me to him."

A low level of anxiety pervaded the atmosphere around Tish Martin and Bob Cannon which prevented them from fully enjoying their last day together. Part of it was the post-holiday let-down, but thoughts of their impending separation kept intruding and brought about frequent moments of distress as they thought about their future. And thoughts of a potential rival for her affections occasionally occurred to him.

The month since Cannon left *Essex* had gone well. Both sets of parents had gotten along very well at the small dinner party arranged by the young couple at Trader Vic's, one of their favorite restaurants, located in Manhattan at the Savoy Plaza Hotel. So did the engagement party given by the Martins just before Christmas in the ballroom of the Indian Harbor Yacht Club with a tall Christmas Tree set up at one end and a roaring fire in the large fieldstone fireplace at the other end.

To no one's surprise, Tish graciously facilitated the flow of introductions between the two families and their respective sets of guests. She made a particular effort to see to it that the two Cannon girls were made to feel comfortable and asked them to join the bridal party as her bridesmaids. A tentative date for the wedding was set for the last weekend in September 1968, on the small island of Chappaquiddick, just off the larger island of Martha's Vineyard. *Ticonderoga* was expected to return to her homeport at the carrier pier at NAS North Island, just across the bay from San Diego by mid-September. Despite all of these positive steps the couple was gloomy.

On the previous evening, Cannon spilled some olives on the rug in front of one of the two opposing loveseats in Tish's apartment. Tish was in the small kitchen preparing dinner while Cannon gathered up their wine glasses and clumsily tipped over a plate when he tried to carry too much. A few remaining olives rolled off the plate and under the skirt of one of the loveseats. When Cannon went to retrieve the olives, he saw several white cardboard signs of the type typically carried by anti-war marchers that bore the words "Stop the War Now!" He examined them briefly, and then he looked over his shoulder and noted Tish was out of sight and busy in the kitchen. Hurriedly, he gathered up the olives, and replaced the signs under the loveseat, and carried the glasses and plates back to the kitchen without saying a word. He knew she was against the war from their very first meeting. Still the reality of seeing the anti-war signs, hidden from his view, was disturbing to him; however, it was no time for another disagreeable discussion about the war.

He had already concluded that the war was far too complex and too ambiguous to try to persuade anyone to see it differently. The impact of television newscasts and casualty reports were more cogent than any well-articulated argument. The war was imposing a physical separation for nearly 10 months and that was sufficiently disturbing to them, and he had no wish to exacerbate the situation and for them to separate feeling angry, hurt and distant.

Cannon was searching for a way to break the mood. He was pretty sure, but not certain, and he did not want to raise false expectations, nevertheless, "Darling, you know I was thinking, to the best of my knowledge, all of the WestPac carriers go to Hong Kong for R and R..."

"R and R?"

"Rest and recreation. And wouldn't it be wonderful if your Easter recess over-lapped *Tico's* R and R period in Hong Kong...I mean if her schedule works out. If your schedule works out."

"You mean that I might be able to join you in Hong Kong, Caro?"

"Possibly."

"Carissimo, I'll come even if taught classes are in session. I'll come to Hong Kong to be with you. We'll make love in Hong Kong!" She skipped towards him in her apron with a spoon and fork in each hand. He threw his arms around her and lifted her off the floor and twirled her in a full circle.

"Hong Kong! Yes! And make love in Manhattan all night, tonight!" He looked up at her smiling face, and she kissed him on the nose and on the ear and kissed him firmly on the lips.

"Yes, Carissimo, all night long but, but, not until you taste my pollo limone with an excellent vino blanco d' Orvieto."

Ticonderoga pulled into Pearl Harbor in early December before proceeding next to Yokosuka, Japan. In the back corner of the main bar at the Enlisted Men's Club, near the golf course of the Pearl Harbor naval base, a dozen or more enlisted men from *Ticonderoga* stood or sat around Chaplain Osborne conversing over a beer. They were wearing the dress white tropical uniform of the day and except for Osborne, who wore three ribbons over the left pocket of his white short sleeve shirt, most of the men were E2s or E3s on their first deployment to WestPac and wore only the National Defense Service ribbon.

Since committing his life to the service of Jesus Christ and becoming an ordained Episcopal priest and subsequently a navy chaplain, Osborne, by choice, never wore his Korean War ribbons which had been awarded to him as a former 1st Lieutenant with the First Marine Division. His combat experience included escaping the death and carnage of the Chosin Reservoir, two Purple Hearts and a Silver Star —facts about his former life that Osborne kept to himself. In due course, like the chaplain, *Ticonderoga's* enlisted men would add the Vietnam Campaign and Republic of Vietnam Service ribbons.

Chaplain Ogilvy Osborne was by rank a commander in the Chaplain Corps, and by tradition, the EM Club was off-limits to officers unless they were deliberately invited, which was an invitation rarely extended and rarely accepted.

"Commander, how many cruises you had to WestPac, sir."

"You can call me O, or Double-O, or O Square. What's your name, sailor?

"Schultz, Norman Schultz, sir...I'm mean O...from New Ulm, Minnesota, sir."

"Made quite a few, Norman Schultz. Quite a few. This is my first with *Ticonderoga*."

"You like *Tico*, sir?"

"Yes. Yes, I do. She's a great ship. And she has a lot of fine fellas on her like you guys, too. Got a good skipper. Straight shooter. You can trust what he says, men."

"You think we're gonna win this thing, sir?"

"You mean the war in Vietnam?" It was a rhetorical question. "Let's remember our mission, men. What we are trying to do is to stop this war.

The Red Chinese proposed dividing the country into two nation states at the 17th parallel during the Geneva Conference of 1954 to end the First Indo-China War. We are trying to stop the war. Stop the aggression from the North upon the Republic of Vietnam. We are trying to give the people of South Vietnam, who lived under French colonial administration and Japanese conquest, a chance to live without being under the control of a Stalin-like dictator in the North." A young electronics technician striker, half the age of the chaplain, spoke up next.

"Sir, isn't it true that South Vietnam is pretty corrupt, too?"

"Yes. That is true." Osborne paused before he added, "You know, men, there are 144 member countries in the United Nations. Only about two dozen can be considered liberal democracies like the United States. There just aren't that many of us." Then Osborne changed the subject and lightened his tone. "What dija do in New Ulm, Norm?"

"Worked on the family farm, sir. Mostly corn and soy beans, fixed cars... chased girls... stuff like that, Chaplain."

"Well Norman Schultz, dija catch any?"

"Catch any?" Schultz was taken momentarily off guard. "You mean girls? Yes, sir. One or two." Schultz nervously took a quick sip from the can of Schlitz beer in his hand and wore a half-proud, half-embarrassed smile as he searched the faces of his shipmates as whistles and catcalls broke out all around.

"Good. That's a lot better'n me. All I ever caught in Minnesota was a coupla walleyes." Easy laughter broke out among the men. A voice in the crowd asked.

"Was that a fish or a woman, Chaplain?" The subject brought on more anxious laughter, but an easy camaraderie prevailed. Someone in the second row of the circle around Chaplain Osborne kibitzed.

"Lucky she wasn't a sockeye or you'd know the difference for sure, O." Raucous peels of laughter broke out among the men of *Ticonderoga*.

'Ha, ha." Osborne laughed genuinely. "Ha, ha. Yeah, I guess I would." He waited for the atmosphere to settle before resuming, "So Norman Schultz, whaddya going tell the folks back in New Ulm about what you're doing in *Ticonderoga*?"

"Haven't told them nothin', sir." He paused sensing he had the audience with them, "Guess I'll tell'em, we're gonna try and stop aggression, and..." He took a dramatic pause before continuing with a huge grin, "an' just like the recruiter said, 'Join the Navy. See the world.' " That brought hoots and peals of laughter all around as someone always made a cynical joke about promises made to them by their recruiter. "Now I'm in Hawaii, and next I'm goin' to Jap-pan!" Osborne got up smiling and laughing, and stepped forward and shook Schultz's hand.

"Here's a five spot, Norm, for a round of fifteen cent beers on me. Make sure you spread them around, will you?"

"Aye, aye, sir!" Schultz was deliberately emphatic. "Thank you, sir"

"Thank you. Thank you all, men, for the nice invitation to your club. And when you see me around the ship, come up and say 'Hello to O.' " He shook hands with several men as he left.

"Enjoy your liberty, men. There are hard days ahead." Osborne left rushing off to his next appointment at the Hickam Officer's Club, a dinner date with Lieutenant Augustine MacD. Campbell, a pilot in Attack Squadron 23 and Osborne's newest chaplain's assistant.

They were seated at a table overlooking the channel to Pearl Harbor. Ships of the Seventh Fleet of every description were moored at the piers of the naval base. They had just finished the main course and were awaiting dessert when they fell into serious conversation.

"I think you probably recall, O, that my father was a missionary in Korea and taught the Bible and ancient history in Seoul."

"Indeed, I do, Ti."

"My father has a Ph.D. in ancient history and he reads Hebrew and Greek. He has a church in Florida now, and he has been writing a book."

"Yes?"

"To my parent's regret, and now sadly to my regret, I wasn't much of a student, so I pretty much avoided those intellectual conversations that my father had with my older brother and wanted to have with me."

"And now you wish you could?"

"Yes...sort of...yes. Anyway, it was my father's observation that no other major civilization placed as much value on the primacy of the individual as Western Civilization. And he believed it was because Western Civilization adopted certain teachings in the Old Testament and carried them forward in Christianity that this was so. In fact he thought that the Bible, the Judean-Christian tradition and Western Civilization were integral.

"Hmm. How so?"

"He believed the very notion of a just God implied that others, especially God's people must have rights—inalienable rights. And that those rights were protected by law. He noted that four of the Ten Commandments were prohibitions protecting the individual rights of men against other men. The right not have false testimony borne against them, the right to possess personal goods, that is the law against theft. The law against murder which implies the sanctity of individual life, and finally the law to maintain the security of marriage and household possessions. God," he said, "gave us the notion of a society governed by law."

"Intriguing. I had not made the political connection." Osborne thought for a moment before he added. "I suppose the stories in the Bible of the rights of masters and slaves and the duties to each other would be part of that."

"Yes. My father would unabashedly declare that the Magna Carta imposed upon King John in 1215 was the logical extension of the rights and duties of masters to slaves as articulated in the Old Testament, and later by Paul, who proclaimed that masters and slaves were equal in the eyes of God. He repeated many times over, that the moral compass of western civilization was inherent at the very inception."

Indeed there were hard days ahead. In just two days out of Pearl Harbor *Ticonderoga* and her escorts were caught in a vicious storm. While *Ticonderoga* was taking every third wave over her bow fifty-five feet above her waterline, the destroyers and their crews were taking such a beating that the screen commander requested permission to leave the formation and steam independently at best course and speed.

Chapter 4.

Cannon took the shuttle from LaGuardia down to Washington National for lunch with Captain Pebbles and Beebe Byrnes. Pebbles was his old boss in *Essex* and had introduced him to Mrs. Byrnes, a CIA case officer, who had certain assignments when *Essex* was deployed to the North Atlantic and in the Mediterranean just before and just after last year's Six-Day, Arab-Israeli War. It was a reunion of old friends—the widow, the former boss, and in a way, their joint protégé. After they were seated in a loud restaurant in Georgetown with the kind of background noise that intelligence officers like, Captain Pebbles began the conversation. "So what's this story that I heard about you removing a senior officer from the conn?" He said with a wry smile.

"How did you learn about that?"

"We have our ways," he winked at Beebe, "don't we Mrs. Byrnes?" So Cannon related the story of how he decided it was necessary to relieve Commander Knight of the conn. Pebbles then asked him, "How did you manage to get *Essex* into station?"

"In a very lubberly fashion, sir. I held her a half to a full degree to port to counter bank suction and slowly brought the turns down until we just about had our refueling stations aligned with *Kankakee*. Then I brought the turns up quickly to 10 knots for Romeo Corpen. It was greasy. Not recommended, but I got away with it without losing steerage." Pebbles nodded.

"So who's your spy, Captain?" Cannon flashed a Pebbles-like smile, one of the many mannerisms that he acquired from Pebbles after working as his administrative assistant in *Essex'* Operations department.

"Not to be repeated, but Captain Meehan called me and asked my opinion on a few related matters. Knight has been served divorce papers by his wife. Her father is a vice-admiral and has probably helped his career along."

"So he loses a wife, *and* a rabbi," surmised Beebe.

"Ah, I always wondered who protected that man," interjected Cannon. "The man has no sense of loyalty downwards."

"I'll not comment on any of that." Pebbles frowned at both of them. "Anyway, Jim Meehan said that you put him on the trail. Something about displaced hostility as a hypothesis, as a possible explanation for Knight's behavior. That's why he called me and others here in Washington."

"So Meehan has a tough decision to make on the future of Knight's career," added Beebe.

"Can't ignore it. Knight committed suicide in front of a dozen people including several peers," declared Cannon firmly revealing a repressed sense of anger. "Pushed me to the limit for no damn good reason. Could have been more serious."

"Sounds like a courageous call. I have it on very good authority, that Meehan thought you handled it well," added Pebbles.

"That's what he told me, and I trust him. Anyway, enough on that, sir." The subject was still distasteful, and Cannon prudently switched the subject. "Speaking of behavior which is hard to understand, what's been concluded about the former captain of K-22?" Cannon was referring to the collision that resulted when a soviet nuclear submarine appeared to deliberately ram a destroyer escort last August in the Eastern Mediterranean. Beebe spoke.

"I don't think we have a better answer than that he was either drunk..."

"Drunk?"

"Yes.

"With nuclear weapons aboard?" asked Cannon incredulously.

"Yes," responded Beebe. "Or we have your theory, if you prefer it. That he was emotionally unstable, and had a nervous breakdown."

Pebbles added, "Don't think we're going to get a more definitive answer from the Russians, but Bob...you and I have discussed this at least once before...we have begun high level discussions with the Russians about incidents at sea. They agree that the games being played are on the verge of getting seriously out of hand."

"Thank God for that."

"The theory of mutual deterrence seems to be working."

There was a brief lull in the conversation before Mrs. Byrnes revealed the real motive, other than genuine friendship, for the luncheon.

"I have heard a rumor that you are engaged, Mr. Cannon."

"And I have heard it, too. And it wasn't from you, Bob." Pebbles was playfully reproachful. "Why didn't you send me a note and tell me directly? That's wonderful news. She's a beautiful, young woman. Lucky, man. Do you know her, Beebe?"

"Just seen photographs of her. She's attractive, Captain." She spoke the words coolly with implied disapproval and understated her beauty. Cannon caught the abrupt change in tone. And Pebbles did, too. He always believed Widow Byrnes's interest in Mr. Cannon was a bit more than totally professional although he never doubted that her conduct was anything but thoroughly professional. On more than one occasion she had characterized Cannon as very like her husband, a tall, well-educated, articulate Marine officer killed early in the war in Southeast Asia. "And the engagement adds further complications."

"How's that, Beebe?" asked Cannon.

"Bob, internal security is not a matter for the CIA. It's a matter for the FBI." She reached down and pulled a brown envelope out of her purse from which she withdrew a photograph. "Your fiancée marches with Columbia University Graduate Students Against the War." She turned the photo so that it was right side up for Cannon. Cannon looked at the photo. It was a street scene, a demonstration of some sort, and it pictured Tish with her sign about to be pelted with something, perhaps an apple or a tomato, and the artsy fellow with the long, blond, Botticelli hair by her side shielding her, protecting her. Cannon imperceptibly winced.

"Yes. What's that to do with photographs of Laetitia Martin?" A twinge of anger passed through Cannon. He was covering his own anxiety, the protective stance of a possible suitor, when he challenged Beebe Byrnes.

"I was asked by a counter-part in the FBI about you."

"Me?"

"Yes, you. When I asked why, they told me they were running a B.I. on you for a top secret clearance. They showed me this picture of her marching with a Stop-the-War-Now! sign. They asked if there was a loyalty issue."

"And what did you say, Beebe?" Cannon's tone challenged the CIA officer again although he invariably took the direct approach which often disarmed people.

"I said, on my husband's grave, 'No way.' I said it was also the opinion of several senior naval officers that you exhibited the highest professional standards and could have an exceptionally fine career as a naval officer if you chose it." She paused, "And, I promised never to discuss the issue with you."

"Thank you, Beebe." He was sarcastic but very controlled. "Did you tell them that I prefer to develop my own thoughts, hunh? Did you tell them that I think for myself, and that I am quite allergic to all forms of pablum propaganda? Did you tell them that? Did you tell them I didn't buy the B.S. about *USS Liberty* any more than I bought the crap about the so called Gulf of Tonkin Incident? And did they say to you, 'Those are the ones who are the least trustworthy. They are the worst kind.' "

"That's unfair. Very unfair. I vouched for you." There was a very long, tense pause in the conversation during which Pebbles kept his silence and watched this new breed of officer which did not accept authority unquestionably and routinely tested its legitimacy. Cannon was quick to anger in such circumstances, and Pebbles waited and observed. Cannon took a deep breath and noticeably let half the air out between his lips before responding—a hopeful sign that he was maturing.

"Mrs. Byrnes, I apologize. I'm sorry that I doubted you. Thank you." Pebbles waited a moment, then he added.

"Bob, I was consulted, too."

"You, too?" Pebbles let the gravity of the message register, then he spoke softly. "Bob, ask Tish if she can be less visible about it. I'm not asking her to change her opinion about the war; I'm only suggesting that it wouldn't be great to see a picture in some tabloid of the two of you cutting a cake together with an opposing picture of Tish carrying an anti-war sign. Move back in the ranks. Lose the sign." Cannon stared blankly into Pebbles face, and then he searched Beebe's expression. He was idealistic, but above all, he was a pragmatist.

"Is that why I was invited to lunch?" Pebbles answered him carefully.

"Yes and no, Bobby, but overall, you were invited as a friend." Pebbles referred to him as Bobby deliberately. It was the first time that he used the name in front of a third person. Heretofore, it was only used in private between the two of them. But he used it dramatically as if he were speaking like a father to a son. "I have 250 lunches to allocate a year, young man. I don't book lunch with junior officers without good reason. You're among friends here, Bob. We're not extremists. But it might be a good time to move your rook and castle your king. Not everyone will be your friend, and someone…someone who can do you great harm, may be less understanding, less tolerant."

"Sir, is this a general admonition…career counseling…or do you have someone specifically in mind?" Pebbles ignored the slight tone of insolence and remained patient with Cannon. Creative minds required sensitive management, and Cannon had a precocious ability to handle the unstructured problem extremely well.

"Bob, you know as well as I do that the war is not going well. A lot of people will do strange and unpredictable things to advance or protect their careers. There will be blaming. Some might exhibit 'displaced hostility.'

Don't make yourself an easy target. Preserve yourself to fight the good fight. You once said you were Odysseus. Be strategic. Don't foolishly fall on your own sword."

"Sir, Tish is a strong-willed woman. In a few years she has grown from being a sweet debutante to being an autonomous, self-directed intellectual. What makes you think that even if I were to request that from her that she would actually refrain from doing it?" Beebe Byrnes was visibly impatient with the direction of the conversation.

"You're a naval officer. You need to control your woman!" Beebe interjected with disgust. Canon's eyes flashed anger.

"Uh, Beebe... um," Pebbles used a calming voice. "We handle things in the Navy a little differently from the Marine Corps." Pebbles smiled trying to relieve the tension. Then he looked at Cannon. "Bob, I'm not suggesting that you sell her out. Certainly it is up to her to decide. And for you, too. But you need for her to know the potential consequences." Then he shifted tack. "I want you to imagine someday that you are being considered by the Senate Armed Services Committee for CNO or for Secretary of the Navy...that could be you...when some senator pulls out a photo of your beautiful wife demonstrating against the war. Being in love, being married, sometimes requires something sub-optimal from the other partner."

"This is a matter or moral principle, religious principle with her...and, and I'm in love with her.... May be a naval career isn't for me. May be the price is too high. If I can be smeared as unpatriotic or untrustworthy with guilt by association, then maybe I should return to civilian life when my contract is up."

"Then, I would say to you, Bob, that your country will be deprived of a very great talent." He paused and looked at his watch. "You need to get going to Andrews, and I need to get back to the office. Give it some thought. I'd like to have you in Washington in about a year."

The chartered, Boeing 707 MATS flight began its descent into Clark Field in the Philippines. Every seat was taken by servicemen of all races from all branches and all ranks. They were seated randomly about the aircraft although the center of gravity in the waist of the 707 was made up of enlisted men in the army. The cabin crew operated with a polite, sympathetic reverence for the men headed for war. Their passengers did not manifest the gaiety of tourists bound for adventure. Most were just out of infantry training; a few were returning for another tour.

Cannon sat by a window in the middle of the aircraft. Next to him was a first class, black petty officer from the Seabees who was returning for a second tour to Danang. Except for verbal pleasantries at the start of the flight, each man remained silent and slept or thought or dreamt to himself. The general emotion in the cabin was sobriety. Gaiety was reserved for another moment. Gaiety, or perhaps, sadness, or a mixture of gaiety and sadness was reserved for the men who were alive, who were otherwise unwounded, the survivors, who would take the reverse trip back home.

Cannon had plenty of time for reflection on the 22 hour flight. He dreamed of his last night with Tish in New York, and making love to her in Hong Kong, and his thoughts ranged from the disturbing topic which he referred to as the Byrnes-Pebbles issue, to his preparation and experience for his new assignment, and speculation about his specific responsibilities.

Cannon possessed a first-rate mind, and he had an unusually keen grasp of geo-politics, and he gave particular thought to the validity of the domino theory—the theory that if Vietnam fell to communists, Cambodia, Laos and Thailand were likely to fall as well. He also calculated the odds of "victory" in Vietnam, and he didn't like them. He knew the US had definite interests in Southeast Asia and that there was a NATO-like treaty, SEATO, that obligated the US to come to the defense of member nations. What bothered Cannon was the fact that South Vietnam had been the target of subversion by the North for nearly two decades, and that the post-colonial government in South Vietnam had undergone a coup and additional changes in leadership and remained corrupt, unpopular and unstable and now faced active guerilla operations across a broad area of the country. He took it to be a cheap war being waged by the northern communists, proxies for the Russians, tying down American forces and consuming resources when the truly serious communist threat remained in Western and Eastern Europe and with oil in the Middle-East.

As intellectually curious as Cannon was, he avoided judging whether the war was a just war. Certainly his fiancée had her opinion. It was a source of tension, and perhaps it was sufficient for him to know that his country was at war, that the decision had been made, that he was now going to be part of it, and it was preferable to win it than to lose it.

In a way he had cleared the decks of his mind for action. Were he not going to a support role stationed, not in-country, but on an attack carrier in the Gulf of Tonkin, far from the killing grounds, he might have been required to confront the subject. On the other hand, leading a platoon in a search and destroy operation was not a time for indecisive contemplation either. He had a profound respect for the distinction, and for those who served in-country, and while technically he would be in the war zone, he steadfastly referred to the location of his assignment as the Gulf of Tonkin.

The plane departed from San Francisco and stopped in Honolulu for refueling and went on to Wake Island where it refueled again for the final leg into the Philippines. He was beginning to feel like Kurtz who felt civilization fading behind him as he traveled up the Amazon River into the heart of darkness.

Dawn was breaking over Wake Island. Across the tarmac Cannon could see the unmistakable black profiles with their large characteristic vertical stabilizers of several B-52 strategic bombers parked in their revetments. At each stop the proximity of the war felt closer to him.

The MATS charter landed at Clark Field with a thump-bump and a loud roar of the engines' thrust being reversed to slow the aircraft on a long runway laden with mid-morning, hot and humid air. Several "cattle-cars" were visible, lined up as the plane taxied up to a basic structure that served as a terminal. Army personnel were called first off the plane and disappeared from Cannon's sight. The last group called to debark from the plane was navy personnel. Near the bottom of the stairs there was an airman with a plain, white cardboard sign with hand-written letters that simply said "Navy." There were about 30 navy personnel, and they were led off to the right of the aircraft and walked to a strip of grass about a hundred yards away and told to wait for a bus to take them to Subic Bay and on to the Cubi Point air station.

They stood, sat, crouched or lay down in the oppressive heat and humidity. Some drew on cigarettes. No one had a bottle of water. Several sailors removed their blue wool jumpers and Cannon removed his double-breasted jacket and cap. Virtually everyone wore service dress blues which were appropriate from their commands back in the US in wintry January and were always an appropriate uniform for reporting to a new command, but the uniform was hardly intended for a tropical environment.

About forty minutes later a tug with a trailer piled full with their checked baggage pulled up, and the group began to operate like a working party to sort the luggage. Cannon redonned his officer cap when he sensed he was beginning to sunburn and walked over to the Filipino driver of the tug and asked him when he thought the bus would arrive. "Maybe in an hour, sir," shrugged the driver with a grin.

It wasn't a bad guess. Shortly before noon, a school bus painted haze gray, driven by a local civilian, appeared and made its way towards them. Silently they filed on, tired, hungry, and thirsty. Cannon tossed his val-pack in the overhead luggage rack and sat in the middle of the bus, in a window seat, and took in all that he could as the bus made its way to their destination.

The rutted road was laden with omnipresent potholes even as they made their way through the main streets of Angeles City. The bus shook and rattled as it made its way, and there was a manual transmission that added a colorful whine to the overall atmosphere. Here and there he could see men in various uniforms that looked like police and private guards with holstered pistols and ammunition around their waists.

The overall impression was of an impoverished country that was still recovering from the Huk, communist guerilla insurrection, and where security was provided by non-governmental groups, and where basic commerce seemed to flourish vigorously. The houses ranged from reasonable wooden structures to huts and hoovervilles, and the women were dressed in bright colors and in general, the mood of the Filipinos was visibly pleasant despite their hardships.

Cannon was the only passenger left on the bus after the stop at the Subic naval base. He moved to the first row of seats but was too tired to engage the driver in conversation. Finally the bus pulled up to the air station operations shack. He put on his jacket and donned his cap as he grabbed his bag and stepped off the bus.

"Good luck, sir." The Filipino driver smiled at him cheerfully.

"Thanks. Thanks for the lift," and he turned to enter the operations shack where he presented his travel orders to an airman. After greeting the officer, who wore only a national defense medal on his uniform, a visible sign that Cannon was new to the theater, he read Cannon's orders.

"Let's see, sir...hmm. *Tico*. COD. Priority high." He paused before speaking. "Okay, sir, here's how it works. We send a message to the ship saying you have arrived at Cubi. They send a message back to us saying which COD flight you will be manifested on. Here's an alarm clock." The airman reached for an almond color, wind-up, alarm clock and handed it to Cannon. "You call in every morning at 0330, sir, and if you are on the manifest, sir, you get here by 0500." The airman wrote down the phone number on a pink chit and handed it to Cannon.

"I've come all this way, priority, says I'm priority...you mean I just sit here and wait!"

"Yes, sir. That's the way it works. Today's COD only took spare parts, sir."

"I see." Cannon was disappointed with the uncertainty of his last leg to *Ticonderoga,* and emotionally he felt somewhat under-appreciated after having traveled so far with highest priority. He also felt suddenly alone.

"Sir, we'll call you a cab, sir, for the BOQ. You got quarters, sir?"

"Quarters?"

"Twenty-five cent pieces, you'll need 'em to feed the cab meter, sir. Don't worry, the driver can make change. Take any berth in any room of the BOQ that you like, sir."

Cannon carried his val-back through the front door of the gray BOQ. The building was empty. There wasn't a soul. He found a room with two of the four bunks taken, and went on to another that he claimed for himself. All of the rooms had wooden louvers for windows and screens. A few of the louvers were missing, and all of the screens were in disrepair and pushed out. It reminded him of a World War II movie in the South Pacific. *Helluva a thing if I came high priority all this way just for a dose of malaria,* he thought as he inspected the screens. *Farther up the Amazon; closer to the war zone,* he mused. It was getting very palpable now.

Cannon spent two more nights in the BOQ and was beginning to feel unwanted before he was scheduled to fly aboard *Ticonderoga.* He needn't have called the operations shack. A messenger woke him around 0300, well-before the alarm was set. He called a cab and was at the operations shack only to find that the COD wouldn't depart until 0700. By now he was getting good at doing nothing, and he went for breakfast in the adjacent cafeteria, read the latest edition of *Stars and Stripes,* and then tried to close his eyes and nap. He checked his calendar watch and read the date. It was January 8, 1968. He had forgotten; it was his birthday.

When dawn broke it was a bright, cloudless, sunny morning, ceiling and visibility unlimited. Two pilots, passengers returning to the ship, were standing in olive, nomex flight suits near the rear ramp of the aircraft when Cannon walked up and said hello. He had newbie written all over him, and he struggled hard to strike a pose of humble self-confidence in front of the attack pilots. They had flown a pair of Skyhawks in for maintenance the night before. One of the COD's crewmen, picked up a duffle bag belonging to one of the attack pilots and tossed it on the ramp. There was the certain sound, though muffled, of glass breaking, and shortly thereafter a colorless liquid ran from the bag. The senior pilot, a lieutenant commander, crouched down and unzipped the bag and began removing pieces of glass of what was formerly a fifth of vodka. He looked up at Cannon and smiled, and then showed a bottle of Canadian whisky to the other pilot who shrugged. Cannon smiled back. *Wet ship,* he thought. Contrary to Navy Regulations, he had heard that it wasn't unusual for pilots who were flying a mission or two a day over North Vietnam to finish the day with a drink in the privacy of their staterooms. *Who could blame them?* These were the most intensive carrier operations in the history of naval warfare against the most heavily defended target in the history of air warfare. The policing mechanism was whether their peers were willing to fly with them the next day, and whether they could handle the combat conditions.

Six seats were set against the forward bulkhead of the aircraft facing the rear separated by the companionway to the flight deck of the C-2. Except for the seats for the two crewman and the three officers, the aircraft was loaded to its weight limit with crates, and boxes.

"Welcome aboard. Ever landed on a carrier before?" asked the plane commander who greeted Cannon as he took his seat."

"Once. An E-1B. Aboard *Essex,* sir."

"Okay, you know the drill. Flight time is about eight hours to *Tico* if we hit the stack on schedule."

"What's the weather like out there, sir?"

"The usual for this time of year. Thousand foot ceiling. Visibility a quarter to a half mile. Monsoonal rain, variably from light drizzle to a soaking rain, winds 5 to 10 knots. IFR recovery." Cannon nodded. "Okay, buckle up."

Cannon heard the pilot lower the flaps and the landing gear on final approach to *Ticonderoga.* He had dozed along the way along with everyone else in the rear of the plane, but now he was wide alert. He laced up his shoes, rechecked his "H" harness, noted the emergency exits, and memorized the location of the fire bottles.

In one coordinated moment he heard the loud thud of the landing gear on the deck, the arresting gear reel out, and the turboprop engines wind up to full power in case of a bolter. The plane decelerated rapidly and the inertia of motion drove the passengers into the backs of their seats. The COD was the last trap in the recovery and taxied to a spot in the middle of the flight deck just opposite Flight Deck Control. The side hatch of the aircraft popped open, and there was the ship's logistics officer in his yellow flight deck jersey and Mickey Mouse ears saying hello. "You must be

Cannon, Lieutenant J.G. I'm Hugh Hanson, air department, JG. Welcome aboard."

"Thanks, nice to meet you."

"I'll take care of your gear. The CIC officer, Commander Jeffreys, wants to see you right away. Ops office. Oh-two level." The ship was turning out of the wind and as Cannon went through the hatch of the C-2, a blast of warm rain hit him in the face. He grabbed his cap and ran for the open hatch in Flight Deck Control. There he was met by broadly grinning Chaplain Osborne wearing a green flight deck shirt with a black cross done in magic marker on the front and back.

"Hi, I'm Ogilvy Osborne, better known as Padre, or O, or Double-O, or O-square to the boys aboard *Tico*."

"Yes, sir. Nice to meet you, Padre." Cannon warmed to the chaplain immediately. The first impression certainly was of a tall, pleasant man who commanded instant respect. He displayed unusual energy, a willingness to get his hands dirty as manifested by his sopping wet flight deck jersey. He appeared very real and genuine.

"I know your fiancée's mother, and her family. Was ordained in Christ Church, Greenwich. Letter from Brooke Martin said you were coming. Asked me to remember you in my prayers." Cannon was stunned. Tish had said nothing about it. Cannon's first reaction was that Mrs. Martin was having someone checking on him. "Heard you know, Ned Chase, also." Cannon was stunned again. He had met Ned Chase briefly before Chase went to OCS and had been introduced to him by Tish. "He's aboard *Ticonderoga*, too. Weapons department. Well, gotta go. Today's my day with the boys on the roof. Have my own green jersey. Arresting gear crew. I try and spend time when I'm not being hauled off to some tin can with the men at their work stations. God is right here on the flight deck with us all, you know. That sort of thing. We'll meet and have a real talk again soon, Bob." Cannon was just a bit overwhelmed by the chaplain's dynamism, but he managed to say, "Thank you, Padre. I'll need the prayers."

Chapter 5.

The way to the Operations office was identical to *Essex* on the 02 level, and the office was laid out identically with two yeomen outside and the operations officer and the administrative assistant inside. Commander Jeffreys was waiting for him and immediately stood up and greeted Cannon warmly.

"Hi, I'm Frank Jeffreys, you must be Bob Cannon."

"Yes, sir." Cannon extended his right hand to meet the commander's right hand, "Bob Cannon, Commander." The aviation navy was informal compared to the black shoe navy. The surface navy retained the hierarchical structure of rank and operated more on a level to level basis. In contrast, in an organization where an ensign was commonly a commander's wingman, competency mattered more than rank. A senior officer with poor flying skills was exposed quickly and was accorded the respect of rank but little more, and the converse was true for junior officers with excellent flying skills.

"How's *Essex*. I flew F-9s off her way back when."

"Korea?"

"Yes."

"She's a CVS now Commander, and well…she's my first ship. She has served her country well."

"Well, welcome aboard *Tico*. You'll find her a damn fine ship as well." He paused before continuing, "Damn fine. Well, we had a little trouble getting you here from Cubi. Sorry 'bout that. But we really need you, and you have a lot of nice qualifications. The navigator has already told me they want you on the bridge."

"Yes, sir."

"And I saw in your jacket that you have experience controlling aircraft including fighters, so what we'd like to do is as follows: One of our strike controllers has moved to Ops admin assistant, and I'd like you to fill that spot. And we'll work you into the watch rotation as a CIC watch officer, and I know they will put you on the bridge. So that looks like you'll be on watch for 12 to 14 hours a day. You'll be on the bridge with the RadNav team during Sea and Anchor detail. See that you have done that before, and for GQ, get to CIC and work it out with Van Kirk how you'll cover strike and let me know. Do you think you can handle that, Bob?"

"Strike controller. I'm not familiar with the function, sir. Could you help me out, sir?"

"Okay. After the strike launches they switch from the tower frequency to strike control. They stay with you until they get to the target area or go feet dry, and they switch to one of the squadron attack frequencies. On the way out, when they go feet wet, they switch back to strike control. That's when it gets interesting. You're sort of the 911 for the air wing. Some of the birds may have battle damage, be low-state fuel, might have a fire, et cetera. Your job is to get'em help. In a shoot down, that may be to hustle up additional ResCap and organize a SAR. You'll just have to be aware of the situation, use your head, and do your best." Jeffreys paused and ran through a mental checklist of the job description, and then he added, "A lot of times, especially during bad weather, like now during the monsoon, the guys will be bringing back unexpended ordnance, and you will have to find a safe place for them to drop it before they come aboard."

"You mean they don't just pickle 'em off somewhere over the North."

"Unh, unh. That's not the way we fight our wars. The rules of engagement require us to identify legitimate targets before releasing any ordnance. No, you'll have to find a safe place within five to fifteen miles of the ship to drop the iron bombs. The lighter weight, expensive missiles, they'll bring 'em back aboard." Cannon made a mental note to bring this last point to his fiancé's attention, but more significantly, he was excited by the challenge of the function, and he could imagine how it could have a critical life or death responsibility, and just as immediately he felt inadequate to the task although he remained confident that in time he could handle the position.

"That sounds like a lot, sir. I really know very little about the mission, the process and procedures, the types of aircraft, but I guess I can learn."

"I know, but you're the best that we have. Hopefully you can come up the power curve quickly." Cannon remained guarded.

"Sir, I have never been on an attack carrier. I have a basic understanding of carrier ops from *Essex*, but there we operated 7 by 24 on a four hour cycle. Can you cover me off on some of the differences?"

"Sure. First we're part of Task Force 77, and we're Task Group 76.1. We have three, sometimes four carriers on Yankee Station. Each of us flies a 12 to 13 hour shift with 90 minute cycles. They give the little decks like us, the *Essex* 27 Charlie class, mostly the days because we don't carry anything that can match the night and all-weather capability of the A-6 Intruder."

"The Grumman A-6...with the DIANE navigation system?" He paused. "Haven't we lost quite a few of those?" It was information that

Cannon had acquired from the reading that he had done for this assignment.

"Afraid so. They often go in as a single plane raid at 50 to 100 feet AGL. They seem to be bagging them on the way out." Both men soberly considered the implications. Cannon envisioned pilots and crewman who were fighting to live, died or were captured. Jeffreys broke the silence. "Anyway, that's nine launches and nine recoveries per ship, with two of us always flying. So the task force flies 24 hours a day, 365 days a year unless we're given an order to stand down. Despite any stand down, we maintain a combat air patrol barrier between us and the MIG airfields for fleet defense all the time. Our mission is primarily the interdiction of logistics and occasionally the Joint Chiefs of Staff will order a major strike on targets in Hanoi and Haiphong. Haven't had many this year. '67 we had two, three Alphas a day. In those cases, each carrier will put up a deckload of 30 some aircraft, and we'll go in with 90 to 100 airplanes. Generally the air force will precede or follow the navy with a similar gaggle of aircraft within 15 minutes. They will also generally put up two or three KC-135 tankers over the Gulf for the navy."

"That's an Alpha strike. Hmm."

"Yup." Jeffreys paused to think whether he needed to add anything. He shifted the subject slightly. "It's been primarily an attack pilot's war."

"I see." Cannon paused to digest what he had just heard, *an attack pilot's war.* Considering it an attack pilot's war coming from an attack pilot added a new distinction to the characterization of the air war. It was the kind of distinction that one heard only if one were close to the air war or close to people prosecuting the air war and not likely to be picked up from his reading and preparation which he began as soon as he received his orders to *Ticonderoga.* He laid the thought aside and moved on to the next question. "You didn't say much about ASW, Commander."

"Your official billet. Well, let's see. COMASWFORPAC has primary responsibility for ASW. There are a couple of attack boats and a couple of patrol plane squadrons who manage that in the Gulf. There's also SOSUS. The threat level is not considered high. *Tico* doesn't do much. An occasional exercise. I'll see that you're on the distribution list for ASW info." Cannon was aware that the two-ocean navy emphasized different threats in their training and preparation. Historically the Atlantic Fleet was oriented to anti-submarine warfare while the Pacific Fleet emphasized amphibious and strike warfare.

"I know the NVN and the ChiComs don't have much, but there's no sweat about Russian boats, sir? No cruise missile, Echo class boats, sir?"

"Not so far," Jeffreys looked around for a piece of wood to knock on but couldn't find any as the ship was stripped of as many combustibles as possible, "knock on wood," he smiled faintly, "but my guess is that they are being trailed if they come within a thousand miles of Yankee Station." He paused and smiled at Cannon. "Since we're on the Russians, I guess you have had elint trawlers with you?"

"Affirmative, and destroyers, sir."

"Gargles is always with us. When you get on the bridge you might ask them how they work 'em. I think there is some sort of understanding with the Russians. Maybe not, but we don't seem to go out of the way for 'em."

"I see." Cannon wondered what if anything was left uncovered. Then he asked, "What sort of collateral responsibilities do you have in mind, sir."

"None. The Ops Boss thought that was enough. We won't give you any division responsibilities, or anything else, although I can't be certain that the Captain's Office won't put you on a court-martial board. We kind of thought you'd be pulling more hours on watch than anyone in the department...or the ship for that matter. You'll be earning your pay. Think you can handle it, Bob?"

"Yes, sir, if I can get the op-order and some OJT, I believe I can handle it." Secretly he was thrilled. He was the classic achiever and the easiest way to motivate him was to offer him a challenge that was rarely done. His assignments were a perfect fit with his personality.

"I have a copy of the op-order. I'll lend it to you. Check with the yeomen later today. Also make sure you keep up with the message boards."

"Certainly. Thank you." But Cannon remained curious about his primary assignment. "Sir, can you tell me anything more about the strike controller position?"

"We like to have officers in those positions. Dick Van Kirk, he's the other strike controller. He's a naval flight officer. He'll break you in."

"Well, okay. I better get over to the Captains Office and check in..."

"Uh, one other thing, Bob. I was a little surprised that you didn't have a permanent top secret clearance. So we put in a request to get the process going."

"I think the FBI has a backlog of background investigations, sir, something over a year. So the East Coast ships were asked to cut the applications back to the bone, sir. And then in *Essex*, I don't think the average ensign or J.G. needed one." He didn't mention that he knew the FBI was acting on his background investigation.

"You should have one here, so you'll get a temporary top secret now, and we have requested a permanent clearance. You may need it depending on our SIOP responsibilities." That was code for nuclear weapons and their targets.

"Yes, sir." Cannon winced slightly.

"So, please, get over to the Captain's Office ASAP, give 'em a new set of finger prints, and fill out the paper work. I'll start you on the CIC watch bill tomorrow. By the way, I checked, and you'll be the senior CIC watch officer when Lieutenant Syzmanski leaves the ship in a few months. I'll coordinate with the navigator."

"Yes, sir. Thank you, sir. I'll try not..." he interrupted himself and remembered Tish telling him "trying" was not a commitment, "I won't let you down, sir," although he wasn't quite sure how he would handle the strike control assignment.

"Good."

"So sir, what did you do before you came to *Tico*?"

"Flew Spads, A-1Ds, off *Intrepid* with VA-176."

"VA-176. I have a good friend from secondary school and college who flew with VA-176, Pete Russell."

"Pete Russell. Sure know him well. Good guy. Damn good pilot."

"Wasn't he one of those Spad drivers," Cannon was clearly comfortable with pilot lingo, "who splashed a couple of MIGs?" Cannon was referring to an air battle between four MIG jets and four propeller A-1Ds two years earlier which resulted in two MIG kills and a third MIG damaged by the navy pilots.

"Yeah, he was part of that little skirmish." Jeffreys' response was in the classical, "aw shucks," stoical style of naval aviation which understated the danger and understated the accomplishment when the outcome was favorable.

"I'll be damned.... Well, I guess I better get going." At that moment, the department head, Commander Killinger returned to the office. Jeffreys introduced Cannon to Killinger who was a fighter pilot with a reputation as one of the more colorful characters in the WestPac aviation navy.

"Cannon, nice to meet you." Killinger had a beery grin, a waistline to go with it, and he actively chewed gum. They shook hands quickly. It was apparent the Operations Boss was in haste.

"Nice to meet..."

"Cannon, Cannon. We're gonna call you Big Gun. Sorry gotta go. We'll talk to you again, Big Gun. Welcome aboard."

"Yes, sir. Thank you, sir." *Unmistakably a former fighter jock*, thought Cannon. *Ticonderoga is going to be really interesting.* Jeffreys chuckled in amusement, in part, at Killinger's high-energy fighter pilot style, and that his newest officer had just been given a pilot's handle.

"Big Gun, geez. That didn't take long" Jeffreys chuckled again. "Bob, go ahead and get settled. Glad to have you with us."

"Sir, one last thing. I'm reluctant to mention this since I've just gotten here. But I'm engaged, sir, and I wonder if there is a schedule of port calls, in particular, Hong Kong, sir."

"Nothing but Cubi Point, Subic after this line period. Ask the bar girls in Olongapo. They usually know before we do."

"Really?" Jeffreys laughed.

"Yeah. It's always been like that as long as I have been in WestPac, going back to my *Essex* days, during Korea. The bar girls always seem to know."

"Great security on ship movements!"

"Oh yeah." He said it with resigned acknowledgment. "Anyway, it's my guess that after the March line period we might pull Hong Kong."

"That would be nice."

"Whaddya thinking of? Having her fly out and meet you?"

"Ay-ffirm. If we can do it."

Cannon was off to a good start with a lot of opportunity to shine. He was officially assigned to a full lieutenant's billet. He would be the senior CIC watch office in a few months now held by a full lieutenant. The strike control position had just been vacated by a full lieutenant, his counterpart was a full lieutenant, and he was very likely to be an OOD. He wasn't sure about his preparation for being a strike controller, but for someone who wanted to be at the center of things or to consider a career in the navy, he could hardly ask for more. He also liked the mood of confidence and sense of purpose throughout *Ticonderoga* and the easy and comfortable style. Pebbles was hardly uptight, but Jeffreys and Killinger, who had flown hundreds of missions over North Vietnam, appeared downright loose.

"Mr. Cannon, I'm Jungle Younger, Ship's Secretary," extending his hand. Cannon shook it, and checked the gold, ensign's bar on Jungle's collar. "Call me Jungle, Cannon." *Middle age. Must be a story there. Likely a mustang with a name like Jungle*, mused Cannon.

"Bob Cannon, nice to meet you, Jungle."

"Bob, they want you up on the bridge. They are short two OODs and don't have anyone ready to move up. Navigator told me he'd like to see you next. Got my guys here to check you in. Think all you need to do is see the wardroom officer and the chaplain. Assume everything in your personnel jacket is accurate. Thought I could save you a lot of time."

"Thank you. Yes, that saves a lot of time running around to the post office and the laundry, and so on getting checked in on the ship. Thanks." Cannon was getting the impression that *Ticonderoga* had an unusual degree of cooperation and was a very well-run and happy ship. A sense of purpose prevailed everywhere, even in the most menial support and housekeeping functions, and he liked the thought that he was going to be part of it.

"I know Commander Jeffreys wants you to get a permanent TS so we're just gonna amend the paperwork and forward a new set of prints with an urgent request to expedite.

Jungle's yeoman rolled Cannon's finger tips on the finger print form before he left to see the wardroom officer and handed him a brown envelope with his name tag and other useful information about the ship.

The wardroom officer took a personal check for $35 dollars and change for Cannon's mess share, had Cannon fill out his W4 form for the IRS, and assigned him a berth in a four-man stateroom with three lieutenants. *Upper berth again.* "I had the stewards unpack your cruise box and place your uniforms and stuff in your locker and chest of drawers in your stateroom. Hope you can find everything. Here's the combination to your safe."

"Thank you."

"You probably want to get out of your blues. Won't need those for awhile." The wardroom officer smiled.

"Probably not," he said as he smiled in return.

"Easiest way to your stateroom, B-304 B, is out the portside door of the wardroom," pointing to the doorway, "forward a few steps where you'll find a ladder down to the third deck."

Cannon found the stateroom quickly and a large head nearby. Behind the stateroom, just inboard, was one of the ship's two bomb assembly rooms where ordnance came up from the magazines below, and the prescribed fins and fuzes were added to match the ordnance to the mission. He found the upper, outboard berth against the skin of the ship vacant and chuckled about rank having its privilege. *Stateroom sure beats the bunk-*

room even with the upper berth. Cannon found his uniforms all nicely hung in the locker and folded in two drawers allocated to him, and quickly shifted into a freshly starched working khaki uniform with brown shoes and garrison cap which he preferred over a cap with a visor. He found visors obscured things like low overheads, pipes, and interfered with using binoculars or hooded radar scopes. It was typical of Cannon. He had a well-thought out reason for everything including the details. He dialed the navigator's phone number and was told Commander Fritz would like to see him in the chartroom behind the bridge.

Fritz greeted him warmly and told him that he was needed on the bridge. Again it was unusual for a CIC officer to stand bridge watches on a carrier but Jeffreys, Killinger, and Fritz worked out a way to use Cannon's skills appropriately. "I'll start you in the watch rotation tomorrow as JOOD for a week so you can get oriented to the way *Tico* operates, Yankee Station, Task Force 77, et cetera. If things go well, we'll move you to OOD next week. I'm sure Frank also told you that we occasionally run an ASW exercise when we leave the line for Cubi. Keep us in the loop when you develop your tactical plan for those, Cannon. I'm a patrol plane pilot. Maybe I can help." Cannon got the message that he would be an OOD unless he failed to win the confidence of the navigator and the captain over the next week. Apparently the navigator also had some sort of unofficial role, or would like to have a role, in ASW.

At dinner in the wardroom they sat roughly by rank at one of four long tables covered with white linen. Cannon was hoping to meet a young attack or fighter pilot and request a NATOPS manual for his type of aircraft which he succeeded in doing. Each type of aircraft had a published manual for use by pilots and maintenance personnel, and it was a good source for general familiarization with the Skyhawk and Crusader jets that he would be supporting. He felt reasonably comfortable with fixed-wing, piston engine aircraft and turbine powered helicopters from his experience with ASW aircraft in *Essex*. Wherever and whenever possible Cannon built his fundamental knowledge via books, and then tested his knowledge against those who had concrete experience to ensure his understanding.

After dinner he checked the "C" mailbox in the portside, forward corner of the wardroom. There were two letters. He read the addressees, and was pleased to find a letter from Tish. A stocky-looking lieutenant of medium height, standing behind Cannon, noticed that Cannon held the mail from the "C" box and strained to read the addressees over his tall shoulder.

"Ti Campbell," he said, "Campbell, A.M., Lieutenant, the other one's for me." Cannon pivoted and handed the letter to the pilot.

"Cannon, Bob Cannon. Just joined the ship," extending his right hand. Campbell shook his hand.

"Ti Campbell, VA-23, nice to meet you…Cannon, hmmm, Cannon. You go to Davidson?"

" 'Fraid not. Columbia."

"Sorry. Went to Davidson. Just thought I knew you from some-where… Pensacola?"

"Nope."

"Very sorry. You just look familiar."

"Well, I'm sure we'll be seeing more of each other. Nice to meet you again, Ti."

Cannon flopped down on a green naugahyde loveseat in the wardroom lounge and began to read the letter from Tish. A new face in the wardroom always provokes curiosity. Several officers from the Operations department came up and introduced themselves and interrupted him from reading Tish's letter.

January 5, 1968
Morningside Heights

Carissimo mio,

You have been gone just the briefest moment of time and I find myself missing you so desperately. I promise to be brave, but next September seems so unthinkably distant, and I have already begun to have fantasies of visiting you in Hong Kong. Please let me know when you can about whether HK will be real or not. I'm saving my money for a plane ticket.

I was crossing the Sundial the other day when I ran into a younger girl from Prospect House, my old house at Vassar, who's in her first year at the law school. She's been dating a guy who might have been in your class at OCS. Like you, he was just trans-ferred to a West Coast ship. (She said "boat." I could hear you groan.) "Nothing exciting," she said, "like an aircraft carrier." Some type of intelligence ship. So when we discovered we both had beaus in the navy, we agreed to see each other for lunch. Not very many people here at Columbia can be dispassionate about the war, nor, I'm sad to say, very civil towards anyone with attachments to it. So Rachel Diemel and I plan to have lunch together. She even speaks a little German.

I started this letter yesterday at noon, Caro. Last night I received a call from BJ Van Vechten. She was terribly upset. Dutch's company left Okinawa just after Christmas and is going first to Danang then on to some place just below the DMZ near Laos, called Khe Sanh. Dutch told her you and Chase would know where it was. Dutch joined his outfit in Okinawa just out of Basic Officer's School to take over a platoon. She thought Dutch seemed worried about it, and that he was covering up and telling her he was well-trained, and the Marines were the best fighting force in the world, and that she shouldn't worry, he'd come out just fine. She asked me to ask you what you know about Khe Sanh. Dutch said they were joining the 26th Marines who were operating in Quang Tri Province.

BJ told me that she thought Ned Chase had been assigned to your ship while it was in the shipyard at Bremerton, Washington. Wouldn't that be wonderful if the two of you were on the same ship? (Ned might even keep you out of trouble, Caro, as I have heard how Asia is the garden of earthly delights.) I hope the two of you get to know each other. I think you will really like Ned. Like you, his mind is first rate although in some respects he lacks your self-confidence.

I have finally decided to give in and purchase a television for the latest news and to keep me company for all the future lonely nights.

I love you, Carissimo, my darling husband to be. Please take care of yourself and avoid doing anything foolish. I want all of you back with me.

> *Tutto il mio amore,*
> *Tish*

There was no easing into the ship's routine. In 24 hours Cannon was pushed off the dock and a lot of people were watching and counting on him being able to swim. On 16 January 1968, Cannon's one week of orientation came to an end when he was called to meeting in the commanding officer's at-sea cabin. He knocked on the door.

"C'mon in." Captain Tarrant was sitting at a small desk. He was a Texan from Galveston and like all carrier skippers a naval aviator. He was a fair man, but he had not quite overcome a regional suspicion of Easterners, and he had little respect for elite colleges and universities that tolerated unruly behavior, this was despite the fact that many of the junior officers in the ship's complement were either Holloway ROTC or OCS products from many of these schools.

"You wanted to see me, Captain?"

"Stand easy, Mr. Cannon. The navigator and I think you have the makings of a pretty good deck officer. Here's your letter as OOD. But, I like to have a short and serious conversation with my deck officers."

"Yes, sir?"

"First, when you're the deck officer, you run my ship." Tarrant pointed definitively at Cannon's chest on the word "you." "Second, I expect you" again he pointed aggressively at Cannon's chest, "to be aggressive and when necessary to take prudent risk. Third," he pointed again emphatically at Cannon and on every subsequent use of the word *you, your* or *you're*, "you're playing with your career and my career. Call me when the situation merits it, and call me soon enough to allow me to take action. But use your damn judgment. I am not delegating my authority to a deck officer who can't solve problems, can't make a decision, needs his hand held all the damn time and can't anticipate and take timely action. Finally, we all make mistakes. Do your damnest to minimize 'em and keep your ratio of attaboys and dumbshits in the right proportion. But, I'm unforgivin' if you're careless, reckless, or irresponsible. Now, is there anything about what I have said that is unclear to you?"

"No, sir."

"Perfectly clear, mister?"

"Entirely, sir."

"*Entirely*," Tarrant chuckled. He was beginning to like the young officer. He regarded his response as confident and unintimidated. "Now, I have another issue to discuss. I have a request from Frank Jeffreys for you to have a temporary top secret clearance. Seems reasonable enough. But explain to me, mister, why you would want to marry a woman who is a war protestor? You couldn't have that as a navy wife." Cannon was flabbergasted and speechless for several seconds. It had been only days since his lunch with Captain Pebbles and Beebe Byrnes.

"Uh, well...sir, no one has ever challenged my patriotism or loyalty to my country."

"I'm not questioning your loyalty. I'm questioning your damn judgment."

"I see." He took several seconds to think before proceeding further. "Sir, you are from Texas aren't you?"

"Yes, I am, and right proud of it, too." Cannon looked Captain Tarrant directly in the eye.

"With all due respect, Captain, first, my fiancée has the courage of her convictions. I don't always agree with her, but she has had eggs thrown at her. She has been spit upon. She has been jostled. She has been groped, and...she remains undeterred. I love a woman like that."

"Second, Captain...if I remember my American history correctly...your Texan forebears applied to join the United States, voluntarily swore allegiance and happily took your seats in Congress as an equal state in the Union. Some 15 years or so later, they took up arms, a little over a century ago in a disloyal, armed rebellion against the very same Government of the United States. The Navy seems to have given you the benefit of the doubt despite the regional indiscretion of your birthplace, Captain Tarrant. May I ask you to do the same for me?"

Tarrant was stunned by Cannon's counterpunch despite Cannon's Pebbles-like smile. There was no weasel in it. The young officer's self-confidence and moral courage were undeniably apparent and rather than offering a mealy-mouthed apology for his fiancée, he effectively defended her. Cannon stood anxiously waiting for the response while Tarrant gave it full consideration. Tarrant took several moments and observed the analogy wasn't quite precise but the guilt-by-association message came clearly through. He chose not to challenge the weight of the logic, instead he was impressed by the junior officer's moxie.

"Damn good answer, young man. You sound like the kind of man I used to like to fly on my wing. Smart, straight-shooting, courageous, but not too-damn brave." Here Tarrant paused to reflect on Cannon's answer again. He shook his head. Then he stood up and offered his right hand to Cannon. "Stand Texas tall, mister. I'll sign your clearance."

Something good happened in the ether of the air. It was an early but critical moment in their relationship. A captain does indeed place his career into the hands of a junior deck officer, often a reserve officer, who has no ambitions for a naval career, and a commanding officer has a right to assure himself that he has approved the recommendations for the right officers for the job. Tarrant tested Cannon and rather than take offense at the brazenness of the junior officer's response, which another senior officer might have easily taken as insolence, he admired the younger officer's pluck.

Men in command often have to take the measure of other men on scant cues and make judgments about their qualities when the stakes are high. To be a good judge of horseflesh was an invaluable talent for every successful officer to possess, and those who were good at sizing up others also knew precisely when they were under scrutiny and responded positively to the challenge. It was an inseparable part of life in the military.

Accordingly, in some inexplicable, intuitive sense, despite the disparity in age and rank and regional backgrounds, the two men sensed they could trust what each had to say to each other, and instead of having an unspoken issue exist between them, it had been confronted, and in the process, mutual respect arose among them. Like Pebbles, Tarrant was looking for talent, and he was willing to look beyond his own biases to find it.

Down in Ready Room Five, the commanding officer of attack squadron twenty-three addressed his pilots. "We have something here that's a little sensitive, Operation Igloo White...Igloo White. CAG wants to know if there's anyone here with night work experience...armed recces at night under flares. It's supposedly classified Top Secret, but the message with the request is Secret." The skipper searched the faces of his senior pilots, the lieutenant commanders.

"Message, skipper?"

"Yeah CTF 77. Apparently they want to add more night sorties and the A-6 capacity is fully utilized. As an airwing, we have de-emphasized night tactics. Haven't practiced 'em. Somethin' had to go. We still had to keep up our special weapons routines. We're thin on night experience. In fact I don't think they have used A-4s for night work since VA-65 introduced the A-6 with *Ranger*."

Nobody really liked the thought of night landings, particularly now, in IFR weather, during monsoon season over the Gulf of Tonkin. There was a lot of conversation, before Ti Campbell raised his hand. Campbell thought some of the lieutenant commanders would have had night work with flares.

"You, Campbell?"

"A little, sir, 'bout 20 missions with VA-155 in '66."

"What boat was that?"

"*Constellation.* Flew wing for the XO. He and the CO believed in night work. Had the numbers to prove it. Everbody thought 153 and 155 were crazy."

"Okay. Well, I guess you're going to fly with the CO, me, Lieutenant. You're gonna make a night recce pilot out of me. 192 and 195 are going to put up a section each to start. Couple of guys did flare work in F9Fs in Korea. You have 20 more missions in night work in Vietnam than anyone else aboard."

"Sir, this won't take me off Iron Hand. I wanna stay with Iron Hand, sir."

"Not to worry, Ti. When we go north for an Alpha, you'll lead one of our Iron Hand sections."

Lieutenant Ti Campbell was reassigned to VA-23 when the Lawcases needed to have some pilots with combat experience, but not too much experience. BuPers was until then trying to spread the risk around, but combat losses were thinning the pilot ranks and many pilots were flying over 300 to 350 missions before they were being taken off flight status. Campbell was not considered green with 60 missions, but neither was he considered highly experienced, but he was smart, courageous, aggressive and an excellent pilot.

He had a reputation as a good stick and was considered brave, but not too brave, which is another way of saying he was courageous but not to the point of foolishness. Those who were selected to fly Iron Hand, the pilots who flew ahead of the bomber formation and engaged the SAM missile sites before the strike force was over the target, had to be good to be chosen, and they had to be good to remain alive. They were the most dangerous missions in Operation Rolling Thunder.

There was another thing about Augustine MacD. Campbell, the son of Presbyterian missionaries who refused to leave Korea and abandon their congregation during the war. It was the Koreans who nicknamed him "The Tireless One." He seemed to be indefatigable and had developed a grittiness and tenacity about him which rarely caused him to give in to a challenge. Young Campbell developed a cold hate for communists of the North Korean and Chinese kind as he witnessed their brutality—the carnage, the homelessness, the disease, and starvation that they vested upon combatants and non-combatants alike.

As a child he was homeless, and sick, and famished as well. He became good at the Korean martial art, Taekkyeon, appreciated the Confucian mind, and spoke Korean. Ti Campbell was also a devout Presbyterian and prayed regularly to Jesus Christ. Sometimes, at the behest of his parents, he prayed to Jesus to help him forgive the North Koreans and the Chinese, but the thought of forgiveness remained in his head and would not reside in his heart.

When the truce was signed, he was sent to boarding school in New England with many sons of ex-patriot missionaries before attending college at Davidson which was affiliated with the Presbyterian Church. Upon graduation, before there was a war, Ti Cambell went to Pensacola to fulfill a boyhood dream—to fly navy. By the time that he progressed beyond Pensacola and drew A-4s, he knew he was going to Vietnam. Virtually all A-4 pilots rotated to Vietnam. He went without mental reservation.

"C'mon with me Ti. We have a meeting with CAG."

Just hours after his meeting with Captain Tarrant, Cannon found himself performing a similar assessment on the two officers assigned to his watch team on his first watch as OOD. The ship had just begun to recover the last cycle of aircraft. *Ticonderoga* conducted two underway replenishments every night after flight operations. One was always bombs and ammunition, and the second was either fuel or fresh stores. Tonight they would take on fuel first.

"Mr. Trout, do you know ATP One Alpha?"

"Signal book, yes, sir"

"Good. How about your steering and engine orders?"

"Fairly well, sir,"

"Had much time conning the ship?"

"Very little, sir."

"Okay, tomorrow night you'll be the conning officer. Know your steering and engine orders faultlessly before you come on watch."

"Aye, aye, sir."

"In the meanwhile, Mr. Trout find out where the oiler is, who it is, and it's call sign, if you will, please."

"Yes, sir."

"Mr. Reposa?"

"Yes, sir."

"Mr. Trout will be the primary conning officer. That means that you will maintain all status boards, encode and decode all signals, maintain the surface watch, and compute courses, speeds, and CPAs on the maneuvering board. You will also interface with Primary Flight Control, Combat and the Engineering Officer of the Watch, got it?"

"Yes, sir."

"Good, but tonight, Mr. Trout will handle signals and the maneuvering board, right Mr. Trout? Right, Mr. Reposa?" Like Captain Tarrant, Cannon not only spoke to be understood, and he had learned from Captain Pebbles how to speak to not be misunderstood. Both officers looked at each other, and acknowledged his directions.

There was no mistaking the new Officer of the Deck as he confidently took control, and it was also clear the watch was being organized differently from the conventional watch organization. The Junior Officer of the Deck assumed the conning responsibilities and all other tasks were being devolved to the Junior Officer of the Watch.

Chapter 6.

"CTF-77 assigned *Ticonderoga* and Air Wing-19 to work with us. Now we get a chance to prove the worth of our technology." The Ghost Squadron, VO-67, was based at Nakhon Phanom Royal Thai Air Base, Thailand.

"You taking the first mission, Skipper?"

"You bet." The words expressed enthusiasm, but they were delivered in a well-modulated manner that more accurately reflected determination. "We're gonna prove that our acoustic and seismic technology is as valuable on land finding trucks and tanks as passive acoustics proved finding Russian submarines at sea. Would make a real contribution to this war and open up a lot more career possibilities for patrol plane types."

"Yeah, we have a helluva psychic investment in this," responded the Squadron Duty Officer. "Been a helluva a development cycle, sir. If it weren't for ARPA I don't think BuOrd and AirPac would have gone along."

Operation Igloo White pertained specifically to missions run by VO-67 flown from Nakhon Phanom Royal Thai Air Base (NKP) in Thailand. The squadron was established from former anti-submarine pilots and airmen who flew the OP-2E, a twin, piston-engine airplane with a crew of 9. This was a modified P-2V Neptune, a long-range anti-submarine patrol plane that was being replaced by the P-3 Orion. Instead of dropping sonobuoys into the sea, VO-67 dropped sensors called Acoubuoys into the jungle treetops to listen for enemy activity, and seismic detection sensors into the ground to sense the vibrations of trucks and tanks. The latter device, ADSID, was aimed from 2500 feet by a Norden bombsight, a device last used by heavy bombers in World War II.

CAG began the meeting. "First, just to be clear, the operation, the existence, the technology and everything about this squadron is top secret. Strictly need to know. This is not to be discussed broadly in the ready rooms. Just the guys flying the missions."

"Yes, sir," responded the commanding officers of his three attack squadrons.

"Well, these ASW types have these sensors that they typically drop during daylight over the known logistics routes used by the NVA. Intelligence reports indicate activity has really picked up in Laos and western Quang Tri Province since the first of the year.

"As you know trucks do not move during the day. They travel at night so that we can't easily see them. Some people believe the North Vietnamese Army is prepositioning for a major offensive in the south. Admiral Weinel wants to reserve the Intruders for missions up North, but he wants to see what we can do working at night against trucks and tanks coming down the Ho Chi Minh Trail."

"How's this going to work, CAG?"

"VO-67, call sign, Lindy, will sew the sensors during the day and the Air Force will have an EC-121, "Batcat," up at night to read the sensor data. They are like our Willie Victors. They will give us a rendezvous point, and we will check in with them, and they will guide us to the sensors which are hot. After that it's like FAC work. You'll use flares, and use bombs and CBUs against hopefully something worthwhile—trucks, tanks, troops."

"Will the ship add cycles or shift her schedule?"

"We're working on the air plan now. CTF-77 thinks moving us back to 12 to midnight works best. *Bonny Dick (Bonne Homme Richard)* will operate from 06 to18 and leave *Ranger* at 18 to 06 with her A-6 Intruders flying at night. It's the least disruptive and gets the job done. Now who has serious night experience?" Campbell's squadron commander spoke up.

"23 has Ti Campbell sir, He's one of our Iron Hand guys."

"Anybody else? Anybody from the Golden Dragons? The Chippies?"

"No, sir."

"Turn around from the last cruise has been short CAG. Just haven't had time to train for it."

"Yep, I know." CAG stoically clipped his words. The attack squadrons based in Lemoore were turning around in three and a half months after a ten and a half month deployment—scarcely enough time to allow squadron personnel to get to know their families again. A lot of their training time was taken up practicing nuclear weapons drops which could not be done while in the war zone and which no one ever wanted to do for real. It required an Immelman or a Half Cuban 8—difficult maneuvers where the plane climbed steeply at maximum power and just before the apogee released the weapon, lofting it towards the target while the pilot abruptly rolled and turned the aircraft away. He shifted his tone. "Campbell, you have about 20 night hops with 155. Is that right?"

"Yes, sir. In '66, from the *Connie*, sir."

"Was Bud Ingley CO of VA-155 then?"

"Yes, sir. Flew on his wing a few times."

"Damn good pilot. Knew him from Korea." CAG paused as if to re-capture a nostalgic moment in time with Bud Ingley. "Okay, so brief me on how 155 would generally run a night mission, Ti."

"Yes, sir. Well, we worked mostly Routes 1 and 15…trucks. The threat environment was a lot better back then. We carried low-level, lay-down ordnance—bombs and CBUs, and, of course, flares. We would launch and join up over the ship, head northwest, and tank before we went feet dry. Usually one of us would be at 4000 AGL and we would coast in to the target, lights out, using only visual navigation, and the lead would get to Route 1 at about 500 feet. We dropped our flares at 2500 feet, and the low flier would wait for the flares to ignite then he would get under the flares. You can't see anything above the flares. You gotta get below 'em."

"Below the flares?" CAG was skeptical. "That's really low. Didn't you worry about guns, about small arms?"

"Yeah, we were afraid of guns and silver bee bees in daylight and would avoid flying below 3500 to 3000 feet, but night was a different story. Back then, they didn't have many radar guided guns on the roads. We felt safe down low at night. It was more a matter of getting used to the dark and looking out for the hills and our ability to put ordnance accu-rately on the target. That was our biggest problem. It's a bitch to line up azimuth, altitude and air speed when you're down in the weeds and very close range from the target. If you back off, you'll never see the trucks at night."

"Gutsy."

"We would get down to 100 to 200 feet and hammer them with snakeyes, rockeyes, or 20 mike mike. On a typical mission we'd get a couple of trucks. Maybe three or four. Once we caught 30 or 40 trucks out in the open near the Thanh Hoa Bridge, but that was kinda lucky. Usually it was nothing dramatic. But not much moved when we were there. We were more productive than guys working at day from higher altitude and dive bombing. That really didn't seem to work that well."

"What about the Intruders?"

"We were better truck hunters than the A-6. They were better against hard targets. The sense in the air wing was that we really complemented each other."

"So how would you suggest that we work with Batcat?"

"Well, if I understand correctly, VO-67 will drop the sensors quite precisely, so Batcat should have a good sense of where the targets are, but we're still going to have to see them to hit 'em. We're still going to have to illuminate. They have more radar-guided guns now. It's going to be hairier. I don't think we want to spend a lot of time flying the axis of the road. Better to come in at an angle, line up on the road under the flare, unload and get off the road. That's what they can do for us. Keep us from flying the axis of the road." Campbell stopped to check if he was registering his points with the senior officers. "Commander Ingley thought two guys flying down the axis of a road in daylight was a bit crazy, sir. Radar is going to reduce some of the advantage of night, though. Definitely no second runs in the same area."

"They're saying that we can DF on the sensors."

"DF? DF?… how accurate would that be at our airspeeds?" asked Jim Hessmann, CO of VA-195. Campbell answered.

"Sir, if they drop their sensors very near the roads, a line of bearing across a known road, a mapped road—that's as good as a fix. That would save us from flying the length of the road. We could focus on the areas where the sensors are hot. If the technology works as advertised, it takes a lot of the reconnaissance out of the recce, if you will, sir. We could set up an IP, if you will, come in on angle and rollout on the heading of the road. The guy up high pops a few flares, the guy down low hunts and drops. Could be very productive and mitigate our risk."

"The air force is willing to drop flares for us," added CAG. Again Lt. Campbell responded,

"I'd rather drop our own flares. Drop them in pairs. Timing the flare drops is kinda critical, sir. It's not just having enough burn time from the flare, but a flare has an initial surprise effect, then it has an alerting effect, and you want to be on them and hitting them before they recover and get a bead on us. That'll require some coordination to get that right."

"Maybe we ought to go over to NKP and meet with 'em on this, CAG," suggested the CO of VA-192." CAG abruptly broke off the discussion.

"Okay, guys. Mr. Campbell, thank you. I'm going to meet with the squadron COs now, and your skipper will get back to you." Ti Campbell left Flag Plot where CAG liked to hold his meetings when there was no admiral embarked which was usually the case because the big decks, like *Ranger*, were better suited to carry an admiral and his staff. "Gentlemen, there's a lot of materiel teed up to come down the HCMT. Maybe waiting for the Tet holiday truce to move it south. We don't have time to train up. It's going to be on-the-job training."

"What I'm going to suggest to the skipper and CTF-77 is as follows: one mission tomorrow night, two the night after, three the third night, and then we go from there. Now as to tactics… Ingley and Campbell flew the A-4C. The Foxtrot version has a superior bombsight. None of this stuff about being below the flares. I want you above the flares where you are not lighted-up for the gunners. Use 30 degree angle dive bombing which reduces the chance of vertigo at night. Pull out at 5,500 feet so that when you level off you are above the small arms fire. We don't need to pay any more in tuition to learn these lessons again. There is no need for the Foxtrot version to be down in the weeds. There is nothing down there worth an Air Wing 19 pilot and his plane. We need to learn our way carefully into these tactics." CAG paused before resuming. "Jeff, I'd like you and Campbell to go first. You work out how you will work together and brief me. I'd like 23 to put up a section every night."

CAG had a second less obvious reason for asking Jeff Gibson and VA-23 to take the lead. The two F-8 fighter squadrons, VF-191 and VF-194, along with the attack squadrons, VA-192 and VA-195, had been together for several deployments on Yankee Station. VA-23, although it was one of the earliest attack squadrons in the war and the first to carry Shrike missiles on Iron Hand missions, and although this was their third combat deployment, they had not yet gained full acceptance with the rest of the air wing. When CAG learned that Campbell was in VA-23, he hoped that choosing VA-23 to be the first in Igloo White would help. He had set it up so that they would initially have more experience with Igloo White, and the rest of the wing would be required to turn to them as a resource.

"Campbell put his finger on a big issue. Aiming the ordnance is a big deal." He paused and joked, "We won't be measuring CEPs" The senior officers chuckled at the gallows humor. Circle of error probable, the shorter the radius, the tighter the circle, the more accurate the pilot. Every attack pilot had a CEP the way baseball players have a batting average. CAG resumed, "I'd like 192 to begin to ramp up the second night, and Jim, I don't know if your guys with the Charlie version should fly these missions…. Debrief the hell out of these missions, gentlemen. Learn every little damn thing that you can. I know 153 and 155 really liked night work. Never got the recognition they deserved, but I never liked night work. And the winter of 1968," referring to the monsoon over the Gulf, " is a helluva lot different from mid-year 1966. The flak is better directed by radar, and the weather over the ship at this time of the year sucks."

"IFR night landings" Gibson said under his breath.

"What was that?" CAG looked around.

"I said instrument night landings in lousy weather, CAG."

"I know. I know." CAG was solemn and took a deep breath as he exhaled he said. "We're professional naval aviators, gentlemen." He let the import of his words sink in before continuing. "Now, frankly, we got a squadron of ASW rookies with a twin engine patrol plane flying below 2500 feet dropping sensors. They have been trained to track and destroy submarines. Not trucks and tanks protected by triple-A. And we have an Air Force Willie Victor monitoring the sensors. A little complicated. Interservice communications. It's novel. But somebody believes it's necessary. Everybody understand?" CAG again looked at his squadron commanding officers one by one. It would be an understatement to say their expressions were unenthusiastic.

"Jeff, you've got a good boy there. Use him as a resource, but squadron commanders lead. You lead the mission. I want you to lead the mission, and I want to see you both back aboard." CAG looked his squadron commanders in the eye. The years of flying in two wars, the stress and strain of flying from aircraft carriers and penetrating deep into enemy territory, left deep creases of experience in his face. "And that goes for all of you CO's. In Naval Air, the commanding officers take the tough missions and roll in first."

"Yes, sir. We'll be careful, CAG, but if we get a chance at trucks and tanks, sir, we're goin' to hit 'em."

"Damn right."

While the winter monsoon weather presents poor flying conditions along the coast and in the Gulf of Tonkin, inland, west of the Annamite Mountains, the weather is better. The monsoon season inland usually arrives in late spring and lasts for half the year. In the Khe Sanh area along the Laotion border, after the morning fog lifted, the visibility was reasonably good.

Over Laos, Batcat loitered in an orbit above a broken layer of clouds at 12,000 feet waiting for the VA-23 A-4s to check in. "Batcat, Batcat, Lawcase 305, 309, flight of two, alpha four foxtrots, checking in."

"Roger 305; we have been tracking you inbound to us. Batcat on station, at base plus angels 6. We'll be about 30 miles north of your target area, copy?"

Lawcase 305, Gibson's plane, answered, "Batcat, Lawcases descending to angels ten. Lawcase 305 will remain high until we eyeball a target; 309 will descend to 5000, be the first flare ship." Gibson wanted altitude separation and he wanted to commence his dive bombing runs from at least 10,000 feet. "What target info, Batcat? "

"Lawcase 305, Batcat has positive indications about 9 miles from you. Suspect trucks and tanks. Interrogative your weapons?"

"Mark 82s, Rockeye CBUs, and 20 mike mike."

"Lawcase 309, flare ship, call Batcat when ready for a vector to the first hot area."

"Click, click." Five minutes later Campbell called the EC-121. "Batcat, Lawcase 309 level at angels 5."

"Roger steer 340 for 8 miles, standby to drop."

"Click, click." Less than a minute passed before Batcat called with a minor correction.

"Come right, 5 degrees; prepare to drop…now, now, now."

"Flares are down, 309, Batcat." Campbell dropped two flares and waited for them to ignite.

"Okay, Lawcases, you have it from here. Call Batcat if you need us. Batcat will monitor."

"Click, click."

Each A-4 carried two pods of eight flares. The flares were magnesium parachute flares that provided two million candle power of illumination, and because they drift with the winds in the target area, they require flight adjustments by the pilot to maximize their effectiveness. They ignited at 3000 feet. Two flares lit up an area about as big as seven or eight square blocks and the visibility was remarkably good although the jungle over the trail offered excellent concealment.

Campbell descended to four thousand feet making 400 knots and began a race track pattern around the area of illumination looking for targets. Within the triple canopy of vegetation, he could see the thin, narrow dirt road that made up this particular branch of the multi-branched trail that was collectively referred to as the Ho Chi Minh Trail, but he saw no targets after several orbits. "No joy this time, 305"

"Click, click. Batcat, did you copy that?"

"Roger… Can we try 500 yards to the north?"

"Ay-firm," responded Gibson. Ready, 309?" Campbell had already returned to 5000 feet and was ready to drop more flares. He flew a little further north and corrected for the wind drift of the flares in the target area.

"Flares down. By the drift of the flares I'd guess maybe four to five knots of wind from the northwest." Gibson made a note to set his bombsight for the winds accordingly. Again Campbell descended a thousand feet to search for targets, but he saw none. Gibson was not surprised. At 4000 feet and at 400 knots, a pilot in a single seat jet airplane had difficulty picking out a moving target on an interstate highway in daylight. Now it was pitch black, and the trail and parking areas along the trail were concealed by thick vegetation which made up a triple canopy of cover. And the enemy had learned its lessons, too. They knew it was wise to be still and motionless as soon as they heard airplanes. "Negative targets, 305, break, Batcat, any suggestions?"

"Maybe 300 meters further up the trail."

"Roger, Batcat." Again Campbell climbed back to 5000 feet. He could see the dying flares from the previous run, and he dropped two more flares, seconds apart, just a bit further to the north. He waited for the flares to ignite at 3000 feet. This time he descended lower to 3500, remaining above the flares, and began looking intently for targets as he flew in a racetrack pattern around the illumination area. Gibson remained above at 10,000 feet waiting for indication of a target.

"Think I have something, possibly a truck. Let me try and confirm that when I turn back."

"Click, click." Gibson straightened up a bit in the cockpit. Campbell turned back and tried to avoid providing indication to the enemy on the ground that they had been spotted.

"Ay-firm. Vehicles. Likely trucks…maybe a few bicycles… Just about 75 yards to the north of the center of the flare umbrella."

"Roger, nosing over, now" Gibson selected the ordnance station where he had three, 500 pound bombs under his port wing and armed the bombs. He set the pipper on the trail at the approximate point suggested by Campbell. From Gibson's altitude it was more of an area drop than aiming for a specific target. The Skyhawk picked up speed in a 30 degree dive. At 5,500 feet Gibson pulled the pickle switch and released the bombs, "Ordnance away." Then he pulled back on the stick, shallowed out of his dive at 4500 feet and began his climb back to altitude. Two 37 millimeter antiaircraft guns opened up at the sound of his engine as he applied power and climbed out, but the gunfire was wildly mis-aimed.

The three bombs detonated near where Campbell thought he had seen the trucks, but there were no secondary explosions to confirm that the bombs had hit a genuine target.

"Batcat, your gadgets pick up the detonations?"

"Affirmative, sir."

"Can your gadget offer any guidance on the next drop?"

"Wait out." Batcat took several minutes. Gibson impatiently orbited the target area. A "wait out" was generally an irritating response to an action-oriented, military pilot flying a jet airplane. Finally, Batcat, came back up. "Negative, 305. The sound volume and vibrations went off the charts."

"Nothing? Nothing useful at all?"

"No, sir. Negative, sir. We need to turn down the gain."

"Juliet foxtrot bravo," Gibson said to himself—a derisive, coded expletive for "just effing beautiful." "309 is low; 305 is level high."

"Click, click." Campbell, who had cleared from the area being worked as a precaution against a midair collision, turned back towards the area. "Gonna try and put the flares just a bit further north."

"Roger that," responded Gibson. Shortly thereafter Gibson called, "Orbiting at angels 10" Campbell proceeded for the fourth time to place his flares right over the trail, a little further north of his last drop.

"Flares down." When the flares ignited Campbell resumed hunting for targets. The 37 mm guns opened up on the flares. The tracer rounds snaked up like drops of water from a garden hose. "I see several vehicles…trucks…pos-sibly armor, tanks. Dead center of the flare umbrella."

"Commencing second run. Three Mark 82s." This time Gibson came from a different compass bearing and made a correction in his run. Again it appeared to him to be an area drop, but he treated the trail as a bridge and approached the trail on a 15 degree offset to its axis and planned to drop his ordnance on a diagonal across the trail. Again the 37mm guns began firing. Gibson held the A-4 steady in the dive. The tracers got closer to him as he got lower and the gunners aimed at the sound, but they could not see his aircraft above the flares. Their brilliance served to blind the gunners.

"Bombs away." Campbell watched the target area looking for detonations, but he cleared the area and began his climb to 10,000 feet. The pilots were exchanging roles and positions for the next run. Gibson again shallowed out of his dive and leveled at 5000 feet as he assumed the role of flare ship.

"On target," announced Campbell, as the attack aircraft repositioned. "Secondaries. Secondary explosions…fuel, maybe ammo." The fires burned brighter. "309 level at 10."

"Can you see the fires, 9?"

"Kinda. Maybe some smoke, dust in the area. Prefer some flares for the first run."

"Okay, you'll get'em. Recommend you treat the target area as a bridge."

"Click, click."

"Running short on time, 9. Do two runs. Mark 82s first. Rockeyes next. Drop everything. I'll follow with a single run with my CBUs."

"Wilco." And that's how the two VA-23 pilots finished their initial work over the target.

"Alright, Batcat, thank you gentlemen. We're going feet wet." There was a sense of accomplishment among the adhoc Batcat-Lawcase team.

"Goodnight, Navy."

"309 are you climbing?"

"Roger, where do you want to meet?"

"Let's go to Panther's 280 radial at 40 nautical, angels 20."

"Roger that 305. Tedious work."

"Yeah. Seems it might have been worth the trip." Both A-4s flew separately making their way south of the DMZ heading east, climbing towards 20 thousand feet, to the safety of the sea.

"309, you still with me?"

"Roger, feet dry, switching button eight," the ship's strike control frequency.

"Roger coming with you." Gibson headed east for the Gulf of Tonkin and ascended for the rendezvous point.

Later, back aboard *Ticonderoga,* Commander Gibson and CAG were on the darkened bridge and just finishing briefing Captain Tarrant on the first Operation Igloo White mission when the captain asked, "Gibby, how'd the young fella work out?"

"He's professional. Extremely cool in the air, sir. What you expect from a guy flying Iron Hand."

"Good. That's good to hear."

"I really like flying with him. He thinks right along with you. Brave, but not too brave, if you know what I mean, sir."

"I do, Gibby. Indeed, I do."

A day later VO-67 lost their first plane as the OP-2E plane criss-crossed several branches of the Ho Chi Minh Trail planting sensors. The plane was reasonably armored but the suspicion was that triple-AAA had taken the

plane down by an alerted gun crew. Due to technical limitations in the
sensing devices, the sensors had to be precisely planted from the aircraft at
treetop level at 248 knots. The precise geographic location for each sensor
had to be known to enable accurate bombing under flares later that night.
VO-67 suspended operations for the next day to review their tactics. Lindy
7 and her 9 crewmembers were officially listed as missing in action. But
as time wore on hopes for the 9-man crew dimmed although no crash site
had been reported.

Four nights later, Lt. Ti Campbell prepared for his third Igloo White
launch at 1930. As he taxied on the dark, rain swept flight deck, he said a
brief prayer. "Lord Jesus, be with me tonight. Lord Jesus, give me the
strength to do my duty and come home."

Augustine MacD. Campbell grew up in Korea during the war where
his parents were Presbyterian missionaries who refused to abandon their
congregation in Seoul. Quiet courage was a Campbell gene. As a young
boy, he was no stranger to the stresses of being a refugee—lack of shelter,
food, clothing and two legs were the primary means of transportation. As
an adult, he displayed an unusual inner richness that synthesized the
harshness of war, Korean culture, a quiet but indomitable spirit, an exu-
berance for piloting airplanes, and above all, a devout and abiding faith in
Christianity. Within the squadron he enjoyed wide respect although he
was sometimes affectionately teased as a "no-fun" guy at the O Club bar
or among the earthly delights of Olongapo and other ports of call in Asia.
He was polite and socially deferential reflecting traces of Confucian har-
mony in Korean culture.

Shortly after the air wing came aboard, Campbell sought out Chaplain
Osborne and asked to be one of the Chaplain's Assistants. He also formed
a friendship with Pete Peterson, also an Iron Hand pilot in the sister squadron, VA-192, and a Mormon from Utah who had spent his mission in Japan. Both were thoughtful, enjoyed comparing and contrasting Japanese,
Korean, and American cultures, their religions with the various Asian religions, and taught each other Japanese and Korean.

As his squadron executive officer, Jack Martini, a Californian, once
remarked after a fitness report review, "Dude, you are one helluva a cocktail." Immediately thereafter he became known as "Cocktail" in the squadron which was an incongruous nom de guerre, totally out of character, but
catchy, and therefore, it stuck with the squadron although Campbell preferred Tireless, a more honorable nickname. Back at Lemoore the squad-

ron even had a contest to find out who could invent the best recipe for the "Campbell Cocktail." Needless to say, it resulted in a smashing good party as sampling each concoction was a mandatory ritual of attendance.

It was a particularly black night. Cannon had the 1800-2000 OOD dog watch on the bridge, and he and the captain looked down on the flight deck and observed the launch. The F-8 Crusaders were first off the ship to relieve the earlier flight of fighters manning the barrier between the MIG airfields in North Vietnam and the fleet in the Gulf of Tonkin. The ear-splitting roar of the Crusaders in full military power and after burner was only slightly muffled by the rain and rattled pencils, dividers and coffee cups on the bridge. Low hanging clouds and monsoonal rain showers made for a very dark night and raindrops could be heard striking the over-head sheet metal that now enclosed what was originally an open bridge. The blue flames from the Crusader tailpipes, confirmation of full power, were reassuring to the catapult crew as the F-8s accelerated down the deck and were then gone into the night.

Cannon watched from the portside of the bridge above the flight deck as the A-4s taxied to the catapult bridles while the blast deflectors folded and were stowed. 18 and 19 year old yellow shirts, thoroughly soaked by the rain, moved quickly to secure the Skyhawks to the catapults which were then set to deliver the required airspeed specifically to each airplane and gross weight. In the mostly dark, low light, he could barely see the side numbers. The pilots flicked on their red, anti-collision beacons to indicate they were ready to launch. Subsequently the "shooter's" lighted wand arced over his head and pointed down the catapult track towards the bow of the ship—the signal to fire the cat.

12, A-4s in all launched but only the first four, a section from VA-23 and another from VA-192, were assigned to Igloo White. As the last plane to launch went off, a KA-3 Skywarrior tanker from Heavy Attack 4, the flight deck transitioned from launch to recovery. Already an A-4 from the previous cycle was in the groove for the first of 18 aircraft to be recovered.

Cannon rechecked the wind indicator which read 30 knots at 350 degrees relative to the ship's head. His junior officer of the deck and the helmsman were conning within a half degree of Foxtrot Corpen at 20 knots making 30 knots of wind over the angled deck as prescribed.

Nothing was more hazardous than a night carrier landing in inclement weather, and they were particularly determined to do their part to facilitate the recovery. Air Wing 19 pilots often said they preferred two minutes over Hanoi to the last 20 seconds of a night landing on a carrier.

After having operated around the Mu Gia Pass to the north the night before without results, the experiment known as Operation Igloo White was back working the Ho Chi Minh Trail in the vicinity of Khe Sanh where the Ho Chi Minh Trail intersected Route 9, an east-west route to Dong Hoi on the coast of the Gulf of Tonkin. The commanding officers of *Ticonderoga's* attack squadrons were up for the mission.

As CVW-19 gained experience with Igloo White they had growing concerns about sequential attack runs on a relatively, geographically confined and defended target, and they wanted to consider what might be done to enable each section to make fewer runs and reduce time over target. This led them to consider adding a third A-4 solely to drop flares, and then employing two Skyhawks, flying together, in a strictly drop mode, to roll-in quickly, drop their ordnance, and get out. This could be challenging as all aircraft would be working in the dark, often flying below 5000 feet AGL without navigation lights, posing a risk of a midair collision at 800 to 900 knot closing rates.

The officers and men of VO-67 were heavily invested in Igloo White and were even more dedicated to prove the concept and to develop codified tactics and express them in their own rules of engagement after the loss of Lindy 7. Gibson and Campbell discussed whether the Lindy 7 crew was over-determined to the point that it affected their judgment, or whether they were simply constrained to very low altitudes at moderate speeds by the limits of their airplane and the sensors.

Experienced attack pilots consider courage a *sine qua non* but there was such a thing as trying too hard to win the war. Shakespeare identified the personality in Hotspur and Laertes, and Custer manifested the trait throughout his career until it ended badly at Little Bighorn.

Both VA-23 and VA-192 were getting more comfortable with the sensor-guided flare work. Tonight they would operate as they had before with one wingman dropping flares and hunting for targets where the sensors indicated probable targets and the other Skyhawk remaining high poised to attack. The squadron commanding officers would make a special effort to observe the strikes and consider what might be the best future tactics.

After several runs the North Vietnamese guns were very active. There were more guns than the previous nights, an indication that the enemy placed a higher value on the flow of materiel. There is an old saying in naval air. "Whatever is worth bombing is worth defending," and the logic could be reversed. Where there were defenses there were targets.

Campbell positioned for the fourth attack run of the raid. "309, coming fast from the north end on a westerly heading." Like the first night, they had no wish to be low and slow. "Speed is life" – another basic axiom of naval air. During the debrief of the first mission Campbell remarked that the Ho Chi Minh Trail was better concealed by jungle canopy than he remembered Routes 1 and 15 being at night. He said the task of sighting the targets was substantially more difficult than where they chose to hunt for trucks on the highways which was precisely the rationale for using air-dropped sensors.

"Click, click," acknowledged Commander Jeff Gibson, VA-23's commanding officer. Campbell saw the string of flares ignite at 2500 feet and pushed the nose over putting his plane into a 30 degree dive as he commenced his run planning to cross the trail on a diagonal where Gibson thought there might have been targets, but he was uncertain. Campbell put his pipper on a dark shaded area. Immediately a radar-guided 57mm gun opened up with well-directed fire. Shortly thereafter two 37mm guns began firing wildly in the direction of the 57's tracers. Campbell had to remain steady at this point in the flight until he released his ordnance as the tracers were passing by his windshield. Campbell had been shot at before. To say the least, it was never pleasant; but he held the Skyhawk steady in the dive on the azimuth and at the air speed required for the gravity-type Mark 82 bombs. He rechecked that he had selected the proper ordnance stations, that the bombs were armed, and that ejectors were set for a string-release of his weapons. As he had done the first night, he came in at a 15 degree offset, heading 185 to the south and dropped all six 500 pound bombs across the trail where they suspected NVA trucks might be camouflaged and hidden.

The Skyhawk jumped ahead when freed of the weight and drag of the ordnance, and as he applied power and pulled off to the right. Now the 57mm opened up again. Campbell tried to stay low but he had to clear a 3000 foot karst ahead, and as he climbed more 57mm rounds from another site intercepted him.

"Negative results," called Gibson, "Damn."

Campbell was too busy flying the airplane to respond. He felt something hit behind him and something hit the underside of his right wing. "Took at least two hits, 305. Not sure. Definite flak. Think I'm hit somewhere in the control surfaces. Possibly the engine."

"Roger. Clean everything up. Drop the empty tanks and bomb racks."

"She's mushy, sir. Losing power, losing airspeed. Controls are stiffening." Campbell reached down to a T-handle near his left knee and pulled it disengaging the hydraulic control system and flew the plane manually. Immediately he felt the aerodynamic forces on his A-4.

"Your heading?"

"West, sir… I can't bring her around. Gotta get over this karst"

"Roger. Don't have a tally on you."

"Trying to fly her in manual. No joy. Have a fire alarm… About 1000 feet is my max rate of climb. Might just clear the karst."

"Stay with it if you can." There were no friendly troops below, "Could you make Khe Sanh?"

"Doubtful. She's very mushy. Probably the compressor…feels like she's ready to stall."

"Got it."

"Just cleared the karst. I can push her over now but the engine is running rough." The stricken Skyhawk just managed to get over the karst, but damage to the right wing was causing drag and the aircraft wanted to yaw to the right. Campbell tried to correct with the rudder and the ailerons, but the rudder's effect was weak and in manual mode he was still fighting the forces on the control surfaces albeit they lessened as the A-4 lost airspeed. The plane was threatening to stall and enter a spin. In the dark, Campbell had difficulty determining damage to his aircraft. What he could not see, his rudder was a third blown away.

"I'll stay with you as long as I can."

"Sorry, skipper. I can't get back to the ship. I think I'm going to have to get out." He shoved his buttocks as tightly as possible against the back of his seat.

"Cocktail, call me. Check in with me as soon as you get down."

"Aye, aye, sir" Campbell reached up, pulled down the curtain and ejected into the night over Laos.

Chapter 7.

"Damn, why me? What did I do to deserve this?" The drogue chute pulled open Campbell's parachute. He ripped off his oxygen mask, pulled down his visor to protect his face and prepared for a jungle landing in the tree-tops. He could hear the words of the instructor, "At 22 feet per second, your parachute's rate of descent, trees break bones. Make yourself small. Keep your elbows tightly by your side. Cover your face. Slightly flex your knees. Keep your feet together. If you should survive landing with your feet wide apart, you'll be a singing soprano in the church choir!" Odd he thought, he should recall the words, the details, the gallows humor, so common in naval air, and the tonality of the instructor like it was yesterday, while he was floating to his fate in Laos.

Campbell crashed into the trees feet first, into the darkest part of night beneath the jungle canopy, then he tumbled forward as his parachute hung up in the trees. He was momentarily disoriented as he continued tumbling spread eagle until some of the parachute cords hung up above him, breaking his fall and causing him to swing like a plumb-bob. A pain in his left shoulder told him he was alive. A tree limb wacked him on the lower left leg and checked his velocity as he swung by. He felt his heart racing madly. He had no sense of his relationship to the ground beneath him. When he hit the tree limb a second time, this time with his left thigh, the radius diminished, and he began to spin in a counter-clockwise direction making him slightly dizzy, and he was again momentarily disoriented. The cords wound up as he spun until the spin stopped and slowly began to spin in reverse direction, but before it had gained speed and completed a revolution he grabbed the tree limb, which had, until that second, been the bane of his primeval existence, and brought himself under control.

Campbell rested in his parachute harness breathing heavily. He noticed his night vision was poor, his left shoulder was giving him great pain, and he could move his left arm only with extreme pain. He became aware that he was breathing with a sense of fear. So as he had often done in martial arts training, Campbell began to meditate to regain awareness and self-control. There he remained in meditation clearing his head of all thoughts, focusing his mind on the pain in his shoulder, ridding himself of the thoughts that produced fear and anxiety, and becoming mindful of the sounds and smells, and degrees of shadow and light in the jungle around him. As his night vision improved, it seemed he was several feet above some sort of phosphorescent vegetation, but the eerie white-green glow in the dark made him uncertain, and he refused to draw any conclusions about his height above the ground. Campbell finished meditating and began a prayer. "Jesus, Lord and Savior, be with me now. Give me the strength not only to endure what is before me, Sweet Jesus, please give me the strength to prevail over this challenge."

"Honey, I'm going to do my best to bring all of the boys back home to Lemoore." It was the last thing Gibson said after kissing his wife goodbye, and climbed the ladder into the cockpit to lead the Black Knights fly-on to *Ticonderoga* last November.

Gibson was not flying well now, and he knew it. *Fly the airplane. Fly the airplane*, Gibson kept telling himself. It was the most basic axiom of flying—a cautionary axiom which meant, despite all circumstances, nothing could be paramount to flying the airplane. Campbell's ejection kept entering his mind. Nothing felt normal to him. The Skyhawk's stick did not feel normal. Mentally he did not feel that he was processing information as quickly nor as effectively as normal. Thoughts and emotions were swirling through the head of the commanding officer of the Black Knights, and they were distracting him from the task at hand which was to avoid becoming a casualty, himself, and to get safely aboard *Ticonderoga* at night in the winter monsoonal rain of Yankee Station.

Commander Gibson left his orbit at marshal and headed for the gate for the final approach to *Ticonderoga* under positive radar control from CATCC, the carrier air traffic control center. Distractions kept entering his mind. Momentarily he began to organize his observations for the mission debrief. Then he was disconsolate over the possible death or capture of the first Black Knight pilot under his command. Feelings of guilt periodically threatened to overwhelm him. *Fly the airplane*. His thoughts went again to Campbell. He was allowing himself to become emotionally involved over Campbell's shoot-down. *Fly the damn airplane*. He missed the latest transmission from the controller giving him the setting for his altimeter. He felt perspiration in the palms of his hands inside his gloves. *Focus or you'll kill yourself, Gibson*.

Without his realization, he was being afflicted by early symptoms of survivor's guilt. He felt a fatherly responsibility for all of his pilots, and especially for Campbell, owing to his stoic willingness to prosecute Operation Igloo White. Gibson admired Campbell's grit, his sense of maturity, his professional airmanship, and his quiet example of devotion to Christianity, which initiated an unfamiliar effect on Gibson who was not particularly religious. These thoughts competed with his attention to the instrument landing. *Damn it focus…Campbell knew the risks. We all know the risks…. Focus, focus before you kill yourself.* Gibson continued to fly down the final leg to the landing and was looking for the familiar yellow and green lights of the Fresnel landing system. *Damn…that guy was exemplary.* The ship's controller kept telling him he was low. "Flaps down; wheels down; hook down; all down." He slipped further below the glide slope when he passed through the plume of hot stack gases from *Ticonderoga's* oil-fired boilers that crossed the glide slope. A wave of anxiety passed uncontrollably through him as he hit the bubble of less-dense, heated air. *He didn't deserve it.* Gibson reacted late to the need for more power. *Add power, nugget.* He pushed the throttle forward and the plane climbed back onto the glide slope, but he over-corrected and now was too high. He sensed palpitations in his heart. The controller was telling him he was high. "Ease your power! Ease your power!" added the landing signals officer. Gibson was feeling the symptoms of anxiety and tried to respond by being hyper-focused on getting aboard.

Gibson strained to see through beads of monsoonal rainwater rolling over and off the windshield and canopy. "305, state 2.6, I have a ball" and he cut back the power to return to the glide slope. Again he sensed his hands shake and his lips quiver and fought his anxiety. Now he saw the ship's round down, and inelegantly dove for the deck and applied full power. Bang! He felt the jolt as the Skyhawk hit the deck and caught the fourth wire. His body strained against the shoulder straps of his harness as the arresting gear rapidly brought the plane to a stop. Suddenly he felt extremely fatigued. *Crap landing,* he said to himself with disgust and self-loathing, *but alive. Damn sight better 'n Cocktail—poor bastard!*

Down in Strike Operations aboard *Ticonderoga,* the air intelligence officers were beginning to assemble the scant information on Cocktail and assess his situation. Batcat had tracked Lawcase 309 until they lost radar contact, and they deduced a rough search area which was transmitted to *Ticonderoga.* They were certain that Cocktail had gone down in Laos, not Vietnam, but there were wide variances in their estimate. For one, Batcat tracked the aircraft but did not know where Campbell had ejected. Second, they knew only that Cocktail was heading west and that he had cleared a known karst, and they would not be able to search for the crash site until daylight. Third, they knew where he had been aiming his bombs. The net of this was a wide trapezoidal area where Cocktail was likely to have gone down. Inside the trapezoid ran a small river—a very important source of water for Cocktail—and at least two small villages. The vast majority of the land was jungle, but here and there the geography showed cleared areas used for agriculture and an array of several elevations and steep karsts.

They reasoned that the NVA had brought in an additional 57mm radar guided gun that was unknown to navy and air force intelligence, and the NVA had located it further south than sites which were known, plotted and briefed. Cocktail's bomb run took him towards this gun. The crew manifested sound discipline and did not betray their position with wild firing and withheld firing until they had a good target within range. When Cocktail pulled out of his bomb run into what was believed to be a relatively safe area, he overflew this newer gun site and exposed himself to deadly fire.

Ticonderoga diverted a section of A-4s with each launch cycle to search the area until they ship ceased flight operations at midnight, but neither the crash site nor the pilot were located. Other aircraft from the Yankee Station carriers would continue the search for Cocktail and his aircraft until *Ticonderoga* resumed flight operations at noon the following day. At daybreak, the air force would put up A-1H search and rescue Skyraiders, better known by their call sign, Sandy, and augment the search.

However, the most perplexing piece of information was the absence of a radio response from Cocktail or a beeper. Gibson reported that Campbell sounded "very together" as he ejected and rogered the request to check in with Gibson when he got down. But Cocktail never checked in despite several radio calls on 243.0 military guard from Gibson or from subsequent *Ticonderoga* pilots.

This gave rise to several hypotheses. One, Campbell had not survived the ejection or was very badly injured. Two, he was alive and his radios or their batteries had failed. Three, he was in the vicinity of people or human activity and could not risk using the radios. Four, he had hidden or destroyed the radios presumably before imminent capture, and five that he had, in fact, been captured by the brutal Pathet Lao communists. None of this was good. Without radio communication the probability of his recovery, never very high in Laos, dropped by 80 to 90 percent and his situation had to be considered dire.

All of this information was summarized and transmitted up the chain of command to CINCPAC and to all army, navy and air force air elements and search and rescue assets in the theater. Campbell was also officially listed as missing in action, and The Reverend and Mrs. Campbell, now serving The First Presbyterian Church in Vero Beach, Florida, were subsequently notified.

In the aftermath of Campbell's shoot-down the mood was sour aboard ship. Poor flying weather, the lack of good targets, an increasing unease with the national leadership and the prosecution of the war, affected the motivation of the air wing. Where in previous deployments there was a sense of being part of a larger effort to defeat the Viet Cong and North Vietnamese and a strong, commonly felt sense of American esprit de corps, the attitude was shifting to one best described as "let's take care of ourselves." It meant that while there was political ambiguity about the strategy guiding the war effort, the air wing would perform their duty, but they would exhibit greater caution and mitigate their exposure to risk. The loss of Campbell reinforced and resolved any and all doubts about the practical wisdom of this course of action. Where in the past young pilots had to be held back by more experienced, veteran pilots, the command leadership was now increasingly challenged to justify the missions and to ask for commitments to efforts that they themselves doubted.

Campbell sensed the dim light of dawn, however lacking in luminosity, beneath the jungle canopy and reckoned that he was nine or ten feet off the ground. The lichens or whatever was phosphorescing were no longer visible as darkness vanished in the gray dawn and Campbell began a more complete assessment of his situation. He noticed that there might be a trail, a trail that he could barely make out in the growth of the jungle, running nearby—a trail which could bring patrols to him as well as offer him a route of escape. Trails are risky and dangerous thought Campbell, and he had been trained to avoid them, but it didn't appear to be any other choice in the jungle.

He took from a survival pack around his fanny a 20 foot piece or nylon rope and fashioned a foot loop at one end with a bowline. He gathered several parachute cords and affixed an aluminum carabiner to them and threaded the other end of the rope through the carabiner, placed his left boot into the foot loop and despite the excruciating pain in his left shoulder began to lower himself hand over hand to the ground. Suddenly whatever was holding the parachute up in the trees abruptly gave way and Campbell fell and rolled on the ground, injuring his shoulder again and increasing the severity of the shoulder pain, but he stuffed the desire to howl and scream out loud.

When the pain subsided he got out both radios, loaded the batteries from other pockets in the survival vest that were neatly contained in the fanny pack, and checked them both with a click-click to ensure they were functioning. He got out a bottle of water and drank it all with two Tylenol pills, and attempted to pull the parachute down from the trees, but it was thoroughly entangled, and he could only capture five or six feet of material before he had to give the effort up. Campbell had made up several rice balls in the Korean manner and now took one out of the vest and began to eat it. He also took out a small scale map, estimated his position on the map and considered his options.

He knew he was in Laos west of Khe Sanh and south of Route 9 which ran west from Khe Sanh across Laos to the Mekong River and Thailand. There were just two possibilities, but in reality just a single choice. He could attempt to head towards Khe Sanh and somehow pass through the North Vietnamese Army, avoid being killed by friendly fire, and pass into the hands of US Marines in Khe Sanh or Army Special Forces at a small camp four miles south of Khe Sanh at Lang Vei. The distances were shorter, but he calculated that the odds of success were shorter still.

Alternately, he could head west over very difficult terrain unless he travelled by roads, an extremely chancy option, some 100 or more miles to Thailand. He reckoned the latter option had better odds, particularly, since he had walked hundreds of miles living off the land as a refugee in Korea.

Campbell considered the crash site of his airplane to be a wild card factor because he had no idea where the site was. He presumed it to be somewhere west within five miles. Normally proximity to a crash site abetted recovery, but it also attracted people who were understandably hostile after being bombed. So his plan cautioned him to be on the look out for pedestrians and signs of a crash. Next he checked for various pieces of paraphernalia—a compass, light sleeping bag, socks, iodine pills, fishing line and hook, and small tools—just to satisfy himself that they were all there. Finally he took his .38 caliber pistol from his shoulder holster, removed the bullets from the cylinder, removed the cylinder which he would toss into the jungle at a further distance, and tied the pistol to his parachute. He presumed the Laotians would eventually find the parachute, and he wanted to indicate that he was unarmed. He also wanted to shed the weight of the pistol. Every ounce of weight above his waist was the equivalent of five or six ounces on his feet. Then he transferred all of his belongings to a lightweight rucksack.

"Jesus, Lord and Savior, lead me west to the Promised Land."

Beebe Byrnes picked up the phone as it rang in her office in Langley, Virginia. The CIA headquarters office was relatively new. Construction had only been completed in 1961. "Mrs. Byrnes here."

"Beebe, it's Sharon." Dr. Sharon Schwartz held a bachelor's degree in bio-chemistry from Radcliffe and a doctorate from MIT. Those credentials offset the anti-Semitic bias in recruiting at the FBI as the bureau's interest in advancing the science of forensic evidence was greater than their prejudice. "I have your answer to the gentleman with Ms. Martin. The one shielding her in the photo."

"Yes."

"Franco Ciorrazzi. Here on a student visa. Departed from Leonardo da Vinci in August 1966 and passed through Immigration at Kennedy. Visa has been promptly renewed annually, and subject has legally registered as an alien at 529 West 112th Street, Manhattan. Status as graduate student confirmed by Registrar, Columbia University. No fellowships. No visible means of income. Born in Orti, a hill town in very southern Italy, on July 5th, 1942." Byrnes read back her notes to Schwartz.

"Thank you."

"We would appreciate a return favor. We're interested in Ciorrazzi."

"And you're curious, because…?"

"His name keeps popping up as an organizer in the anti-war protest movement. And the one's that he is associated with are very well organized…too well organized."

"Unh-huh."

"And there's one more thing," Sharon Schwartz paused before she added, "Interpol indicates that he was arrested on charges of assault and battery…"

"Yes."

"…and the charges were dismissed."

"Hmmm."

"Needless to say, you can't say anything to Ms. Martin."

"Yes, Sharon, that is needless."

Campbell crawled on his hands and knees through the dense undergrowth towards the trail that he had seen earlier while his parachute was entangled in the trees and suspended him in the air. The growth was very thick and he had to go around or forcibly make his way through vegetation of all sorts including tree trunks, stems, and vines. He stopped to rest when he

was within one to two feet of entering the trail. He was breathing heavily
from the exertion required to squeeze through the undergrowth, and he
stopped to catch his breath before entering the trail. His breathing was audible, but it subsided as his heart beat returned to a resting pulse rate.

Suddenly he heard sounds of conversation coming his way, and he
tried to shrink back into the jungle behind him, but movement was difficult and noticeably audible. The voices came on towards him, at least two
distinctly different voices. On they came, until he could tell there were
four of them. One was on the trail, virtually unseeable but directly in front
of him, when another man shouted in Laotian, and all four of the men let-
down quietly off to the sides of the trail and quickly camouflaged themselves with leaves and fronds that they cut with machetes. Campbell could
hear the nearest man's machete and here him grunt with each swipe of the
machete. When the Laotian settled down, he could hear the man breathe
until he came to rest.

Campbell figured the men were concealing themselves from something, but from what, he could not determine. So the five men, the American who had grown up in Korea, and four Laotians, who were probably
searching for him, lay there hiding in close proximity. In the distance,
Campbell began to hear the sounds of airplanes, propeller driven airplanes.
He could tell as the pitch rose the planes were approaching his position,
but they turned away and the pitch dropped and the sound faded. Minutes
passed and no one moved. Again Campbell could hear the approach of
planes, A-1Hs he reckoned, USAF Sandy aircraft, likely searching for
him, but he was in no position to call them by radio or attract their attention with reflections from a mirror which he also had in his rucksack.

Ants began to crawl over Campbell and into his flight suit and they
began to bite him severely. He fought the temptation to scratch, or swat
the ants for fear that he would be heard. They covered his neck and ears
and went down his back biting him and producing painful stings. Campbell submitted to the agony of the ants and their fiery bites rather than
move. Now he heard the sounds of propeller driven aircraft again, and
again he could not signal them. Again the planes withdrew from his position.

After the planes were no longer heard for several minutes, the Laotians
got up and retraced the trail in the direction from whence they came.
When Campbell was certain they could not hear him, he forced his way
through the underbrush carrying the stinging ants with him. There he undressed, smacked, swatted, and brushed away the ants from his body and

his clothing with his good arm, "Bastards," and treated himself with a salve for the substantial quantity of ant bites that he endured before re-dressing. "Little bastards." In the process he examined his shoulder which was badly swollen and bruised. He could not raise nor rotate his arm with-out extreme pain, and then only with reduced mobility, and Campbell could not effectively apply salve to certain bites which were beyond reach of his right arm. He also took out another water bottle and drained it as he felt thirsty and sensed the early stages of dehydration. He needed to find water. Campbell got up and began to walk in a westerly direction after the Laotians thinking that they would lead him to a source of water.

He began with a silent recitation of parts of the 23rd Psalm and added a walking meditation, focusing his mind on his breathing while his senses began the process of attuning themselves to the primeval, Laotian jungle. He became aware of birds and animals, especially chattering monkeys, swarms of insects, one of which, a large insect, landed on his shoulder, which he grabbed and promptly ate what he thought was a good source of protein. It was the first insect that he had eaten since he was a boy of ten in Korea. He noted occasional scents, aromas, and odors from various plants, and his booted feet discerned slipperiness and dryness and various textures beneath him just as his Taekkyeon, a Korean martial art, instructor had trained him to raise the alertness and keenness of his senses. "No thinking! You must leave your mind to come to your senses, Tireless One."

Cannon's orientation period was over with a two-fold affect on the young officer. The first and more obvious was his quick ramp up the learning curve, and he was now standing all of his watches without supervision. Depending on whether his schedule included two-hour, dog watches, he was on watch 12 to 14 hours a day in CIC, as strike-controller, or officer of the deck. The remainder of each day was spent eating, sleeping, groom-ing, or reading messages, but he was spared the duties of a division officer or administrative collateral duties.

The second affect might be referred to as a shift from a conceptual sense that he was in a war zone to a concrete internalization that it was very real. The downing of Cocktail, and the death or capture of half a dozen other Yankee Station pilots from the other carriers in the brief pe-riod that he had been aboard *Ticonderoga* drove any sense of romanticism about war out of him if there were any need to do so. The effect was to motivate him to perform at the highest level of professionalism which emanated from his natural sense idealism and a pragmatic understanding that he was a small but potentially important part of a complex, sea-based, aviation weapons system, and an enormous navy and air force effort referred to as Operation Rolling Thunder. He exhibited profound respect for the pilots and what they did, as did all of the officers in the ship's company, and within their personal limits each was determined to operate the ship with maximum proficiency.

Nevertheless Cannon felt undernourished and dissatisfied with his sense of the big military picture, the strategic backdrop, and where, how, and to what degree the magnificent effort being made by *Ticonderoga* and Air Wing 19 mattered. He thoroughly understood the geo-political arguments for the war, and he was experiencing the operational aspects of the naval air war. But he had a void in his understanding about the justifiability of the American effort, the cost in American blood and treasure, and the cost and benefit to the South Vietnamese population—in part the answers to the questions of the war's morality posed by his fiancé and the notion of a morally just war.

Chaplain Osborne saw Cannon having breakfast and asked him to save the seat next to him while he procured his breakfast. The Chaplain frequently seated himself with the junior officers rather than at the commanders' table. He returned promptly with coffee and juice in hand. "You're a tough guy to run down. Every time I call the Ops office you are either on watch or racked out. How's it going, Bob?"

"Pretty well, O. I've gotten into the swing of things pretty well."

"Little faster pace than *Essex*, I gather."

"Entirely." Cannon hesitated before asking the padre the next question. "O, how well did you know Campbell…Cocktail?"

"Interesting fellow. Grew up in Korea as a young boy during the war. Very nice young man." He paused parenthetically before mentioning, "We were both veterans of that war." Cannon apparently missed the significance of the statement. Osborne paused momentarily before resuming. "But he didn't wear his religion on his sleeve; he was very devout, and exhibited a quiet humility despite the fact that he was an officer. And as I gather, a damn good pilot." Again Osborne paused for a moment before he added, "He admitted that he was a mediocre student, but I actually found him to be quite philosophical."

"How so?"

"Korea was obviously a formative experience, and he thought a lot about a favorite subject of his mother and father during the war, about civilizations that lacked a moral and just organizing principle. He thought that was Christianity's gift, God's gift to the world, and he thought it's absence in the Soviet sphere of the world accounted for a lot of cruel, egregious perpetrations by the North Korean state against its citizens."

"Huh. I had a Jewish professor at Columbia, who, half in jest, and half in truth, said a great part of the history of Western Civilization could be explained as the History of Christianity."

"Now, there's a thought," chuckled Osborne. "I'll use that in a future sermon when I'm asked back to preach at Yale."

"Do you happen to know where he went to school?"

"I do. As his parents were Presbyterian missionaries in Korea, it was quite natural for him to go to Davidson. Older brother went to Princeton."

"Uh-huh. Do you happen to know where he went to school before Davidson?"

"Westbridge Christian School, in the Berkshires," he paused before he added, "He was one of my lay chaplain's assistants."

"Damn. Thought I knew him from somewhere! There was this guy from Westbridge who knocked me cold in a lacrosse game. Just a couple of minutes left to play, when 'Wham!' the lights went out."

"Campbell?"

"Yeah, they told me later. After the game was over, so they told me, this guy jogs over and bows and wishes me well. Of course, I was so damn woozy I only remember what they told me later. But I wanted to know who the guy was. Totally clean play."

"I think you would like him."

"Yeah…well, I guess that's not going to happen for awhile." He was subdued as he spoke and reflective before he excused himself. "Sorry, O, but I gotta get to CIC."

"Sure…how 'bout dinner at my club in Cubi?" Osborne tried to lighten the atmosphere.

"Your club? Which club is that?" Campbell asked with surprise as he got up from his chair.

"Whom do you think they named the O' Club after?"

"Oooo! That's bad, Padre. Very, very, very bad…okay. But only if we go dutch."

On the morning of 21 January, *Ticonderoga,* operating as TG 76.1 with her commanding officer the Officer in Tactical Command, received the following operational immediate message.

1. UPON RECEIPT THIS MESSAGE CEASE FLIGHT OP-
   ERATIONS ON OR BEFORE 1800 AND RECOM-
   MENCE CYCLIC OPERATIONS AT 0600 22 JANUARY
   IN SUPPORT OF US MARINE BASE KHE SANH AS
   PART OF OPERATION NIAGARA.

2. TG 76.1 SUPPORT OF OPERATION IGLOO WHITE IS
   SUSPENDED IMMEDIATELY

3. CVW-19 TO CHECK IN WITH CONTROLLING
   AGENCY HILLSBOROUGH, USAF TACTICAL CON-
   TROL GROUP, AND ORBIT IN STACK AT 500 FOOT
   INTERVALS UNTIL DISTRIBUTED TO FORWARD
   AIR CONTROLLERS

4. MOUNT MAX EFFORT IAW A/C AVAILABILITY.
   TARGET ORDNANCE LOADS AGAINST TROOPS,
   GUNS, CAVES, COMMAND POSTS, MATERIEL

The second message, an after-action summary from Headquarters, 3rd
Marine Expeditionary Force, explained the shift in mission.

1. KHE SANH COMBAT BASE UNDER COORDINATED
   MULTI-UNIT ATTACK AFTER MIDNIGHT IN WHAT
   IS BELIEVED TO BE THE OPENING SKIRMISHES OF
   EFFORT BY THE NVA 304TH, 320TH, AND 325TH
   DIVISIONS TO OVERRUN KSCB AND CONTROL
   AVENUE OF APPROACH TO QUANG TRI PROVINCE

2. HILLS 861 AND 881S WERE ATTACKED AFTER
   MIDNIGHT AND REPULSED IN TOUGH BITTER
   FIGHTING WHICH SOMETIMES INCLUDED HAND
   TO HAND COMBAT.

3. SHORTLY THEREAFTER MAIN BASE CAME UNDER
   HEAVY 82MM MORTAR AND 122MM ROCKET AT-
   TACK WHICH WAS EFFECTIVE.

4. MOST STRUCTURES ABOVE GROUND AND MAIN AMMO DUMP WERE DESTROYED INCLUDING STORES OF CS TEAR GAS.

5. HEAVY GUNS IN NVA REAR BEYOND RANGE USMC 105 HOWITZER COUNTER-BATTERY FIRES MOST TROUBLESOME

6. NVA SAPPERS ATTEMPTED SEVERAL BREACHES ACCOMPANIED BY ASSAULT TROOPS BUT IN EACH CASE WERE DRIVEN OFF BY WELL-POSITIONED INTER-LOCKING FIRE AND THE COURAGEOUS OFFICERS AND MEN OF THE 26TH MARINE REGIMENT.

Chapter 8.

The 22nd of January began with another step up in tempo for *Ticonderoga*. If there was a sense of monotony or waning commitment, the call to arms to defend Khe Sanh changed all of that.

The air plan indicated nearly a deck load of aircraft would be launched on every cycle. While one deckload was launched and airborne, the remaining deck load was being armed and refueled on the flight deck or hangar deck. Virtually all pilots were scheduled for two missions during the day, and the squadrons were collectively putting up 16 to 20, A-4 Skyhawks per cycle, generally loaded with eight Mark 82, 500-pound bombs and two Mark 81, 250-pound bombs. Six or eight F-8 crusaders were armed with rockets for air strikes and ResCap in addition to the standard launch of fighters which were tasked for BarCap—the barrier combat air patrol for fleet defense. In addition to *Ticonderoga's* own airborne tankers, the KA-3 Skywarriors and A-4 Skyhawks with buddy tanks, the air force provided three KC-135 tankers over the Gulf of Tonkin for navy aircraft.

Jeffreys called the CICWO, Ltjg. Meyers, standing the 04 to 08, and asked Ltjg. Meyers to send a messenger to Cannon's stateroom. "Have the messenger apologize for me, for waking Mr. Cannon and tell him that I think it would be a good idea for him to attend the brief at 0430 in Strike Ops. I know Cannon runs short on sleep, but I think he needs to get the big picture plan for Khe Sanh."

"Yes, sir."

Strike Operations was packed with squadron COs, XOs, Operations Officers, the squadron air intelligence officers, and every pilot above the rank of lieutenant who could find standing room in the compartment. Commander Jeffreys and Lieutenant Van Kirk, and Ltjg. Cannon attended the briefing. Cannon and an ensign air intelligence officer stood in the rear. The white lights in the overhead felt especially bright to Cannon that morning. The Strike Operations compartment was lined with maps and photographs of new targets and recent bomb damage assessment. The mood was businesslike and rational which is the way the best and the most successful at strike warfare like it. While the attitude was sober, it was abundant with well-calculated optimism and confidence.

Commander Wertz, Strike Operations Officer, began the mission brief. "Gentlemen, the air power mission over Khe Sanh is being designated Operation Niagara. The mission today and for the next several days will be to attack troops, guns, caves, command posts and any valuable materiel of the North Vietnam Army presently conducting offensive operations in the Khe Sanh area. The overall direction of Niagara is under the command of the Seventh Air Force. The plan today is for us to launch, form up in divisions over the ship and proceed inland climbing to at least angels 24 by the time you cross the beach. Then, check in with 'Hillsborough.' That's an Air Force C-130 tactical control ship who will assign you an altitude bloc and a location to orbit until he is ready to hand you off to a FAC."

Wertz saw the first hand go up with a question and anticipated the answer. "You want to know the radio frequencies, right. Gentlemen, we will give you all a frequency card, and your AIOs will have extra copies. There are a lot frequencies as this is a tri-service operation, and we don't have the crystals. You'll have to put 'em in manually. Please hold your questions to the end of my part." Wertz paused briefly before continuing. "After that, it is standard FAC work. It's been suggested that they will ask you to use a shallow, 10 degree angle dive and drop with snakeyes. A good tactic against troops, but stay within your ROE. There is one exception. You will have mostly iron bombs, and you'll drop all of your ordnance, repeat, all of your ordnance in one run in a single salvo and get your asses back here and safely aboard. We are going to binge on ordnance and economize on American lives."

"Gentlemen, there are about 7000 US Marines down there under attack from nearly three NVA divisions. For once Washington is not screwing around. Now, please hold your questions until the Air Intelligence Officer completes his briefing. Jack, take it away."

Jack Neilsen, lieutenant commander, began his brief. "Okay guys I think we all know the weather. It's still the northeast monsoon that has certain affects on Khe Sanh. There will be a high layer, broken to overcast, and until mid-morning there will likely be fog. The fog tends to be in the valley and over the base which has an elevation of 1500 feet. Winds are generally from the south... less than five knots. You can always expect haze or dust over the target area. Trust your FAC. There will be a lot of air traffic in the area. Be damn careful. There are C-130 transports going into and coming out of the base air strip. There are helos down low. There are Air Force F-4s, F-100s, 105 Thuds, and B-52s. Yes, B-52s will be dropping from above 30,000 feet. And there are Yankee Station aircraft from *Kitty Hawk*, and *Ranger*. It's going to be an effing rock concert out there. While the area is virtually vacant of civilian population which allows us to be more aggressive, at all times remember, there are friendlies on the ground."

Neilsen now used a pointer on a map of the Khe Sanh area. "We'll get more maps ASAP for you to put up in your ready rooms. Hopefully, you'll have 'em before you return to your ready rooms. Now about 6000 marines are inside the base here," using the pointer, "which you can easily pick out by the air strip. There is also an augmentation battalion of marines going in by helo this morning, when the fog lifts, due west of the base. To the north and northwest there are four hills ranging from about 2000 to 3000 feet in elevation containing deployed Marine units blocking the avenue of approach to the base. Generally the tops of these hills lack vegetation. There are also various elements of 3rd Marine Recon in the area so you cannot assume that there are no friendlies in the valleys. We need good discipline in the air at all times. Drop only when and where you're cleared to drop by your assigned FAC."

"Hills 881 South, the most western, Hill 861, closest to the base, Hill 861 Alpha, just to the north of 861, and Hill 558 lower in elevation and almost due north of the base are all controlled by elements of the 26th Marine Regiment." Neilsen carefully pointed the hills out. "Runway 28 points to the general direction of these hills, and there are three reasonably sized rivers that run through and around these hills." Neilsen pointed out these terrain features with deliberation before resuming. "You should be able to see them from the air to locate these hills and your relationship to them. These hills with our marines are blocking the 325th NVA Division from accessing this natural avenue of approach to the Khe Sanh Combat Base. This is where we expect the enemy to come first in force, and where the CAS (close air support) missions are likely to be most intense. Incidentally this is the first time the three battalions of the 26th have been fighting together since Iwo Jima and Okinawa." Neilsen paused to drink from a glass of water before resuming.

"Up here, north of 881 South lies 881 North, and north of that, is where we believe the main body of the 325th lies. South and west of the base between the base and Lang Vei, the Special Forces camp over run about two weeks ago, lies the NVA 304th Division. Two smaller NVA units lie to the east of the base, the 95th Regiment and the 6th Battalion. Now, let's not use the word 'surrounded.' 7000 marines are tying down about two and a half divisions, one, an elite division from Dien Bien Phu, but be advised… these are all highly capable forces representing the corners of a potential triangle about the marines." Neilsen again paused before beginning again. "Okay, air defense. The situation is fluid. You have to assume there are guns everywhere. Your FAC will give you the latest on gun sites. Any questions?"

"Yes, Jack." It was Gibson, CO of VA-23. "What makes this different from the French at Dien Bien Phu?"

"Good question. Three things. American air mobility and maneuver, American fire power, and the French never controlled the hills and were pinned down in a valley. As you can see, the marines control the high ground—still a strategic advantage since before the days of Caesar. Anybody else?" Neilsen looked around the Strike Operations space.

"Any sense of the NVA intentions?"

"Didn't I brief that? Shame on me; 'nother good question. One, they would like to blow open the doors and move south in mass. Two, they want a Dien Bien Phu-like propaganda victory. And three, they would like to foment mass desertions among the ARVN. Next question." Neilsen looked for questions. "None? Okay CAG, your meeting."

"Gentlemen, I think this is the battle that we have been waiting for. You know damn well when Marine Air asks for navy, and, believe it or not, air force CAS, the Marines are damn concerned. This is a massive response, many times larger than Con Thien, last year. This is a JCOS deal all the way. We are not going to let those marines down. Lead your pilots like the professionals that you are. Bring credit to the ship and your squadrons, and…and" he repeated, "bring all of your boys home."

Lcdr. Neilsen asked for questions one last time. "Jack, anything new on Campbell?" CAG answered the question.

"I'll take that one, Jack." He turned directly and addressed the squadron commanding officers. "Gentlemen, the answer is negative. There is nothing new." He paused for deliberate emphasis. "Now, it's tough to say it, and it is harder to hear it. We all care about Campbell… but under the circumstances, we have to put Cocktail behind us like every other air wing out here. January has been a lousy month. We have all lost good pilots since the first of the year. If Cocktail is alive, he is alone, down in Laos, on his own. The Air Force SAR units are looking for evidence of his fate. There is nothing more that Air Wing 19 can do for him right now. Our focus needs to be on marines at Khe Sanh who are in harms' way. Now let's get on with the work we have to do."

The ensign AIO looked over at Cannon and raised an eyebrow. Cannon narrowed his steel-gray eyes, bore him a quick, grim look and nodded twice in comprehension. CAG's answer was part of the calculations and decisions that men who lead other men must make in war.

It was very hot and humid in the jungle although Campbell was sure it was not as a hot as being in an open field. He perspired moderately although even light perspiration accelerated the onset of dehydration. He made his way carefully over the jungle trail, pausing every twenty or thirty yards to listen for signs of Pathet Lao or Laotians whom he presumed he was following towards water. He could also hear the sounds of distant detonations which he presumed were the results of air attacks on parts of the Ho Chi Minh Trail in Laos. It didn't occur to him that some of the sounds came from North Vietnamese artillery. The direction that he was traveling kept the sounds to his back.

In time there was a fork in the path and one fork seemed to slope away and Campbell chose that direction hoping that was an indication of a watershed. As he continued, insects, in particular mosquitoes, became more prevalent, and Campbell sensed relatively cooler, more moist air and came upon a river, perhaps thirty or forty feet wide. The river had steep banks and had been eroded over the ages five or six feet lower in elevation from where Campbell was standing, and the water was brown and flowed slowly. He remained hidden in the jungle while his eyes and ears were hyper-attentive for indications of human activity. Across the river where it turned to the right, perhaps 250 yards away, he observed a herd of water buffalo along the opposite bank, and he searched the herd and the area around it for a herdsman or a farmer but saw none, nor any signs of movement, only the vegetation and the animals were apparent.

Campbell sat down and pondered his next step. Should he risk exposure in daylight or wait until dark? However, he noted early symptoms of dehydration—extremely yellow and pungent urine and headache. The decision made, he chose to go for water and slid down the riverbank whereupon he filled the empty plastic water bottles that he had retained, dropped in an iodine tablet and moved to return to the jungle edge.

Campbell slipped and slipped again. With his injured shoulder, he could not climb back over the edge of the riverbank. He moved now in the opposite direction of the water buffalo looking for a fallen tree or log which he then dragged back to where the trail neared the river and made his way back into the concealment of the jungle pulling the log up behind him and collapsed breathing heavily. He rested until shortly before darkness to bathe. He drank both bottles of water after allowing them to sit for thirty minutes. The water settled some of the mud to the bottom of the bottle, but the water carried a heavy flavor of iodine. Later he would refill the bottles and repeat the iodine treatment.

When it became dark, he moved the log to where he could use it again, slid down the bank to the river bringing all of his gear with him. He removed his boots, clothing, and examined the ant bites, several of which were infected by the ant's venom. He waded into the river and soaped down and rinsed off by squatting over the water, and he washed his underwear. As he returned to the riverbank he noticed several leeches had attached themselves to his ankles and legs, and it took his survival knife to scrape them off although he continued to bleed from their attachment points. Campbell seemed to recollect from his training that the leeches produced an anti-coagulant to maintain the blood flow of their hosts, so now he tried to use the soap to wash his skin thoroughly and prevent new leech attachments. Again he treated himself with a penicillin salve where his skin might be open to infection, but his sore left shoulder limited his ability to cover all of the openings. Campbell did not redon his hot, nomex, flight suit, but rather, he brought clean, olive green utilities and one pair of skivvies to wear and put them on, laced up his boots and gathered up his things.

When he climbed again up the riverbank into the jungle, he ate another rice ball and rolled out the light sleeping bag. There was no place to sleep but in the center of the trail. There Campbell said The Lord's Prayer and spoke with God. "Heavenly Father and Your only son, Lord Jesus, grant me the power to overcome these challenges. Protect me from mine enemies, and guide me safely unto caring hands, in your name, Jesus, and in the name of the Most Merciful Father, I ask it. Amen."

Campbell was exhausted and trusted in the notion that there would not be any Laotians along the trail at night. The AIOs said the Laotians feared spirits in the jungle at night and avoided entering it. He checked the date and time on his watch, January 22, 2010 hours, zipped up the sleeping bag as best he could to breathe and keep the mosquitoes off him, and promptly fell asleep.

Around midnight he felt something heavy on his leg. He kicked it off with the other leg and heard several squeaks of alarm as, whatever it was, scampered off. He thought it might be a curious monkey. Thereafter, for the longest while every sound in the jungle provoked anxiety in him until he got hold of himself, and meditated, and centered himself on the present, and returned to sleeping.

Again and again, Cocktail incorporated certain practices from the Korean martial arts that he had practiced as a boy growing up in Korea and drew upon his Presbyterian religion which he had learned from his missionary parents which taught him his faith in God, the Father, and in Jesus Christ, his only son. The blend of certain Eastern practices and his Western religion so far appeared to serve him well.

He had evaded capture for nearly two days. But it was two days of the beginning of a trend of physical deterioration brought about by insufficient food, water, and rest, a badly bruised shoulder, and insect bites that carried infection.

Chippy 502 launched on the 1330 cycle and was leading a flight of four A-4s flying the older Charlie version and was inbound to Khe Sanh at 24,000 feet. "Hillsborough, Chippy 502." By early afternoon the Yankee Station air wings had the Khe Sanh routine down.

"Chippy 502, Hillsborough, go ahead."

"Chippy 502, inbound to you with a flight of four Alpha four charlies armed with eight Mark 82, snakeyes."

"Roger Chippy 502 your 500 pound iron bombs with retard fins. Break, proceed Kilo Sierra 170 radial at 40 miles and hold at angels 20. I'll have a Bird Dog shortly."

Chippy 502, proceeding to hold at Khe Sanh's 170 at 40, descending to angels 20."

"Roger, call me when level on station" Chippy leader responded with a click, click of his microphone. Several minutes later Chippy leader called Hillsborough.

"Hillsborough, level angels 20."

"Roger, Chippy 502, switch frequency 286.6, Nail 24 waiting for you."

"Switching 286 point 6 for Nail 24, break, Chippies let's go to 286.6." The A-4C division from *Ticonderoga* positioned themselves as requested

"Nail 24, Chippy leader is with you."

"Roger Chippy leader, your call sign Chippy One; break, your angels?"

"Passing 14, descending."

"Uh… Chippy One, I have troops, mortars, guns and maybe supplies on a 1300 foot hill about 4500 meters east from the threshold for runway 100. They're in slight defilade behind the summit. Proceed to 120 at 5 from the base. Run in will be about 350. Pull off to the east. Requesting 10 degree dive. Am proceeding to mark target with white rocket smoke."

"Roger, that, we're turning right and inbound."

"Roger, this is the NVA 95th Regiment. They have been active, and this is the first strike of the day against them. Break, rocket away." There was a long pause while the rocket flew to its destination. "Good smoke."

"Chippy One sees it."

"Target is 100 meters north and 50 left of the smoke."

"One is in." Thirty seconds later, "All stations armed for a one-run drop." A minute later, "Bombs away... One is out."

"Nail 24 followed your detonations. Chippy Two, your target 50 meters north and 25 right of One's blast. Chippy Two repositioned himself to change the run in heading. In actual practice a lot of time lapsed between transmissions where the pilots were silent.

"Two is going in. All stations armed... Two's bomb's are away... Two is off target."

"Good drop. Several secondaries. Three, lay your load 25 left of Two's drop."

"Chippy Three repositioning... Three is in. All stations armed, single salvo." Chippy Three delivered his ordnance and pulled off the target obtaining more secondaries. Nail 24 had fortuitously discovered either an ammo dump or POL dump. The results were excellent. However this time a 23mm gun opened fire although the rounds were poorly aimed.

Chippy Four, tail end Charlie, lined up for his run-in to the target. Again he repositioned to attack on a different heading "Four is going in, all stations armed." The 23mm crew was now looking towards the south where the Chippies had been generally coming from. Against the overcast it was possible to see the dark exhaust of the A-4 jet engine. A second 23mm opened fire. "Bombs away... Four is off the target." Again more secondaries erupted.

"Chippy Four, Nail, were you hit by tracers?"

"Roger, left wing tank. I've got smoke and fuel trailing from the left wing."

"Four this is One. I'm closing on you. Let's go for altitude and let's go for the Gulf ASAP. How's your power?

"Power is fine, but I'm leaking fuel."

"Chippy Two and Three head for the ship as briefed. Call Strike and tell'em we're gonna need a tanker."

"Three roger."

"Nail 24 thanking you for your services. Excellent BDA. Good luck, Chippies"

The VA-195 Dam Busters switched back to their squadron frequency, reverted to their standard call signs, and climbed out staying south of the DMZ heading for the safety of the sea. Chippy 502, the squadron's operations officer, came up on 507's wing, the stricken plane. "I'll look you over 507." 507 was flown by a J.G. with combat experience from the deployment the year before. "Looks like just one hole. The fire is spreading. After we get up to altitude and get plugged in, let's check your control surfaces... your flaps."

"Feels pretty good, 502. If I can get her to thin air at altitude, I may be able to starve the fire of oxygen. I've transferred most of the fuel into the fuselage tank. Maybe get higher and try a power dive."

"Roger on that. I think you have a good chance with this one. Your control surfaces look pretty good."

"Panther Strike, this is Chippy 504 flight of two with 511, feet wet." Cannon was the strike controller.

"Roger 504, hold you on Panther's 290 radial at 65."

"Panther, 507 took a 23 mike mike tracer in the left wing. 502 is on his wing. They are climbing to altitude to try and get the fire out. They're gonna need a tanker." Adrenaline shot through Cannon. He had planes with emergencies before, but this was the first with combat damage and the first since arriving aboard *Ticonderoga*.

"Panther Strike copies, your fuel state, 504?"

"My state 2.9."

"Roger 2.9." Cannon then turned to the CIC Watch Officer. "Chippy 504 reports Chippy 507 with a fire in the left wing, going for altitude. 502 is with him. I need a tanker. Will it be one of ours or one of the KC-135s?" Accordingly the bridge and the Air Boss were informed. It was the Air Boss's call although he might want to discuss it with Captain Tarrant. Cannon doubted that an A-4 buddy tanker would carry enough fuel for a low state A-4 and expected one of the ship's KA-3 Skywarrior tankers, affectionately nicknamed the Whale, to be allocated.

"Panther Strike, this is Chippy 502 with 507. 507 is low state and is burning in the left wing. We have a good chance of getting the fire out. We're passing through angels 22. The bird is flyable. We need to check the flaps before we try to come aboard."

"Strike copies. Question for you. Can you make Danang with a tanker?"

"Probably, but we prefer to come aboard." Word came back down from the Air Boss. "Give him Holly Green 6." Cannon then relayed the information to 502. Holly Green 6 was one of *Ticonderoga's* KA-3 tankers.

Chippy 502, Panther Strike holds you on my 285 at 75. Holly Green 6 will be your tanker. Standby for vector… Holly Green 6 is in orbit. Vector 110 at 25."

"Roger 110 at 25. No smoke now. Fire appears out."

"Click, click." Cannon rogered with his microphone and passed the last piece of information again to the CIC Watch Officer who in turn relayed it to the bridge and the Air Boss.

Chippy 507 stabbed at the tanker's basket twice before he settled his nerves and connected to the drogue and took on fuel from the Skywarrior, KA-3 tanker. Chippy 507 remained plugged into Holly Green 6 as both planes flew down the final approach to *Ticonderoga*. Two miles from the ship, 507's pilot unplugged from the tanker, flew steadily through the bubble of stack gas, calmly called the meatball and uneventfully brought the Skyhawk aboard.

Cannon checked the mailbox in the wardroom and found a letter from his fiancée, Laetitia Martin, which he immediately read before taking his dinner.

January 17, 1968
Morningside Heights

Carissimo mio,

I miss you Caro. Your departure seems so long ago, and I feel so alone and as if I'm living in a shrunken world. Your energy and aliveness, your intellect and expression are absent that so much expanded my life. I feel my stoicism is quenching my own aliveness. How I miss you and daydream about your return, or Hong Kong together. How you might hold me and how I would be kissing you and telling you how much you mean to me, and how much I want to be with you and spend my life with you, Caro. That probably sounds very selfish and needy, but it is an honest reflection of me. How I hate the war and the navy for taking you from me.

*The war is all around me. Well, not in the way it is around you.
But there are desks on College Walk soliciting signatures for
SANE and all manner of anti-war resolutions. And one silly issue
protesting a gymnasium to be built in Morningside Park for use by
the university and local residents. Antiwar Teach-Ins are regularly
scheduled, and there are appeals for participants in endless demonstrations.*

*Weighty columns are written about the war by Richard Reston,
and by Harrison Salisbury who writes against the war while Hanson Baldwin assesses it. Cronkite covers it every night with live
footage from Morley Safer and Marvin Kalb. Everybody on the
Columbia campus seems to be obsessed with it all of the time. And
it is certainly bringing out the undergraduate radicals and the
"professional" radicals like C. Wright Mills, Amatai Etzioni, and
Eric Bentley.*

*I can hear you expressing the real politik point of view, which
just seems so soulless and amoral, so arithmetic. You'll tell me that
Uncle Ho liquidated a million North Vietnamese on his way to
power, and how he was in Moscow in June 1950 when the North
Koreans attacked the South, and he likewise obtained Russian and
Red Chinese support for the First Indo-China War against the
French colonial government. And you'll go on about tens of thousands Cochin-Chinese and Annamese Roman Catholics being
forced to flee for their lives to the South, and how the Red Chinese
orchestrated the accords of 1954, and how they created two separate nation states and that reframing this war as a civil war, a war
of national liberation, is North Vietnamese propaganda of which
you will be entirely dismissive*

*And so on and on will go the killing, the wounding, and the
maiming with each side arguing and asserting the "rightness" of
their position and justifying their homicides. I'm sorry, but you
know how much I detest the killing, and how much I am against the
war, and how much I wish that you had nothing to do with it.*

*I've just reread this letter to you, and I apologize for it being
such a cheerless drag, but as Walter Cronkite would say, that is
the way it is this dreary January 1968 with snow and slush on
Morningside Heights.*

I miss you darling. Ti amo, amore mio.

Tish

Cannon shrugged off the melancholic mood of the letter, finished dinner, and stood the second dog watch, the 1800-2000 on the bridge. He was relieved just as the ship broke away from taking on bombs and ammunition from the ammo ship alongside and went below to his stateroom to grab a few hours of sleep before taking the mid-watch in CIC.

He arose in time to read about 30 or 40 confidential and secret messages in the Operations office. Cannon made a mental note of one message that indicated that an assassination attempt had been made on the president of the Republic of Korea and suspicions were raised that the attempt had been carried out by infiltrators from North Korea. He checked his watch which read 2325. He had 15 minutes before reporting to CIC and went below to the wardroom to grab a cup of coffee to which he added, as was his quirky habit, a pinch of salt.

It was a little after 0200 in the Combat Information Center and things were routinely quiet. Only a surface watch team manned CIC when *Ticonderoga* stood down from flight operations. The men chatted and easily kidded and bantered back and forth in what is usually a calm watch that verged on boredom. Cannon was speaking to Nowatski, the petty officer of the watch, who came from Brooklyn, and the two were comparing and contrasting Brooklyn and Hoboken when a messenger from Communications arrived with a metal box that contained a pink, top secret message for the CIC Watch Officer. It was the first of just two top secret message that he would ever see.

Cannon lifted the lid and read the message carefully from the Commander of US Strike Forces, South Pacific. The subject was ominous.

OPERATIONAL IMMEDIATE
TOP SECRET

1. USS PUEBLO (AGER-2) UNDER ATTACK BY NORTH KOREAN AIR AND SURFACE UNITS WHILE IN INTERNATIONAL WATERS, 16 NM FROM ISLAND OF YO DO, PROK.

2. USS ENTERPRISE (CVAN-65) WITH AIR WING 9 GETTING UNDERWAY FOR SEA OF JAPAN.

Cannon checked the distribution list which was lengthy and observed that it ran from SECDEF, to CINCPAC to SEVENTH FLT to CTF 77 and finally to CO USS TICONDEROGA CVA-14. The six-digit, date-time group suggested that the message was several hours old. Then he checked where the Communications department routed the message aboard ship which included virtually everyone in the ship's chain of command and to the watch officers at critical stations like the bridge, CIC, and strike operations. The addressees were undoubtedly being rousted out of their bunks to read and acknowledge the message, so he felt no need to notify anyone, and he maintained the watch as before. He acknowledged the message with his signature, flipped the lid of the Top Secret box to close it and handed the box to the messenger.

Shortly thereafter two yellow, secret messages followed which were originated by *Pueblo* and were rebroadcast by COMSTRIKEFORSOUTH. The first indicated that additional torpedo boats were now approaching *Pueblo,* but the ship was ambiguous whether they were about to be engaged. The second and last message indicated that *Pueblo* was about to be boarded and that they had only partially destroyed sensitive information, codes, and ciphering machines. He retained these messages and looked down at Nowatski, RD2, from his console.

"Ski?"

"Sir."

"Ski, please take an inventory of all charts that we have for waters between here and the Sea of Japan including the Sea of Japan. Make sure we have everything that we are supposed to have on our required chart list. Make a list of anything that is missing."

"Yes, sir. Something wrong, sir?" Cannon ignored the question.

"If you don't complete the inventory on this watch, make sure your relief on the 4 to 8 continues to take inventory on the next watch."

"Something gone wrong, sir?"

"Sorry, Ski. That's all."

"Aye, aye, sir."

Cannon's fertile mind immediately recalled the conversations that he and Captain Pebbles had about the attack on *USS Liberty* last summer. Cannon was certain Pebbles would remember how Cannon asserted that the failure to come to *Liberty's* aid and punish the attackers, even if they were Israeli allies, would be observed and exploited by the Russians. He had also seen *Liberty* and some of her scars while she was under repair in

Malta when *Essex* and her task group visited Valletta. Cannon had no doubt that the North Koreans were Russian proxies and would never have seized *Pueblo* without Russian instigation or endorsement. A sick, helpless feeling immediately possessed him as his prediction now became true, and as he recalled that a member of his OCS class was an officer in *Pueblo*, too.

When the watch was over Cannon, briefed his relief on what would become known as the "Pueblo Incident" and said that only as a precaution had he asked the petty officer of the watch to see to it that CIC was carrying all required charts if for some reason they were ordered to operate off North Korea.

Chapter 9.

Over breakfast in the wardroom Cannon learned *Ranger* was being sent to North Korea and Operation Igloo White was suspended. There was much speculation about what would happen next among the ship's junior officers and the air wing pilots. The undertone was one of anxiety for a widening war in Asia and concern for themselves. *Ticonderoga* would revert to the status quo ante and conduct flight operations from 0600 to 1800 hours. Now he was reading messages in the Operations office which arrived since his mid-watch before he relieved Lt. Van Kirk on the strike control watch at 0900. The key message was as follows:

>   OPERATIONAL IMMEDIATE
>   034623JAN1968
>
>   FM COMSEVENTH FLT
>   TO USS RANGER CVA-61
>
>   INFO CNO
>   JCOS
>   CINCPAC
>   CTF 70.1
>   CTF 77
>
>   SUBJ TASK FORCE 70.1 BUILD UP, SEA OF JAPAN
>   SECRET
>
>   1.   UPON COMPLETION CYCLIC FLIGHT OPERA-
>   TIONS 23JAN1968 PROCEED AT BEST SPEED
>   WITH CVW-2 EMBARKED FOR THE SEA OF JA-
>   PAN. RENDEZVOUS WITH USS ENTERPRISE
>   CVAN-65, AND REPORT TO CTF 70.1 FOR DUTY
>   NLT 0800 LOCAL 26JANUARY1968.
>
>   2.   TF 70.1 NOW BEING FORMED COMPRISED OF
>   ENTERPRISE, USS PROVIDENCE CLG-6, USS
>   YORKTOWN CVS-10, USS BANNER AGER-1,
>   COMMUNICATIONS RELAY SHIP, AGMR-2 AND

THREE DDS, ONE DDG, ONE DE. ADDITIONAL
UNITS TO BE ASSIGNED,

3. EXPECT TO CONDUCT COLD WEATHER OP-
    ERATIONS. PROVIDE LIST OF EQUIPMENT, POL,
    WEATHER GEAR, ETC TO COMNAVAIRPAC,
    COPIES TO NAVSUPPLYJAPAN AND
    COMSERVPAC PEARL ASAP. EXPECT TO UNREP
    ENROUTE SEA OF JAPAN FOR NFSO, AVFUEL,
    STORES, EQUIPMENT, BOMBS AND AMMO.

Though the US Navy was built for hostile conflict, it didn't wish it, but it
looked like more was coming its way.

Cannon was impressed with both the sobriety of the navy's reaction
and the ability to pull three carriers together with a few messages and form
Task Force 70.1. But, he also observed that TF 70.1 was short on anti-
aircraft support ships. In a word, she needed more AA missile ships, and it
was apparent that the US Navy was stretched beyond its resources by
commitments in the Gulf of Tonkin, the Pacific Sea Frontier, as the homeland of the West Coast was referred, and US Government treaty commitments in the Pacific.

Enterprise was enroute from the States to begin her deployment on
Yankee Station. She had sortied in haste from Sasebo to the coast of North
Korea in the Sea of Japan, and *Ranger* had been clearly pulled off her line
period on Yankee Station with her A-6 Intruders, which were the only
truly reliable, all-weather, naval bombers against North Vietnam during
the winter monsoon. The navy was also stretched for personnel especially
first class petty officers, lieutenants, and potentially the most serious of all,
combat losses were leading to a shortage of pilots.

"Good morning, Bob." Cannon looked up from reading the message
board and saw that it was Commander Jeffreys.

"Good morning, Commander."

"What do you think, Bob?"

"You mean *Pueblo*? You mean CTF 70.1, sir?"

"Un-hunh."

"Damn troubling stuff, sir. We need *Ranger's* A-6s down here. And it
looks to me that we are short of assets for fleet defense in the Sea of Japan."

"How so?"

"Well, we're short missile ships… poor depth of defense, easily saturated by a moderate number of bogies. That means we'll have to hold more fighters back for fleet defense than would otherwise be available to cover the bombers on the way in and out of the target area."

"That's probably true. You're picking up this strike warfare stuff pretty fast," concurred the former attack pilot.

"You know, Commander, I don't think this was a coincidence."

"What do you mean, Bob?"

"I have always thought that the Russians noted last summer how *Liberty* operated unescorted, that she was vulnerable, that our aircraft from *Saratoga* were called back while they were enroute to support *Liberty*, and so long as we operate our AGERs that way, they could take an intelligence ship like her anytime they wanted. And the Soviets are happy anytime they can humiliate the US Navy and pick up codes, ciphering equipment and sensitive material to boot. So I have several questions."

"Yes?"

"In addition to seizing *Pueblo*, it looks like the North Koreans attempted to assassinate the President of the Republic of Korea the day before yesterday. Then they just caused us to divert one of our front line carriers with a state of the art air wing—A-6s and A-7s—from the Indo-China theater of operations. All of this just happens to coincide with more than a skirmish at Khe Sanh. Seems reasonable to ask if there is another shoe to drop in the Southeast Asia theater of operations."

"Second, what does *Pueblo* have that the USSR could want? I'd guess the Russians may have a need for ciphering equipment and obsolete codes."

"Why'd they need that? We've already changed our codes around the world."

"Yes, sir. But the Russian's might possess a trove of older, unbroken messages that they want to decode."

"Hmmpf. Good questions. Guess we'll just have to wait and see, and be ready for anything."

"Yes, sir. Sir, is there anything new on Cocktail?"

"Campbell? Not a damn thing. Haven't even found the crash site yet. Coupla Sandys and a C-130 been looking for it. No damn joy."

"I see." Cannon greeted the news with a grimace. After remembering where he had known Campbell, Cannon began to identify personally with Campbell.

"By the way, Bob, everybody thinks you're doing a damn fine job. You've come aboard here and come up the curve lightning fast. Don't let these big questions distract you. We have the Pentagon and the CIA to answer those questions." A quick wave of anger passed through Cannon.

"I appreciate that, Commander. Please, have no fear, sir, I can handle both." The Ops Boss, Commander Killinger, entered the office. His big personality immediately filled the Operations compartment—all fighter jock posing as a desk-jockey Operations Officer—a necessary step if he coveted a fourth stripe. But it was well-known that Killinger had a decided preference for the cockpit of an F-8 Crusader, whiskey, and women. And he was pretty handy with all three.

"Hey, it's Big Gun. How's my newest officer doing?"

"Just great, Commander, just great. Sorry, sir. Excuse me, gotta go, Boss. I have to get to my strike control station." Cannon left the office quickly. The don't-think-too-much message really annoyed him.

"Hmmm, that was quick. What's wrong with him?" asked Killinger

"Cocktail," answered Jeffreys. Killinger responded with a grunt.

"Other than that, how's your boy doing?"

"Good as advertised. Very smart...make that damn smart. Very professional. Everybody's very happy with him. Bit of a big thinker though, Killy."

"Hmmm. Don't need any of those around here."

As Cannon took the few steps from the Operations office to CIC he thought about North Korea and wondered what kind of support could be had from the US Air Force, which would undoubtedly be mobilizing, and the Republic of Korea. The ROK forces were widely respected by the American military.

Cannon's ability to comprehend the breadth and depth of an issue and to quickly draw broad, reasonable and uncanny implications was the rare trait that intrigued Pebbles most about Cannon. Pebbles did not diminish the value of courageous men of action, but he saw the role of American foreign policy and the future of technological complexity changing the requirements for the type of officer that would be needed to lead the United States Navy. Pebbles observed that Admiral Rickover was operating under similar assumptions and was himself an example of the requirement for different skills and abilities. Moreover, he saw Rickover's difficulties fitting into the naval establishment as an indication of the need for the Navy to create an environment where change-agents and visionaries could thrive. Rickover was implementing like-kinds of thoughts in of-

ficer selection for the nuclear submarine service. Pebbles acuity to spot
unusual talent and to envision where it fit in the future US naval establishment distinguished him from peers like Killinger, and was one of the
attributes that destined him for flag rank.

Cannon relieved Van Kirk just as the 0900 cycle was launching aircraft, many bound for Khe Sanh as part of the tactical air component of
Operation Niagara. As the aircraft checked in with Strike Control after
launch, he interrogated their IFF-SIF gear, identification system friend or
foe with special information feature. These were referred to as parrots and
parrot checks. The launch was fairly standard—a dozen or more attack
aircraft, fighters for fleet defense on the barrier between the MIGs up
north—most of which were now based in the sanctuary of Red China but
posed a potential threat to Task Force 77—and various supporting aircraft:
tankers, electronic counter measure, photographic reconnaissance, logistical fixed-wing aircraft and helicopters.

The Laotians renewed the search and were back near the scene where
Cambell had landed in the trees with his parachute. One of the men who
carried a machete and wore a loin cloth caught sight of the light olive
green parachute as they moved slowly and deliberately through the jungle.
They hacked their way into the jungle until they stood under the tangled
canopy of the chute. Another, using his AK-47, pointed towards Campbell's .38 caliber pistol and emphatically pointed out that the cylinder was
missing. Eventually with all four men pulling, the branches gave up the
parachute, and they gathered it in with the pistol before returning to the
trail.

Another, also in a loin cloth, also with just a machete, pointed out
tracks undoubtedly made by a pair of flight boots, and they began tracking
in the direction where Campbell had gone. The four of them then broke
into an effortless jog and picked up their pace until they came to the fork
where Campbell had gone left towards the river. They stopped only to examine more tracks that indicated Campbell was heading for the river.

Campbell continue to hear detonations day and night as he tried to
move west, but before leaving the river on the third morning since his
ejection, Campbell held a conversation with himself and considered again
his options. Despite his training on evasion, until he left the jungle environment, he decided that he must rest by night and travel by day, the opposite of what he was taught. Next he considered the need to find food—
rice, some eggs, perhaps a small chicken. This would bring him near small

villages and would increase the risk of being sighted and captured. Like-wise, despite the risk, he would also attempt to find a clearing and make contact with a plane by radio. He was certain that his squadron mates would be continuing to search for him or that an air force plane flying be-tween Vietnam and Thailand would cross overhead.

By mid-morning he came upon a thatched structure built on wood pil-ings that he barely caught sight of as he walked by because it was over-grown with vegetation. He spent several minutes surveying the area for signs of occupancy before he carefully climbed the ladder with difficulty. His left shoulder was particularly painful and rather useless when he reached up with his arm as he struggled to climb and enter.

Several bluish balls were gathered on the floor about the size of pota-toes which he recognized as opium balls that his father had once pointed out to him in Korea. He searched further and found the equivalent of a half a cup of uncooked rice and emptied the rice with maggots and rodent droppings into one of his socks before descending and proceeding towards the west along the river.

Shortly thereafter he approached several thatch huts on stilts along the river with an open area used for agriculture surrounded by a very large expanse that he judged to be several acres of elephant grass, and some other, small structures that he eventually learned were coops for chickens. He could make out distant voices that sounded like a group of women on the riverbank, but he saw no children nor adults in the vicinity of the huts, and he proceeded cautiously towards what he hoped were chicken coops surrounded by fences made of vertically thatched reeds. This he believed was fortuitous as he could search for eggs partially hidden by the fence.

The chickens made no unusual sounds as he made his way and reached under each sitting hen feeling for fresh eggs. Immediately he cracked the shells and swallowed three eggs raw before he tried to break the neck of a chicken and take it to be cooked later. He selected a young hen, and as he laid his hands on her neck, she tried to peck and bite, and flapped her wings raising dust and letting out with a screeching alarm that was mim-icked by other hens in the immediate area.

He wasted no time wringing her neck despite the pain in his shoulder and snapping it with a quick jerk, again, just as he had done as a young refugee in Korea, and he gathered three more raw eggs before he moved swiftly to leave the vicinity of the village. An old woman in a nearby hut rose with the sound and commotion of the hens and caught sight of his backside as he hurriedly circled behind a patch of young, planted corn and moved onto the trail leading to the tall elephant grass wearing his olive, unmistakably western utilities. He checked the compass on his watch and noted that his direction was north towards multiple karsts that appeared blue and purple in the humidity. He believed that a northerly course would eventually intersect Route 9 which ran westerly towards the Mekong River and Thailand. His survival training was seriously flawed as long distance travel was entirely prohibited by the jungle, steep karsts, and the Annamite Mountain Range. There was no indigenous alternative to rivers, trails, and roads in Laos.

When he was well-down the trail and deep into the tall, elephant grass, Campbell carefully cracked the shells of the purloined eggs and sucked the caloric value of their contents into his mouth. He listened to hear if he was being followed. He was still carrying the freshly killed chicken in his left hand, and now he packed it in his rucksack and hoped he might later find time and a place to cook it over a fire. It was now afternoon and the temperature was rising to a high temperature causing his body to perspire profusely in the unbearably hot, stifling Laotian heat, but for the first time in three days he did not feel hungry. He moved on more slowly to conserve energy and fluids.

Awhile later Campbell began to hear the welcome sound of piston-engines and presumed it to be a section of air force Skyraiders looking for him. He got one of his personal radios out and turned on the homing beacon which was carried over 243.0, the emergency frequency, monitored by all NATO military aircraft. The plane seemed to come closer as the pitch rose slightly. Moments later it was clear the plane was getting closer and louder until it passed overhead at altitude well-above where it could be reached by small arms fire. It wasn't easy to identify the plane. It had four engines and looked like an older transport, like something he had often seen in Korea. The plane circled back towards him, and he thought it might be a C-54, but he didn't know who would be flying a World War II plane in Laos. The plane now began to circle over where he was and Campbell was concerned the plane would attract attention and give away his position.

"Aircraft overhead, over." There was no answer. Campbell tried again, "Aircraft circling overhead, this is Cocktail, over?" This time there was a very staticky response with a weak sound of a voice. "Aircraft overhead, this is Cocktail, standby to copy, over." Given the circumstances, Campbell was incredibly composed.

"Am...rica 2, ... ahead."

"Amrica 2, you are cutting in and out with static, information follows, information follows:" he paused for the pilot to take down the information, "Cocktail, designated naval aviator, Panther, 6-8-3-3-4-7, how copy?" There was a long pause before the aircraft overhead responded.

"…num-ers, -gain."

"What, what? …numbers again, numbers again…oh, rog; okay, okay, affirmative: 6-8-3-3-4-7, repeat 6—8—3—3—4—7—how-copy?"

"Air-merica has—r num-ers." The C-54 rolled out and headed west towards Thailand. Campbell's mind flashed through several moods from anxiety and uncertainty to elation to back to uncertainty. He just wasn't sure the C-54 had copied his transmission accurately, but he put the thought aside realizing that it would do him no good, shut down his radio to conserve the battery power, took a careful look around, and then continued north towards a distant tree line.

When he got to the tree line, he saw that there was a seasonal stream that had been improved for irrigation, and he followed it north until it led him to the jungle where he decided to spend the night. He back-tracked and gathered wood for a fire and set about roasting the chicken hoping that the jungle canopy over the fluvial area of the seasonal stream would mask the smoke from the fire.

Several hours later a message was received aboard *Ticonderoga* that buoyed morale around the ship and raised expectations that Campbell would be recovered the next day. Air America was the cover for a small, special operations and logistical air force run by the CIA from Thailand that supported various indigenous groups in Laos and Cambodia. Like all propeller aircraft in Thailand it was based at Nakhon Phanom just west of the Mekong River separating Laos from Vietnam.

SECRET

1. AIR AMERICA C-54 REPORTS EMERG BEEPER AT APPROX 100 RADIAL NKP AT 120 STATUTE MILES AT APPROX 1340 LOCAL 23 JAN.

2. CONTACT ON GROUND IDENTIFIED SELF AS COCKTAIL / PANTHER / 683347

3. BELIEVE THIS MAY BE TICONDEROGA MIA PILOT

4. PLEASE VERIFY. FORWARD SECURE IDENT QUES-
    TIONS FOR COCKTAIL ASAP.

5. 602 SOS INTENDS TO SEARCH AREA AT FIRST
    LIGHT, CALL SIGN SANDY

In the dark at 0600 the following morning and in anticipation of daylight, two USAF A1-H Skyraiders rolled down the runway in a section take off at NKP and climbed out on the 110 radial in search of Cocktail. They leveled at five thousand feet above the ground, adjusted their cowl flaps and leaned out the carburetor. At that altitude they were above small arms fire, had a good field of slant-range vision and the outside air temperature was several degrees more comfortable than on the surface.

Campbell arose with first light and broke camp quickly doing his best to hide any signs of fire. He wrapped the uneaten pieces of charred chicken in his spare skivvies and placed the chicken inside, near the top of his rucksack, and retraced his route along the tree line to a junction that he noted the day before that ran north. He took the risk of being in the more open meadow of elephant grass than traveling in the jungle to increase his chance of sighting friendly aircraft or being seen by them.

He could hear the Skyraiders before he could see them, and then they appeared to be loitering in a circle over a distinct area—possibly the crash site of his A-4.

"Sandy, Sandy, this is Cocktail, to the south of you."

"Cocktail this is Sandy One, over…."

Further to the south an eight man party, made up of four partly uniformed men with rifles led by four men in loin cloths with machetes, now ran cautiously but faster than a jog when they heard the A-1s. They where following a trail marked by heeled boots left by an airman.

Campbell sat on the trail hidden by the tall elephant grass and answered correctly the three personal identification and authentication questions for the air force pilots.

"Okay, Cocktail, stay put. We'll make a high pass over you and get some Jolly Greens in here for you."

"Roger, Sandy One. Sounds very good to me." Shortly thereafter the A-1s passed overhead. Campbell's hopes were rising. *Please, God, help me. Please Lord Jesus, save me.*

Campbell thought he heard sounds of movement behind him. He could also hear the sounds of helicopter blades so he wasn't sure. The chop, chop, chop of the helicopters drew louder, but now he definitely heard Laotian voices behind him.

The Laotians were now in a sprint to reach Campbell. If they could get very close to Campbell, better yet, capture him, the planes would not take them under fire.

Campbell now began to run towards the north away from the Laotians in hot pursuit and called on the radio. "Sandy, have hostiles following me at my six o'clock" Campbell then began a sprint.

"Roger, Cocktail, Sandys are in a buster to you. How many hostiles?"

"Half dozen, may be more." Campbell looked skyward, not watching carefully where he was running as he dashed searching for the A-1s and the Jolly Green helicopters. The helicopters were now quite loud, when, whoompf. Cannon crashed through a camouflaged animal trap and somersaulted forward. He tried desperately to extract himself but bamboo stakes on all sides prevented him from scaling the wall.

"Yute, yute, yute!" The first of the Laotians with a machete reached him. In several seconds he was surrounded. Hastily Campbell reached for his combat knife and stabbed each personal radio, with disgust, several times destroying it as the tip of the blade broke through the thin casing of each radio while the Skyraiders roared helplessly overhead. Then Campbell looked up and saw the rifles pointed at him and raised his right arm in surrender overhead, but the left arm could not be raised above his shoulder. He heard the helicopters with their distinctive chop, chop, chop bear off while the Skyraiders circled in frustration overhead without being able to fire a round in defense of their countryman.

Campbell received a rifle butt to the head knocking him to the ground. His rucksack was pulled from him and immediately his left arm, the one with the bad shoulder was yanked up behind his shoulder blades and subsequently lowered to his waist and was tied with a rope which was then wrapped a full turn around his neck. He was kicked twice and signaled to roll over whereupon his right hand was also tied at waist level. The remaining 12 to 15 feet of rope were held by another man with a rifle slung across his shoulders. He was then jerked to his feet, and the nine men began to run at a fast jog, retracing their steps towards the tree line and then turning, as Campbell had, towards the jungle.

The Skyraiders continued to orbit in futility overhead until Campbell was taken into the jungle and disappeared. The group proceeded to cover ground quickly for a mile or so into the jungle before they stopped and listened for the Skyraiders. They could still hear the aircraft in the distance, but they halted and again knocked Campbell down with a rifle butt to the side of his head and hid in the jungle until there was a total absence of sound from aircraft.

Campbell believed he had been captured by four Laotian guerillas and four Pathet Lao regulars. The guerillas deferred to the Pathet Lao who wore various pieces of brown uniforms and were equipped with rifles or semi-automatic assault rifles. The leader wore a brown shirt and trousers and a brown hat that resembled the style that Campbell had seen pictures of Mao Tse Tung wearing. The guerillas, with loin cloths and bare skin tops, were armed, as it were, with machetes and appeared to serve as local guides.

Then they went through the contents of the rucksack and the first thing to come out of the rucksack was the uneaten chicken wrapped in Campbell's underwear which brought about an excited conversation among the Laotians. Immediately one the men in a loin cloth jumped to his feet and began to beat Campbell with a bamboo rod. Campbell rolled over to protect himself but he continued to receive blows about his head and shoulders until the leader halted the thrashing. His assailant stopped with two swift kicks to his ribs. While he was lying on the ground, blood now flowing from a cut above this right eye, another local guerilla removed his watch with compass from his left wrist. The leader kept the survival knife, the map, and Campbell's identification card. One of the men wearing a loin cloth was given the rucksack to carry, and again Campbell was deliberately jerked to his feet and the group resumed running with the man with the rucksack in the lead until they arrived at the next village.

Each time that he was abused, he did his best to mask any signs of pain, or when there was a gesture to humiliate him, he attempted to preserve his dignity, or perhaps, more accurately said, to preserve "face" in front of his Oriental tormentors.

Campbell's captors sat down to lunch, in part, made up of his chicken and some rice shared by the villagers while one of the villagers guarded Campbell with a Kalashnikov. Sitting on the gravel and dusty earth, he was something of a spectacle and attracted a large group of curiosity-seekers who came to observe him. A young girl, perhaps eight or nine years old, smiled at him, and brought him a young puppy dog to hold. Cmpbell cradled the puppy between his crossed legs, and gently petted the puppy with his right hand which brought nervous, approving smiles to the faces of the villagers around him. Then another child brought him a kitten which he also stroked gently until the kitten scampered away, again bringing smiles and laughter to the small crowd.

Abruptly the Pathet Lao leader dispersed the crowd with a remonstration, and a few chicken bones and pieces of rice were thrown on the dirt in front of him to eat. He contemplated whether the chicken bones had nourishment value if he ground them with his teeth, but he chose not to eat them fearing that he might choke and picked out the few kernels of rice to eat with the fingers of his right hand. He was given water to drink which he did without hesitation and asked for more. He was beyond concern for contracting water-borne diseases. As before, he was sadistically jerked to his feet, and the party left for the next village with two new local men and the four Pathet Lao soldiers. Again the pace was somewhere between a jog and a run.

By noon aboard *Ticonderoga* the ship learned of Campbell's capture.

CONFIDENTIAL

1. REGRET ADVISE COCKTAIL CAPTURED ABOUT 1000 25JAN1968. SANDY AND JOLLY GREEN AIRCRAFT IN CLOSE PROXIMITY WHEN CAPTURED. PILOT WAS IDENTIFIED AND AUTHENTICATED.

2. SANDY AIRCRAFT MADE SEVERAL PASSES OVER COCKTAIL. BELIEVE HE HAD FALLEN INTO A TIGER TRAP AND WAS SURROUNDED BY 6 – 8 HOSTILES WHEN SANDYS FIRST REACHED COCKTAIL AND COULD NOT STRAFE DUE TO PROXIMITY OF COCKTAIL AND CAPTORS.

3. PILOT REPORTS THAT HE BELIEVED COCKTAIL DESTROYED BOTH PRCS. BOTH BEEPERS CEASED JUST BEFORE COCKTAIL WAS OBSERVED RAISING HANDS IN SURRENDER.

4. SANDYS REMAINED ON SCENE AND OBSERVED COCKTAIL BEING TIED UP AND MARCHED OFF IN

THE DIRECTION OF ROUTE 9 UNTIL COCKTAIL
AND HOSTILES DISAPPEARED IN JUNGLE

5.   WRECKAGE OF SKYHAWK WITH SIDE NUMBER
     309 FOUND 290 NKP 105.

The Laotians and Campbell continued travelling throughout the end of the afternoon, through the heat and humidity, until they arrived at another village where upon his captors ate, and again he was thrown scraps from the table. Campbell held up to the stresses remarkably well although he feared he would be losing weight as a result of the energy that he was expending and the substandard caloric intake of the few morsels of food that were given to sustain him.

That night he was staked out on the ground with his extremities tied in a spread eagle. He moved and wriggled his body to try and get comfortable on the gravelly ground, but he could do nothing to protect himself from ants and mosquitoes. After a brief prayer to God, the Father, and to Lord Jesus, asking for strength to endure and prevail over his captors, he shortly fell asleep with exhaustion.

He was awakened at dawn with a kick in the ribs, and his face was badly swollen from insect bites and the swelling around his eyes partially reduced his field of vision. He was given a small handful of rice to eat and water before he and the Pathet Lao regulars with two new guides left for the next village. One of the regulars now carried his rucksack and as was now routine, he was triced up with his left arm behind his back, the rope encircling his neck, the right arm bound in front, and a long tether held by one of the soldiers.

Chapter 10.

Cannon received Laetitia Martin's letter on January 24, the day after the siege of Khe Sanh began. The disconnect between his environment and her environment could not have been greater.

January 18, 1968
At My Apartment

Carissimo Mio,

    The City is getting its first real snow of the year, and I have just come in from the weather where I have gotten a thorough facial from the snowflakes melting on my face. How glorious. I'm feeling especially warm with pink ears and cheeks due to brisk circulation of my blood through my veins stimulated by the cold air after the walk from Avery Hall. It's about 25 outside, and Mr. Weatherby is calling for ten inches tonight, but I'm feeling very cozy curled up on one of the loveseats with a glass of rich, red brunello in my hand. With the exception of your absence, darling, life is near perfect.

    It's perfect because I have finally found the painter whom I want to make the subject of my dissertation. Sorolla! I had a conversation last weekend with Daddy, and Money Bags was not so very keen on my being in London and Dublin doing research on Jack Butler Yeats and the Pre-Raphaelites, and, frankly, neither was I. So my choice will now be Joaquin Sorolla, Spaniard (February 27, 1863 – August 10, 1923). He's perfect. High quality, under-appreciated painter, in need of rediscovery.

    It will be nice to work with a normal adult.—monogamously married, children, successful, well-behaved. I must say after a year of living with my poor, bi-polar Caravaggio, I began to feel as though I were suffering from major depression disorder, myself. I'll bet you have never heard of The Hispanic Society at 155th Street and Broadway.

    It's the biggest and best, least known museum in the world. It has the largest collection of Iberian art outside of Spain, and Money Bags will be pleased to learn it's just a fifteen-cent ride on

*the subway and museum entrance is totally free. I'm taking you
there when you return to me in September, lover.*

*Rachel and I are having lunch next week. He's the guy from
your OCS class. Can't remember his name or his ship. Should be
fun. Two war widows who know nothing about the US Navy.
Probably a very good idea if both of us keep the war out of our letters.*

*Think I'll take the train to Greenwich tomorrow just to frolic in
the snow and have dinner with Mom and Dad. I'm trying to stay
normal without you.*

All my love, Robbie
L.

Cannon's life aboard *Ticonderoga* fell into a predictable, daily routine that
generally included two three-hour shifts as strike controller, a four hour
watch in the Combat Information Center and four hour watch on the
bridge. When he wasn't on watch he ate, slept, groomed, or read messages. If he had any free time he skimmed magazines and newspapers that
were received in the wardroom—*Aviation Week, Navy Times, Stars and
Stripes, Time, Newsweek,* and his own subscription to *The Economist.*

On the 29th of January he received a letter from his mother.

January 24, 1968
Castle Point, Hoboken

My dear son,

*It's not been quite a month since you left for San Francisco.
Your father and I appreciated your phone call from Travis Air
Force Base. We suppose that you have probably been very busy
now that you have arrived on Ticonderoga. I do hope that you will
have a moment or two to write us every so often, although I suppose, rightfully, that Laetitia has first claim on my baby boy's time
now. Your birthday passed poignantly in your absence. Like the
time now, you were born in a time of great uncertainty during your
father's war.*

Your father was saying that Walter Cronkite reported a major battle was shaping up somewhere in Quang Tri Province where 7000 Marines were surrounded by three North Vietnamese divisions and that the marines were supported by the Air Force in Thailand and by three aircraft carriers in the Gulf of Tonkin. Dad said he presumed that one of them was Ticonderoga and that your ship must be in the middle of it. He said when it comes to the Pacific Theater the Marines seem to get the tough ones. He's reading everything more closely now that you're part of it. The news reminded him when he was at BuOrd in Washington during the battles for Iwo Jima and Okinawa.

Dad says, "Do your job well, acquit yourself with Cannon pride, and take care of yourself." Of course he loves you, too, as I do, only its just harder for him to say so.

All our love to you, Robbie,
Mother

Cannon responded with a letter to his parents at his earliest opportunity on a mailgram that he wrote from his small desk in this four-officer stateroom which was located portside, amidship, on the third deck.

Dear Mother and Dad,

Much regret for not writing sooner. Apologies. Please do not worry about me. I stand 12-14 hours of watches a day as either Officer of the Deck, Combat Information Center Watch Officer, or as one of the ship's strike controllers. Tico is a great ship, and we have a very experienced air wing that can penetrate, hit the target, and return with minimum of risk, and fleet defense here on Yankee Station is highest priority.

Yes, we are in the middle of the Battle of Khe Sanh and we are putting up at least 300 sorties a day. The air activity over Khe Sanh with the USAF tactical air from Thailand, B-52s from Guam, and three carrier air wings may be the most intense, most focused, air armada in history. All navy aircraft are dropping their ordnance loads in a single salvo—that's one small indication of MACV's commitment to Khe Sanh. Between all US forces we probably have at least one airplane dropping several thousand

*pounds of ordnance every minute at NVA targets around Khe
Sanh. The JCOS have supposedly committed in blood to LBJ that
Khe Sanh will not be another Dien Bien Phu. Nothing is being held
back; if anything, it's overkill.*

*While the senior officers here feel pretty comfortable about the
outcome at Khe Sanh, we are less sanguine about the war. There's
just something I can't figure out about our rules of engagement—
what's off limits. The average officer just feels that LBJ and
McNamara are micro-managing the war and won't trust the flag
officers to run it. This smacks of frustration and blaming. Clearly
MacArthur's politically reckless advance towards the Yalu River is
on everyone's mind. Nobody wants to see the PRC enter the war,
but I keep thinking there is something else.*

*Well gotta go. Tell Dad not to worry—his boy is on the ball.
And tell him I love him.*

*Love to you all,
Your son, Robbie.*

Captain Robert Pebbles had just turned off the lights and slid into bed next
to his wife in their Arlington, VA, home when the phone rang. It was a
little after 10 P.M. on the 31st of January. Lieutenant John Stevens, personal aide to the Chief of Naval Operations, called.

"Sorry to disturb you, Captain. Have you heard the reports out of
MACV, sir?"

"Just preliminary indications, Jack."

"Hundreds of attacks across the South by the Viet Cong in violation of
the Tet holiday truce. The US Embassy Saigon, Ton Son Nhut, Hue—
many others. Serious reports of hundreds of political assassinations, too,
sir. The Chief would like you in the office by 0600, sir, and to meet with
him, in his personal conference room at 0800."

"Let me see. That's *Pueblo*, the attack on Khe Sanh, and countrywide
battles in violation of the Tet truce. One, two, three—hmmm. Thank you,
Mr. Stevens. Assure the Chief, I'll be there."

The admiral's steward served Captain Pebbles black coffee with a sweet
roll. Pebbles took the salt shaker and shook it twice over his coffee.

"Your cardiologist know you're still doing that, Bob?" spoke the CNO
light-heartedly.

"I'll bet he doesn't," said Vice Admiral James. "No cardiologist, not even a doc at Bethesda, would suspect a captain in the United States Navy following such an arcane practice."

"You know, Bob," Captain Mueller, the fourth member of the meeting, "I believe I'll try my coffee your way this morning. The reports from MACV aren't that good. Please pass the salt. Must be something to it." That got a good chuckle all around the table.

The gallows humor tended to help relax the tension, nevertheless, the mood was tense. Everyone had read the messages and battlefield reports.

"Mack…you on the line?"

"Yes, sir."

"CINCPAC holding together?"

"Yes, Chief, our initial response to the multiple Tet attacks has been good and effective. The attackers in the Saigon embassy have been killed or repulsed. Hue is the principal hot spot where the enemy is in force, and it is urban, door-to-door warfare. Spoke with General Walt, this morning for about twenty minutes, and he says he figures Hue might take about three weeks to pacify. He could move faster if necessary but he is trying to pacify Hue with a minimum of friendly casualties. I concurred with him but told him Washington might have other thoughts. Walt's view is that while we have been surprised by the breadth of the coordinated attacks, the breadth contains the seeds of the enemy's weakness as they are, in fact and in effect, contrary to the concept of concentration of forces."

"That's an interesting point. Thank you, Mack. Let's discuss things further after this meeting." The CNO paused before introducing the purpose of the meeting. "Gentleman, this meeting is completely between us. The fact that I'm holding this meeting is itself confidential. I have gathered you because I think you are some of my most thoughtful officers not otherwise engaged, and as you can observe, I have not adhered to the formal organization structure. There are no stripes in this meeting. Everyone stands on equal ground, or I would not have invited you. Understood?" The small group of officers nodded. "Good. Now I'm very disturbed when I hear that MACV wants another quarter million troops on top of the half-million plus that we now have in-country. I've become even more disturbed when I hear that Westy believes that we should consider using tactical nuclear weapons to defend Khe Sanh and sabotage virtually all of our efforts to control these weapons and their use since Nagasaki."

"Moreover, when you consider that *Pueblo*, Khe Sanh, and Tet might be coordinated events involving Russia, Red China, and North Korea with the North Vietnamese, and likely, too, their irregulars in Cambodia and Laos, there's a grave risk of both under-responding to this kind of coordinated threat *and* of over-reacting. At 1400 today, the Joint Chiefs are meeting to provide a point of view to the President and SecDef. So I'm asking you gentleman to share your thoughts and help me pull together a sound and persuasive point of view. Historically the Navy carries more weight in the Pacific Theater, and I'd like to keep that way." The Chief looked around the conference table in his office. Nobody stirred as they took in the import of the CNO's words and although the Chief said there were no stripes in the meeting, that was not completely true, and rank, ambition, and protocol operated to varying degrees in every meeting in the navy. "Okay, Bob Pebbles, what's your reaction."

"Yes, Admiral." Pebbles cleared his throat. "I think the size of the Tet offensive is very significant politically. It suggests that our belief that there is a schism in the leadership of North Vietnam, that they have there own division of hawks and doves, like we do, that there is, or perhaps, *was* a difference of opinion in their leadership, that it has been resolved or at least temporarily resolved. It seems to suggest that our policies, that is, our tempo, the level of intensity, the rules of engagement, our signals to the North Vietnamese moderates probably have, I'm sad to say, gone for naught."

"Bob, may have something, here." Captain Richard Mueller, a naval intelligence officer, spoke now. "I think we have all been a little puzzled by reports of a series of arrests in Hanoi. To the best of our knowledge, it's the moderates and those who have advocated negotiating a peace with us who have been rounded up and placed under house arrest over the last four to six weeks. This suggests that the hawks are in control. General Giap has not been arrested although we have reason to believe he is one of the moderates. Again, to our knowledge, Ho Chi Minh has not given any indication of a position. So, the hawks have likely pushed for the country wide attacks. They are probably impatient, and they may have over-estimated the weaknesses in the South."

The Chief of Naval Operations then asked CINCPAC, a question over the secure phone line to Hawaii. "Mack, if General Walt is correct, that there's a strategic flaw in the North's plan, such that we will prevail, and inflict serious casualties on the VC and NVA, does it follow that the hawks will in due time be discredited?"

"Interesting thought, Chief. Yes, that's a possible outcome, maybe the most likely outcome, but it leaves me uncertain as to our proper course of action. Do we begin to stand down our effort or do we act to the contrary and increase the level of violence?"

"Yes, Mack, I think that is the 64,000 dollar question. Admiral James, you've been silent."

"Yes, I have, Chief. I've been thinking… if we look at this as a decision problem, qua decision problem, operating in an environment of partial information, our criterion is minimum regret. If we fail to achieve peace, which would we regret least? A reduction to a lower plateau of violence, or an escalation to a higher plateau of violence and destruction for some definable period? Keep in mind that we probably do not have to make this choice for several weeks or months. There will be time to learn more, to increase our confidence in our assumptions. Time to make more observations and gather findings which could tip the balance in favor of one strategy versus the other."

"Very good points, Gene. But is the set of decision options limited to just two?"

"Basically, yes Chief. We're not going to cut and run. We're not going to use nukes. We are not going to increase draft calls for another 250 thousand men, train them, equip them, and commit more blood and treasure, and the public is not going to tolerate the current status quo beyond the next federal election."

"Haven't you just argued against escalation?"

"Not quite, sir. We could do a lot more with air power. We've really held it under wraps trying to support the North Vietnam moderates. The harbors remain to be mined. We could take out the Red River system of dykes. We can reduce the thirty mile sanctuary along the Chinese border. There's a railroad that's been left intact that runs from Hanoi to the PRC. We could get serious about untouched strategic targets up North. We can use strategic air resources more intensely. There's a lot more that can be done, sir."

"Yes, I've heard privately that that's the essence of Nixon's secret plan to end the war. Thank you, again, Gene." The conversation continued over several other issues before the matter of the *Pueblo* response came up. "Gentlemen, when each of you joined my staff, at our first meeting, I asked you all if there were an issue or two which you thought warranted attention at my level. With hindsight, Bob Pebbles brought me two that I wish I had spent more time on. The first was the increasing number of incidents at sea with the Soviets and their proxies—the shoulderings, the flyovers, the missile-control lock-ons, et cetera, and the concern that they could rapidly escalate out of control. The State Department has that on their agenda, and I've heard that the preliminary response from the Kremlin is encouraging.

"The second issue was our policy of running AGERs without escort. It was Bob's opinion that the *Liberty* attack last June would not have occurred if we had given her a Tartar-equipped, anti-aircraft ship—a missile equipped destroyer—as an escort. Moreover, Bob told me that one of his bright junior officers opined that the Russians were very likely to have made note of our policy of relying on the international law of the sea for protection and to exploit that at a time and place of their choosing." The CNO spoke as he surveyed the faces around the green felt conference table in his office. "Well, they've gone and done it. Their proxies seized *Pueblo.*" He paused again. "So the questions are what should be done about it? What can be done about it? And whether anything should be done about it?" He checked for understanding around the table. "Dick," he turned towards the intelligence officer, "lets level the room. Please give everyone an assessment of what we lost."

"Yes, Chief," Dick Mueller began in a monotonic, somber style. "Well…in addition to the ship and crew, we lost various codes and means of encoding and decoding—cryptographic machines. The codes themselves have all been switched to new codes which differ in degree and kind. So that is primarily an operational nuisance as we have contingency plans for potential incidents like this. Second, however, the various pieces of communications intelligence equipment aboard *Pueblo*, when analyzed, will serve to give them a near sense of certainty about our capability for intercepting and breaking their messages and for characterizing their air defenses and how we might exploit certain weaknesses that we believe they have in those air defenses. The CIA has confirmed that Russian technicians were flown to Wonsan within 24 hours of *Pueblo's* arrival in Wonsan. Accordingly, we can expect them to remedy these flaws. Most critically, in my opinion, is the loss of the encryption-decryption equipment. I say this because we know in some cases, and suspect with reasonable confidence, that certain undecoded messages have been intercepted or stolen by Soviet espionage operations that can now be broken with the equipment that was aboard *Pueblo*. The *Pueblo* crew, much to my consternation, did not destroy the system."

"Then, there is the not insignificant matter of 30 highly trained, globally knowledgeable, NSA personnel. Taken collectively this group fully understands our global communications intelligence collection effort, and our sources and methods. We must assume the worst case and assume that the KORCOM, CHICOMs and Soviets will gain this information." Mueller paused here. He had spoken euphemistically. In reality he was thinking of these men being subjected to torture. "In all candor, our losses must be evaluated as severe. And finally, there is the matter of all 82 *Pueblo* personnel now being held in North Korea as hostages."

"Excellent summary, Dick. A lot to consider there." Next the CNO directed his attention again to Vice Admiral James. "Gene," James had extensive experience as an attack pilot in three wars, "would you summarize where we are on a plan for a retaliatory air strike, please?"

"Yes, sir," he paused briefly before beginning. "Gentlemen, as you know, the safes here in the Pentagon are full of plans from tit-for-tat retaliation to full-scale war plans. The plan today being put forth is believed to be appropriately measured. It consists of simultaneously striking seven airfields where approximately 200, MIG 17, MIG 19, and MIG 21 fighters are based. Against these targets we have two carrier air wings from *Enterprise* and *Ranger. Yorktown,* I'll remind you, has been converted to an anti-submarine carrier, and the 4th Air Force Tactical Air Wing consisting of three augmented squadrons at Kunsan Air Base, South Korea. Moreover, they have excellent tanking capacity for air force and navy needs. Now, the estimate is that at least 100 MIGs will be airborne by the time the first strike aircraft reach their targets. This is highly problematic because even if the air force readiness factor is 100%, the navy, practically speaking, can only put up a combined deck load of 65 to 75 aircraft of all types, several of which must be retained for fleet air defense, Chief. Practically speaking, Chief, the combined strike force wouldn't have more than 60 to 65 bombers and 24 to 30 fighters for TarCap. And that's assuming 8 fighters are sufficient for fleet defense. That puts the MIGs 4 to 1 or 5 to 1 against our fighters, Chief."

"That sounds pretty unhealthy, Gene."

"Absolutely, Chief. You're basically going to send two carriers back to CONUS for two more air wings, assuming we got'em."

"I suppose we can't reduce the number of airfields to be struck for fear that those which are not struck would come after us like a mess of angry hornets."

"Yes, sir. That's the thinking."

"Well, I'm going to have to hear what Bill Momyer, Seventh Air Force, has to say." He turned towards Captain Pebbles. "Bob, I'm very uncomfortable about this plan. Naval Air is already running short of pilots due to our Rolling Thunder losses over the last three and a half years. I want the final proposed plan to be fully vetted and evaluated by the operations research group. Make damn sure they note our helo, SAR and ResCap resources. Make damn sure that they consider the survival time in icy cold water. I want to know our expected losses in aircraft and pilots, and our expected results. I want to see an acceptable risk-reward ratio on any *go plan*. Most of all, I want a sound argument that convinces me that an air strike will get 82 men back. It looks to me like our best suit is diplomatic action not military action. Anyway, the SecDef likes numbers. Let's see what the numbers say." Pebbles nodded. "And Mack, CINCPAC, you still there, Mack?"

"Yes, sir."

"Mack, you would like to task *Ticonderoga* to relieve *Ranger.* You said you wanted *Ranger* back on Yankee Station and wanted to bring *Ticonderoga* north, didn't you, Mack? You want those all-weather A-6 bombers back in the Gulf, right? As a result of Tet, right?"

"Yes, sir. We're stretched. *Tico* and Air Wing 19 are not an equal exchange. We're basically exchanging A-4s for A-6s. The payload of an A-4 is about a quarter to a third of an A-6 and it's only performs well in daylight."

"Yes, that's clear. I covered off the SecDef and explained that *Enterprise's* A-6s are sufficient to execute the Wonsan harbor mining option if ordered. So let's go ahead and send Panther up for Grayeagle." Like admirals James and CINCPAC, the CNO was also a former naval aviator. "It's zero-sum. What Operation Rolling Thunder picks up, our *Pueblo* retaliation strike gives up. All of this makes me believe that Khe Sanh, *Pueblo*, and Tet were coordinated and damn well-orchestrated. Very shrewd plan, wouldn't you say, Mack?"

"Damn straight, sir. Looks like Soviet fingers are all over it."

"And as far as you know, Mack, Bill Momyer says the White House wants a "go plan," is that right, Mack?"

"That's what he told me last night."

"I've heard the same from Earle Wheeler, too, but I'll take that to mean they want the military to have at least one, executable option other than nuclear weapons."

Campbell was developing a dehydration headache when his legs cramped, and he stumbled and fell giving out an anguished yell of pain as he could not use his arms to break his fall, and he landed on his bad shoulder. One of the Laotians in a loin cloth kicked him viciously and screamed at him, signaling to him to get up. But the Pathet Lao leader waved him off and massaged Campbell's legs until the cramping was gone, and then he was jerked to his feet again and swatted across his shoulders with the flat side of a machete and commanded to run. Shortly they came to a small stream running through the jungle where he was given several cupsful of water to drink. They all drank the water and rested briefly before resuming their pace until they came to the next village. Again the table scraps and rice were thrown on the ground for him to eat before he was staked out on his back for the night. Again he was a feast for mosquitoes and ants throughout the night.

Campbell and his Pathet Lao captors, with new guides each day to lead them from village to village, would continue like this for several days. They had crossed Route 9 and to the best of his ability, lacking the small compass that was on the wristwatch taken from him, he believed they were traveling in a northwestern direction along jungle trails near streams in the valleys between karsts and mountains.

Chapter 11.

The quartermaster of the watch handed Ltjg. Cannon, Officer of the Deck, a green confidential message from CINCPACFLT. "Looks like we're headed to the Sea of Japan, sir... Korea... relieving *Ranger*."

"Surprise, surprise. They want those Intruders back on Yankee Station." His mind pondered the implications. "Plotted our course?"

"Yes, sir"

"What's the transit distance?"

"About 1900 nautical miles, sir."

"Hmmm. Three days at 25 knots," Cannon calculated.

"Yes, sir."

Cannon skipped over the message header and focused on the body copy.

1. UPON COMPLETION FLT OPS PROCEED IMMEDI-
   ATELY TO 17-30 N, 111-20 E TO UNREP FUEL AND
   STORES USS SHENANDOAH AFS-1 AND ORD-
   NANCE USS MAUNA KEA AE-22. PREPARE TO UN-
   REP AT 0630

2. THENCE PROCEED AT BEST SPEED TO 39-00 N, 129-
   00 E AND RELIEVE USS RANGER CVA-61. CHOP TO
   CTF 70.1 EMBKD USS ENTERPRISE CVAN-65

3. PREPARE FOR COLD WEATHER FLT OPS AND AD-
   VISE COMSERVPAC, COMNAVAIRPAC, EARLIEST
   OF POL NEEDS, DEICING MATERIALS, COLD
   WEATHER PERSONNEL GEAR, ETC.

Cannon made four mental notes from the message. First, it was obviously winter in Korea and that influenced all options. Second, the strategic objective of their mission was undeclared. The reasons given to strike all air fields in North Korea was driven by the judgment that one or two airfields could not be struck without being vulnerable to reactionary attacks from the five or six remaining airfields. Third, *Enterprise, Ranger*, and *Yorktown* were operating north of the 38th Parallel, the dividing line between North and South Korea, and the rendezvous point was at the 39th parallel which could be perceived by the North Koreans as provocative. Finally, given what the intelligence reports were saying that the Russians had already flown in technical experts, the only viable objective remaining was the repatriation of the crew and *Pueblo*. He could not imagine how air strikes would support either objective, yet the strike planning proceeded without abatement, nor any signs other than that they were seriously intended.

Again, he remained angered over the Navy's policy of operating the AGERs without a destroyer escort. He had been in the Norwegian Sea in *Essex* when *Liberty* was attacked in the Eastern Mediterranean Sea and had seen the ship when she was under repair in Malta last summer. Even an old *Fletcher* class would do, and the cost of an escort was nothing compared to the cost in life, property, and classified assets that would result from the *Liberty* and *Pueblo* incidents. The argument that the AGERs were officially classified as "environmental research" ships by the US Navy was not persuasive with him, and he continued to disparagingly refer to the notion as some sea lawyer's laughable idea of protection.

Campbell noted the terrain was changing. For the last two days they had been climbing and now appeared to be emerging from the jungle to a very expansive plateau where the heat rose to more than 110 degrees without protection of the jungle canopy. He noted he was now in an agricultural area with distant mountains to the north and west. Around noon their party was met my two vehicles with better dressed and equipped Pathet Lao soldiers, and Campbell was turned over to their custody. An officer received Campbell's documents and demanded that all of his personal effects be turned over to him which included his knife and watch. He treated Campbell with respect for his rank, and, in general, appeared to be more civil and refined.

Campbell was blindfolded and placed in the rear of a military panel truck with two soldiers as guards, and the two vehicles proceeded towards a regional city and turned briefly onto an improved road and crossed a bridge shortly before stopping. Campbell was then taken to a stucco building where his blindfold was removed. There Campbell received his first solid meal in over two weeks and a pair of clean black pajamas to wear. He was placed in a dimly lit, spartan cell in the basement of the building with a straw mattress. To the best of his knowledge there were no other prisoners around him. Despite the dank, humid air and the stifling, heat, he lay down upon the mattress and promptly fell asleep.

On the following morning he was given fresh eggs to eat and a piece of fruit, and then he was taken to a meeting room on the second floor and left alone, although a guard was posted at the door. Campbell tried to keep his defenses up, but after the stress of the past several days, he couldn't help but relax. The room had a small table, two chairs and two small windows on a side wall. Here and there plaster had broken away from what appeared to be concrete construction and the interior of the building had been recently white washed.

In walked a thin, somewhat taller than average, middle-age Laotian man with wire rim glasses. He wore a French blue shirt and trousers and wore European-style, brown, leather shoes. He offered his right hand to Campbell and Campbell despite his bindings shook hands. "Je parle francais. Parlez vous francais?"

"Un peu. Parlez vous anglais?

"Non. Pas de tout. Continuez a vous en francais, s' il vous plait."

"Oui, si vous parlez lentement, tres lentement, peutetre je comprenerai a vous, mais avec beaucoup de difficile." Campbell was taught French by his mother, and he had taken conversational French at Davidson, but it seemed so very long ago, and he was hardly fluent and spoke the language with a limited vocabulary and many grammatical and syntactical flaws. His interviewer was cordial and the conversation went something like the following.

"So, Lieutenant Campbell, I trust you have been well-fed and slept well."

"Yes. Thank you."

"And you have clean clothing more suitable to our climate."

"Yes. Again thank you. May I have my old clothing returned?"

"Yes, of course, I am having them washed for you."

"Thank you."

"You are an American pilot, no?" Campbell paused before responding while he considered the implications. This could be the first slippery step towards compliance with his captor.

"Yes."

"You are from aircraft carrier 14, no?" Again Campbell paused while he considered the situation.

"Yes."

"And you were shot down while attacking us on the Ho Chi Minh Trail at night, no?"

"You seem to know a lot about me. Yes."

"You were a member of number 23 attack squadron, no?" Campbell was surprised by the interviewer's knowledge about him, and how easily the interviewer had gotten him to converse agreeably with him, but he saw no harm in acknowledging what was obviously painted on his airplane.

"Yes."

"Thank you. You are wise to cooperate. And because you have been helpful you may write a letter to your parents, and if you agree not to return to a combat flying status, we will send you back home to America in ten days." The approach that Campbell was experiencing was not like anything that his SERE training had led him to expect. He recognized its seductiveness and kept his defenses up. "Doesn't that sound good to you, Lieutenant?"

"Oui, monsieur."

"Tres bien," The interviewer stood up and shook Campbell's hand saying "Maintenant, vous ettes un ami." Campbell was given paper and pen and the interviewer left the room leaving him to write his letter.

He began his letter...*Dear Mother and Father, I was shot down near Khe Sanh and parachuted into Laos where I was subsequently captured by the Pathet Lao*.... However he was writing the letter in the Korean *Hangeul* characters and instead of writing in columns from the right side of the page to the left, he wrote the characters horizontally as some Korean writers had begun to do after World War II. This he did because he assumed that the Laotian characters like the Korean characters had common Chinese roots, but he presumed that the Laotians would find many characters unrecognizable and harder to translate if he departed from the traditional columns and spaced his characters carefully. He went on to discuss his experience of the last two weeks, and ended by asking his mother and father *in the name of Jesus Christ, our Lord for their prayers for my safe return*. Except for the admission of his Christian faith, he tried to avoid giving his captors any information that might be used to manipulate him or extort information from him for propaganda purposes. He addressed the unsealed letter in English and gave it to the guard for posting.

At the invitation of the interviewer, which he began to suspect was a ranking communist official, perhaps a provincial chief, the two dined together. Two guards remained outside the dining room while they conversed in French. The conversation never touched on military or political matters. The interviewer subtly fished for personal information.

"Lieutenant Campbell, you wrote your letter in characters. I'm unfamiliar with them. We have our own characters which were originated in the fourteenth century. Yours seemed to look Chinese in some cases and not in others." As Campbell suspected, the letter was another way for his captors to obtain personal information.

"My mother is Korean. She is a Korean War bride. I was born in Korea and grew up there." This was only partially true as his mother had indeed met his father in Korea, but like his father, she was an American Presbyterian missionary.

"So, Yankee imperialism runs in the family, no?"

"No. My father was a missionary bringing the word of God and of His son, Jesus Christ, to the Koreans when the North Korean *imperialists* crossed the 38th Parallel and invaded the south."

"Come, let us not be adversarial. Are you married?"

"No"

"Engaged?"

"No."

"Perhaps you would like to write a second letter to a sweetheart?"

"No. I do not have a sweetheart."

"Too bad. Where is your home?"

"Keokuk, Iowa," a lie.

"Sounds very small. What type of car do you drive?"

"A Henry J."

"Henry J? Is that a Ford?"

"No, it's a Kaiser"

"Kaiser? Caesar? I must be missing something in transalation."

"I'm sorry that my French is so poor."

"Do you believe in God?"

"Yes, of course, I have said my father was a missionary."

"Are you then, a member of a church?"

"Yes."

"When did you learn to fly?"

"I began at age six."

"Six. That's quite young isn't it?"

"Yes, I began at the age of six flying kites."

"Kites? Is that a rudimentary flying machine?" Campbell continually answered these questions elliptically and cordially without any indication of falsehood. The food was particularly good and consisted of two hard-boiled eggs and a rice ball that was covered with honey. Fruit and tea were served, and the interviewer repeatedly offered him French Gauloise cigarettes from a blue package which Campbell declined, "*Je ne fume pas. Pas merci.* " Meanwhile the interviewer lit up continually in his presence when he wasn't eating. After the fruit was served, Campbell was offered French cognac. He negotiated a small amount and sipped about half of the snifter. The interviewer reiterated that it was possible for Campbell to return to America if he continued to be a cooperative prisoner and would not return to combat flying.

"Please consider the People's gracious offer to free you despite the crimes that you have committed as an American pilot." Campbell ignored the comment but took it as a signal that his interviewer was driving towards some sort of confession as a war criminal. So far, the methods had been kindness and isolation and the interviewer had not yet shown a coercive or interrogating style.

"Thank you for dinner. Thank you for the conversation. I will consider the People's offer. Good evening."

"We will meet again, tomorrow, no?'

Campbell was then returned to his cell where an old woman was waiting for him with hot water to bathe him. She also cleaned his wounds and treated them with herbs and gave him a massage before she left. He knelt before his mattress and said The Lord's Prayer before he prayed directly to Jesus. "Lord Jesus, my Savior, thank you for the blessings of the day. Thank you for the peace to rest and sleep, for the nourishment that might sustain me. Strengthen me, Lord Jesus, to withstand the entreaties of my captors and to keep faith with my fellow squadron mates and to keep faith with my fellow Americans. I ask You, Lord Jesus, to free me from the torment of my captors and to return me as a free man, alive, to my country. In your name Jesus, Lord and Savior, I ask it. Amen."

Campbell lay on his back trying to figure out what kind of game he was up against. All of the information that the US Navy had learned indicated that POWs were beaten, tortured and humiliated and made undeniably aware of their dependency upon their captors for survival. "Thin Man" either hadn't gotten the word, or he was operating from another book—a Laotian book that was different from the North Vietnamese book.

Beebe Byrnes picked up the phone and dialed Dr. Sharon Schwartz over at FBI.

"Good morning, Sharon, it's Beebe."

"Gosh! What a morning, Beebe. Jonah came down with a 104 fever this morning. Some damn virus! One of the 200 viruses the little people contract. Just when Herb has to go up to the Hill, and pitch that new treaty wrinkle in the talks with the Russians to the Foreign Relations Committee, and I'm being deposed at one this afternoon."

"Well, this isn't a request. I'm calling to respond to your request. An official memo is in the mail. Our boy, Franco Ciorrazzi…"

"Oh, yes?"

"He's worth watching. He's a registered member of the Communist Party in Italy. That's not very unusual in Italy. Some 60% of the vote in 1960 went communist. But it seems Ciorrazzi left the University of Salerno where he was an art student after two years, and showed up in Yaroslavl to study politics and English. That would kind of make him a more ardent Italian communist. After two years, he returned briefly to Salerno, before heading for Columbia. We suspect that when he was in Yaroslavl he received training with the KGB, but we don't think he was accepted as one of theirs, too volatile. He's what I would call a lightweight recruit. He's not the type for industrial or military espionage. He's here to make trouble in the streets."

"Unh, huh."

"He's also got a nasty streak in him. Thinks he's a Lothario, but when things don't work out, he beats the hell out of them."

"Uh, oh! Should we tip off the Martin girl?"

"Hell, no. She's supposed to be a big girl. Her debutante days are over. Let her manage it." Sharon detected a bit more energy in Beebe's answer than seemed appropriate.

"Okay, but any woman getting a Ph.D. at a first class university should matter to us, Beebe." Schwartz had a Ph.D. from MIT and the CIA officer had gone to Georgetown and took a master's degree in Russian from the University of Pennsylvania.

"Whatever…." There was a pause. "Okay, gotta go, Sharon. Hope Jonah gets better soon."

Cannon opened his latest letter from Tish.

Carissimo mio,

I have a new neighbor. A husband and wife, Jackson and Keesha Clifton, have moved in next door with a two year old son. He's an army major who just came back from Vietnam and is now pursuing a master's at the School of International Affairs. I mentioned that you had taken several graduate level courses there be-

fore going off to OCS. He's big. I mean big. He's an African American who said he was the second "lonesome end" at West Point. I'm having them for dinner next week. You guessed it. It will be Italian night!

I spent last Saturday at the Hispanic Society of America at 155th and Broadway. The Seventh Avenue IRT is very convenient with stops at both 116th and 155th and Bway. Joaquin Sorolla is my man. He's my dissertation. More on this to come.

Had lunch with Rachel the day before we got the terrible news of the Pueblo. Her fiancé is the First Lieutenant. You probably know what that means, and now he's a POW. I called her after we got the news, but I just didn't know what to say to her. What can anybody say, but, "I'm so sorry for you." I understand that two aircraft carriers are being sent to Korea, but I didn't hear Ticonderoga's name.

Well darling, I'm off. It's cold here, Brrrr! I'm jealous for some of that tropical weather that I see on TV about Vietnam.

All my love,
Laetitia

Ticonderoga and her three destroyer escorts were halfway to Korea and preparing for cold weather operations. The maintenance crews were busy changing the fluids and lubricants in the aircraft and in the catapults and arresting gear. Similarly the crews on the carrier's four, 5 inch 38 caliber guns were changing their lubricants for sub-freezing weather. After four previous cruises to the Gulf of Tonkin and limited stowage space on the World War II, 27 Charlie class attack carrier, virtually no one aboard *Ticonderoga* was carrying a full sea bag, and out of necessity, cold weather clothing had been flown aboard and was being distributed to lookouts and flight deck personnel.

Down in Strike Operations plans were being developed and redeveloped to find an acceptable strike plan. Operation Formation Star looked increasingly like a suicide mission, and the mood was grim. If orders were received to launch, the squadrons would fly, but anyone who wasn't afraid of dying in Korea or in the South China Sea wasn't mentally fit to fly an airplane. Pilots were writing letters home, many thinking these might be their last. Other letters would be held in trust by a close squadronmate in the event of their deaths or capture. Letters they fervently hoped no one would ever have to post in their behalf.

The old woman appeared again the following morning at Campbell's cell with two wooden buckets of hot water, and Campbell washed and groomed himself before he was given fruit and tea for breakfast on a tray in his cell. After breakfast he was left alone until late morning when he met again with Thin Man. He began to sense his isolation and aloneness. He didn't know where he was? He didn't know who Thin Man was? He didn't know what was happening next, the status of the war, how likely he would stay where he was, and he had absolutely no sense of whether he would ever return to his parents, to freedom and to the United States. Whenever there were Steel Tiger missions over Laos, his fellow squadron mates often made cautionary statements followed by "Be careful. No one ever comes back from Laos." His mind was starting to undermine his self-confidence.

"Bon jour, Lieutenant? Comment allez vous?"

"Bien, et vous?" Again they shook hands. Thin Man asked a guard to remove the bindings. Campbell brought his left arm forward for the first time since he was captured and found the pain was less severe in his shoulder. Thin Man lit up a Gauloise, took a puff, and began the conversation.

"You Americans have so many problems. Why do you presume to tell the Vietnamese how to act? Isn't that arrogant?" Campbell paused and then shrugged his shoulders.

"Look how you Americans treat black people. Is that the kind of democracy that you want for Indo-China?" Cannon did not answer. After a long pause Thin Man spoke.

"I'll take that as 'Non.' You sense the hypocrisy and cannot answer, no?" Campbell simply shrugged and stared at the table.

"You have wealthy capitalists like the Rockefellers with two, three, four cars. Wealthy capitalists like the DuPonts with two, three, and four houses, while others have no food, have no home. They have no money. No money to pay for a doctor when they are sick. No money for medicines. This is the system that you want for us, no?" Again Campbell just stared at the table and shrugged.

"You are silent, mon ami, Campbell. The truth of my statements embarrasses you, no?" Again Campbell simply stared.

"Are these the reasons that you came to bomb us, no? Are these good reasons to kill us? To kill our women and children, mon ami?" Thin Man paused for several minutes before continuing. Campbell was tempted to respond with an explanation of the rules of engagement, but he realized that their disclosure would be useful information. Already the North Vietnamese had placed SAM launchers amidst the population centers around Hanoi and Haiphong knowing the Americans would not bomb them for fear of creating civilian casualties. So, he continued to stare at the table. Thin Man changed his tone.

"Tell me, what would your Lord Jesus say if you couldn't look me in the eye, mon ami, eh? What would your Lord Jesus, say, eh? He would say that you have sinned, would He not?" Thin Man's words were spoken softly and soothingly, but Campbell was both angered and embarrassed by Thin Man's words. "He would call you to repent, would He not, mon ami? He would say to you to, confess your sins, no, mon ami?" Campbell remained silent.

"We are not Jesus, mon ami. We are comrades and do not call your misdeeds, sins. We are a country ruled by law. We call these sins, crimes, mon ami. Crimes against humanity. Shouldn't you confess your crimes, Campbell?" Again Campbell just continued to stare in silence while he admired Thin Man's devilish ability to twist logic. Thin Man was a clever adversary to be taken seriously. He was seductive and clearly not a man from the Laotian peasantry.

"I see that it might be better for us to stop and give you time to think… to "examine your conscience"… like a good Christian." Thin Man got up and walked out of the room. The guard returned and this time slapped handcuffs on Campbell's wrists and led him down the two flights of stairs to his cell.

Campbell remained in the dimly lit cell. Aloneness closed in around him. He grew hungry but no food was brought to him. He perspired in the sweltering heat, but no water was brought to him. He lost all sense of time and fell asleep. He awoke again in the pitch, dark night hungry and thirsty. He relieved himself over a latrine, that he had jokingly heard referred to as "a French bomb sight," but the roll of toilet paper had been apparently removed and the stench was overwhelming. He was awakened and a few crumbs of rice were thrown on the floor for breakfast. Campbell ate them slowly and finished his breakfast with a cockroach that crossed the cell floor. He smacked it with his shackled hands and ate it. He laughed at the irony that he had the power over the life and death of cockroaches in his cell. Then he returned to the mattress.

In time he was awakened and taken to the meeting room where he was left alone. After what seemed like a long time to Campbell, Thin Man appeared, but he did not shake hands as he had before. The conversation resumed in French.

"Have you been thinking, Campbell?"

"No." Thin Man slowly removed a cigarette from the package of Gauloise, lit the cigarette with a lighter, and exhaled as he asked the next question.

"You haven't given any consideration to the People's generous offer?"

"No." Again Thin Man took a long puff, and exhaled slowly, dramatically.

"Not at all?"

"No."

"I'm very sorry to hear that." Thin Man stood up, snuffed his cigarette out in an ashtray, walked to the doorway and spoke quietly to the guard who promptly entered the room and stood over Campbell who remained sitting in the chair. After several minutes he led Campbell back to his cell. When Campbell arrived he saw right away that the mattress had been removed. So he sat on the floor against the wall in the corner with his knees pulled up to his chest. *Isolation and deprivation… that is my adversary's game*, thought Campbell, *and now he is reinforcing who is top dog, bottom dog. It's about his power, about control and dependency, compliance and non-compliance. The ultimate threat is to leave me here, starve me, have me die alone.*

Campbell was left alone for a full day and given only a thin watery soup and a handful of rice to eat. He had not been given any means to bathe himself. His beard was itchy and began to smell foul and his body smelled ripe. He began to detest his condition which was a kind of repudiation of the self and self-loathing.

On the following day he was rousted off the cell floor where he had been sleeping and kicked and pushed and shoved into a small courtyard. There he was stripped of his black pajamas and ordered to stand naked at attention. At first he stood proudly at attention, mustering what he could to maintain his dignity and face. But in time he weakened, and he began to realize that he was working against himself. It was the schizophrenic's classic double-bind. When he weakened and collapsed on the courtyard ground, he was kicked and beaten for his disobedience until he struggled to his feet. The guard then kicked his legs out from under him, and then beat him severely for not obeying and standing at attention before taking him back to his cell.

Later that day he was taken to the room where before he had first met Thin Man. Two uniformed guards were by the doorway waiting for him. Again he sat for a long time waiting and wondering about whatever was coming next. In time, Thin Man entered the room carrying a briefcase and a lighted cigarette.

"Mon ami, Lieutenant Campbell, do you think you are going to die here?"

"Maybe."

"Good, you have found your tongue today. No, you are not going to die here, I promise you. But, mon ami," he drew on his cigarette and exhaled, saying, "you are going to find that dying is easy. Dying is very easy. Staying alive is very hard." If Campbell had not figured it out or was in denial about the apparent threat and hoped for a better fate, Thin Man had just unmistakenly delivered the threat. "The People's patience is not infinite. We all have schedules and timetables to meet. The People have offered to return you home in exchange for certain agreements. Perhaps you would not want to return home. We can arrange for you to fly airplanes in China. Perhaps you need more time to think about that, no?"

"No."

"So you want to be cooperative. That is good, because I have other things, more important things, to do than to meet with you, mon ami." He drew on his cigarette again. "You should not be ashamed for your true feelings. Thousands of your countrymen are in your streets demonstrating against these imperialist policies and war crimes. The good people are in the streets of Washington and on all the university campuses asking your president to stop the war. Even your religious leaders and churches, Presbyterians, too, are marching against this criminal war. There is no shame in agreeing with them, mon ami. I think it is clear to you that we are peace-loving people, and yet, you American imperialists bomb us. You can visit Vientiane and see for your self. You can go to Hanoi and see for yourself. You can go to China and see for yourself, and as I said, fly for them." Campbell interrupted.

"No thanks."

"Now, I have a paper." Thin Man reached for a paper in his brief case. "Sign it and you will be released. You have my promise." Campbell read the document written in English while Thin Man smoked. It was a concocted confession of war crimes and an admission to American aggression and imperialism towards the peace-loving people of Vietnam and Laos.

"I respectfully decline."

"That is very unwise." Thin Man took a very long puff on his cigarette, held the smoke for effect, then he said very, very softly and exhaling, "I am giving you another chance to sign. You will be released in ten days. Here is a pen. Take it."

Campbell shook his head, "No, thank you." Thin Man, slowly picked up the piece of paper and carefully placed it in his briefcase. Then he stood up as if he were leaving for another meeting. He stopped at the doorway and spoke briefly to one of the guards, and then he was gone.

Immediately both guards rushed into the room. Campbell felt them grab him by the arms and shoulders and drag him down the stairs and across a parking area to a small grove of trees. They flung him to the ground and began kicking him. He kicked back from his position on the ground, but this served only to infuriate his tormentors, so he went limp and tried to protect himself from blows to his head and face. Several kicks struck him in the ribs and kidneys. They continued pummeling him until he passed out.

When Campbell regained consciousness, he sensed his pajamas top was wet from water that they had apparently thrown on him to revive his consciousness. He also felt them tying his feet and shortly they jerked him feet first into the air, having thrown the other end over the limb of the tree. Campbell could look down and see that his head was only 24 inches or so from the gravelly soil below. His cuffed hands almost touched the ground. There was only a pause in the brutality.

Now Campbell felt the blows from a thick bamboo stick. With no way to protect himself, the blows landed heavily about his arms, shoulders, ribs, his thighs and lower legs, and he screamed in pain with each new blow. Blood began flowing from his mouth and nostrils making it difficult to breathe. His thoughts turned to dying, that he would be beaten to death, or that he might suffocate or drown in his own blood. He could see his blood draining and pooling on the gravelly surface below him, his precious bodily fluids draining vitality from him. Then he felt an excruciating blow across his feet before passing out for the second time.

They summarily cut him down and gravity brought his body down in a twisting motion jamming his neck. He lay there unconscious, lying in his blood which had pooled on the ground beneath him, until another bucket of water was thrown on him. When Campbell regained consciousness for the third time, he tasted blood in his teeth, which served to heighten his senses, and he feared again that he was bleeding internally, and that he was severely injured and losing essential fluids. He lay on the ground totally limp, badly beaten, and in severe pain. Everywhere his body was covered with bruising and swelling from the beating, and he relapsed into unconsciousness.

When again he regained consciousness, he found himself in a dimly lit cell. It was very much smaller than his last cell, perhaps only three feet by six feet. It had neither a mattress nor a latrine. And it overwhelmingly smelled of excrement in the sweltering, humid, tropical environment of Laos. He was bleeding in several places. His body was wracked with pain, and he had cuts and abrasions over his body in addition to the swelling and bruises, and on the concrete floor of the cell, he could not find a position where he wasn't in extreme pain.

He lay there, figuratively licking his wounds, not really sure whether he was dying from internal injuries. He gave thought to praying to Jesus, but his anger thwarted him from doing so. Instead he challenged God. *"Have you forsaken me, as your only son thought He had been forsaken? What have I done to have deserved this? Haven't I led a humanly righteous life? Haven't I honored You as You have asked? Didn't I share food and give clothing to others, to refugees in Korea when I was myself famished and chilled to the bone from the winter winds?"* Campbell paused to gather new thoughts. His faith was now in doubt. *"Job asked You if You were the one and only authentic God. And You answered him by asking him if Your power wasn't self-evident. You answered a question with a question. Is it a conceit to ask You, God, if You are evasive, and if Your power might fail? Is it a conceit to say that if you are not moral and just that You are not my God. I'm feeling very like Job. Like Job I am left to wonder where is the moral and just side of my God... the God of Amos? Is that self-evident? Where is the loving God of Hosea? Is that self-evident? How, in the name of a moral, and righteous and loving Almighty God, are You asking me to suffer like this?"*

His mind briefly shifted back to his life as a young boy being taught the Bible by his mother. He was nostalgic and momentarily wept at the thought of never seeing his mother or father again.

Was his mother wrong? The remaining questions did not suggest that he had as yet repudiated his faith, nor that he was fully prepared to do so, but he remained questioning it. *"Do I not, Your humble servant, deserve an answer? How did Job's suffering serve You? How does my suffering serve You? You, who has given me life, are You now taking my life away? Have I been left here to die, ... to die alone, ... forsaken, ... and to suffer, to suffer alone, in vain? "*

Chapter 12.

They kept Campbell in the small cell for days. Once a day he was given a shovel and a bucket to remove the excrement from his cell and to exercise briefly although the slightest movement brought on excruciating pain. He lost track of time. For days he was fed only a watery soup and a few grains of rice. For days he lay in the corner of the cell keeping himself as far from his own excrement and urine as he possibly could, enduring the stench, until he wasn't able to care anymore. For days his body ached from the beating and the black and blue marks all over his body, and he had lost interest in healing. For days he subsisted in the semi-light, semi-darkness of his cell so that it was apparent that his vision, despite his swollen eyelids and cheeks, was dimming, and what he could see seemed uncertain and ambiguous. Mentally he felt abandoned and sensed the beginning of withdrawal into depression and passivity and despair.

His faith in God was in doubt and the notion that God had a plan for him, or that his suffering served some higher purpose, seemed cynical to him. The thought that he might return to life as it was, was remote and pessimistic, if not the apparent truth. The notion that he might ever get out of Laos was dubious and would be entirely a matter that he seemed to have abandoned to fate. All of this suggested to him that his sense of himself and the notion that he might simply survive and live seemed evermore hopeless. "Dying is very easy," said Thin Man. "Staying alive is very hard."

In the quiet of his cell, in the sweltering, dank humid air and putrid stench emerged a deep sob. At first he tried to suppress it, but it would not be suppressed and the sobbing continued and deepened and brought on thoughts of his mother caring for him as a young boy, feeding him in the warmth of the kitchen, and huddling with him in the snows of Korea which brought on a greater sense of grief and forsakenness until exhaustion took him off to sleep.

Such was Campbell's deteriorating emotional, spiritual and physical condition. After days of isolation he was close to breaking down. After several days, a guard awakened him with a kick, and he was taken to another, better lighted room in the basement with a single shower. The old woman appeared again and motioned him to give her the soiled, stinking pajamas and gave him a bar of yellow soap. Totally naked and in complete pain, he began to wash with a cold-water, hand shower. It took him several minutes before he could bend over and wash his legs. Everything, every joint, every muscle, and deep into every bone, he ached. It was the first time that he could see and examine the entirety of his body which was open in tens of places to germs, and disease. Here and there were pockets of white pus indicating skin infections which the old woman drained and treated with Laotian herbs.

If the communists wanted to maintain the fiction of neither killing nor murdering prisoners, all they had to do was to weaken the defenses of the mind and the body and expose them to isolation and germ-ridden, filthy conditions.

The old woman left and returned with his green utilities and clean socks and for the first time since he arrived at this destination, his flight boots were returned to him. She also brought him a banana. Later he was granted permission to use the "bombsight" latrine which now struck him as a comparative luxury.

Campbell was then taken once more to the interviewing room, and as before, he was left alone in the room for an indeterminate period of time with a guard at the door. He could detect the distinctive residual scent of Gauloise cigarettes as, ever so slowly, his eyes became accustomed to the light, and he regained vision. His eyes hurt from bruising, but they hurt less and his field of vision was acceptable despite the swelling in his face. After what seemed well over an hour, Thin Man arrived. Their conversation resumed in French.

"I have been negotiating with your jailors for better conditions for you, mon ami. They say you kicked them, and that they had to forcibly restrain you. You look terrible. In all ways it is in your interest to be cooperative, Lieutenant. All of this is so unnecessary. You have the power to save yourself. Your jailors are not under my control, but the higher authorities have assured me that you can be sent home. Did you get something to eat this morning, mon ami?" He lit a cigarette. "You have your clean clothes as I promised you. And your boots, no?"

Campbell nodded yes slowly.

"This is the last time we shall meet. I shall miss you. I have enjoyed our conversations, but all good things must come to an end, no?"

Campbell just looked dazed and barely comprehended the French.

"Today, Lieutenant, you can choose prison for the duration of the war, perhaps for the duration of your life. My Vietnamese comrades will never concede to the South, nor will we. They began their struggle of national liberation in 1950. It is now 18 years later. You would not consider it likely that a movement so dedicated would concede easily, no? No, of course, you would not. Think, Lieutenant; think about your future in captivity." Thin Man waited for thirty or forty seconds, peering satanically through his French wire frame glasses, smoking his French cigarette, before resuming.

"Or, today, you can choose freedom, mon ami. Freedom wherever you might choose to live. Freedom to know the soft touch of a woman. Freedom to have children and to preserve your line. You want a woman and the joy of children, no?"

Campbell stared blankly.

"You want your life to have meaning, no?"

Campbell continued to stare straight ahead without affect.

"We do not have endless time, Lieutenant. Make the right decision now, Campbell. I do not want to return you to the beasts who are your jailors." Campbell answered in English very softly, flatly and very slowly. There was an absence of aliveness in his replay.

"The answer, monsieur, is 'no.' The answer, sir, when I arrived, was 'no.' My answer, now, is 'no.'" His speech was barely a monotonic whisper, but it quickened, and his voice strengthened, and he would not lose face in the presence of his adversary. "And my answer will always be, not only 'no,' but 'hell no!'"

"You foolish man!" Thin Man said as he abruptly stood up.

"The difference between you and the Nazis is that the Nazis perpetrated the big lie; but you, you communists, are forced to live the big lie." Thin Man slapped Campbell across the face with the palm of his hand and walked out.

Two guards grabbed Campbell and dragged him downstairs where they kicked and beat him while Campbell screamed in pain. Then they removed the iron handcuffs and bound his hands with his left arm pulled behind his shoulder blades, a coil of rope around his neck, and his right hand across his chest, and jerked him, always they jerked him, to his feet and shoved him down a trail heading back towards south central Laos.

Ticonderoga relieved *Ranger,* and *Ranger* proceeded to return to Yankee Station remaining at sea for 61 consecutive days. No other navy in the world could support a combatant ship at sea for any similar period of time, let alone an operational carrier strike group with air wing and escort ships. Most could only supply their ships in port for ten days, perhaps, for two weeks at sea. It was also a tribute to the American sailor's performance under high stress conditions for extended periods of time when circumstances called for it.

Operation Formation Star remained in a "ready" status although Task Force 70.1 was sent further to the south of the Tsushima Straits below the 38th Parallel—a sign that perhaps the diplomatic course of action was under viable consideration.

Padre Osborne was praying for guidance in his stateroom. Before him was a green confidential message that Captain Tarrant had handed him the night before. Captain Tarrant asked the chaplain to come by his at-sea cabin after giving the ship's evening prayer over the 1MC. "O," he said, "you needn't feel that you should do this," handing the confidential message to him, "although I doubt that there is a better man in the fleet to serve these marines. You do not need to do this, O. You served your time in hell." The message was from Commander, Third Marine Expeditionary Force to all major navy and marine commands in theater.

1. THE 26TH MARINE REGIMENT IS COURAGEOUSLY ENGAGED IN A MAJOR BATTLE IN KHE SANH, QUANG TRI PROVINCE JUST EAST OF THE LAOTIAN BORDER AND BELOW THE DMZ.

2. THE COMMANDER OF KHE SANH COMBAT BASE HAS REQUESTED THE AUGMENTATION OF A ROMAN CATHOLIC AND PROTESTANT CHAPLAIN TO MEET THEIR SPIRITUAL NEEDS.

3. ANY COMMAND HAVING A RELEASABLE TEMDU VOLUNTEER FOR THESE ASSIGNMENTS SHOULD FORWARD CANDIDATE NAMES WITH APPROPRIATE PERSONAL INFO TO 3MEF AS SOON AS POSSIBLE. PRIOR COMBAT EXPERIENCE PREFERRED.

Only Captain Tarrant and the executive officer had prior knowledge of Osborne's service as a marine infantry officer in Korea. The communicators routed the message for what they considered routine information purposes to the two senior officers without suspecting there was a potential candidate aboard.

The following day Chaplain Osborne visited the captain again in his at-sea cabin. "I think I need to do this, Skipper. It's what I have been uniquely prepared to do. It is what God is calling me to do. To be with men under fire… in a desperate battle. To bring what little comfort only a man of God who has survived combat can bring."

"Very noble, Padre. Very, very damn noble, just too damn noble," his voice rose with each phrase. "Supposing I say, 'no'"

"You're testing me, Captain." Padre Osborne was very calm and collected. "But I would not expect you to contravene the wishes of an Episcopalian priest who believes he has been called by God. I am needed. Those marines need an understanding chaplain. Khe Sanh sounds like this war's Toktong Pass. You know this."

"Yes, yes, I suppose I do, Padre. I just wanted to make damn sure that you were volunteering for the right reasons before I let you go." Tarrant extended his right hand to Osborne and said, "Go with God, O. You're a damn fine human being, and He has a damn fine servant. We'll miss you in *Tico*. I'll make arrangements to get you to Korea or Japan on the next COD."

"Thank you, sir."

"And I'm gonna personally miss you, O." Tarrant, a former veteran pilot of the Korean War, had tears in his eyes and threw a big Texas bear hug around the chaplain, and pulled him close to hide them.

Cannon was flipping through the messages reading the various bomb damage assessments covering the tactical strikes and B-52 Arc Light strikes in the Khe Sanh area and those messages that pertained to Formation Star. He also read the general reports about the Tet offensive. Only Hue remained unpacified as General Walt predicted and MACV was trying to assess what remained of enemy capability. However, the mail and normal periodicals arrived less frequently than on Yankee Station so Cannon had no sense of the public reaction of shock and dismay back in the States to the Tet offensive. Unbeknownst to him, if the communists intended a propaganda victory, they had gotten it. He flipped over a few more messages until he read one that totally surprised him and totally surprised virtually everyone on board.

FROM: CO TICONDEROGA CVA-14
TO: 3MEF
INFO: CTF 70.1

            CTF 77
            CINCPAC
REF: YOUR LAST

1. OGILVY T. OSBORNE, CDR, CC (PROTES-TANT/EPISCOPAL), USNR, 622432, NOMINATES HIM-SELF FOR SERVICE AT KHE SANH COMBAT BASE.

2. CO TICONDEROGA FULLY ENDORSES HIS CANDI-DACY. BEFORE CHAPLAIN OSBORNE BECAME A MAN OF GOD HE WAS A FORMER US MARINE CORPS IN-FANTRY OFFICER WHO LED HIS MEN ASHORE AT IN-CHON, WAS AMONG THE FIRST UNITS TO LIBERATE SEOUL, SERVED AS ACTING COMPANY COMMANDER HOLDING THE TOKTONG PASS, CHOSIN RESERVOIR AREA OF OPERATION ENABLING 3K MARINES TO WITHDRAW TO THE SEA.

3. CAPT OSBORNE, USMCR WAS AWARDED TWO PUR-PLE HEARTS AND A SILVER STAR FOR CONSPICUOUS GALLANTRY UNDER FIRE.

Within hours 3MEF accepted Osborne's candidacy. The message was personally sent by the CO, 3MEF.

1. GEN WALT WELCOMES CHAPLAIN OSBORNE ABOARD. PLEASE ARRANGE TRANSIT TO OSAN AFB ROK EARLIEST AND ADVISE. THE MARINE CORPS WILL ARRANGE TO GET THEIR MAN OF GOD TO KHE SANH.

2. GEN WALT SENDS

When Cannon read the message, he thought immediately of Dutch Van Vechten, and he quickly jotted a note to Osborne and stuffed it in the chaplain's mailbox on his next trip to the wardroom.

O... Please introduce yourself to my old roommate and good friend, Dutch Van Vechten. 2nd Lieutenant, India Company, 26th

Marines. I'm led to believe they are on Hill 881 South. He's big.
6'-3" 235#, played center linebacker at Yale. No one has more
courage or a bigger heart. Please give him my regards, and watch
over him for me. Please take care of yourself. Your work on earth
is not done. Rob Cannon.

Chaplain Osborne was easily the most popular man in the ship and his impending departure evoked extensive scuttlebutt in the wardroom, on the
mess decks, and in the berthing spaces. His personal magnetism drew
more and more men to Bible study and to services aboard *Ticonderoga*.
The fact that virtually no one knew about his Korean War experience, nor
that he had been a decorated combat officer, caused virtually everybody
on board to reconsider the man that they had known only as a chaplain in
new light, and the new information served to endear the chaplain evermore
to the men. Regardless of their faiths, the men aboard appreciated his force
of personality and his open, and visible sense of caring for each and every
one of them. Few pastors anywhere had as devoted a flock as Chaplain
Osborne in *Ticonderoga*.

Bong, bong....bong, bong... "Commander, O.T. Osborne, US Naval
Reserve, Chaplain Corps, Flight deck, departing." Seventy or eighty men,
mostly made up from catapult and arresting gear crewman, the grapes, the
fuel handlers in purple shirts, and ordnance handlers in red shirts, filled the
space between the ship's island structure and the COD parked on the port
catapult. The hatch at Flight Deck Control on the island was held open for
the chaplain. When he emerged, two men followed behind carrying his
personal effects in a duffel bag and a trunk containing a combination fold-
out altar and small organ. The throng on the flight deck parted and gave
him way to the twin engine C-2.

Osborne shook hands with the men nearest him as he strode forward
and waved to everyone else as he approached the plane. Just before he got
to the plane's hatch, he turned to the men and asked them to bow their
heads in prayer. There was a moment of silence while he gave the men
and the ship his blessing. He looked up and waved towards the ship's
bridge with his right hand and then he mouthed the words, "I'll be back."
Then he snapped to attention, saluted the bridge in crisp, Marine-style and
turned and saluted the national ensign flying at the truck. Osborne stepped
into plane and the hatch closed behind him. The starboard engine was
cranked up to join the port engine which was already turning as the plane
sat on the catapult. Then the crowd moved away, the COD pilot saluted

the Catapult Officer, the salute was returned, and the cat was fired accelerating the COD down the deck and off the bow into the air carrying God's shepherd to his next flock.

Late in the afternoon the Pathet Lao regulars turned Campbell over to the custody of the Laotian irregulars who proceeded to take him to the next village. They proceeded at a brisk walk but at a lesser pace than they had before. When they came upon a flowing stream, one the guerillas took a hand grenade and tossed it in the water. It detonated and killed many fish that floated to the surface belly up. All of the men, captors and captive, roasted the fish on green sticks over a small fire. He seasoned the fish as the Laotians did by rubbing fiery red ants over the fish. He welcomed the bulk of the food, its warmth, its admittedly flavorful seasoning, and it being the first significant source of protein for Campbell since he had been fed by Thin Man.

After feeding on the fish they continued on to the next village where Campbell was displayed as a spectacle and was spit upon by several villagers. After the show, he was staked out as he had been before, on his back, in spread eagle fashion. A middle age male villager, naked except for a loin cloth, came up to Campbell and spat on him before he alternately jeered and taunted him, at least that is how it seemed to Campbell. Then the villager wiped Campbell's face with something sticky that tasted like honey, and pointed at his face, and screamed, and laughed at him sadistically before running off. In short order the honey attracted stinging ants, flies and mosquitoes which crawled over his face and began biting and stinging his bare skin everywhere as he lay without defense on the ground.

When he awoke in the morning he had been terribly bitten by insects and his face was thoroughly swollen as were his eyelids. Campbell was effectively blinded to the degree that when it was time to leave the village, his arms were placed over the shoulders of one of the Laotians in front of him to guide him along the path. Still he stumbled and fell several times, each time receiving several kicks as punishment for slowing the group down. In time they descended down from the plateau, and he sensed they were back under the canopy of the jungle.

After another day the swelling subsided and Campbell regained a partial field of vision. This was fortunate because by mid-afternoon they crossed a stream and came upon a clearing in the jungle. Campbell arrived at what was to be his prison, and this would be the only chance to make mental notes about its layout and disposition from outside the prison.

Campbell's senses were heightened, and he keenly took in what was before him. The prison compound was laid out in a clearing with a high stockade fence, more than twice his height, he reckoned, made of bamboo enclosing a space of about 30 feet by 90 feet. Outside of the fence were five huts and a watch tower, 20 to 25 feet high. As he approached the prison compound, he could just see the peaks of two thatch roofs within the prison fence. They led him around half the compound, past one hut that served as shelter for the guards off one corner of the prison compound, down the length of the compound to the next corner where the high watchtower stood, to the next corner where there was another guard hut. There the irregulars chatted briefly with at least three, possibly four guards, at least, that is what Campbell thought, as one man seemed to be heard from the rear of the hut. Around the corner of the compound, he could make out at least two more huts along the long wall of the compound, and a fifth hut several feet into the jungle that gave off the smell of burning charcoal and boiling rice. He mentally noted that there was essentially a guard hut or tower on every corner of the compound with a food preparation hut off to the side. The two remaining huts, he hypothesized, were berthing quarters for the prison guards.

He was marched down to use a latrine, and then shortly thereafter, he was taken to one of the bamboo thatch structures inside the compound. His rope bindings were replaced by wood foot stocks and French-made, iron handcuffs. The foot stocks became very uncomfortable around his ankles as he lay on his back, but he was off the ground, and he considered his situation preferable to being staked out on the ground. His hands were bound across his waist by the handcuffs.

Twice in the past day the Laotians halted to camouflage and hide themselves in the jungle at the sounds of aircraft. Now he heard distant airplanes again. These sounds were encouraging signs to him, and Campbell began to shake off his sense of despair and think for the first time about escape. However, he knew first he had to heal and recover from his recent beatings, but all the while, he remained alert and observed his new surroundings.

"Hey, buddy." Campbell heard a voice, soto voce, in English. "Keep your voice low."

"Yes." Campbell was bewildered. "Where are you? Who are you?"

"We're in the Waldorf Astoria, next door, where else?... Air America, two pilots and a crew of four... Thais and Hmong Montagnards."

"Navy pilot, off *Ticonderoga*... Holiday Inn."

"Next time go first class, and pay up for the American plan." Campbell laughed for the first time since his shoot down, but it hurt to laugh.

Task Force 70.1, led by *Enterprise,* steamed north through the night up the Tsushima Straits towards a launch point off the coast of North Korea. The strike was on. The launch would commence at 0630. At 0600 the task group would go to general quarters.

It was now just after 0430, and Cannon had showered and shaved. Since a teenager he preferred to be clean-shaven for all of his athletic contests and critical events. He found a day or two's growth a distraction when the situation mandated his undivided attention. He felt a perceptibly solemn tone as he entered the wardroom. The pilots were easily distinguishable in flight suits while the ship's officers wore working khaki. A line had formed for the morning's offering of steak and eggs, the latter cooked to order.

"Morning gents," Cannon tried to be friendly but respectful. He was answered with a grunt from one of the pilots. Thereafter, he remained quiet, and avoided looking anyone in the eye. After breakfast he went below to Strike Operations for an updated briefing by the strike planners for the senior squadron officers and the air intelligence officers.

The joyless atmosphere was even heavier in Strike Operations. Other than updated photographs of the targets and the latest weather, which was acceptably clear for the mission, there was nothing new. The various probabilities for losses and expected values were unchanged and dismal. *Ticonderoga* had two airfields to strike, *Enterprise* three, the USAF had two target fields and were flying from Osan and Kunsan, and the USAF would restrike all seven fields fifteen minutes later.

Senior pilots who had flown hundreds of combat missions and returned alive and unharmed, many of those missions over the same Korean peninsula, were grim as they looked at each other and worked out their tactical plans knowing that many of them would not be making it back aboard.

The squadron leaders went about their conversation with aye-aye-sir professionalism, but they could not help thinking if this weren't the day that their numbers were coming up. And how about the younger pilots, most married, many with children? Was it going to be worth telling thirty or forty families scattered around Lemoore and Miramar, California, that their husbands and fathers had been killed over North Korea, or died of exposure after making it back to the sea, or perhaps, worse, simply advising them that so and so was missing in action.

"Okay, gentlemen, that's about it. I'll be flying TarCap with VF-195. Let's get to the ready rooms and work out your tactics. Good luck." CAG then shook hands with his squadron CO's and with virtually all of the senior officers. The room had mostly cleared when last he came to Killinger. The two veteran fighter pilots met each other and stood shaking each other's hand, their faces weathered and creased, both knowing the gravity of the situation, both having led men on many missions before, both having had to deliver bad news before. CAG spoke softly in Killinger's ear, "It's a beaut, Killy. Do me a favor, Killy. When you get to Washington, tell 'em Air Wing 19 went out and did their duty today."

"Fuckin' a right, CAG." That was Killinger, the archetypical fighter pilot without any ambitions other than to fly—angry, profane, whiskey-drinking, cigar-smoking, womanizing—a warrior who had been shot down by a MIG, survived, was recovered, and went on to even the score with his own MIG kill. "I'll punch the sonuvabitch that ordered this strike right in the fuckin' mouth!"

CAG nodded, smiled weakly and patted Killinger on the shoulder, "Good-bye."

Cannon left Strike Operations for the Combat Information Center which was several decks above on the 02 level in the island structure, and he passed through it without speaking making his way to the Operations Office to read the latest messages. Several officers were there and the two departmental yeoman, when he arrived. Commander Jeffreys handed him the secret message board. "Thank you, Good morning, sir." Cannon began flipping through two or three messages when Killinger arrived. Everyone stood aside for the Operations Boss as he strode to his desk without saying hello and picked up a file folder. He wheeled around and looked directly at Cannon.

"Ever see anything like this Big Gun?" Cannon, who had been leaning with one buttock up on a file cabinet as he had been reading, rose to both feet.

"No, sir. It's quite new to me, sir."

"Quite new…quite new! Boy, Big Gun, you got the words and phrases. It's a giant cluster fuck. A bloody, fuckin', no-chance, cluster fuck, and it is *quite new* to me, too! Never seen anything like it in all my fuckin' years in naval aviation. What do you think of that, Big Gun?"

"Yes, sir. I think I grasp the gravity of the situation, that is, as vicariously as a black shoe can, sir."

"Just how do you grasp it, Big Gun?" It was a challenge and Cannon was fully aware of the intensity of Killinger's anger, and proceeded cautiously, noting that Killinger had singled him out in front of the other department officers, but he answered candidly.

"Sir, I don't mean to sound disloyal, or disobedient, sir, but the risk-reward ratio, frankly, sucks, and…

"You got that fuckin' A right! And what else?"

"Well, sir, it sounds like we are about to compound the situation and hand the Russians a fourth victory and a fourth round of humiliation for us."

"Keep talkin'. How so?"

"First, they captured a commissioned vessel of the United States Navy without us firing a shot. A deep psychic wound, a terrible tarnish on our naval tradition for nearly two hundred years—don't tread on me; don't give up the ship."

"Right. Right."

"Second, they captured codes and very high value crypto equipment which we know the Russians are now earnestly studying which we must assume gives them the capability to break any stolen or intercepted messages from the past that they may not have been able to break."

"Right, right again."

"Third, they are holding 82 hostages which they can use to humiliate us and manipulate us and make us look powerless in the eyes of the world. Which down the road is likely to become a popular activity for any two-bit country that wants to flaunt American military power. Mind you, this follows ransoming the Bay of Pigs prisoners, and failing to retaliate after last summer's attack on *Liberty*."

"That's pretty good, Big Gun, What else?" Killinger's tone changed There was even a sense of admiration.

"Fourth, sir, we know the North Koreans are likely to have half of their air force, a hundred MIGs, in the air before the strike group can get to attack their airfields. We calculate that our strike plan has very low odds of succeeding and very high odds that the North Koreans will score many air victories against us. In addition we are led by the world's first, and only, nuclear aircraft carrier—the greatest visible symbol of American naval power. The story will be that little North Korea humiliates the U.S. and shows us to be a paper tiger." There was a long pause. "I know it is ours to do or die; not ours to question why. But this is just fuck-*ing* stupid, sir." Cannon emphasized the *ing*. Everyone was looking at Killinger waiting for a response to Campbell's accurate summation—a rather audacious criticism for a junior officer in front of his seniors.

"Alright, men. Let's all do the fuck-*ing* best we can to get as many of our boys back as possible." Then he turned to Cannon, and tapped him twice on the chest with the back of his left hand, "Not fuck-*ing* bad for a black shoe, mister."

"When do I get to see you?" asked Campbell.

"Shhhh. Keep it low. Coupla, three, maybe four days. After you're interrogated."

"Ahhh, hell...again." Another interrogation became a prelude to another beating in Campbell's mind. The scent of Gauloise cigarettes wafted through his memory.

"Don't take another beating. Tell 'em something. Anything. Design a new weapon, a new airplane, a ship, anything. Use your imagination. The interrogators are North Vietnamese, speak bad English. Not too savvy."

"Thanks. My name is Campbell, Augustine Campbell."

"Red Browne."

"You kidding?"

"No. Used to have red hair before I turned bald. You can call me Brownie."

"Hey, how do you sleep like this?"

"We'll show you how to take care of that. Okay, Campbell, goodnight." Campbell lay back and began to meditate by focusing on the pain in his ankles. After 15 or 20 minutes he began to think about escaping. He was thinking clearly and thoughts began flowing quickly. He had met Dieter Dengler at Lemoore when Dengler spoke to all of the squadrons about his survival and ultimate recovery in Laos. Dengler was legendary. The only man ever to escape during SERE training, and one of only two navy pilots to escape from Laos.

He remembered what Dengler said. "Your real prison is the jungle. You need to think through very carefully what it takes to survive in the jungle. Forget what you have been told at SERE. The only way that you can travel in the jungle is over existing trails. It could take you a year to hack a mile trail in the jungle. You cannot travel at night in the jungle. It is

simply pitch black. Your absolute essential requirement to survive is water. Do not climb away from water. There is no water on the tops of karsts
or mountains. On the other hand, the enemy knows this. Approach any
source of water carefully. Wait for the monsoon season to escape. That is
when water is plentiful nearly everywhere." Dengler went on to say that
the Laotians were afraid of the dark, especially in the jungle. If they must
go out at night, they go out at least in pairs, and frequently hold hands.
They also sleep soundly and snore like drunken barons. Further he said,
"They are very skilled with the machete, but few know how to handle firearms well, although they all seem to carry a weapon. They carry a funny
mix of firearms, not only AK-47s as you would think, but I also saw
NATO carbines and rifles." Campbell knew these weapons and had fired
them as a teenager at army ranges in Korea.

However, Campbell had been temporarily confused and overlooked
that there are two, distinct monsoon seasons in the Indo-China theater.
There is the winter monsoon that they contend with along the coast and in
the Gulf of Tonkin, and then there is the summer monsoon that covers
inland Indo-China and begins in late May or early June. He lost track of
time, but he figured it must be at least mid-February. The monsoon might
be three months way.

God then became the subject of his last conversation. *"Almighty God,
have you forsaken me? Is my suffering for naught? Have I not been a
humble and obedient servant? Yes, I have sinned against you, and I have
confessed, and I have repented. And what is sin but anything that detracts
from one's love of You, Almighty Father. I have asked you to shroud me
with your grace. Have my prayers gone unanswered?"* He lay quietly
thinking about God, and then he returned to meditating, this time gazing
steadfastly at the ridgepole of the hut. When he finished meditating the
second time, he whispered aloud, "Please God, do not forsake me. I am
asking you in the name of your son, Jesus Christ, please do not forsake
me. Is it arrogant of me to suggest that You must have some higher purpose in store for me other than to rot and die of starvation here?"

Chapter 13.

It was February 6, 1968, and *Ticonderoga* was at general quarters, her practice for full deck-load strikes. It hadn't been the typical frantic dash to battle stations commonly pictured in the movies, but a calm, purposeful, deliberate manning of the ship's battle stations and aircraft in one of the most complex, man-machine weapons systems ever sent to sea. It was final preparation for implementing the actions ordered by civilian authority in Washington.

The flight deck had been de-iced and most of the aircraft were fueled, armed and de-iced. Plane captains were making the last few wipes to clean gun sights and windshields while ordnance men were making final checks of the arming wires and removing red danger flags from the bombs and missiles. Pilots were performing their pre-flight, walk-around checks in the frigid, gray dawn of winter in the South China Sea.

Around the fleet, missile launchers and fire control systems were running through the pre-firing checks and routines. Five-inch 38 guns, which had not been fired for air defense in anger since World War II, were traversing and elevating and the gun control directors were checked while ammunition was brought up from the magazines. Five-inch shells were being fuzed for anti-aircraft protection.

Virtually all of *Ticonderoga's* 20 and 40 mm guns had been removed in response to the age of fast-moving jet aircraft and missiles, but she still carried four, five-inch 38's now being cleared and readied for action as flak guns. At the top of her mast, she carried, as the last line of defense, a system to overwhelm and hypothetically melt the circuitry and disable inbound missiles.

Below decks, Condition Zebra was set closing all of the ship's watertight compartments, and damage control parties and fire-fighting teams were strategically deployed about the ship with their equipment. So, too, were the corpsmen deployed with first aid packs. Secondary Conn, up forward in the ship's fo'csle, was manned with a complete bridge team and the navigator, who would serve as the ship's captain in the event of casualties to the bridge and her commanding officer.

All of the ships across the cold, gray sea in TF 70.1 were similarly manned at general quarters and poised for action. The tension felt aboard *Ticonderoga* was felt everywhere, and nowhere was it likely to be more tense than within flag plot in *Enterprise* where the Commander of Task

Force 70.1, and Operation Formation Star, the admiral and his staff were at battle stations.

Presumably fleet air-defense was to be centrally directed by the guided missile cruiser, *Providence*, acting as the fleet air defense control ship, but the fleet was mixed, some with a modern, computer-controlled, networked, tactical data systems and many others like *Ticonderoga, Yorktown*, and Fletcher and Gearing-class destroyers which operated with anachronistic, manual, World War II methods and procedures which 20 years earlier had proven inadequate against a guided missile of sorts, the kamikaze.

There was no give 'em hell; no witty chalk writings on the bombs. There were only sober thoughts of the mission, of not screwing up, and in the back of every mind, thoughts of death, dying, or capture. If there were a mood from the movies, it was more like the cavalry being sent out against overwhelming numbers and being told to hold until relieved.

Cannon was above the flight deck in the interior darkness of the Combat Information Center seated behind a radar scope with his radio microphone looped around his neck. *Ticonderoga, Enterprise,* the guided missile cruiser, *Providence,* the nuclear powered frigate, *Truxton, Banner, Pueblo's* sister ship, the ASW carrier, *Yorktown,* and a dozen or more destroyers and destroyer escorts in company, perhaps as many as twenty ships, all at general quarters, all plotted on the surface status boards as radarmen relayed their ranges and bearings to men writing in reverse on the backside of the plexiglas boards. So too, was *Gidralog* plotted, a Russian electronic intelligence trawler equipped not unlike *Pueblo*, that shadowed the force. Task Force 70.1 was deployed in Formation 40, an air defense formation for fleet defense. The heavies, the three carriers and the cruiser, were spaced about the center of the formation, and the remaining ships were in a skewed array about the threat axis oriented towards the nearest MIG field in North Korea.

Enterprise, the TF 70.1 flag ship, flying the Foxtrot flag at the dip, served as formation guide, and every ship keyed their maneuvers to her signals and their formation stations were arrayed in ranges and bearings from her. *Enterprise* closed up Foxtrot and the entire task force began turning together to Foxtrot Corpen and maintaining the integrity of the air defense formation.

In a way, the establishment of the task force itself was no small feat. In a little less than 10 days a force of 20 ships was assembled off the coast of North Korea comprised of three aircraft carriers with anti-submarine and air defense escort ships. All of these ships were maintained at sea by a steady supply of food and fuel from service ships steaming out of Japan.

Many of these ships had never worked together before. Their officers and men, especially those in the lower ranks and rates, were just months from civilian life and naval schools and were performing key tasks in a concerted effort to project American naval power thousands of miles across the globe from the homeland. All of this was happening while America's navy was engaged in a bitter war in Southeast Asia, maintained a force of 30 or 40 combatant ships in the Mediterranean Sea, protected the Atlantic and Pacific sea frontiers of the homeland, and sent to sea a strategic force of nuclear submarines to maintain a policy of nuclear deterrence. While the Soviets had captured a valuable pawn in *Pueblo,* they could not fail to heed the strategic strength of the US Navy as it was deployed around the globe, nor how quickly it could react to idiosyncratic and unpredictable events.

Cannon was tense, everyone was tense, and everyone was doing their best to mask the tension and to exude calmness and confidence. It was a kind of psychological mind game that one played with oneself. He watched hypnotically as the sweep of his radar circled his radar scope. He flipped the switch back and forth between the surface radar and the air search radar. He looked at the chronometer on the bulkhead and compared it to his wristwatch. He looked at it again and thought to himself, *"This is just one helluva a long way from OCS and Nimitz Hall, Naval Base, Newport."*

The ship was turning into the wind and heeled slightly to starboard, her plane guard destroyer following a thousand yards astern in her wake. The Angel helicopter was ready to lift off as soon as the ship steadied on Foxtrot Corpen. Now Cannon could hear the aircraft turning up, the whining, screeching sounds of revving jet engines. Those first off were taxiing to the catapults to have their bridles attached. *"Liberty, Liberty,"* he said to himself. *"Another effing war about to begin, because some asshole sent Pueblo out without an escort. Weakness invites aggression!"* Cannon was livid. He mostly only swore when he was angry, and when he was swearing, it was a signal to give him a wide berth because, while the man was getting better at it, he still had difficulty controlling his temper.

Cannon's mood swung from somewhere between rebellious anger to foreboding doom, and he tried to control himself by telling himself that many other men must have had these feelings before dire missions like opposed amphibious landings—Iwo Jima, Normandy, Okinawa. Grainy images in black and white of solemn men in Higgins boats flashed through his mind. He reminded himself that unless the ship was somehow attacked, he wasn't going to die today, and that evolved to an embarrassing sense of guilt when he considered the fate of the pilots in the air wing. These sobering thoughts moderated his mood.

He got up and drew himself a cup of black coffee in a paper cup, and returned to his general quarters station. There were long moments as he looked around Combat. He sipped the coffee. It tasted bitter, and checked the chronometer on the bulkhead and scanned the status boards. He searched the faces of all of the men and officers, checked the bulkhead chronometer and took another sip of coffee. It tasted no better. He particularly watched Jeffreys, the only veteran attack pilot in the compartment. He was calm, expressionless—a man who seemed to understand what he could not control and did not worry about it. Like the pilots flying today, he shared the same understanding of the naval aviator's contract, the one with the unwritten clause that said, "When your number is up, shut up, and die like a man." Cannon drained his coffee. It tasted sour, stared at his radar, checked the chronometer, compared it to his wristwatch again, squeezed the cup, and tossed it in a nearby chit can. And he waited and watched the second hand of the bulkhead chronometer tick down to launch.

"Combat, bridge," the Officer of the Deck was calling CIC.

"Combat, aye."

"The strike is off. We're standing down. You can secure from GQ." Moments later Captain Tarrant addressed the ship over the ship's public address system, better known as the 1MC.

"This is the captain speaking," his voice was going out to all compartments in the ship. "About five minutes ago or so, we received a message from the Joint Chiefs of Staff cancelling the air strike scheduled for 0630. Accordingly, *Ticonderoga* is standing down, and we will shortly return to Yankee Station. *Enterprise* will return to Sasebo, Japan, and then proceed to relieve *Ranger* who will return to CONUS. Operation Formation Star is concluded and Task Force 70.1 is being disestablished."

The Pueblo Incident would become a problem for the US Department of State to resolve.

"I want to thank each and every man aboard, especially the men and officers of Air Wing 19, for your professionalism during this very tense and stressful period. As we transit back to the Gulf of Tonkin, it is a good time to rest up and to prepare to resume Operation Niagara in support of the marines at Khe Sanh. For the period that *Tico* is on the line, we will be the sole navy tactical air support for Khe Sanh. We will be totally dedicated to supporting the 26th Marines. People will be counting on us. So, we have an important job to do. Take the time now to rest up and to prepare."

"Again you are a wonderful crew, and it is my privilege to sail with you. Thank you. Take care. Be safe. That is all."

There was no rejoicing. There were just the expressions and looks that men give each other knowing they had just been excused from a potentially ugly, catastrophic vicissitude in their lives. The same aircraft that had lit off their engines were now shutting them down. It was a grateful, anti-climactic spin-down through lower frequencies to silence—a perfect metaphor for the ubiquitous sense of relief as the crew unwound from general quarters about the ship.

Cannon slumped over his radar scope. He lay limp over the scope for a minute or two gathering his strength after the release of stress and tension. Onboard just 28 days, it occurred to him that he might have experienced some of the more critical moments of the decade at sea over the last year aboard *Essex* and *Ticonderoga*. *Pueblo,* Khe Sanh, Tet, and last summer's anti-submarine operations, when he was in *Essex,* against the Russians in the Mediterranean after the Six-Day, Arab-Israeli War—a very short war with profound, long term, geo-political implications for foreign policy around the globe. His last eight or nine months did not lack for big moments, seriousness nor tension.

Cannon left for his stateroom for a brief rest with his clothes on. He had the 08 – 12 watch on the bridge. Shortly before he was due to relieve the watch at 0745, the phone rang. It was the navigator, Commander Fritz.

"Bob, Commander Fritz."

"Yes, sir."

"We've been trying to qualify the First Lieutenant, Lieutenant Popplewell. It would be good for Poppy's career. He's a mustang, as I'm sure you know. I'm assigning him to your team during our transits as JOOD. Do your best to get him qualified, please."

"Yes, sir." Cannon barely knew the First Lieutenant and had no official contact with him. Wilton Popplewell was a West Virginian, probably twenty years older than Cannon, had been in the service perhaps for 25 years, held the rank of Lieutenant while Cannon was a J. G., and dined with the senior lieutenants and lieutenant commanders in the wardroom.

"When we get to Yankee Station, Ensign Chase will replace Popple-well."

"Hmmm."

"Couldn't give you two more different people." Cannon laughed.

"No, sir. You really couldn't."

"You'll still have Reposa. How's he doing?"

"Very well, sir. I'd say outstanding. Fast learner, motivated, a natural seaman. You can trust him. He's ready for JOOD now, sir, though I'd hate to lose him, but I don't want to hold him back, sir."

"Thanks for the evaluation. I'll keep it in mind. I like him, too, but I also like the way you train your team. Another month or two with you won't hurt him." He paused, "By the way, I like your watch team organization. I'm coming around to making it SOP in *Tico.*"

"Thank you, sir."

"Ever thought of making the Navy your career? You could go a long way."

"I'll consider it, sir. Thank you."

It was an easy watch. *Ticonderoga* steamed with her three destroyers out front in a screen at 25 knots. There was a poignant moment when the Quartermaster of the Watch, who was looking down at the flight deck full of parked aircraft turned to Cannon and said, "There's no O-run today, sir." He was referring to Chaplain Osborne who would normally lead a 12 minute jog up and down the flight deck on days when the ship stood down or was in port and ended with the men bowed in a 3 minute prayer on the Number Two elevator. Now just a few pilots jogged in the frigid winter air. The flight deck, devoid of the chaplain's band of 70 or 80 "holy joggers" who detoured around airplanes and tie-down chains, reflected the absence of Chaplain Osborne's personality and life force.

Cannon let his watch team coast after the intensity of the past week, but he quizzed and observed Popplewell dutifully in an effort to design a training plan for him. Cannon tried to be fair and objective, but he carried the mutual skepticism that most college-educated officers have for mustangers while the mustangers viewed the reserve offices as short term interlopers. The up-from-the ranks mustang officers were viewed as competent specialists who were correspondingly narrow and possessed limited upward mobility.

The First Lieutenant is a critical but unglamorous billet on every naval ship and is responsible for the exterior maintenance of the ship, her ground tackle, replenishment winches and associated gear, and her boats. On a carrier this is a very big job, and it is never done. Like the ship's engineers, a good day is never having an equipment casualty nor receiving a complaint. More than any other assignment in the ship, the First Lieutenant's responsibilities are exposed to the natural elements of the sea. His job represents a classic struggle of man against nature.

Lt. Popplewell appeared uncomfortable on the conn despite having been a helmsman and Boatswain Mate of the Watch as a white hat, and he was not facile with the signal book nor with simple problems on the maneuvering board. Cannon believed Popplewell was reluctant to move outside of his comfort zone and reluctant to accept the anxiety and tension that is an inseparable part of the growth experience. While Cannon thought it was unlikely that Popplewell would be promoted to lieutenant commander or to be given command at sea, he would like to assist him in his career without compromising his standards.

"Okay, gentlemen, on our next watch, I'd like Reposa on the conn. Make sure you know you engine and steering orders."

"Yes, sir."

"And, Mr. Popplewell on the maneuvering board and signal book. Refresh yourself on ATP 1 Alpha and BrevTac, please, sir."

When the watch was relieved, Cannon went directly to the wardroom for lunch. The COD had come aboard during his watch, and he saw the flight deck crew unload several orange bags of mail. He checked his mail box and was delighted to find a letter from his fiancée, Tish.

January 30, 1968
Morningside Heights

Dear Carissimo Mio,

The Clifton family came for dinner last night. Jackson and Keesha and little Jackson Jr. who conveniently slept between two pillows on the rug. They are very nice. Jack, as he prefers to be called, is quite formal and very military, but also very friendly, and he has a pretty good sense of humor. The Army is his career, and he sees a degree from Columbia as career-enhancing and broadening his perspective in preparation for senior officer rank. His wife is quiet, perhaps a little shy, and she was quite taken with how I decorated the apartment. Jack offered to help me if I needed to move furniture or boxes. He said he is looking forward to meeting you. I prepared osso buca and served a brunello with the main course. I think Jack left a little underfed. He is such a big man. I just underestimated what he required and next time I will start with a pasta course.

Was invited to a party down in the Village last week. Fairly serious group of artists and intellectuals. The initial purpose of the meeting was to explore ways to link various protest groups together to create bigger and broader demonstrations. But along the way some interesting questions were asked.

As the apparent WASP woman, I was asked why there weren't more white, middle-class, Protestants and Catholic students protesting the war. I responded by asking whom they thought were making up the protest movement. The answer came back that Jewish students were overwhelmingly represented in the protest movement and that universities with large Jewish minorities were the origins and continuing source of energy.

Someone added that the two politically active student groups were blacks and Jews—both persecuted minorities and persecution animated protest. Another added that Eastern European Jews emigrated from mostly monarchic/totalitarian states and had no means of political expression except protest, the labor movement, and radical and underground political parties—they had a tradition of protest.

I answered that perhaps injustice and exploitation were the answer as WASPs protested for seven years in 1776, and made up the bulk of the abolitionist movement while French Catholics did similarly in 1789. Moreover, I said that by labeling police as pigs and soldiers as baby killers, we were alienating WASP and Catholic constituents who overwhelmingly populated and embodied those institutions.

There was some agreement around the latter point and frustration was expressed at controlling the more radical and hostile elements who get the ink because of their extremism. Someone else added quite profoundly, I thought, that if the theory were correct, we ought to see a kernel of protest among women and homosexuals. Anyway it was a pretty interesting discussion.

Got your latest letter from Yankee Station. I guess if we have agreed not to discuss the war in our letters, that doesn't leave you a lot to say.

Oh, yes! The snow has melted away. Will update you on So-rolla in the next letter.

Miss you greatly.
All my love, Tish

"Good grief. Save me." he said to himself. *"Just what I need, a discussion on the theory of protest... and admonishment that my letters are too short."* It wasn't really a letter to fit his mood.

Chaplain Osborne spent the night in the BOQ at Danang. Things moved so quickly that he did not have time to write his wife who was visiting friends in Florida or his children.

February 7, 1968
Danang, South Vietnam

My Darling Fiona,

What I am about to relate to you would have been better done a priori in person or at least by telephone. Alas, you are in Florida, but I'm not really sure where, so I can't even call you and be-latedly discuss things with you. The decision that I have made might, under untoward circumstances, affect us both greatly. Nevertheless, the expedience of war removes many options which are the niceties of refined civil life and tests the trust of a responsible marriage partnership, as certain events, decisions and actions often overtake them

Such was the case when I felt compelled by the Holy Spirit to meet the need for a chaplain with the 26th Marines in Khe Sanh. Undoubtedly you are aware that they, about 7,000 strong, are under siege by three NVA divisions and a regiment amounting to perhaps 20-30,000 troops. This is, of course, more hazardous than duty in Ticonderoga, and many more lives are in jeopardy in the Khe Sanh area of operations, which is precisely why I have been called to serve them. When I vowed, after the carnage at Toktong in the frigid cold of Chosin, to serve Almighty Father, I did not have it in mind that I should return as a priest to combat. But, I am many things which include being a former Marine Corps officer as well as an Episcopalian priest, and the fusion of these two life-changing experiences uniquely qualifies me to serve at Khe Sanh. I believe it is all part of God's plan for me.

So Darling, I am currently in Danang, and when the weather clears, a young Roman Catholic chaplain, who also volunteered for Khe Sanh, and I shall go to the combat base at Khe Sanh (KSCB).

I regret that God's plan for me should bring separation to us and additional stress to you and the children. Why you, the innocent, should suffer is a very problematic issue which has vexed theologians forever, but I apologize to you and the children for it.

Nevertheless, please know that I love you and the children dearly. I shall write them when I can; however, in the meanwhile, please do your best to explain their father's compulsion to them.

All my love and the Lord's blessing upon you,
O

P.S. I will send the address for KSCB as soon as possible.

Ogilvy Osborne did not sleep well that night. The nightmares which afflicted him and virtually all veterans of combat were particularly bad tonight. He did not question his decision to volunteer, but he feared witnessing again the horrors of combat.

At 0900 Osborne walked out to the tarmac in his field gear complete with flak vest and steel helmet. In a strange way, Osborne felt good being back with the Marines. *"Once a Marine, always a Marine,"* he said to himself.

The Catholic chaplain, tall and lanky, watched as two crewman loaded Osborne's altar and organ into the C-130 Hercules. Osborne walked up and extended his right hand, "Hi, I'm Ogilvy Osborne, pleasure to meet you, Father."

"Seamus Shea, nice to meet you, sir." He had a soft, Irish accent, typical of the educated Irish around Dublin. Shea noted the black oak leaf insignia on the collar of Osborne's utilities.

"Seamus, Seamus Shea... with that name and accent you must be Italian." Osborne chuckled.

"Ogilvy, Ogilvy Osborne… that has a very Italian ring to it, too." Shea chuckled in response. "Come ca va?" Instantly both priests liked each other and began laughing.

"Bene! Well, I'm better known as O. You can call me O, double O, or O squared."

"Well, I'm sometimes called Say Hey Shea."

"How'd you get that handle?"

"Came to America as a young lad. Learned to play sandlot baseball. Played center field for Boston College. You know, Say Hey, Willie Mays."

"Say Hey Shea does have an assonantal ring to it, doesn't it? C'mon let's say hello to the crew." Both chaplains introduced themselves to the crew. The pilot, a young Air Force captain, briefed them on the flight.

"Should take us about 15 to 25 minutes. Khe Sanh is about 70 miles away. We're waiting to hear if the fog has burned off before we leave. It will be a hot landing. We're expecting to be shot at when we land. We are going to be on the ground for 10 seconds. If you are not off this aircraft by then, you better know how to fly. There's a few extra flak vests. Put one under your feet and the other under your butts. The stewardesses have told us the passengers find them more comfortable than blankets and pillows." The pilot could see that Shea was non-plussed and hadn't quite caught on to the gallows humor in the military. "Our own experience suggests that's a smart way to fly, Padre."

"When we get to the base you should expect the base to be under fire by mortars, rockets, artillery, machine guns and snipers. Stay low and get to the trench line ASAP. When you get there, stay there until someone tells you it is safe to move."

"Seen a lot of combat in your years, Commander?" asked Shea.

"Enough, enough, yes, I have… Father, keep this under your steel pot will you? I don't want it spread around. I was a Marine infantry officer in Korea. I haven't fired a shot in anger since. How bout you?"

"Coupla skirmishes. Just been in-country for a month." Shea paused then he said, "O, if you wouldn't mind, give me the benefit of your experience. Train me up, will you, sir. I can't help anyone if I become a stupid casualty."

"Are you afraid, Seamus?"

"Yes, yes, I am." Father Shea was a honest man.

"Good. That is the first lesson in combat. Know that you are afraid. Know that everyone around you is afraid including your enemy. Stay in touch with your fear, but don't let it paralyze you. Fear helps keep you alive. The heedless or the too brave are reckless and dangerous. Now, for example, I check to make sure I know all the ways out of this airplane, and I check where the fire bottles and the first aid kit are."

"Thank you, Father."

The pilot shouted back, "Okay, we have good weather. We're clear to go."

The C-130 descended for landing at Khe Sanh Combat Base which was nearly always under continuous attack from sunrise to sunset. The C-130 Hercules was an excellent flying machine that was built for un-improved and short runway situations. The NVA did not disappoint. The plane landed with a couple of thumps, the turboprops were reversed, the plane slowed to a near stop, the ramp went down, and the two chaplains scrambled to the tarmac while artillery shells and mortars rained down around them. Pallets of cargo streamed out after them including Osborne's altar and missionary organ.

Shea was slightly disoriented with the sound of explosions and the concussive effects, but Osborne grabbed him by the flak vest and indicated the way to the trench line. Shea was the younger man and had an easy, elegant, outfielder's stride and arrived several paces ahead of Osborne as the two men took cover. There they were huddled together briefly before Osborne told Shea they should remain in sight but no closer than 5 meters apart. Shea's eyes were saucer-like, and he was breathing heavily and wouldn't leave Osborne's side. Finally Osborne said, "You stay here. You'll be okay. I'll move up the line."

Osborne surveyed the terrain. There were craters and pockmarks from artillery and mortars everywhere and red clay, ubiquitous red clay. There were no structures above ground. It was a subterranean, Cappadocian-like community of 7,000 marines living below ground level. Outside the base there was little vegetation, all of it apparently blown away by air strikes and artillery, which, he noted, provided excellent fields of fire for the defenders. Out beyond were greenish, bluish, purplish hills that were bald on top. Here the 26th Marines controlled the hills and beyond were the jungle and the enemy. He watched as a jet released its ordnance and pulled off the target. Behind it, perhaps no more than a thousand meters away, mushroomed an orange fireball. Napalm. Osborne imagined that he could smell it.

The similarities and dissimilarities between the Toktong Pass and Khe Sanh were apparent to Osborne. It was tropical here; it was frigid weather there. It rains here; it snowed there. But the similarities outweighed the differences. In both cases the Marines were maintaining a static defense blocking the advance of an enemy force. Both shared hardship, fear, death, and dying. Both had that palpable grittiness and proud history of the US Marine Corps that somehow made bearable the sense of being separated from the larger war, and made the shared suffering tolerable. The Marines had an esprit of being Marines among their own kind of men that made Khe Sanh endurable. *"God was right,"* thought Chaplain Osborne, *"I belong here."*

Just then an incoming mortar struck the pallet with the missionary organ and altar, and it was gone in a fireball and a cloud of smoke. Osborne shrugged.

"Sorry 'bout that, Father." Shea smiled sheepishly. He was picking up the sardonic, understated vernacular of men in combat.

Osborne glanced back at Shea, athletic, youthful, accepting the challenge to be tested in the hell of combat. *"Now, Lord, give us the strength to do Thy will."*

Osborne and Shea were sitting in front of the base commander, Colonel Donigan. They both scanned the command post which was well-bunkered, below ground and the overhead was supported by stout beams.

"Welcome, gentlemen, to the 26th Marine Regiment and KSCB. Hope you enjoy the fireworks courtesy of General Giap." The sound of nearly continuous detonations was omnipresent, and the chaplains strained to hear the base commander's words. "In case we get interrupted, you are being billeted with several docs who serve in Charlie Med. My orderly will take you there when our meeting breaks up." Colonel Donigan then paused and shook hands with the chaplains before he began his briefing.

"I thought it would be a good idea to have a little chat and to lay out some ground rules. We need you, *and"* he exaggerated the word, "we need you alive."

"I lost two chaplains in the last three weeks. Our Catholic chaplain, Father Shea, was killed in action by sniper fire while ministering last rites. My Protestant chaplain was one of our very first casualties, Father Osborne, because he was a little casual about getting below ground during a rocket attack. He was evacuated with shrapnel wounds and eventually, so I'm told, lost his leg. Now, Commander Osborne..."

"Yes."

"I understand you prefer to be known as O."

"Yes, Colonel."

"I understand that you know what it means to be in combat."

"Yes, I do, but I prefer that my former capacity remain between us."

"No problem there. However, would you please share your experience with Father Shea, and take him under your wing."

"I can do that, sir."

"Now, Father Shea, I'm a Catholic myself... I'm about to give you an order."

"What might that be, Colonel?"

"I am forbidding you, you will not, under any circumstances, leave either our medical stations or our casualty collection points when the base is under attack. You are not to go to the wire when we are under attack. Do you understand me? You do not go near the wire when we are being attacked, Father!"

"But sir, as a Catholic priest, you must surely understand the need for me to administer the three sacraments associated with Last Rites."

"Need I explain how and where Father Zinni was killed."

"Sir, with all due respect, is that a legal order?"

"Father Shea, since World War II, Catholic chaplains have the highest casualty rate of any faith, well-above the incidence of Catholics in military service, because of their compulsion for delivering Last Rites on the front lines. They have also been awarded more Navy Crosses and more Medals of Honor, of which, the vast majority were awarded posthumously. There is a shortage of Catholic chaplains in the Vietnam theater. If you are killed, you will not be administering the grace of any sacrament of any kind to anyone. Do you understand me, Father?"

"I understand the thought, sir." Shea looked at Osborne and then back at Colonel Donigan.

"I didn't hear you say, 'Aye, aye, sir,' Father Shea."

"With all due respect, Colonel Donigan, I'm not certain that I can obey that order. You are, I'm sure, aware of the concept of higher law."

"Listen here, Lieutenant, let's be very, very damn clear. Saint Aquinas is not here at Khe Sanh. I'm the law here. I'm the convening authority. I'm responsible for the lives of 7,000 men here. I'm doing my damndest to bring as many men back home alive as I can. We will get as many people back to the aid station or to the casualty collection points as possible. You serve God there. That's where you serve God's children. You serve God there. If you can't, or you won't follow my orders, I'll have your holy ass outta here."

"Uh, Colonel," Osborne broke into the conversation, "as you asked, I'll take Father Shea under my wing, sir."

"Thank you." Facing Shea and pointing his finger directly at him, Donigan added, "You stick with Commander Osborne, pardon my French, like stink on…uh, like white on snow, until you understand what war is about, do you hear me?" There followed a long, tense pause, before Osborne spoke again.

"Colonel, did you know that back home Father Shea was known as Say Hey Shea?" Colonel Donigan looked puzzled for a very long minute, before he recognized the name.

"Oh, no. You're not that guy. The kid from Ireland. The priest they did an article on in the Boston College alumni magazine, are you?"

"Afraid, so."

"So we are BC alums?"

"Seems that way, sir."

"Thought you were headed for a career with the Red Sox. Good jump on the ball. .285, .290 hitter with the Pawsox. What happened?"

"God gave me those skills, and He gave me others to serve Him. God just had a little more pull than Tom Yawkey."

"Well, I'll be damned." The colonel glanced at his watch. "Okay, gentlemen, that's it on this subject. I'm glad that you are here. Commander Osborne take charge of Lieutenant Shea." He smiled at them both, and winked at Osborne, "It seems that Say Hey Shea might be a bit of a challenge."

When they were settled in their bunker, Shea turned to Osborne, "What do you think, O, can Donigan give me that order?"

"Frankly, Seamus, I think it may be irrelevant. We're deployed in a static defense with hostile forces pretty much all around us. Unless you

are the equivalent of a medieval saint who reportedly had the capability to be two places at the same time, from a very practical perspective,
centrally located at an aid station or a CCP might be a better place to
serve our boys. And Father, may I remind you, we are US Navy chaplains, and, as such, we are called to serve all faiths, although it is understood, only an ordained priest may administer the sacraments to
Roman Catholics." Shea nodded and was quiet. His eyes slowly
searched the bunker.

"What are those?" Osborne followed the direction of Shea's
pointed index finger.

"Why I believe those are rat traps, Father."

"Rat traps!"

"Yes, Father, God gave rats brains, too. Why should they want to
stay outside the base where the B-52s bomb them when they can stay
here in comfort with us." Shea eased up a little bit more and laughed.

"In that case, Father Osborne, perhaps you'll join me in a Blessing
of the Animals." Shea was smiling.

"I shall. I shall. All in good time, Father. C'mon, let's check out
Charlie Med."

Chapter 14.

Browne and the other prisoners presented a shocking sight to Campbell. They were gaunt and underweight and their clothing was tattered. Most had very poor, red, scaly skin, and some had several teeth missing and all had beards, and if they were not bald, they had badly matted hair. One, an Asian, limped badly and appeared very weak, and several had serious sores on their bodies. All of them smelled very badly.

All of these characteristics were the result of malnutrition, dysentery, malaria, yellow fever, beatings and torture. Campbell's reaction was to say to himself, *"You are looking at your future if you stay here."* He thought he had already dropped 15 to 18 pounds, and he could feel his strength waning.

Campbell followed Browne's advice and avoided another beating by concocting a new aerial weapon which was carried in a canister on one of the bomb rack stations. He described a weapon, that when released, a balloon inflated and a television camera and microphone suspended to send reconnaissance data to a satellite and back to the ship.

When he was asked, "Could it be shot down?" Campbell introduced an unexplainable and unintended serendipitous element of ambiguity. When he added that the balloon's interior was filled with a cellular structure like Swiss cheese, the concept was unfathomable to his interrogators. The interrogators did not know what Swiss cheese was, and he spent the rest of the first session drawing pictures in the dirt of cheese with holes in it.

First, he showed it in a wheel, then a wedge form, then a slice. Each picture further puzzled his interrogators. The combination of translating between English and Vietnamese, even French, "fromage de Suisse," the visual representations of the cheese, the confusion over the notion that Swiss cheese was merely an analogy for a cellular structure as opposed to a food, and the general complexity of the concept served to make the interrogator's believe they had obtained a trove of data. Accordingly, they extended the interrogation session to a second day obviating the need for a beating or torture. The net impression taken away by the interrogators was that their latest prisoner was cooperative.

As Browne indicated, after the interrogation, the Laotians separated the Americans from the Thais and Montagnards. The Asians, as they were collectively referred to, could understand Laotian to varying degrees and speak some basic English. Campbell welcomed the company of other prisoners, and they served to raise his spirits further, however, in critical

ways he would find that neither the guards nor the prisoners would conform to the expectations of the Geneva Convention.

SERE training assumed that the POWs would be primarily American
servicemen and that a formal rank structure would exist. Here there were
two civilian, Air America pilots, both Americans, two Thai, and two Mon-
tagnard prisoners all under contract to the CIA which presented Campbell
with several issues. First and most obviously, his fellow prisoners were
civilians and only Campbell was obligated to attempt escape. Second, all
of them had been imprisoned for two to three years, and they had no sense
for the escalation nor the duration of the Second Indo-China conflict. They
had all tried escape once and had been recaptured, beaten and tortured,
and, as a result, they had decided to sit out the war and wait for peace and
repatriation of prisoners which they falsely presumed would be reasonably
forthcoming. Fortunately, as it would turn out for Campbell, they were all
eager for news of the war and the chances for peace which served to make
him the apparent authority on the subject and provided him with immediate stature in the group. His officer rank also helped establish his credibility and potential authority, and as a carrier-qualified pilot, he gained immediate respect from the pilots.

Browne also warned him about saying anything that he wanted kept
secret as virtually no one could stand up to more beatings and torture, and
everyone would avoid accepting more beatings, torture, and isolation.

Red Browne grew up in Iowa corn country and escaped working on
the family farm by learning to fly. After graduating from Iowa State University he became a crop duster, but when the thrill wore off, Red went
looking for more excitement with better pay. Air America wrote him a
ticket to Southeast Asia.

His co-pilot, Mike Sekulovich, formerly flew transports with the air
force reserve and was similarly attracted to an offer to fly for Air America
after flying float planes for fisherman into and out of Canadian and Alas-
kan lakes. Like Browne, he fit the CIA profile for experienced pilots who
were resourceful and flew in remote places. It was readily apparent that
they were resourceful, seat-of-the-pants, stick-and-rudder pilots who loved
to fly airplanes and possessed a yen for adventure.

Bundit spoke several languages and formerly served as a sergeant for
eight years in the Royal Thai First Marine Reconnaissance Battalion when
he signed on as a radioman with Air America. He was attracted by the pay
which was modest by American standards but several times his pay with
the Thai Marines. He was strongly motivated to sit out the remainder of

the war, and he spoke Laotian and got along well with the guards. He was also well-versed in squad level and commando tactics and skilled in the martial arts and with small arms.

The second Thai, Thanawat, was a Thai army reservist as all Thais had a military service requirement. He came from a small, remote village, and was very knowledgeable about the jungle and how to survive and live off the land. Thanawat deferred a lot to Bundit's judgment as a former non-commissioned officer.

The Montagnards were brothers. Drang, the elder, and Dit, his younger brother, were cargo kickers. Basically they shoved pallets of supplies out of airplanes which then floated to the ground by parachute. Drang acquired an injury to his knee during the plane crash and limped badly; moreover, he was especially malnourished and was presently suffering from undiagnosed tuberculosis.

All six of these men had survived a fiery, near-death crash together when their C-47 had been shot up and Browne and Sekulovich brought the burning aircraft to the ground on a plateau in central Laos. They escaped dying in the crash only to be immediately captured by Laotian irregulars, but they developed an unusual bond by commonly sharing an uncommon experience together.

As Campbell laid low and recovered from his beatings, he thought back to a course that he had taken in social psychology to meet a graduation requirement at Davidson. He chided himself for not having been more attentive. He was never a scholar. How could he have conceivably imagined that he would find himself incarcerated in a cross-cultural environment with prisoners from different cultures, with various status, roles, and motivations? In addition there was apparent conflict and dislike between the Air-America co-pilot, Sekulovich, and the senior Thai crewman, Bundit. The problem of escape was much more complicated than being more clever than the Laotian guards.

The solution began with being accepted by the Air America group, and then establishing himself with the group's leadership, and ultimately building escape as a common purpose among an informally affiliated group of individuals. A critical step was to bring the Americans on board with the hope that their crewmen would follow the pilots and join the plan, too.

The total contingent of guards numbered seven, and they had been given names like Fat Boy, who was the cook, Stalin, Vicious, sometimes called Shrimpy, Toad, Pawn One, Pawn Two, referred to as One and Two for short, and Nay, which was not a nickname. Seven against seven; Campbell liked the odds provided that he could build a committed team with the objective of escape.

Cannon, Popplewell and Reposa were standing their second watch together, the 1200 - 1600, afternoon watch. *Ticonderoga* was roughly abeam Taiwan and several hundred miles northwest of the Philippine Islands proceeding south towards Subic Bay. The plan of the day called for a 1300 launch of two F-8 fighters, two A-4 attack aircraft, and a KA-3 tanker. The aircraft were headed for Cubi Point for maintenance.

The destroyers, except one for plane guard duty, were detached to return independently to the Gulf of Tonkin gun line. *Ticonderoga* was headed for Cubi Point for an overnight stay before returning to Yankee Station. At 1300 the ship swung to the southwest and increased speed in a light breeze to 25 knots for Foxtrot Corpen. Immediately this created a risk of collision. A large radar contact at 30,000 yards was making 15 knots on *Ticonderoga's* reciprocal course. It tracked CBDR, constant bearing decreasing range. The ships were headed for collision at a closing rate of 40 knots—one nautical mile every minute and a half. In 23.5 minutes, left unmanaged, the ships would collide. Under these circumstances the International Rules of the Road for Avoidance of Collision at Sea do not grant a right of way to either ship when two ships are pointing at each other in a meeting situation.

The Rules have existed in some form for centuries, at least since the Age of Sail, and have been successfully adapted for mechanically driven vessels. Along the way, rules were created to give the right of way to vessels that were less maneuverable, such as sailing vessels have the right of way over mechanically driven vessels, and vessels engaged in various activities where maneuvering is difficult or hazardous. For example, vessels towing, dredging, trawling fishing boats with lines and nets, all have privileges over otherwise unembcumbered vessels.

In the mind of the US Navy and its government, the notion of an encumbered vessel should apply to aircraft carriers when conducting flight operations. But the US Government, one of only a few nations in the world that operated aircraft carriers, and since the majority of nations do not have aircraft carriers, the privilege for aircraft carriers has never been approved for inclusion in the International Rules of the Road.

The radar target was designated Skunk Golf. The electronic signature from its surface search radar identified Skunk Golf as a Japanese super tanker of equal length and greater displacement than *Ticonderoga*. It was the policy of the US Navy, and the duty of its officers, to act as if it had the right of way during flight operations until the ships were *in extremis,* that is, when the maneuvers of one ship were insufficient to avoid collision. This was the situation now facing the bridge team.

"I believe it was Thucydides who wrote, 'A collision at sea will ruin your whole day,' " exclaimed Ensign Luis Reposa.

"Not today," replied Cannon confidently. "Unless this guy panics and turns left into us, we have this one under control." However his response assumed a smooth, timely launch.

Cannon watched as the plane guard helo lifted off. At 1258 the first F-8 Crusader, a supersonic, jet fighter plane, taxied to the starboard catapult followed by his wing man on the port catapult. The catapult bridle was fitted to the F-8, and the blast deflector was raised behind the F-8, and she powered up for launch. The F-8 pilot spent more than the usual 20 or 30 seconds to make a final check of her flight controls before popping into after burner producing 10,000 pounds of thrust at full military power and making a deafening roar. Then power was eased off. The pilot recycled his launch procedures again and hit full military power and sustained it for nearly a minute creating again an enormous noise level. Again the pilot failed to salute the catapult officer for launch. Something apparently failed to check out.

The F-8 reported a gyro failure and the launch was scrubbed on the catapult and would not go to Cubi Point. This consumed precious minutes. It was now 1308. Skunk Golf was still CBDR at 18,000 yards, 9 miles away. More time went by before the decision was made to launch the other F-8. It would now form up with the A-4s for the flight to Cubi Point Naval Air Station.

Additional time was being taken getting a tractor and fitting a tow bar to tow the F-8 off the catapult and down the forward elevator to clear the way for the A-4 launches.

"Lou, keep feeding me the range to Skunk Golf."

"16,000 yards, sir."

Finally the second F-8 launched. Popplewell was beginning to sweat, and Cannon was thinking it might be a good time to call the captain when Popplewell spoke, "You want to take over the conn?"

"You're doing fine. Just keep the wind down the deck." Cannon dialed the captain in his at-sea cabin which was just 10 or 12 steps behind the bridge.

"14,000 yards, sir."

"Captain, we have a CBDR situation here at about 13,000 yards with a closing rate of 40 knots." Cannon was studying Skunk Golf with his binoculars for the first sign of bearing drift.

"Please, take me off the conn, Mr. Cannon."

"Negative." Cannon moved to the pelorus for a better indication of bearing drift—the first sign that risk of collision would mitigate.

"Please take me off the conn…

"12,000 yards, sir." The first A-4 launched followed 30 seconds later by the second A-4.

"Please, Mr. Cannon," begged Lt. Popplewell. "Take me off the conn. I have children." Cannon looked quizzically at Popplewell.

"What the hell do you mean?" Cannon could hardly believe what he heard, and he never finished the sentence. "Stand your post…

"11,000 yards."

… in a military manner, Mr. Popplewell."

"Please sir, I have children; I have a pension," whined Popplewell who feared that if a collision occurred while he was on the conn he might be court-martialed and punished.

"Stand your post in a military manner. That's an order, Mr. Popplewell."

"Please, please…"

"10,000 yards, sir." There was another delay. The KA-3 tanker sat on the cat when it should be readying for launch.

"I have…

"How dare you disgrace Dixie Keifer's bridge."

… children."

"Get the hell off Dixie Kiefer's bridge, you, you, you," Cannon hunted for the word, "damn apparatchik."

"9,000 yards."

"Lieutenant J.G. Cannon has the conn."

"Lieutenant J.G. Cannon has the conn, aye sir," came the reply from the pilot house.

The Boatswain Mate of the Watch looked in disbelief at the messenger while the helmsman concentrated on steering. Popplewell looked out of sorts with his binoculars around his neck. He didn't quite believe Cannon's reaction. He didn't know Cannon well, and he had never seen an officer in the US Navy appear so vehemently livid. But Cannon was genuine enough. He was red hot and his skin matched his mood.

Popplewell had taken an unforgivable, dastardly posture that simply offended everything that Cannon stood for and what Cannon believed all officers must stand for. Things that Dixie Keifer stood for, and to do it on the very bridge where Dixie Keifer lay bleeding, refusing to leave the bridge, directing the damage control efforts to save his ship and the care of the wounded after it had been stricken by two kamikazes south of Okinawa in January 1945, was just totally unthinkable to Cannon. Keifer, awarded the Navy Cross as *Yorktown's* executive officer when she went down after being struck by a Japanese torpedo three years earlier. Keifer, who risked his life as a test pilot and made the first night catapult launch in naval aviation.

"Get off Dixie Keifer's bridge now before I bring charges against you... you poor sonofabitch. You are disgracing hallowed deck space. You are a disgrace to the uniform...."

"8,000 yards, sir."

"Get off! Get out of my sight, now." At that moment Captain Tarrant appeared on the bridge, and Lt. Popplewell shriveled against the after windshield on the starboard side of the bridge out of sight behind the pilot house. "Bosun Mate, sound the danger signal. Five short blasts. Pause. Five more short blasts till I tell you to stop, please." The Rules of the Road defined four or more short blasts as the danger signal, but Cannon always specified five blasts to guard against a miscount since three short blasts meant the ship was backing down— possibly adding to confusion in an *in extremis* situation.

"Bosun Mate aye, sir." The deafening sound signals commenced immediately.

"What do we have, Bob?"

"7,000 yards"

"Sir, we got a Jap maru tanker. Big one. Hundred thousand ton class out here. CBDR. He's probably on Iron Mike. I figure we're in serious *extremis* somewhere around 4000 yards... about 3 minutes for us to take evasive action and have our rudder bite." Tarrant picked up the phone to PriFly.

"Is the F-8 still on your button?" The captain asked if Primary Flight Control, the equivalent of the tower in a civilian airport, had communications with the fighter.

"6,000 yards."

"…Have the Crusader make a low pass over the tanker in burner." Within seconds the F-8 passed over the longitudinal axis of the tanker in full military power at 200 feet making an extremely loud noise. At the tanker's stern, he commenced an Immelman, climbing sharply, turning left, making a complete loop and coming back across the maru's bridge with a second low pass. Shortly thereafter the tanker began a slow turn to the right. Whoever was sleeping on watch got the message.

Finally, the KA-3 Skywarrior began moving down the deck. She had been waiting to carry paperwork from the ship's commanding officer. Cannon and Reposa watched briefly as the KA-3 Skywarrior's aluminum skin flexed and rippled as she absorbed energy from the cat shot. The KA-3 typically seemed to lose altitude after clearing the deck before climbing out.

"5,000 yards, sir"

"I have bearing drift, Captain." Captain Tarrant nodded.

"Thank you, Lou. You can belay that. I don't believe that will be necessary any longer. Bosun Mate, cease sounding danger signals."

The US Navy had asserted its claim to privilege while conducting flight operations. Ensign Reposa crossed over to the 5MC.

"Signals Bridge, Haul down Foxtrot."

"Signals, aye."

"Come left to new course one, nine, zero. Change speed to two zero knots." *Ticonderoga* still had to pass Taiwan before turning for Cubi Point. "Ensign Reposa has the conn."

"Ensign Reposa has the conn, aye, sir."

Ensign Luis Reposa said not a word about Lt. Popplewell. Like Cannon he was shocked by Popplewell's display of cowardice, and he fully understood Cannon's sense of outrage. The circumstances were tense, but Reposa wasn't certain how he would have a handled it. Cannon might be forgiven his temper, under the circumstances, possibly forgiven for publicly shaming an officer in front of enlisted men, one of which, the bosun, was in Popplewell's division, but it was a tasteless and cruel thing to do. And it marked one of the very rare moments when Cannon lost self-control.

A messenger from the Navigation department presented a handwritten note to Mr. Cannon. Cannon unfolded the note. *Meet me in my stateroom immediately upon the relief of your watch. CDR Fritz.* Cannon figured the captain had taken in part of the scene with Popplewell and had asked the navigator to look into it. Judging by the tone of the note, he was either to be queried for information, or have his ass chewed, or both. Most likely both, he concluded.

"Luis, I wanted to spend some time on the mess deck today since we have to sample the food anyway. An RD2 by the name of Burroughs and two others are on watch in Combat now and were going to join me. Would you mind substituting for me? My presence has been requested in the navigator's stateroom."

"Certainly, sir." Ensign Reposa avoided looking at Cannon. It didn't figure Cannon was being invited for afternoon tea. He figured Cannon was going to be given a demonstration that ass-chewings are meant to be held in private.

Cannon updated the status board and prepared for the oncoming watch team. He called Burroughs on the phone and explained that Mr. Reposa would be going to dinner with him. Burroughs expressed disappointment. Cannon, while not wildly popular with the men, was, nevertheless, generally liked and widely respected. However among professional career sailors, he was greatly liked and admired. To the latter, he embodied the role of what a professional naval officer was expected to be.

Cannon made his way down to the third deck, starboard side forward in the "A" section of the ship and knocked on the navigator's door. "Enter."

"Lieutenant Junior Grade Cannon, reporting as requested, sir." Cannon had removed his garrison cap and was standing at attention.

"Actually, Mr. Cannon, for the record, I didn't *request* your presence, you were given a written order."

Cannon swallowed hard. The navigator in an instant had very deftly knocked him down a peg. "Yes, sir."

"Stand at ease. Now suppose you tell me in your own words what disposed you to publicly humiliate a commissioned officer of the United States Navy this afternoon, an officer, I might add, who is senior to you."

"Well, sir," Cannon began very shakily, "under moderately challenging circumstances, Lieutenant Popplewell asked to be relieved of the conn while we had a meeting situation, while on Foxtrot Corpen, with a hundred thousand ton, Japanese supertanker at a closing rate of 40 knots." Cannon was recovering his confidence. "His expressed reason was he was afraid that a collision would blemish his career and threaten his pension and benefits. That is the reasoning of a bureaucrat with a yellow streak down his spine, not the fabric of a United States naval officer who is supposed to express concern for his ship and his men. He's unfit as a bridge officer, and I will not have him on my watch…"

"Whoa. Just a minute! Hold it right there, mister! That's one helluva a load of charges. And, what's more, you don't get to decide, mister, who is to be on your watch team. You are to take the resources and personnel assigned to you and get the job done. Do you understand me?"

"No, sir, respectfully and honestly I don't." Cannon was definitely hazarding being called for insolence, and he was taking a posture generally not recommended when being called on the carpet by a senior officer. But he knew that he had achieved a certain kind of stature, not quite to the point where he could define his role in an organization, but where he could advance a point of view. "Any line officer so lacking in courage is unfit for naval service. Maybe I shouldn't have kicked him off the bridge, but his example of cowardice in front of the men wasn't exactly in accordance with the highest traditions of the naval service either."

"Dammit Cannon. Just who the hell do you think you are making judgments like that about senior officers?"

"Sir, such judgments," Cannon was now extraordinarily brazen, "are made… routinely." Cannon pressed his point and the navigator sensed how fiercely Cannon felt about this and let him proceed. "The concept of leadership, in part, recognizes that other people, enlisted men, junior and senior officers are making judgments about oneself all of the time and requires a certain awareness of a manner of conduct to lead effectively. Show me an officer who cannot judge people quickly and objectively, and I'll show you an incompetent officer. As for senior officers, I think you will agree that we must size up every commander who takes the conn on a replenishment approach. Some sweat and are anxious, some are cocky, over-confident and express false bravado, and others, most others, get it just right."

"Cannon, you are cleverly redefining the issue. The issue today is your conduct and your gross breach of self-control resulting in the humiliation of another officer. And I strongly suggest that you take your own statement of mindful, self-observation and apply it to yourself. You may not realize it, but you also seriously diminished yourself with everyone on the bridge today. And that will continue as word spreads around the ship. You are to get the job done within the limits of civil behavior. Both of you conducted yourselves in a manner unbecoming of a naval officer, but you, you are different. Both the captain and I expect more of you."

"Yes, sir." Commander Fritz had effectively countered his argument by using his own words against him, and it was time to withdraw. "I apologize, sir. It won't happen again, sir."

"Thank you." CDR Fritz felt a sense of relief. Reprimanding an officer of Cannon's caliber was uncomfortable, and, in an unexpressed way, this junior officer contributed to the ship in ways that exceeded his rank. In every way he effectively held down the assignments typically given to lieutenants. "Mr. Cannon, make very damn sure not to ever let this happen again. If such a situation should ever occur again, find another way to deal with it, Mr. Cannon, or I will deal with you. Am I clear on this subject?"

Cannon snapped to attention. "Aye, aye, sir."

"Now, you will also write a personal note of apology and clear it with me prior to delivering it in person to Mr. Popplewell. I want to see the note by 1745 today."

"Aye, aye, sir." It was spoken this time with less enthusiasm and more gravitas. The heat of embarrassment went down his neck. He had been caught off base in a stupid base-running move in front of the stadium crowd. He certainly did realize that he had diminished himself both in the eyes of the ship's company and in terms of his own self-respect.

"You're excused, Bob." The personal use of Cannon's first name in this situation indicated that Cannon's point, in part, had been taken.

"Good day to you, sir."

The navigator held a fact-finding session with Ensign Reposa. Reposa confirmed Cannons' basic story and added that Cannon had on at least three occasions prior to "losing it," in a moderate tone attempted to remind Lt. Popplewell of his professional responsibility. Reposa went on to tell the navigator about Cannon's reverence for Dixie Kiefer, and that he first made a point of Dixie Kiefer's Navy Cross during the *Pueblo* affair. "Mister Cannon never criticized Captain Bucher, CO of *Pueblo*, but he kept putting Captain Kiefer out there, and left it unmistakably clear that Kiefer was the paradigm. Lieutenant Popplewell," Reposa said, "just stepped on a landmine." Reposa paused and then he added. "Mister Cannon's just smart as hell, sir. He just doesn't know how sometimes everyday folks can't stay up with him. He's very broad, very deep. But if you care to learn, he'll teach you about things you never even thought about." He paused again. "Gave me a good personal tip several weeks ago sir. Said as a Portuguese American I should read up on Admiral Jocko Clark. Said Jocko Clark was a half Cherokee Indian, who didn't let it prevent him from becoming the Navy's best carrier admiral during the Korean War."

"You like Cannon, Mister Reposa?"

"Yes, sir. Runs a very smooth watch, sir. Good officer, well…except for that temper, sir."

"Learn what you can from him while you can. The needs of the ship may limit that at some time in the future. Thank you, Mister Reposa."

Lt. Popplewell was also summoned to the navigator's stateroom. The navigator began by saying, "I have the word of two naval officers that you wanted to be relieved of the conn, today. Is that true?"

The navigator's directness unnerved Popplewell. "Uh…uh…uh." Popplewell felt trapped.

"Is that true, Mister Popplewell?"

"Uh…yes, sir."

"Can you explain yourself, Mister Popplewell?"

"Sir. I have a child who is autistic sir, and sir… and, and I, I just can't lose my benefits. I've been in the navy for 27 years, sir."

"I am very sorry to hear that. I sympathize entirely with your difficulties Mr. Popplewell. That is a particularly heavy burden for any man to carry." The navigator was genuinely sympathetic and paused and changed his tone, "If you were in my position, Mr. Popplewell, should I continue to keep you in the watch rotation?"

"I don't know, sir."

"I see." There was a long pause. The navigator was disappointed by his answer. Popplewell did not take the opportunity to assure the navigator that this would not happen again. Instead he continued to think like a bureaucrat and worried about the downside. "Mister Popplewell, it might be good for you to know, that the Officer of the Deck cannot delegate his responsibility to another officer. He may delegate tasks such as conning but not the responsibility. The OOD is theoretically responsible for everything on the ship during his watch, but he is always responsible for whatever the ship's captain is responsible. If Mister Cannon wanted you on the conn, you should have accepted that task and performed it to the best of your ability. If you thought the situation made you nervous, how helpful do you think it was to ask off the conn in the middle of those circumstances?"

Lt. Popplewell just stood there in silence. His next words indicated that he still did not understand the issues involved. "Where will this go, sir?"

"I don't believe it will go very far, Mister Popplewell, but I don't think you will be standing bridge watches, but I will let you know if that changes. Good afternoon, Mister Popplewell."

Popplewell seemed relieved. "Thank you, sir. Good afternoon, Commander."

Commander Fritz called the captain and gave him all aspects of the story. Captain Tarrant responded by saying, "Figure out a way to give them both a pass on this." In other words, let's handle this aboard *Ticonderoga* and not get this into the fitness reports of either officer. "However, I agree with Cannon. I don't see how we could trust Popplewell on the bridge again or ever give him the deck underway. As for Cannon, impress upon him that he cannot do this again."

"That message has already been delivered, Captain."

"Well, good. This young fellow is pretty good material. He had things pretty well calibrated today. He had the situation under control. He's got a future, but not if he's a damn hot head."

"Captain, he has a temper, but he is not a hothead. He rejected Popplewell's request for relief on the conn very professionally, on a measured basis, at least three times. But Popplewell just would not drop it."

"Well, Dave, you know what I mean. I'll mention it to Cannon, too and, maybe Killy has to speak with him."

"Yes, sir."

Chapter 15.

It was dusk in the late afternoon near the end of February when winter begins to loosen its grip on the City of New York. Daytime temperatures
creep into the low forties, but winter regains control after dark as the
winds whistle through the concrete canyons dropping the chill factor to far
below freezing.

Franco Ciorrazzi was ostensibly walking Laetitia Martin to her apartment to pick up a handful of stop-the-war-now signs for the weekend's
demonstration.

"Give me the key, Laetitia"

"Please wait here. I'll get the signs for you, Franco."

"Give the key to me, Laetitia." Ciorrazzi was mercurial, his tone was
insistent, and he grabbed her by the collar. "You want me, Laetitia. You
have been teasing me, Laetitia."

"I think you misunderstand, Franco. It's America."

"No, Laetitia. It is a woman and a man. You want me. You have been
teasing me. No longer. I'm going to take you now." He ripped the keys
from her hand. Several keys were on her key chain. She tried to get free,
but he increased his grip with his left hand and pressed her against the
door with his body while he tried several keys in the lock with his right
hand.

"Please, Franco, No. No means, no!"

"Silence. Don't make me hurt you, you little teasing bitch." And he
changed his left hand grip to cover her mouth and shoved her head hard
against the door while he continued to try to find the right key for the lock.
She scratched at his face.

"Help! Help! Help me!" Ciorrazzi responded by slapping her left
cheek with the keys in his hand and backhanding her on the opposite side
of her face.

Jack Clifton looked up from his reading and looked over at his wife as
if to say did I hear something. Then he heard the cries for help and recognized his neighbor's voice. In an instant he was up out of his chair and
moving through the doorway of his apartment and into the hallway.
Keesha followed him into the hall.

Laetitia Martin was slumping from the physical blows and the psychic
shock of the blows when Ciorrazzi shouted, "Scratch me, bitch!" and he
struck her hard with his fist with the keys in his clenched hand breaking
her jaw. Martin screamed in pain and dropped to the floor. Ciorrazzi didn't

see the very large figure of Clifton coming at him. Clifton now had a good sense of the situation, and he was on Ciorrazzi before he could react, and he grabbed Ciorrazzi, and with his strength easily threw him across the hall, headfirst into the wall, stunning Franco Ciorrazzi. Then he turned to examine Laetitia. He saw she was groggy, but crying, perhaps better said, sobbing, and bright, scarlet blood was flowing from her nostrils and her mouth, over her lips and chin and dripping onto her ivory wool scarf. "Call 911, Keesha. Tell them we need the police and an ambulance." Jackson Clifton turned back to Laetitia Martin. "Are you alright, Tish?" She did not answer, again he asked, "Are you alright?" He sat her up against the apartment door so that the flow of blood would not block her airways, but she had difficulty speaking and she held her chin in place to ease the pain while she continued to sob.

Ciorrazzi managed to get to his feet and started for the stairway, but Clifton wheeled and caught him and delivered a chopping blow to his shoulder fracturing Ciorrazzi's collar bone. Ciorrazzi went down on the floor in pain. Clifton stripped him of his belt, turned him over and lashed his arms together. Then he rolled Ciorrazzi over again on his backside, unbuttoned his jeans and pulled them down below his knees effectively hobbling him. Ciorrazzi could not get to his feet and run.

Officers Foley and Fortuna were patrolling north along Riverside Park in their unit at 110th Street and Riverside Drive when they received the call and were on the scene quickly. Keesha had described the scene to the 911 operator as a possible rape. Foley raced up the stairway to the sixth floor. He was slim and wiry and was a runner. Despite his winter coat, his weapon, radio, and other pieces of equipment, he arrived without losing his breath while his partner took the elevator. Both ensured that neither the elevator nor the stairway could serve as an escape route.

Foley saw a large black man kneeling over a white woman. He hadn't yet seen Ciorrazzi. He pulled his .38 caliber pistol from the holster, "Freeze, you black bastard." The words flowed out of his mouth, unchecked, reflexively. "On the floor! Face down!" and pointed the weapon. Clifton saw the weapon and judged that this was not a moment to push back, and he complied.

"You're making a mistake, officer."

Keesha screamed, "He's my husband! He's my husband! He saved her!"

"Shut up and stand back, ma'am," and Foley slapped the cuffs on Jack Clifton.

"Be calm, Keesha. Do as he says." Jack Clifton turned his head sideways to try and make contact with Foley. He offered no resistance and remained calm. It wasn't the first time that he had been rousted or cuffed by a white policeman. "The assailant is over there…behind you." Foley got to his feet and slowly backed away holstering his weapon, and looked in the direction behind him. The doors of the elevator opened and Officer Fortuna rushed to where Foley was standing. He could see Ciorrazzi lying trussed up and Clifton face down on the floor and Laetitia Martin lying on her side, in pain, sobbing and bleeding. "What have we got here, Des?"

"Perp rapist here," pointing at Jack Clifton. "The other guy, dunno. Probably just happened to come along at the wrong time." Laetitia Martin groaned, raised her head, and shook her head in dissent.

"No, no. My husband saved her. He's an army major. That's the bad guy there. I'm the one who called 911." Officer Mario Fortuna looked around surveying the scene; then he looked at Foley.

"You sure you got this straight, Desmond?"

Later, back in the squad car, Fortuna spoke. "This is goin' to be a regular incident, Dessy. This is goin' to cause a problem."

"Easy for you to say. You moved out to the Island. I got 'em movin' inta the neighborhood in the Bronx. We got a lot of problems with the niggas."

Cannon was fully aware that the Popplewell incident on the bridge was traveling fast through the ship in the various working spaces, berthing compartments and on the mess decks. People avoided looking at him as they met in the passageways and various compartments of the ship. He reckoned that he needed to take his medicine and facilitate an ending to the scuttlebutt as quickly as possible. He gave a lot of thought to the wording in the written apology and how it would be delivered. He wrote two drafts before he made a final copy and handed it to one of the Operations Department yeoman for typing. He retrieved it by 1745 and called Commander Fritz's stateroom. The commander was available to read the letter and hopefully sign off on it.

Fritz read the letter and handed it back to Cannon, saying, "Approved." He really wanted to say that Popplewell would not be standing any further deck watches, but he refrained. He didn't want to undermine the message that had been delivered to Cannon, or that he was in any way vindicated. Word would get around the ship fast enough that Popplewell's name was missing from the bridge watch bill.

Cannon now took the letter and walked the few steps from the commander's stateroom to the wardroom. He knew that Popplewell and several other mustangs usually attended the 1800 seating in the wardroom. Cannon lingered in the TV lounge waiting for Popplewell to be seated and for the table to be served iced tea by the Filipino stewards. He also waited for most of the places at the dinner tables to fill before he entered the wardroom and took his seat at the table on the portside usually used by ensigns and jay gees. He looked over and saw that the commanders table was full which included the executive officer, Fritz, Killinger, Jeffreys, most of the department heads including the ship's medical officer, and CAG and the squadron commanding officers.

Cannon got up very slowly and walked around the end of the junior officer's table and approached Popplewell's table holding the letter very visibly in hand. He stopped behind Popplewell's chair. Fritz just caught Cannon out of the corner of his eye, and he nudged Jeffreys who was sitting next to him, and Jeffreys signaled Killinger who had to turnaround to see what was going on. Now most of the commanders had their eyes on Cannon.

"Mr. Popplewell," began Cannon, "may I have a word with you." Popplewell was stunned. "May I have a word with you before dinner is served, sir?"

"Uh, uh, I guess so."

"Thank you. That is very kind of you, sir. Please follow me, sir." Popplewell followed Cannon to the forward bulkhead of the wardroom next to the movie screen. By now virtually every eye was on the two officers and the wardroom was buzzing with conversation. Some knew what was going on, most did not, but those who had not, figured something unusual must be happening, and word got around the tables quickly. Certainly all of the commanders by now knew what was happening.

"Mr. Popplewell, I owe you an apology. I was out of order earlier today. My behavior failed my own personal standards and was unbecoming of an officer and a gentleman." Popplewell was still off-balance.

"Yuh...yuh." He nodded his head with each syllable.

"Please accept my apology, sir."

"Uh, yuh...sure."

"I was particularly out of order, given your rank, sir. Please accept my humble written note of apology." Cannon again made certain to expose the letter so that it could be seen throughout the wardroom as he offered it to Popplewell. Popplewell remained off balance and was generally ill at ease and was deficient in certain social skills. There was a long embarrassing pause before Cannon said, "Will you accept my written apology with deepest regrets, sir?" Popplewell finally reacted and received the letter.

Commander Killinger, who had been straining to watch what was happening, turned back towards Fritz and Jeffreys. "I'll be a sonuvabitch. Big Gun has just finessed the shit out of this. Balsy as all hell."

Fritz who was more elegant and still had flag ambitions simply said, "Not exactly what I expected, but it's a coup for Mister Cannon, alright. Nevertheless, it serves my purpose."

"I'm sorry to have delayed you from your meal, Lieutenant. Again, thank you for your courtesy, Mr. Popplewell." Cannon returned to his seat where the junior officers were sitting. They were embarrassed and avoided eye contact with him. Likewise, Popplewell retook his seat at the lieutenants' table and opened the note.

"What's it say?"

"It's an apology," and handed it to one of the officers to read. Cannon caught this act from his place just two tables away which he thought was tasteless, but it played to his motive of apologizing to Popplewell so publicly. Best to get this over and done with and back in the good graces of the ship's senior officers.

One of the lieutenants read the note silently and handed it back to Popplewell saying, "Hell, looks like he did everything but perfume it for you, Will." This brought about nervous laughter that helped break the shared sense of embarrassment. These were Lt. Popplewell's peers and friends, but they also knew that he had shirked one of the inviolable tenets of what is expected from an officer in the US Navy.

There were plentiful comments in the wardroom over the days and weeks that followed. And the averted eyes and quick glances and whispers behind Cannon's back continued to embarrass and humiliate him throughout the line period.

"The boys offer you coffee, major?" On the following morning Jack Clifton was sitting in an oak chair in front of the captain of the 24th Precinct. A bronze placard on his desk, a gift from his last precinct when he made captain and took over the 24th Precinct, read, "Capt. John 'Whitey' White, NYPD." White's desk was cluttered with papers and file folders and the office smelled of stale cigar smoke. The second floor windows, protected by heavy wire screens, hadn't been cleaned in years.

"Yes, thank you."

"How d'ya like it? Coffee reg'lar?" In New York everybody knows coffee regular means two sugars and cream. It's as standard in the City as black coffee is in the navy. Clifton assented. "Mikey, two coffee reg'lars, hanh." He turned back to Clifton. "I understand you're just back from 'Nam, Major. Is it true it's not goin' too good?"

"The Tet Offensive? Looks like it's a political victory for the communists and a battlefield defeat. It could be going better, but they will never defeat the US Army in the field. Here in the streets, maybe, but never in the field."

"I was in Korea wit' the army…an MP unit. That's really how I decided to join the NYPD. After that I went to John Jay College on the GI Bill." He paused a moment, " 'Nother bitchin' war, huh, major?" Major Jackson Clifton, US Army, nodded. The coffee arrived and White said to a rather corpulent, gray-haired sergeant, "Thank you, Michael. Meet Major Clifton, here." Michael and Clifton shook hands.

"Very nice to meet you, Michael."

"Same here, sir"

"Okay, Mikey, give us some privacy, will ya? Please close the door as you go out." He watched as the door closed. "Thank you, Michael." Then he faced Clifton. "I was hopin' that we could talk about this regrettable incident. I apologize for my uniformed officer. I was just hopin' that maybe you would settle for a personal, written apology, sir."

"I'm afraid not, Captain. Your officer drew on me."

"Yeah, very regrettable. Very, very regrettable. It wasn't right. He thought he was answering a call for a rape in progress. His motive was pure."

"Not quite. He referred to me as 'you black bastard.' "

"I know. I know. We tell these guys about race relations, but sometimes, you know, in the heat of the moment…." He looked at Clifton searching for an indication of sympathy.

"Your officer presumed because of my color that I was the rapist. Prejudged based on my skin that I was the perpetrator. I don't think a formal letter of apology will do it. You black bastard and drawing and pointing his weapon at me requires more. No, it won't do."

"Please, major, I don't need an incident like this. The 24th Precinct is number one in crime. Morningside Heights, Riverside and Morningside

Park, parts of Harlem. I have my hands full. We're number one in homi-
cide, number one prostitution, number two in drug dealin', and number
two in rape. You have any idea what a 24 hour day is like here, major? It's
a jungle out there."

"I can sympathize with you, Captain. We have our hands full in Southeast Asia and plenty of racial issues in the army, too, but we have been
working on them seriously since 1947. You need to send your guy to racial sensitivity training and anger management, then, I'll accept an apology."

"Major, please. This isn't the LA police force. Every guy with a college degree and a crewcut. Neatly pressed uniforms where the sun shines
everyday. This is Nu Yawk. There are eight million stories here in Naked
City."

"I'm sorry, Captain, but…"

"Major, please. We don't have the resources. Go down to City Hall.
Tell it to the Maya." It was getting tense which was contrary to White's
objective. They fell silent, and White thoughtfully gazed out the window
while Clifton looked over the office in more detail. There were family pictures. A first communion photograph of the precinct captain with a little
girl dressed in white, probably his daughter. Pictures of moments in
White's career. One with Mayor Wagner standing next to him in uniform.
A plaque about a parish hall and the CYO and with a picture of a priest in
a black cassock and White holding a basketball with multi-racial, black
and white, middle-school kids gathered around them.

There was a very long break in the conversation, before White spoke
again. "You know, major, we're not so different. The NYPD is getting exhausted here with the crime rate in the City. We never know when or
where all hell will break loose, and what not. Where one of your guys will
get hurt or killed. I don't have the patrolmen or the detectives to clear the
blotta. You got the same problem. The army is getting very tired… every
night on TV…firefights, ambushes, countin' bodies, and what not…and
your boss, what's his name… Westmoreland. He keeps asking for more
troops. You had all hell break loose, the Tet thing. You don't know where
them Viet Cong will show up next, right?"

"What are you driving at?"

"Can you meet me halfway on this, major? You know this Doctor
Martin Luther King is doin' some good. Let's reason togetha. I get my
guys to come in, say for an hour, an hour and a half. Maybe around eight

in the morning, when things out there are slow. You come here to the precinct house and talk wit' 'em."

"Save the soft soap, Captain."

"C'mon, major. Yer askin' for what I can't deliva. Meet me half way…please." White implored him, was almost begging him. Clifton was silent as he thought through the options, then he responded.

"Okay, tell me more, Captain White."

"Good…alright. Now, maybe we're startin' to get somewhere. What if you was to come here and talk about the slights, the prejudice, what it's like being black, and what not. You know what I mean. Then you tell 'em how black people want what they want. Nice family. Nice house. Safe neighborhood. Good schools. See your kids grow up and be successful. Not have no barriers in front of 'em. Somethin' along those lines, huh major?"

"I dunno."

"Please, major. Just meet me halfway on this. Halfway. I'm askin' ya… we gotta start somewhere." Clifton saw that White had a strained, sad look on his face, and he took White to be genuine, and he was probably telling the truth about the absence of remedial programs.

"Tell you what, Captain. I'll agree on three conditions."

"Oy! It's always the conditions. It's like wit' the transit union."

"I get the written letter of apology from the patrolman."

"Yeah, of course, of course."

"And you agree to do my introduction including all the facts from the beginning of this incident until now."

"Yeah. I can do that, too. Sure. Consider it done. What's numba three?"

"You married, Captain?"

"Of course. Twenty-eight blissful years."

"Now, there's a lie." White laughed.

"Well sorta." White chuckled again. "Me and the missus has had a few words, but over the years, it's been pretty good. What's the catch, major?" White asked skeptically.

"You and your wife come for dinner at my place."

"Okay, okay, invitation accepted," then he teased with an Irish twinkle in his eye, "You sure you live in a safe neighborhood, major?" Clifton laughed with the precinct captain.

"Can I use your phone, Captain? I want to check with my wife."

"Sure. Sure. Dial nine for an outside line." Clifton got his wife on the phone and got three possible dates and gave them to White, and then he said to his wife clearly with the intention that White would hear him, "So we'll have ham hocks, okra, maybe some collard greens, and grits."

"Oh, now yer layin' it on. Now, yer gettin' yer pound of flesh."

"And get this, Keesha, his nick name is Whitey."

"Oh, boy. Yer layin' it on real good."

Chapter 16.

March 1, 1968
Greenwich, CT., Hospital

My Dearest Darling,

Please sit down and take a deep breath before you read on. First you should know that my prognosis is excellent.

Two days ago was a very bad day. Franco Ciorrazzi, the Italian sculpture student, attempted to force his way into my apartment with intentions to rape me. Jack Clifton, the army major (and his wife and son) whom I entertained for dinner, my next door neighbor, came to my rescue, but not before Franco punched me and fractured my jaw in two places. The restorative surgery was done yesterday morning here in Greenwich, and I have more wires in my mouth than the Brooklyn Bridge. They have prescribed Darvon for the pain, and I'm recuperating well and expect to be released in a few days. I will not be able to eat and chew solid food for many, many weeks and my diet will consist of liquefied food that can be sipped through a straw. Under the circumstances Daddy said a trip in April to Hong Kong was unwise. I'm crushed.

I so wish you were here to hold me. I'm feeling so alone, and I need you and your strength and tenderness right now. Carissimo, I love you. Please come back to me. Please take care of yourself. I love you so in more ways than one, my darling. While I'm healing physically, I'm pretty shaky emotionally. I am at once angry as hell and hope they throw the book at him including deportation, and I am extremely angry at myself for not reading him for what he was. I feel so dumb. I treated him like a friend not just another anti-war activist. I keep replaying in my mind all of the conversations that took place between us for clues that I missed. He had an easy charm and, in retrospect, a degree of hostility that always seemed to be aimed against the war. Perhaps it was some general alienation that was coalesced and aimed at me.

Anyway, I just keep crying and feeling so embarrassed over all of this and just how will I face everybody back at Columbia. I'm just so damn lucky that Jack and Keesha Clifton are my neighbors and that they were home and heard my cries for help.

To make matters worse, the cops arrested Ciorrazzi after some complications involving Jack Clifton due to an "unreconstructed cop" from the Bronx who automatically presumed a black man was my assailant. Very nasty scene.

Anyway, Ciorrazzi is in jail and will be charged by the Manhattan DA with assault and battery, first degree, and possibly attempted rape if they can get sufficient evidence for the second charge. The latter is mostly a matter of my word against his.

It has also been suggested that I have a few therapy sessions given that this was a somewhat traumatic event, but other than the fact that I'm feeling stupid and embarrassed for not reading Franco better, I'm not feeling the need right at the moment.

Mother, of, course, thinks the whole Columbia doctorate idea is a lunatic waste of time and money, and is very upset as she thinks we are already late planning our wedding in September. She simply denies the seriousness of the rape attempt and the physical violence and plows along still insisting on six bridesmaids. Neither does she get it that we have a serious war with over a half million troops engaged in Vietnam. I told her that you might have a hard time finding six ushers and a best man. I don't think she gets it that some of your best friends, like Dutch, are involved in the war.

Next, I'm enclosing a transcript of Walter Cronkite's recent remarks after visiting Vietnam this month. I thought you would want to read it. He thinks the best that can be hoped for is a stalemate and suggests that we negotiate an end to this four-going-on-five-year war.

Valiant II, the new Etchells 30 will arrive shortly. I was so excited before all of this. I hope I can get my head right. It's a terrific boat. Hard Sails will provide a full suit of sails. Becky Simpson was planning to rejoin my crew this year which would be great because she's been sailing with the Pembroke varsity this year. We were both looking for a third girl because we wanted to continue to be an all-girl crew. It was so-o-o much fun beating the men last year in the Luders. Anyway, I have a letter from Amy Cross in Darien, presently at Abbot Academy, who would like to sail with us. She's heard about us and is related to Bill Cross (very famous blue water racer), so that sounds encouraging.

Well, Carissimo Mio, I'm so sorry I'm going to miss seeing you in Hong Kong. I hope you understand. Daddy suggested seeing you

in Manila when Ticonderoga is in Subic Bay, but I'm thinking that
is around exam time. Anyway, think ushers and a best man. I love
you and miss you dearly; I need you, my darling.

  All my love,
  T.

Life in Campbell's prison camp was hard, and life was at the most rudimentary level of survival, far, far below what Professor Maslow could
have possibly imagined when he constructed man's hierarchy of needs—
the highest being self-actualization, the most ludicrous of notions that an
imprisoned man could possibly imagine.

All of the prisoners' personal effects such as they had—identification
cards, dog tags, mosquito netting, sleeping bags, and shoes and boots were
taken from them. However, they managed to free themselves each night
from the foot stocks and pick the locks on the French manacles which held
each prisoner manacled to each other. The lock picks were creatively cast
from molten toothpaste tubes. By dawn they would slip back into the
stocks and manacles before the guards opened the doors to the huts.

The day started with exercises led by one of the guards for ten minutes. They then had about an hour to walk around the prison yard perimeter before they were returned to the stocks. Incongruously, they were
given Chinese toothbrushes and toothpaste. The latter they swallowed after brushing for sustenance. They had bamboo cups for drinking foul water
and another to collect urine during the night. About mid-morning, they
were led, one by one, to a latrine outside the prison, but with dysentery so
prevalent, the area around the latrine was covered with fecal matter and
toilet paper was non-existent. If one's bio-rhythm didn't conform to the
schedule, one had little recourse other to relieve oneself in the hut. The
stench was barely tolerable. If someone had dysentery he would lie in his
own mess and would further suffer from dehydration. They all had dysentery at some time and tolerated the effects of a fellow prisoner reasonably
well, although in more ways than one, they were all medically jeopardized
when any prisoner was ill.

Every other day they were taken down to the muddy stream to wash
themselves and their clothing. They did their best to scrape the leeches
from their bodies with a small scraper made of bamboo. During these occasions the guards often sadistically kicked and butted the prisoners with
their rifles.

At noon they were let out to sit at a wooden, picnic-like table where they were given a half cup of boiled rice and a watery soup. Two village dogs would lick the sores on their legs, which they permitted the dogs to do since they found it aided healing. Then they were returned to the stocks until they were released for the evening meal around five in the afternoon. "Dinner" was similar to "lunch." After dinner they were returned to the hut and put in foot stocks and manacles for the night.

The lock picks and anything else considered contraband were kept safely in one's underwear as a Laotian taboo would not allow the area to be searched. Similarly, the prisoners were never bothered at night given the Laotion fear of the dark and spirits in the jungle, and they tended to snore heavily.

In a sense, freedom occurred after dark, and dreaming was one of the few pleasures available to the prisoners. Snakes frequently dropped from the overhead, and it was not uncommon to wake and find a snake had crawled down a pant leg. Rats ran across their legs at night.

As it got closer to the end of the dry season all of these conditions worsened. The nearby stream became a trickle and more infested with pathogens. There was no such thing as safe, potable water. Bathing was very difficult. Rice portions grew even smaller.

Disease was a major, omnipresent problem—not only dysentery but the prisoners had frequent bouts of yellow fever, and fatal cases of pneumonia and tuberculosis emaciated the prisoners and took lives.

The prisoners felt weak and had frequent dizzy spells. Any incremental degree of exertion brought on dizziness and a sense of weakness. It seemed that their captors wanted them too weak to escape, but not too weak to die.

To supplement their diets they attempted to catch insects for protein. Occasionally the guards would hunt a deer and throw the scraps to the prisoners—intestines, testicles, the penis, an ear—which were eagerly devoured including undigested grasses in the deer's intestines. The guards would keep the meat for themselves until it spoiled, turned green with mold, and was infested with maggots. When they would not eat it, they gave it to the prisoners who would eat it. Needless to say, the meat had an extremely putrid smell. When they vomited, they would do their best to eat their own vomit. Any calorie, any source of protein, was precious to them.

Their routine and maltreatment again brought on a sense of despair and depression with Campbell and caused him periodically to doubt his faith. The theme remained constant. It was less a plea for help and was more a search for understanding. He became progressively weaker as each day passed. He prayed to God to reveal the purpose of their suffering. He asked God how a just god could permit the inhumanity that they were enduring to continue.

To maintain their sanity, the Americans told Bible stories, at which Campbell excelled, and recalled moments of American history. Together they reconstructed scenes from memorable movies. Campbell invited them to whisper the Pledge of Allegiance which they did each morning as they slid back into their shackles. At night they would whisper evening prayers. They would relate to each the dreams and fantasies that they experienced. Once a week after dark they would hold a Christian service after they freed themselves from the manacles and stocks, and they alternated who would deliver the sermon. Singing during the day amused the guards, and the Americans took pleasure in singing hymns, patriotic songs, and popular, rock and roll hits.

They organized hunts and contests with the Asians for anything edible—ants, mosquitoes, roaches, fish, tadpoles, snakes, even rats, which they succeeded in catching and eating.

After a suitable time for recovery, Campbell focused his energy on escape. He saw escape as the easy part, evasion as more difficult, and making it back to friendly control a serious challenge. Nevertheless, he knew he was losing his strength daily, and viewed the alternative as dying via a state of increasing starvation and exhaustion. He began a series of one-on-one conversations, a different prison mate each morning after the exercises, which were more like Socratic dialogues.

"Morning Red. How're doing? How's your weight today? Over the yellow fever chills now? Feeling dehydrated? Think you'll ever fly again? What was it like when you used to fly? What's Iowa like, Red?

He made similar inquiries of Sekulovich with a slant towards Alaska, Canada and fishing. Always he would ask them how they viewed the state of their health and ask them if they remembered certain activities when they were free men.

With Bundit he was more direct. "What were the Thai Recon Marines like? What was training like? What weapons would they typically carry?" When he felt he had Bundit's confidence he would add more direct questions. "Is that an AK-47 that such and such guard was carrying? Anything unique about using one? If you wanted to booby trap a path, how would it be done? You see anything here that could be useful for a booby trap?"

He and Thanawat would walk together when they were permitted to bathe by the river. He asked Thanawat to point out edible plants. Thanawat described how certain tree trunks could be cut open for drinking water, how certain young shoots could be eaten. And where they could find edible roots.

With Drang, who was seriously ill and coughed blood and sputum, possibly from tuberculosis, he asked Drang about his symptoms and his family and asked him to describe his village. Drang asked Campbell if he would bury him if he died, which Campbell assured him he would, and see to it that his family would learn his fate, and ask the CIA to send his back pay to his family, if and when, he was "repatriated."

Drang mentioned all of this to Dit who asked Campbell if he would do the same for him. Of course, Campbell agreed, but he also told Dit that his health was better than Drang's, and someday he might return to his village.

By April, Campbell was able to add the thought of escape to these questions, and he did it ever so adroitly in the Socratic way, posing questions, so that each prisoner was beginning to accept the logic of escape as their only reasonable alternative.

"Have you ever thought about escape, Red?" "Mike, if you were to escape would you return to flying airplanes?" To Bundit he would ask, "If we were to escape how would we make it to Thailand?" Similarly he asked Thanawat, if the edible plants which Thanawat described could be found along the way if they were to escape and head for Thailand?

Sometimes he would ask them a question and ask them to think about it for a day or two before answering.

By mid-April, the prisoners created small peep holes in their huts and in the stockade fence and began a concerted effort to observe the routines of their captors and to hypothesize about an escape plan. The sounds of overflights raised some possibilities. However later that month Drang died, and they buried him near the stream in a bamboo coffin. Campbell led a brief service recalling several passages of the Bible and concluding by reciting the 23rd Psalm from memory.

Dit became despondent over his brother, Drang's death, and was reluctant to participate in the escape plan until one day the guards teased him about his despondency. The guards went further and played a version of Russian roulette with them laughing each time Dit flinched at the click of the rifle.

Bundit, who spoke good Laotian, overheard the guards talking about an increasing shortage of rice and that there was insufficient food for both the guards and the prisoners. They were considering shooting the prisoners and taking their bodies and hiding them in the jungle. That threat brought both Thais on board.

Browne and Sekulovich came aboard when Stalin shot at Sekulovich just as he was beginning to squat over the latrine, and laughed at Sekulovich as he hurriedly hitched up his pants. Stalin prodded him with his rifle back to the prison compound without permitting him to relieve himself.

The men came aboard in reverse order from Campbell's initial expectations. Candidly, the cruel Laotian excesses were more effective bringing everyone aboard rather than Campbell's effort of persuasion. Thanawat suggested that they become blood brothers which they did at the next noon meal pledging loyalty to each other.

There is a very long tradition of tribes taking in blood brothers and creating tribes of blood brothers. Browne gave the group a name, SixBro, and developed a fraternization ritual wherein the remaining six prisoners exchanged blood by pricking their thumbs and sequentially pressing their thumbs together.

Campbell thought they were making good progress, but he worried that there remained six to eight weeks until the monsoon—a long period to maintain morale. Projects often begin with high morale and sag in the middle and fail. If and when the group senses that they will be successful, near the end, morale rises. Campbell began to think about how he could avoid the U-shaped morale curve, and he offered a brief prayer asking for God to give him guidance and for Jesus to be with them and give them all the inspiration and strength that they needed to attain freedom. This became a continuous theme with the Americans in their evening prayers and weekly service.

Campbell believed God had spoken to him one night through Jesus. Jesus said focus the brothers on an escape plan, on a survival plan in the jungle, and making their way in 40 days to Thailand. Jesus reassured him that that would suffice to maintain the group and keep it working effectively against the objective of regaining freedom. Campbell thanked God for His direction, and asked forgiveness for doubting Him again.

Campbell saw the next steps clearly and directed SixBro to study the routine of the guards and time it using one-Mississippi equal to one second, and to build a model of the prison as preliminary steps to developing an escape plan. Of course, they had to teach the Asians how to say Mississippi which was not without its humorous moments. Browne said an "Asian Missisippi" was more like a second and a half. Sekulovich even gave the plan a name, Operation Modeerf, which was simply referred to as Mo-deerf, which was freedom spelled backwards.

Cannon reread the letter from Laetitia Martin. He was at a total loss as to how to feel nor how to respond to the perpetration of an attempted rape upon his fiancée. He felt inadequate and helpless to do anything half a world away. He recalled a certain discomfort watching Ciorrazzi pass Tish through the door to Avery Hall while he went to a meeting with Professor Meaney. His golden, flowing, Botticelli-like hair, the color unusual, but not unknown for a southern Italian, but nevertheless the hairstyle was in his mind an affectation—a sculptor's fantasy—rationalized Cannon. Also rooted in his memory was the FBI photograph of Ciorrazzi at Tish's side protecting her at one of their anti-war marches. The image of Ciorrazzi, the protector, shielding his vulnerable fiancée struck at the center of his sense of manhood. He hated the picture and hated it even more that Beebe Byrnes brought it to his attention, and even more so in front of Captain Pebbles. He had tried to shrug it off at the time, but the photograph had a castrating effect upon him, and his discomfort with Ciorrazzi grew to a cold hate for Ciorrazzi although he was a person whom he hardly knew.

But he was also angry at Tish and blamed her judgment for letting Ciorrazzi get so close. She was miffed at him when she started off to Avery Hall, and Cannon thought, at the time, that she might have been flaunting that other men found her attractive in front of him. His emotions were jumbled and confused, but over the next day anger towards her dissolved, and his feelings turned towards sympathy for her and an understanding that she needed reassurance and support from him. Cannon never sensed these things emotionally, but he eventually got to the proper response after an intellectual exercise. It was just the way he was, and it was a classic example of an excess of a strength becoming a weakness.

USS Ticonderoga CVA-14, at sea, Gulf of Tonkin
March 7, 1968

My Dearest Darling,

Your letter shocked me to the spine. I know you are badly injured, but I'm so glad that it was not worse and that you might have been extremely battered or killed. I'm so glad that you can recover from the injury to your jaw and that means more to me than missing you in Hong Kong. Not to say that I wouldn't love to see you in Hong Kong, nor to travel to Greenwich for that matter, but knowing that you will be alive and well when I return in September to marry you means so very much more to me. I love you, Darling, and I regret that I am not with you.

I confess I'm feeling quite inadequate being helplessly apart from you, but please thank Jack Clifton and his wife for me. He sounds in every way like my kind of guy, and I'd like him to serve as one of my ushers. Would you convey that for me?

I have a few fraternity brothers and oarsmen from my varsity boat that I would also like to have with us, so I think I can make your mother's number. I'll get on it as soon as I put down the phone after calling you at your parents home from the O Club at Cubi Point a couple of days after this letter arrives.

I'm also going to ask Dave Johnston to be my best man, since I'm sure Dutch just won't be available. Dave was my big brother at Northfield, and we both ended up at Columbia. He was two years ahead of me. Looks like Tab Hunter. Also played lacrosse at Northfield, and rowed crew at Columbia, and is a fraternity brother. And he's a naval officer, too—an all around great American. Last I heard he was XO on an ocean-going tug out of Guam and should finish his active duty tour with the Navy by midsummer.

Listen, Tish, I don't think it would be a bad idea to seek out somebody for professional help. How about the psychiatrist who helped you with your master's thesis diagnosing Caravaggio? Maybe she has a name or two for you. You've survived a very traumatic incident and there's a lot of new stuff coming out now about post-traumatic, after-effects. You can be emotionally wounded in ways that are potentially more injurious than a broken jaw, not the least of which might be an unrecoverable ability to trust men. Don't dismiss it too quickly; please give it a little thought.

Thank you for the Cronkite piece. The Viet Cong and the North Vietnamese Army will never defeat the US military in the field, nor can we ferret out every last guerrilla fighter or straighten out the South Vietnamese government. So I think he is right on both a stalemate, and its time to seek a peace, although I don't see us having any leverage in a negotiation. Not likely to happen soon. More on this some other time.

Darling, I love you very dearly. I'm so grateful to have you alive and well and in my life. Get well. We have a lifetime ahead of us.

All my love,
Your Robbie

By mid-March, *Ticonderoga* had completed her second line period. Including her trip to Korea, she had been at sea for 41 consecutive days. She would go to the Philippines for a brief stay overnight in Cubi Point, and then proceed to Singapore for a port visit.

However, when she was to leave Yankee Station, she was scheduled to perform an anti-submarine warfare exercise, an ASWEX, on her way to Cubi Point. Jeffreys asked Cannon, whose official billet was Anti-Submarine Warfare Officer, to develop the plan, and he emphasized that it must be a plan for the entire task group as *Ticonderoga's* commanding officer was also the Officer in Tactical Command of the Task Group 76.1.

"Think you can do this, Bob?" This was normally a task handled by an experienced lieutenant commander attached to an admiral's staff.

"Pretty sure I can, sir. Saw a lot of them when I was in *Essex.*" Cannon loved a challenge and an opportunity to shine.

"Ever done this before?"

"No, sir, but I understand all of the latest ASW concepts and how to apply them. How to layer them. How to integrate them."

"Okay, have at it. When can I see it?"

"I have the mid-watch in CIC tonight. We're not flying; I'll develop the plan then. Have all the pubs I need. Yeomen can type it in the morning. How 'bout 1200 tomorrow?"

"That will work just fine. Thanks."

"No problem, sir."

The exercise was to commence as soon as they replenished from *USS Shenandoah* AFS-1. *Shenandoah*, six destroyers, a P-3 squadron of patrol planes, and *Ticonderoga* were all part of the exercise as well as the diesel-electric submarine, *USS Tang*, SS-563 which served as the hostile submarine. These were substantial resources that lacked only the SH-3 Sea King, sonar-equipped helicopters, available in anti-submarine hunter-killer groups.

Cannon put together an imaginative, task-group level plan using the P-3's passive acoustic capabilities with Jezebel sonobuoys and two E-1B Tracers and an EA-1D from *Ticonderoga* for long range visual and electronic surface search. Diesel-electric submarines often transit at snorkel depth or completely exposed on the surface, and they use electronic counter measures equipment and radar on the surface to detect targets as well as passive sonar when they are submerged. He assigned three destroyers each to *Ticonderoga* and *Shenandoah* to screen the heavies, designated them Search and Attack Units Alpha and Bravo, and asked the Screen Commander to assign the escorts to the SAUs. The exercise limited the speed of the surface ships as it was clearly designed to force contact with *Tang*. All ships would abide by an emcon plan (a plan to minimize electronic emissions), utilize zig zag steering and turn count masking. After the replenishment was complete, *Shenandoah* and *Ticonderoga* would separate into two units, each with three escorts, and *Shenandoah* would cross in front of *Ticonderoga* while *Ticonderoga* launched the requisite aircraft in an effort to mask the identity of the two heavies.

However, the legitimate replenishment lasted longer than planned and extended well into the ASWEX area. The ships had no sooner formed up to begin the exercise when *Tang* fired two green flares signaling that she had a successful simulated torpedo solution on *Ticonderoga*. Cannon was disappointed. He thought the plan was well-conceived, but he wanted to see how the plan, essentially an experiment, would turn out.

As required Cannon sent the plan and an assessment of the exercise in a message to COMASWFORPAC, CTF 77, Seventh Fleet, and CINCPAC. Three days later a message was received on *Ticonderoga* commending the CO for the imaginative plan. Captain Tarrant held the message in a file folder on the bridge for the next time he would see Cannon.

"Thank you, Bob. Very well done. I'll see that mention is made of this in your fitness report."

"Thank you, sir."

"Maybe the way to manage some of you bright young fellas from top civilian schools is to give you tougher assignments and move you through the lower ranks faster. Might make the Navy more attractive to you. Whaddya think?"

"It might, sir. Some of us might grasp the concepts more quickly, but there's no substitute for experience. I'm not sure that I could have done this plan if I hadn't seen a half dozen tactical plans last year when we were doing it for real against the Russians in the Med."

"Didja see where Seventh Fleet sent your plan to all carriers."

"Yes, sir."

"Boy, I better get ready to be razzed by all of the other carrier COs when they catch up to me." Tarrant laughed. "Anyway, keep up the good work… and Bob, I don't want to hit this too hard while I'm givin' ya 'n attaboy, you could go very far in the Navy, but you gotta watch that temper of yours, you hear, son."

"Yes, sir."

"Okay. I don't want bring this up again. The Navy needs more people like you."

"Aye, aye, sir." Cannon's reply was the proper response to an order. He must have chosen the words deliberately rather than "yes, sir," to emphasize with Tarrant that he understood the personal criticism and taken it too heart.

Ticonderoga proceeded to Singapore for six days of R and R before returning directly to Yankee Station and continued her support of the marines at Khe Sanh. Part of the fun was deliberately steering a course crossing the Equator affording a couple hundred shell backs the opportunity to initiate several thousand shipmates into the Realm of Neptunus Rex. After mild hazing, the Pollywog initiates crawled through the length of a garbage chute containing rotting garbage across the flight deck, were washed off with a fire hose and finally got to kiss the Baby's Belly which was played by a perspiring, corpulent chief petty officer who had protected his body from the burning equatorial sun with ample supply of suntan oil. The matter of becoming a shell back was dutifully recorded and copies were sent for inclusion in every officer and enlisted man's personnel file at the Bureau of Naval Personnel in Washington. Apparently the US Navy did not treat the maritime tradition of becoming a shell back as an entirely trivial matter.

Osborne and Shea hiked swiftly under cover of fog with a squad of marines hoping to make their destination from Khe Sanh HQ to Hill 881 South before the morning fog lifted. The grittiest of the grittiest marines in the 26th Regiment were the proud marines of India Company who held the hill. India Company fought off some of the first NVA probing attacks which in some cases involved hand to hand fighting. Holding a position close to the enemy and blocking their advance into Quang Tri Province, made them critical targets for fire missions, and they came under daily artillery, rocket and mortar attacks.

Dutch Van Vechten greeted them with a big smile when they arrived at a heavily fortified bunker.

"Hello Padres, First Lieutenant Dutch Van Vechten at your service, sir."

"Hello Dutch, I'm known as O for Ogilvy Osborne and this is Father Shea." The three men shook hands warmly.

"India Company is delighted to have you as overnight guests with us gentlemen. Haven't had any men of the cloth visit us. You're the first. Welcome."

"We like to get out and around when we can, Dutch. We can't very well save souls in an empty church, if you will, so we bring the church to the souls, right Father Shea?"

"Certainly. Father O and I make up the Alpha and Omega MCU for the 26th Marines."

"MCU? What? What was that Father?" asked Dutch.

"The 26th's one and only, all-faith, Mobile Church Unit." Dutch chuckled.

"Good you have a sense of humor, Father. It helps out here. The CO should be here shortly."

Captain Maney stepped into the CP bunker, and Van Vechten introduced the CO to the two chaplains. "Captain Maney, these two chaplains go by their nicknames, Father O, that's O as in Osborne, and Father Say Hey Shea, as in Roman Catholic." Maney was all business. Very professional, but rather humorless, and combat had drained whatever affect had been present within him.

"Welcome, gentlemen. Real good to see you here. Got the word you would be willing to hold services. Good. We appreciate that. We can get 20, maybe 25, men in our aid station bunker. That's 8 to 10% of the men here. When can you start?"

"Right now, Captain. I'll hear confessions and say mass from now until 2400, except for timeout for chow, and again at 0630 tomorrow."

"Excellent. How 'bout you Father Osborne?"

"Same thing. Father Shea and I developed a joint service for Catholics and Protestants. We have worked out where we can sing hymns together, recite the Lord's Prayer together. I can serve the Eucharist separately for

Episcopalians when Father Shea provides Holy Communion, et cetera. Works well, except for Jewish Marines. Do you have any?" Maney shrugged his shoulders. "The Protestant service is non-sectarian although we modeled it around a typical AME-Presbyterian-Methodist-type service. We usually have them sing something everybody knows like *A Mighty Fortress is Our God* while Communion is being served. The lessons and sermons are abbreviated. It's a little tricky for the congregants but we talk them through it. Every service ends with the Navy Hymn. *Eternal Father*. Most of them think it's pretty cool."

"Sounds good to me. How about adding the Marine Hymn as a recessonal?"

"Excellent thought, Captain. Conside it done," said the former marine officer.

"We'll get the word out. First service, 1330 hour okay with you?"

"Yes, that will please the Lord. Thank you," said Father Shea.

The chaplains went right through to midnight as promised, and they lost count when over 200 marines attended service. Bright and early they conducted the last service on 881S the following morning and finished in time for Colors.

Captain Maney, in a daily act of defiance, conducted Colors every morning at precisely 0800. They lowered a radio antenna and secured an American flag to it. Then a bugler sounded *Attention to Colors* while the whip antenna was raised. All around, the marines popped their heads up and saluted the flag. All of this took no longer than 20 seconds before the NVA mortars rained in on them in response. Osborne glanced over at Shea at the next bunker. Shea had a group of men around him, and they had obviously been telling jokes. Shea had a huge smile on his face as he stood proudly with India Company and saluted the American Flag. Then like everybody else he got below in a bunker.

Osborne turned to Van Vechten, "How often do you do this?"

"Everyday. Understand you know my old roomie, Cannon?"

"Sure do, very fine officer. Stands a lot of watches. Widely respected. Gave me a note to look you up." He paused. "Damn, Dutch I just counted 9 incoming. How often does this happen?"

"Everyday, everyday, several times a day. We have everyone count the incoming like you just did. And we have them count the souls in the bunker." They sat quietly for a few moments then there was a succession of three heavy artillery rounds nearby. "Shit, the bastards are adding a dose of artillery today." Dust and sand filtered down from the overhead with the concussion. "We'll see how long it takes Carroll to silence 'em."

"Carroll, Camp Carroll, the firebase?"

"Un-huh."

"Hadn't realized they were that close."

"Just up the road, Route 9, a few klicks" Three more rounds struck near them and shook the ground. "Jeeezuzz.... Oh, sorry, Padre. Those were close." Father Osborne just nodded and was as calm as the rock beneath Peter's church.

"Captain Van Vechten, sir," a lance corporal appeared in the bunker, "a bunker collapsed from the concussion, sir."

"Which one?"

"The one with the Catholic chaplain, sir." Van Vechten was up and heading for the exit exposing himself to fire. Osborne was right behind him.

When they arrived, two marines managed to escape entombment by crawling out of a hole between several timbers. Several other marines were frantically trying to raise a timber when Van Vechten and Osborne, both men over six feet tall, joined the party. All of the men were exposed to mortar fire, but the counter battery fire from Camp Carroll apparently had their effect on the NVA artillery while tactical aircraft engaged the mortar positions either destroying them or causing them to keep their heads down. Van Vechten and Osborne and all of the marines knew they had just a brief, few minutes before the mortars would likely move to a new location and take them under fire again.

"What's the count?"

"Two out, three to go, including the chaplain. Total of five, sir." The addition of Van Vechten and Osborne moved the timber. Several men began pulling at sandbags and were able to pull two more marines out from the bunker.

"Where's the Chaplain?"

"Southside bulkhead, sir," answered one of the marines who was in the bunker. "We asked him to pray with us. Just got his rosary out when three heavies landed. The overhead fell directly in on him. Three. Maybe four timbers, sandbags, sir. Lot of weight on him, sir."

"Think he is alive?"

"Slim, sir. Couldn't get a pulse." The marines could hear the thunk, thunk, thunk of more incoming mortars. "Alright, everybody get below in my bunker."

Down in the bunker, Osborne's hands began to shake uncontrollably. "Three rounds," he said, "in the name of the Father, and the Son, and the Holy Spirit...." Osborne was overcome with grief and despite his training as a marine officer for retaining a command presence, tears began to flow visibly in front of the men. "The Holy Trinity," he spat out the works sarcastically, "three effing rounds of artillery." Then he got on his knees wiped his face with the back of his hand, "C'mon men, pray with me for Father Shea."

Chapter 17.

Later that day the marines, without further casualties, were able to clear the timbers and sandbags that crushed the life from Chaplain Shea and take him to Charlie Med. Osborne climbed down into the Charlie Med bunker where Father Shea now lay. The men had rolled Father Shea on his back and removed his helmet and closed his eyes. The rosary beads were still in his left hand. Osborne looked upon Shea's face which was once vibrant and was now exhibiting a bluish cast and prayed silently for several minutes. Then Osborne reached for Shea's rucksack and took from it Shea's missal. In the missal he leafed through the pages until he found the appropriate prayers for the day in the encyclical calendar, and then said the Roman Catholic funeral mass without Communion over Father Shea's body. Then he slowly closed the missal and returned it to the rucksack.

As Chaplain Shea's body was zipped in the body bag, Father Osborne prayed, "Lord of us all, please accept your humble servant and grant that perpetual light shall shine upon him. Do not hold it against him that he did not receive Last Rites, nor that his funeral mass was not conducted by a Roman Catholic priest. We mean no blasphemy. We do not profess to know Your ways nor Your plans and purposes for all of us. Here lies Your humble servant, Seamus Sean Shea, who did his best to serve You, by serving Your children who are engaged in this terrible conflict."

"He saw pain and tried to ease it. He saw suffering and commiserated with it. He saw the need for the expression of faith, and he led it. He felt fear and faced it. He saw tragedy and sympathized with it. He saw death and dying, and now, Almighty Father, he has joined others who have died here at place called Khe Sanh."

"Lord, I knew him too briefly, but in all respects, Heavenly Father, I can give testimony that Seamus Sean, who took the name of Jesus' brother, James, and of John the Baptist, was a fine priest, and had the makings of being an exceptionally fine representative of the Roman Catholic Church." Osborne's hand trembled as he made the sign of the cross over the body bag, and he winced as a thought from Toktong Pass moved through him. In his mind he had just lost another of his men. "In the name of the Father, and of the Son, and of the Holy Spirit. Amen."

Osborne returned to the bunker that the two chaplains shared with four doctors and gathered Chaplain Shea's personal effects. Later he would write a letter for Shea's parents which would arrive with his personal effects shortly after official notification that Lt. S. S. Shea, CC (Roman

Catholic) USNR, had been killed in action, 17 March 1968. It had not occurred to Father Shea, nor any of the marines around the bunker, that the
day was St. Patrick's Day.

On March 31, 1968, President Johnson, offered another olive branch to the
North Vietnamese and ordered a halt to all bombing north of the 19th Parallel. MACV believed that both the Tet offensive and the siege of Khe
Sanh were major military losses for the North Vietnamese, and it was
hoped that the doves in Hanoi were vindicated and rehabilitated although
there was little evidence to suggest this.

    In the aircraft carriers and air wings on Yankee Station this was re-
ceived with mixed emotion. On the one hand, the authorized target list up
North was so insignificant that few thought they were worth the risk anyway, and there was a corresponding sense of relief. Others were cynical,
and felt deceived that there had been any bonafide value worth the losses
in men and treasure that had accumulated over nearly four years of combat
flying. Psychologically, the pilots withdrew even more into the sense that
they needed to watch out for themselves and to execute every mission with
a high level, if not, an extreme level, of caution. This was further reaf-
firmed, when coincidentally, after 77 days of siege, the badly battered
North Vietnamese Army withdrew from Khe Sanh licking its wounds as it
traveled north, and the Marines shortly thereafter abandoned what had
been presented as so critical to defend—the Khe Sanh Combat Base.
There was hardly any talk about winning the war now. They thought privately of not dying in it. They spoke only of ending it.

The Reverend Ian Campbell, his son a casualty of the defense of Khe
Sanh, arrived early for the Military Parents Prayer Group held each Thurs-
day afternoon at his church, the First Presbyterian Church of Vero Beach.
The meeting was open to all faiths and was composed primarily of parents
and relatives of military personnel serving in Vietnam from Indian River
County. It also included the names of those who were identified as missing in action, killed in action, of, if known, prisoners of war. Generally
there were more names of servicemen than attendees, and the participants
drew the names of those who were not represented until all servicemen
were represented by a participant. The attendees were also mostly women,
some of them African Americans from Vero Beach and Gifford, and gave
rise to the nickname, Military Moms Prayer Group.

Sitting in a circle in the church hall, the service usually began with the 91st Psalm, sometimes referred to as the Soldier's or Warrior's Prayer, read in concert, then each participant offered a prayer for their loved one and for any of the names that they had drawn. After the round was concluded, the participants said The Lord's Prayer and the meeting was ended by reading the 23rd Psalm responsively.

Mrs. Campbell, who had cared for her son through war on the Korean peninsula, offered the prayer for her son in Laos. "Almighty Father, we ask that Thou should watch over our son, Augustine, and protect him, and strengthen his faith, that he shall do Thy will, and serve Thy purpose. In the name of Your only son, Jesus Christ, we ask this. We also ask You, Almighty Father, to assist us with thy grace, so that his father and I might endure the absence of word of our son and the absence his presence among us." She paused before she added the word, "Amen." Esther Campbell stifled her tears as best a mother could.

Air Wing 19 adjusted to the new routine of the air war being restricted to targets below the 19th Parallel in Route Package II which contained few lucrative targets other than the MIG base at Vinh, and most of the MIGs had been long ago moved to a sanctuary in Red China. The air plan stepped down the number of daily sorties, and the missions were generally defined as armed reconnaissance without predefined targets or missions to work with forward air controllers in South Vietnam, generally referred to as FAC work. Pure reconnaissance flights continued over North Vietnam and revealed, to no one's surprise, that the North Vietnamese capitalized on the opportunity to rebuild their air defense system and the infrastructure that had been brought down in the prior years of Operation Rolling Thunder. None of this was received well and morale declined further.

On April 5th, it was April 4th on the other side of the international dateline in the United States, Cannon was at his strike control station monitoring flights in and out of Vietnam and Laos, when a loud, sustained roar of cheering and laughter broke out in the Combat Information Center. It was so loud that Cannon could not hear the radio transmissions from *Ticonderoga*'s aircraft. He looked up smiling, expecting to hear that some popular sports team had achieved a major victory. PO2 Burroughs, the watch petty office standing over the dead reckoning tracer, had his back to Cannon when Cannon asked what was happening.

"What's going on, Burroughs? What's going on? Somebody win something?" Burroughs turned around and said.

"No, suh. Mahtin Lutha King 'ssassinated." The shouting and cheering continued without abatement.

"Say again, Burroughs. I can't hear you."

"Mahtin Lutha King 'ssassinated, suh."

"What? What was that? Martin Luther King was assassinated?"

"Yes, suh."

"How do you know that?"

"Ahmed Fawces Radio, Saigon, suh." Cannon looked over at the CICWO, Lieutenant Commander Reeves, a patrol plane pilot from South Carolina. Reeves seemed oblivious to what was going on and gave no sign of reaction nor made any effort to quiet things down.

"Panther Strike, this is Water Wagon 55, inbound to you." Cannon, shouted back.

"Wait out!"

About a handful of the 60 men in the OI division were African Americans, and he looked at the black faces on watch in Combat. They were in a double state of shock as they watched the carryings on of about half of the white radarmen on watch. Other men looked on and were embarrassed. But the noisemakers were made up of many, but not all Southerners. Given the Southern military tradition in America, many of these men were well-motivated and had career ambitions in the navy.

Cannon stood up, and shouted, "Pipe down! Pipe down! Settle down!" But he was either unheard or unheeded. Now he got up from behind his radar scope and waded into the middle of the cheering men, and shouted again. It was a risk, to leave his watch station if aircraft with an emergency could not have their calls received in *Ticonderoga.* Again Cannon shouted. "Pipe down, all of you! Now! Or I'll put every damn one of you on report." Cannon snarled at Burroughs. "I want every damn name of every sailor with a smile on his face. I want nothing but professional naval decorum from these men. Do you damn well hear me, Burroughs?"

"Aye, aye, sir."

"And I am personally disappointed in you. Burroughs." Cannon was fond of Burroughs, who was otherwise an excellent petty officer. The noise subsided but sheepish smiles continued as Cannon returned to his station.

"Water Wagon 55, this is Panther Strike, over...." Water Wagon was the daily Fleet Logistics Group C-2 coming in from NAS Cubi Point. Some of the men continued to smirk silently among themselves creating an uneasy atmosphere in CIC.

After watch, Lieutenant junior grade Cannon crossed the passageway and entered the OI Division office to speak with Master Chief Faulk. He recognized another sailor, in the office, and Cannon was still angry and abrupt. "You, Sorenson, take off. I need to speak with the chief, please."

Master Chief Bobby Lee Faulk had curly blond hair and was a Southern Baptist from Mississippi. He looked a bit like Fearless Fosdick, but Cannon knew him to be a fair-minded man who was a devout Christian.

"Chief, did you hear that noise in Combat about an hour ago?"

Yes, sir, I did. I was just about to go and see what it was about when it stopped." Chief Faulk was articulate and displayed excellent manners. His soft "r-less" Mississippi accent was always syntactically correct. In a word, he was professional and both Faulk and Cannon admired each other.

"They were celebrating the assassination of Martin Luther King, and Burroughs was just celebrating right along with the rest of them. We can't have this, chief." Cannon pointed at the deck and jabbed his index finger with each phrase to punctuate his remarks. "Not in this division, not in this ship, and not in the United States Navy!"

"Yes, sir. I agree with you completely. It's not Christian, sir."

"Good. We both agree on that. What do you think should be done about it?"

"Well, sir, off hand, I'd say I need to take every petty officer between me and the seamen first and have a counseling session with every petty officer in the division. Tell 'em if they can't or won't treat people fairly, and respectfully, and can't or won't lead effectively to improve race relations that this will affect their careers negatively."

"Excellent. Very good. Sounds very good to me, chief. Please do it. Thank you."

"Yes, sir."

"Please relay our conversation to Mr. Pierce, your division officer. Tell him I'd like to chat with him about this. Please tell him about our conversation."

"Aye, aye sir,"

"Thank you, chief. You're a damn fine man and a helluva a human being." Cannon left the office slamming the door behind him. He was still hot under the collar.

Ticonderoga thereafter had few if any racial incidents, although an uneasy calm existed throughout the ship. Junior officers, who were division officers and assistant division officers, acted on their own initiative to improve race relations and were vigilant to nip problems early. The new breed of officers, who were mostly white and had a strong sense of fairness, came from integrated schools and communities, acted quickly before the department heads assessed the situation and provided direction. Their effort was abetted by the intense workload of the carrier navy which kept everyone busy, and the crew needed to depend and rely on each other. On the flight deck and on the replenishment stations where the work was particularly hazardous, the only thing that mattered was competency and race was a non-issue. In the information-oriented functions like CIC, attentive supervision was desirable.

Ten days later, as *Ticonderoga* approached Subic Bay, Commander Killinger was meeting with the captain on the bridge during Cannon's watch, when someone said that the ship would be arriving at the Cubi Point carrier pier only slightly before the end of happy hour at the O Club.

Commander Hessmann, commanding officer of VA-195 and one of the most experienced strike leaders in the Pacific Fleet, was also in conference around the captain with Killinger. The three men huddled together. Apparently the meeting had something to do with air wing morale, when all of a sudden Hessmann, who was the most junior officer, was tasked to get off a message to the O Club management ordering 2500 Stingers to be purchased before happy hour prices expired. Hessmann grabbed a phone and called his squadron duty officer to get the message out.

Word spread rapidly through the officers of the ship. 2500 Stingers at happy hour prices! Imagine 2500 Stingers at ten cents apiece. It was the quantity and the shrewdness to place the order before happy hour expired that gave rise to the levity. The quantity, about 8 Stingers per officer, was outrageous, but it did the trick. For $250 the sour mood was broken. Levity prevailed, though not without some unintended consequences.

Cannon invariably exchanged duty with some other officer desperate to hit the beach on the day the ship made port. So he missed the Stinger party and the trashing of the officer's club that ensued. The next morning Captain Tarrant was summoned to the base admiral's office, was "preached to down by the riverside," and was told that all of his officers were denied the privileges of the three officers clubs in the Subic naval complex while they remained in port. Further, upon their future return to Cubi Point, *Ticonderoga's* officers could only attend an officers club if they posted a full commander as special shore patrol officer at each club. A perverse pride in being naughty boys temporarily prevailed and the air wing and ship's officers agreed to boycott the club rather than to accept the provisional conditions on their next visit to Cubi Point.

If Captain Tarrant was upset about his reprimand he never said so to anyone aboard *Ticonderoga*. Nevertheless the word went out that nothing less than good behavior would be tolerated and the next officer who stepped out of line on the beach would find himself in hack for every in-port period between here and San Diego.

In contrast to the crew's morale when leaving the Tonkin Gulf, morale was high as the ship left Cubi Point for Hong Kong. Everybody on board was excited. If one had been there before, one was overjoyed to return. If one hadn't been there, the scuttlebutt about the ship created high expectations.

At Point Oscar, the carrier met the six screening ships. A destroyer leader or frigate, a modernized Gearing class destroyers (FRAM II), two Fletcher class destroyers including *Fletcher* herself, DD-445, and two Dealey class destroyer-escorts.

Cannon's watch team had the 1200-1600 watch with a 1400 recovery of four aircraft that were coming in from Cubi Point after maintenance, an F-8 Crusader, two A-4 Skyhawks, and the ship's COD which was bringing mail.

The ships formed what was technically known as a 5 Charlie screen which meant 5 ships were arrayed in a fan-shaped screen separated by the effective sonar range in front of the carrier. The destroyer leader, within which the screen commander rode, was in the center. To her starboard hand was a Gearing class destroyer, to port was *USS Fletcher* and the destroyer-escorts were on opposite wings of the screen. *USS Nicholas* DD-499, the other *Fletcher* class destroyer, was assigned plane guard for the recovery and followed in *Ticonderoga's* wake 1000 yards astern. *Ticonderoga* was formation guide. The ships fell into formation smartly and proceeded on a northwestern course at 20 knots for Hong Kong some 800 nautical miles away until *Ticonderoga* needed to turn to Foxtrot Corpen for the recovery.

Cannon's bridge team was now made up of Ensign Luis Reposa, and Ensign Chase. Ned Chase was a brilliant officer and had become a kind of trophy for the Second Division boatswains. The refined Harvard graduate from several generations of Bostonians had a wry sense of humor and impeccable manners that stood in extreme contrast to the men under him. The bosuns, like the snipes, were known to be a rough bunch. Like Cannon he was tall and bright, but his experience on the bridge had been shallow, and he had not been pushed and given responsibility in the way that Cannon trained his team.

In contrast, Luis Reposa had fish oil in his veins and came from generations of Portuguese fishermen. He was an instinctive, natural seaman. Although junior to Chase by date of rank, he was ahead of Chase in meaningful experience and was an excellent bridge officer. Cannon had a special affection for Reposa. Of the three officers, only Reposa had committed himself to a naval career, and Cannon wanted to do everything he could to qualify him for Officer of the Deck Underway. Much in the way that Pebbles had managed him, he gave every reasonable responsibility possible to Reposa and stretched him. Cannon had spoken to the navigator and asked him to list Reposa as the JOOD.

About 1300, the bridge team started to see the tops of a series of small dark clouds on the horizon to the southwest in the direction of Foxtrot Corpen. Cannon asked Chase to check the radar for weather. Chase saw nothing.

"Increase the range on your radar scope," said Cannon firmly. Chase wound the scope's range out to 40 nm, well beyond the range of the SPS-10 surface search radar.

"Still nothing, sir."

Cannon got on the 1MC squawk box to CIC. "Combat, Bridge."

"Combat, aye, sir."

"Check for weather on your air search radar to the southwest and advise, please."

"Aye, aye, sir." Combat did not respond for several minutes so Cannon called Combat again on the 1MC.

"Combat, Bridge, what do you have for me?"

"Uh, sir, uh, the SPS-43 is down, sir."

"Down?"

"Yes, sir."

"Okay have the officer of the watch call me on the phone and explain why it took five minutes for you to tell the bridge that you were down." The phone rang promptly. The voice at the other end belonged to Ensign Brestovansky.

"Mr. Cannon, it's Ed Brestovansky…"

"Ah forget it Bresty," interrupted Cannon. "Just meet me in the wardroom after the watch." After a hard line period and a very deserving R and R period in Hong Kong, it became apparent that the first string had been pulled out around the ship for a rest. Players were coming in off the bench in relief to gain seasoning.

"Yes, sir." Cannon went over to the 5MC squawk box.

"PriFly, Bridge." There was no answer. "Primary, Bridge," Cannon repeated. Several seconds later a slightly flustered aviation boatswain mate second class, responded.

"Primary, aye, sir."

"Is the Air Boss around?"

"No, sir. The Assistant Air Boss will handle the recovery, sir." More of the same, thought Cannon, the first string was being given a rest.

"Where is he?"

"I don't know, sir. He hasn't come to Primary yet, sir, but I will find out, sir."

"Okay have him call me, Mr. Cannon, OOD on the bridge ASAP."

"Mr. Cannon. Yes, sir."

"Ned," that was one sign that one had made the cut with Cannon as a bridge officer, being addressed by one's first name on the bridge, "let me know as soon as that weather paints on the scope. Track it for course, speed, CPA (closest point of approach). Assume we'll be on fox corpen, 240 at 20 knots at time 1358. Get Combat to assist you and maintain a track. And Ned, have signals handy for a corpen to fox corpen and alternatively for detaching the screen and letting them steam independently. I'm very afraid there is a damn good chance that we're going to have serious weather over the ship at recovery."

"Aye, aye, sir." Until that moment neither Reposa nor Chase took in the potential gravity of the situation.

The Assistant Air Boss called back. "Mr. Cannon, Commander Handy, sir, how can I help you, sir?"

"Commander Handy, if you will look to the southwest right where we are going to head on fox corpen, sir, it looks like we have multiple cells, you can just see the tops, of a hellacious squall line, sir…." Chase signaled Cannon with one hand and pointed to the scope with the other.

"We have the leading edge of the weather, sir." Cannon nodded.

"Do we have any flex in the recovery time, sir?" asked the OOD.

"Let me see," thinking out loud, "the aircraft have already left the beach for the ship. We don't have any tankers airborne. I'd say no."

"Are you sure, sir?"

"Yes, I'm fairly sure." *Fairly sure,* wasn't exactly a crisp conclusion, thought Cannon. Cannon then called Meteorology and asked them what they knew. *Ticonderoga was* hundreds of miles if not thousands from friendly weather information. Meteorology had nothing to add to the radar plot.

"Ned, do you have a CPA yet?"

"Yes, sir. Sorry, it will be right overhead at 1400."

"I'm not going to be half as sorry as those pilots." Cannon reached for the phone and called the captain in his at-sea cabin. "Captain, we have a challenging situation. We have what looks like a serious squall line that we will be passing through just as we begin recovery at 1400, sir. I expect convective storms, possibly embedded thunderstorms, wind shear and having to carry left rudder to keep the wind down the deck, sir." Cannon was crisp.

"Crap!" Captain Tarrant was emphatically crisp.

Cannon resumed. "The assistant air boss doesn't think we can afford to delay the recovery because he has no way to get a tanker airborne."

"I'll come directly to the bridge."

"Yes, sir." Cannon hung up and seconds later the captain appeared on the bridge and immediately dialed the assistant air boss on the phone and discussed the situation with him. Tarrant was angered. He slammed the phone down and directed Cannon, "Prepare for recovery as scheduled."

"Aye, aye, sir." Then Captain Tarrant turned to Cannon.

"Do your best to keep the wind down the deck. Worry less about air speed, just eliminate the cross-wind factor. Those boys see that weather up there. They know what they're in for. If we can keep the wind down the deck, I think we'll be alright." It proved to be excellent direction. Cannon had been trying to resolve that very trade-off and welcomed the Captain's advice.

"Yes, sir."

"Mr. Cannon, I'd like you to have the conn." Apparently the captain wasn't yet sold on Cannon's watch organization.

"Yes, sir." Cannon stepped towards Reposa. "I need to take the conn."

"I heard." Reposa announced, "Lieutenant J. G. Cannon has the conn."

"Lieutenant J. G. Cannon has the conn, aye." Cannon glanced at the chronometer which read 1345. Cannon would have preferred to have had Reposa on the conn and to be free to manage the watch without the burden of giving detailed steering and engine instructions and waiting for the helmsman's response to ensure that orders where being executed properly.

Conning was the perfect position for a JOOD. He continued to believe most officers, including Captain Tarrant, confused control of the helm with optimal ship management, and did not consider the benefits of effective division of labor for managing *Ticonderoga* and assigned ships under her tactical command.

"Lou, put FOXTROT CORPEN 245 TACK 20 TACK 245 CORPEN, SPEED 15, execute to follow in the air please."

Reposa complied using PriTac and the task group call sign, Truculence. Each ship acknowledged the signal in alphabetical order of their call signs. Then he went to the 5MC and told the signal bridge to "Dip Foxtrot." At 1348, Cannon told Reposa to execute the signal. Reposa used the task group call sign.

"Truculence this is Panther, 245 CORPEN TACK SPEED 15, Stand by… Execute." Again he spoke to Signals on the 5MC. "Two-block Foxtrot."

Cannon gave the rudder order, "Left 10 degrees rudder."

"Left 10 degrees rudder, aye sir. My rudder is left 10 degrees, sir."

"Very well, change speed to 15 knots."

"Sir, 15 knots are indicated, sir."

"Very well." The three bridge officers watched the destroyers very carefully to confirm that they all turned left which they did as *Ticonderoga* started to swing left. They could clearly see the squall line approaching. First the Dealey class destroyer on the distant port wing disappeared in the heavy rain, then *Fletcher*, then the destroyer leader. As *Ticonderoga* steadied up on Foxtrot Corpen, she entered the squall line. Wind-driven, torrential rain made it virtually impossible for the bridge officers to see the bow of the ship. The sound of heavy rain drops drummed on the bridge overhead, and they were driven against the windshield. Rain came in heavy sheets and lashed the ship and the men exposed on the flight deck. These were dangerous flying conditions, and things became immediately worse.

Chase screamed out, "Sir, *Fletcher* is dropping out of station, rapidly! Range 3900 yards."

Simultaneously, the 1MC squawk box barked with alarm, "Bridge, Combat… *Fletcher* is DIW (dead in the water) at 3800 yards, sir." Like Cannon, Reposa's mind was still running ahead of the problem. He crossed to the 1MC and told Combat.

"Mark *Fletcher's* datum on the DRT."

"The DRT is down for maintenance, too, sir."

"Bob, she looks like she is DIW," Chase spoke. "Shit, she is dropping into the sea return." Chase rarely used profanity. Captain Tarrant became alarmed.

"Skyhawk in the groove," blared the 5MC from PriFly. The first A-4 was close-in on final approach with visibility below minimum ceiling and distance. The wind indicator showed 340 degrees at 45 knots. Cannon ordered 15 degrees left rudder, but the wind was not coming back to 350.

"Increase your rudder to left 20 degrees."

"Sir, my rudder is left 20 degrees."

Cannon stepped over to the 5MC. "Primary I'll be carrying a helluva lot of left rudder in these cells until we get behind the squalls."

"Primary, aye." The wind indicator started moving right towards 350 and indicated 50 knots of wind velocity. He was carrying constant 20 degrees of left rudder to keep the wind down the deck. This required the pilot to make a constantly descending left turn to land on a constantly turning ship in substantially reduced visibility, and it presented Cannon with another very serious problem. He was steering *Ticonderoga* directly into the last known position of *Fletcher*.

Cannon grabbed the phone mike for PriTac and dropped all tactical call signs and sent everything in the clear. "All Truculence ships, immediate execute SPEED 10, I say again, SPEED 10, stand by… execute.

He handed the PriTac phone microphone to Reposa. "Louie, tell *Fletcher*, in the clear, to light off her Grimes light and tell us the color.

"*Fletcher* this is *Ticonderoga*," Reposa dropped the call signs as directed, "Turn on your Grimes light immediately and interrogative color." *Fletcher* did not answer. Cannon went over to the 1MC and asked Combat if they had *Fletcher* on the CI net, combat information net. The answer was negative. She hadn't responded for several minutes.

Reposa then added "Make sure the lookouts sing out with accuracy if they see her." Reposa was adding value. It was clear that he not only understood Cannon's intentions, he could think with him and add value. He became extraordinarily valuable in this crisis management situation.

"Louie, keep sending in the blind this is an emergency, give her our rudder and engine orders. Maybe she can receive only."

"I doubt it sir, if she doesn't respond on the CI net. I think she has had a massive power plant failure, sir."

"*Fletcher* is in the sea return, sir, at 350 relative, 1700 yards, still DIW, sir." Given the reduced visibility and *Ticonderoga's* almost constant turning and speed changes the error factor in a dead-reckoning plot made an accurate DR virtually impossible and now she was in the sea return of *Ticonderoga's* radar. *Fletcher* could not be distinguished from the radar echoes coming off the waves and the sea. They had no real idea where *Fletcher* was except that they knew she was ahead of them... somewhere... and probably perilously close.

Cannon was straining under the mental overload and doing his best to exude confidence. "Very well. Boats, sound emergency signals. 5 short blasts. Pause 10 seconds, give me a continuous set of emergency blasts until I tell you to stop."

"Aye, aye, sir."

"When you pause between series, pass to all hands, "Rig for collision."

"Aye, aye sir."

"If we collide with *Fletcher* we are going to general quarters. Don't wait for an order from me."

"Bosun Mate, aye, sir." The ship's horn was now blasting a series of very loud emergency blasts. The cacophony on the bridge was incredible.

Cannon shouted, "Captain, I'm increasing my rudder to left 30 degrees to avoid *Fletcher*. We need a wave off, sir."

Tarrant grabbed the phone to PriFly. "Give him a go round. We've got risk of collision with a destroyer. *Ticonderoga was* slowing to 10 knots but she was heeling in excess of 10 degrees.

Either the A-4 never got the word or the pilot decided he wasn't going around. The A-4 dove for the heeling deck, hit it hard, the hook skipped over the third wire and miraculously caught the fourth wire.

"Louie, check the starboard side for *Fletcher*. If I don't hit her with the bow I may hit her with the starboard quarter. I'll need to shift my helm." Reposa moved quickly to the starboard wing of the bridge.

Cannon grabbed PriTac, "*Nicholas* this is *Ticonderoga*, recommend that you come left inside my wake to avoid *Fletcher*." Cannon thought that it was possible that *Ticonderoga* could miss *Fletcher* just to have *Nicholas* strike her. *Nicholas* would be having virtually the same difficulties locating *Fletcher* visually and in the sea return of her radar.

"This is *Nicholas*, wilco, my rudder is left, sir." The rain was beginning to moderate and visibility was improving to 200 yards or so.

'Very well, *Ticonderoga* out."

"Bob" Reposa shouted at the top of his lungs, "*Fletcher*, *Fletcher*, close aboard, close aboard, 020 relative. Shift your helm. Shift you helm, now, now, now!" *Fletcher* was now off *Ticonderoga's* starboard bow. They could only make out her superstructure. Her hull was partly in the blind spot of *Ticonderoga's* bow and now could be struck by *Ticonderoga's* starboard side like the rear end of a weathervane as *Ticonderoga* turned left about her pivot point.

"Helmsman, shift your helm, Right emergency full rudder."

Tarrant was on the phone to PriFly, "Wave off, wave off, wave off, dammit wave off or I'll have his damn wings." The sound of an A-4 applying full military power passed overhead as *Ticonderoga* checked her swing to port and starting coming back to the right.

"Sir, my rudder is emergency full, right, sir."

"Where is she Lou?" Cannon heard the helmsman but didn't have time to respond."

"50 yards abeam the number three elevator. It's going to be close."

"Aspect?"

Just as the helmsman was trained, until acknowledged, he repeated, "Sir, my rudder is emergency full, right, sir."

"She's showing her port side to... Her stern is closer in... Our rudder is biting... our stern is moving left... We're opening.... We're gonna miss... We're clear! We're clear! Thank God. We are clear."

Cannon, fully aware that he still had aircraft to recover, immediately started the ship back towards Foxtrot Corpen, "Left 30 degrees rudder to new course two zero zero." There remained three aircraft without a refueling option to recover.

"Sir, my rudder is left 30 degrees. I'm coming left to new course two zero zero."

"Lou, on PriTac advise the formation we are returning to fox corpen in the clear." Cannon squeezed in a response to the helmsman. "Very well, steady up on new course two zero zero."

"New course two zero zero, aye, sir."

"Got it." Reposa gave an unmistakably clear but unmilitary response.

"Captain, I recommend that we detach the screen now and let them steam independently. We want them the hell out of the way when we have to come right on the backside of the squall line so we don't steam through them," advised Cannon.

"Do it."

"Lou, in the clear all ships except *Nicholas*, repeat except *Nicholas*, screen commander take tactical command of your ships and steam independently for destination. On *Nicholas*, KILO ROMEO ONE TACK YANKEE WHISKEY ONE." Cannon knew about 30 signals from memory. He automatically "thought signals" and unconsciously lapsed into signal speak.

"Bosun, cease all sound signals. Pass secure from Collision Quarters."

"Aye, aye, sir." The cacophony ceased, near chaotic conditions began to subside and normalcy was beginning to return on the bridge.

Reposa repeated the instructions, and then added "Transmit your steaming instructions, then minimize this circuit." Continuing in the clear "*Nicholas*, I am taking you under tactical command, follow in my wake." Reposa knew the signal and gave it in the clear.

The screen commander rogered. He detached the starboard wing Dealey class destroyer escort to stay with *Fletcher* and formed a simple column astern and set course for Hong Kong with three ships.

Meanwhile *Ticonderoga* was now on the backside of the squall line. The rain had almost entirely tailed off, visibility was improving rapidly and the sun was beginning here and there to dart through the remaining clouds. Cannon now chased the wind to the right and increased speed to 20 knots to bring the wind down the deck at 350 at 30 knots. He carried right 10 degrees rudder through the rest of the recovery.

The second A-4 landed anti-climatically as did the F-8 and the COD. They recovered the plane guard helo and turned for Hong Kong at 25 knots with *Nicholas* in their wake. To the east the sky was black from the squall, and to the northwest, their course for Hong Kong, the sea gave no sign of the terror that they had just steamed through. It was placid and accurately reflected the ocean's name—Pacific.

Cannon gave Reposa the conn and his hands began to shake involuntarily. They shook for about five minutes. Captain Tarrant gave the team a profoundly grateful, "Well done" and summoned the Assistant Air Boss to the bridge. Tarrant virtually interrogated Handy. "Who was responsible for the air plan? Why no tanker? Not even a buddy tanker? Why couldn't one of the A-4s have been configured as a buddy tanker? Why couldn't we take a 15 minute delay in recovery?" Why no contingency plan? Et cetera."

Handy lacked for good answers.

Captain Tarrant finished the dressing down by saying, "Previous, prior, proper planning, prevents, piss-poor performance. We're just damn lucky that we didn't lose a pilot today and that we didn't collide with *Fletcher*. Build Murphy's law into every air plan in the future, do you understand me?"

"Aye, aye, sir."

Tarrant started to ease off. "Awright, go on, get out of here," he said with lowered volume but with decided disgust.

A chastened Commander Handy shot a glance at Cannon, "Yes, sir. Thank you, sir." Cannon's expression suggested to Handy the conversation with Captain Tarrant would be held in confidence. Handy left the bridge followed by Tarrant. Tarrant paused and put his hand on Cannon's shoulder. "Good job."

"Thank you, sir. I think the pilot house might like to hear that from you, too, sir."

"Yes, of course." Captain Tarrant stopped by the pilot house with Cannon standing behind him and complimented the Bosun and his watch team for their flawless performance, and then left for his at-sea cabin.

Cannon spoke. "Gentlemen, as far as you are concerned that conversation between Commander Handy and the captain never happened. Bear in mind, Murphy's law can be squared. You both were magnificent. Helluva a fine job. Bravo Zulu. And Lou, thanks for the rudder commands when *Fletcher* was passing down our starboard side."

"Sorry, sir. They should have been recommendations."

"Forget that. The point is you know how to handle this ship and you called it right. Damn fine effort. Couldn't have done it without you."

"Thank you, sir."

Cannon stepped over to one of the pilot house portholes, "Boats, give me the full name, rank and rating of everyone in your watch team. One more time to you, to the helmsman, to the quartermaster of the watch, and to the alternate helmsman, "Four-Oh. Bravo Zulu, men"

Several, "Thank you, sirs," followed.

Cannon was emotionally drained. He let his watch team carry the load the rest of the watch. He sensed that this watch team was different, and today, in the crucible of a near-collision during flight operations, in extreme weather conditions, the three of them sensed they had bonded uniquely.

Cannon had not seen the navigator arrive on the bridge, although he thought he had glimpsed the navigator at the plotting station on the starboard side of the bridge clear out to allow Reposa uninhibited access to the starboard wing of the bridge. Now he stepped forward and said, "Charlie Romeo Charlie, Chase, Reposa, Cannon, that was a triple A effort. Well done, gentlemen."

"Thank you, sir." They fell silent as they steamed a steady course without surface traffic for Hong Kong. Each officer, singly, silently, began to process and reprocess what they had just gone through. The remnants of the screen were about 16 thousand yards ahead steaming at 25 knots. All ships awaited a casualty report from *Fletcher*. She would not get underway again until midnight.

Towards the end of the watch, Reposa spoke first. "You know a second time around I wonder if we could have asked the screen commander to give us *Fletcher*'s range and bearing to us?"

Cannon responded, "You mean because she wouldn't be in their sea return? Helluva 'n idea, Lou." He paused just a second, "Why the fuck didn't you mention it earlier?" That brought about an immediate response of belly laughter from the three deck officers.

Chase asked, "What was that alliterative admonition the captain used?"

"Previous, prior, plan, something," tried Reposa.

"Previous, prior, proper planning, prevents piss-poor performance. It's a Marine Corps thing," said Cannon.

"I like it. Oughtta be a navy thing," said Reposa. Chase nodded in agreement.

"Lou, tomorrow many will say that I saved *Ticonderoga*. Few will say the truth. *Fletcher* was saved by Lou Reposa. Well done again, Lou. Bravo Zulu, Bravo Zulu."

At 1930 that evening Captain Tarrant addressed the crew on the IMC. "Good evening Tico Tigers. This is the captain speaking. I want to express my sincerest thanks and convey those of ComTaskForce 77, Admiral Hastings. Admiral Hastings is a naval aviator and flew from the deck of USS *Enterprise* during World War II. I have a message from him and I would like read it to you now:

"On behalf of myself and my staff, I would like to extend my grateful appreciation and gratitude to the officers and men of *USS Ticonderoga* CVA 14 and Air Wing 19. Your return from Korea and re-entry into the Gulf of Tonkin with your aircraft has been decisive in breaking the NVA siege at Khe Sanh. You can be certain that our US Marine brothers welcomed every one of your four thousand sorties flown in their support. The intrepidity of your pilots, the extraordinarily high availability of your aircraft and the flawless operation of your ship are remarkable. *Ticonderoga* is indeed well-respected around the fleet and her performance has been peerless. *Ticonderoga* is comparable in every way to the legendary World War II *Enterprise*. Thank you, men, and well done."

Captain Tarrant resumed, "Over the last line period of 41 consecutive days at sea, beginning on Yankee Station, and then our reassignment to Korea, and followed by our return to Yankee Station, during Operation Niagara, we launched and recovered 4,123 aircraft and dropped over 6,300 tons of ordnance on targets in and around Khe Sanh where we believe some 25 to 40 thousand North Vietnamese Army troops surrounded 7500 US Marines. Air Wing 19 pilots, working with B-52 Arc Light missions out of Guam, have inflicted a serious cost upon the enemy in personnel, equipment and materiel. In the process, US aviation forces have destroyed hundreds of targets comprised of forward observation posts and command posts, POL and ammo storage areas, numerous tanks and trucks, numerous 37, 57, 81 and 100mm gun sites trained on our marines and inflicted unknown, but you can figure significant, casualties on NVA troops.

"During this time we took on fuel, stores and ammo while at sea on 52 separate occasions and in turn refueled our escorts 15 times. We have operated without a major personnel accident, knock on wood, without a major equipment casualty, and without going on water hours. Our accident rate and discipline rate are among the lowest in the fleet. Our long hours of training, preparation and dedicated professionalism are paying off.

"Today we had a situation brought about by very dangerous weather and a casualty to one of our escorts, *USS Fletcher* DD-445, where once again our training paid off. Our pilots safely brought aboard four aircraft in weather that would have temporarily shut down most civilian airfields. Bosun Mate Werner Schmidt and his watch team in the pilot house today did a superb job and his helmsman, Seaman Second Class Roosevelt Green, did an exceptional job on the helm to avoid a possible collision in the middle of a recovery. Our bridge officers handled this situation in a thoroughly professional manner and with some good luck that we may have created for ourselves. Through thorough preparation and training, we avoided what might have been a collision with serious loss of life.

"*Ticonderoga* had the right people in the cockpit, the right people in the pilot house and the right people on the bridge. But we do this every day as you know in *Ticonderoga*. Well done." Captain Tarrant paused and his tone changed before resuming.

"Next, on a lighter note, I'm very happy to say that Chaplain O will be rejoining the ship in Hong Kong, and I ask you all to give him a warm

Tico Tiger welcome when you see him. Finally, I want to compliment you. As far as I am concerned, you are the most professional crew in the US Navy, and I am extremely proud to serve with each and every one of you. You should be justly proud of yourselves. Your families should be proud of you, and Admiral Hastings is proud of you. Bravo Zulu. Enjoy a good, well-deserved liberty in Hong Kong. Thank you and good night."

Chapter 18.

Adam Smith would have loved Hong Kong. A hugely vibrant economy grew by leaps and bounds relatively unfettered by regulation. Thus, everyone pursuing his own self-interest propelled an economy and a democracy in the British Crown Colony that was the envy of the Pacific Rim. Hong Kong had the fabulously rich British and Cantonese and the wretchedly poor squatters who had sneaked in from the Peoples Republic of China to make their way up in the world in accordance with their abilities. The relatively low, thick-walled, gray Victorian style, colonial structures were giving way to the most modern, gleaming skyscrapers in the world.

Even the People's Republic of China had a huge retail shop covering an entire floor of the Ocean Terminal. Enormous quantities were displayed everywhere of marked down statuary of the recently disgraced Chairman of the People's Party, Liu Shao Chi.

The harbor bustled with activity. There was every kind of vessel imaginable from sampans and junks and luxury yachts, in quantity, to modern freighters and tankers, and men of war. The Star Ferry plied her way back and forth from the Kowloon terminal on the mainland to the island of Hong Kong. At night the city glowed in its own light and the colored signs of commerce shown brightly in neon logos atop every building.

Cannon took a room in the Mandarin Hotel on Connaught Road on the island of Hong Kong. It was a deluxe, first class hotel and affordable on a J.G.'s pay when denominated in Yankee dollars. As luck would have it, the heavens opened up for three solid days as if to provide a final drenching before the monsoon went into abeyance for another year. The clouds hung low obscuring the summit of Victoria's Peak. Cannon confined his activity to his shopping list which was by now standard for young naval officers—a Nikon camera, hi-fi tuner/amplifier, speakers, record player, and tape deck. The Cantonese shopkeepers were superb and did well by doing good and ensured that each customer had his main item and all necessary peripherals such as filters, lenses, lens covers, batteries, flash attachments, camera bags, etc. Cannon's 35mm Nikon, however, came only with Japanese language instructions. He spent the better part of an afternoon using trial and error and basic knowledge of photography figuring out how to operate the Nikon. The bulky electronic equipment was delivered directly to the Fleet Landing by the merchant and into the ship's supply officer's custody for delivery to the ship.

He telephoned Tish several times when he thought he might reach her during the day, but he missed connecting with her and fell into a lonely mood. The gray skies and nearly continuous rain reinforced this saddened mood and sense of aloneness. When he thought what her visit might have been in contrast to what was, he withdrew and felt sadder and more alone. The bustling vigor of Hong Kong rather than drawing him out served only to heighten the sense that he was an Occidental visiting Hong Kong and didn't quite belong.

After fiddling with his camera, Cannon got a coke from the mini-bar, and clicked on the television in time for the evening news. He watched a BBC news summary of the recent history of the war with President Johnson announcing that he would not run for re-election. Cannon took the repudiation as a sign of shifting public opinion towards the war. Johnson also announced the halt to all bombing north of the 19th parallel as an enticement to negotiation putting Hanoi and Haiphong and most of North Vietnam off limits. Cannon thought the North Vietnamese would see this as a sign of weakness, particularly with the protest movement gaining strength in America's streets in the spring weather, and would protract negotiations while events played to their advantage in America—exactly the opposite of Johnson's intention.

He had dinner in the Mandarin's restaurant, drank several Tsingtao beers—a remarkably good beer from Red China from a brewery originally founded by Germans in China—and returned to his room. He was lonely and bored and drank several miniatures of Scotch whisky of various brands from the mini-bar until he got a buzz on and fell into a deep sleep.

The phone rang shortly after eight the next morning. It was the CIA officer, Beebe Byrnes.

"You're difficult to track down. I thought you might return each night to the ship. It took a lot of persuasion to get your duty officer to give up the name of your hotel. He couldn't accept that I was CIA."

"Where are you calling from, Washington?"

"No, right here in Kowloon."

"Really?"

"Yes, really."

"Okay…. Well, what's up?"

"A few things. Just like your thoughts. Your point of view."

"Un-huh."

"You alright? You sound down. Not like you."

"I'm okay."

"You know, we could have warned her. We knew about Ciorrazzi. My error."

"Broke her jaw in two places."

"Ouch. Didn't know that. Just heard there was a thwarted rape attempt."

"Yeah. Couldn't join me here now."

"That's too bad. Sorry to hear that." She paused, then asked, "Well, in that case, why don't we meet for a drink and dinner? Could you meet me at The Peninsula in Kowloon, say, about six? I'll get dinner reservations for eight."

"I can do that." He replied flatly.

The guards occasionally raised animals for food and were currently feeding a pig from table scraps. Red Browne noticed an eaten corn cob lying on the ground as he was led to the latrine and kicked it to the side of the path. On the way back he bent over and picked it up and began to chew on the cob when Stalin saw him do it. Stalin started shouting and running towards Browne, and swung his rifle butt striking Browne full force on the side of the head. Browne dropped to the ground unconscious, and Stalin struck him several more times with the full force of the rifle butt before kicking him several times. Blood flowed from Browne's scalp and ear and from his nose and mouth. Vicious joined in kicking and beating Browne.

The prisoners inside the compound were ignorant of the cause of the beating, but they could hear the shouting, and Bundit could make out from the Laotian shouts the cause of the beating and whispered it to Campbell and Sekulovich.

"About corn cob. Corn cob for pig, not for Brownie."

After several convulsions that night, Browne died in Sekulovich's arms. He had been murdered by Stalin and Vicious who valued feeding a pig over his life. Campbell was saddened and escaped his sense of despair and sorrow by being philosophical.

"Mike, what sort of civilization produces such cruelty? Is there no sense of morality? Is there no moral compass? What value do they place on life?"

"They're all a fuckin' bunch of bastard communists." They both fell into silence and were subdued.

However, the effect of Red Browne's death was to further solidify the group which was now down to five.

"Should we rename ourselves FiveBro?" asked Campbell.

"Certainly not. We're SixBro, in memory of Brownie. When we make our break, Stalin is mine." Sekulovich had changed. He previously indicated that he wanted no part of killing the guards, particularly in cold blood, as he saw it that way, taking the guards by surprise. But the unjustifiable death of his friend and fellow pilot changed his position. "I want to shoot the sonuvabitch. Sadistic bastard."

Browne's murder brought about another challenge to Campbell's faith. Again he had a serious dialogue with himself. *Almighty Father, when my mother taught me the Book of Amos, she showed me how You are a moral and righteous as well as a strong and powerful god. From the prophet Hosea, we learned that You are moral and righteous and a loving god who shall come to judge the living and the dead. I believe in one god—moral, just, loving, and all powerful. But when Job, who was miserably tried, as we are now, when you gave Job over to Satan, and when Job asked You in his suffering and misery, if You were the authentic God of our faith, You answered him evasively with a question, by asking wasn't your power self-evident? It is the last time that You spoke to Your children in the Old Testament, and You did not affirm your moral and righteous character.*

I was taught that a god who may be powerful but is not just, who is not moral, is not our God. In the name of God, how was it that one of your children should die over a corn cob? Did not Browne, have not all of us, suffered enough? To what purpose does our suffering serve? What sin have we committed that justifies this cruelty? Are You saying the American intervention is unjust? Are You saying the war has gone beyond the limits of a just war? Campbell turned momentarily angry. *What message do You deliver to the communists? to the Pathet Lao?* He paused, and he contemplated his circumstances with a sense of near resignation. *Almighty Father, what more do we have to give but to die here without any sense of dignity? How Almighty Father does our dying here serve You?*

They buried Browne the next morning alongside Drang near the stream, but for several days Campbell remained disturbed and little progress was made planning for their escape.

Eventually, despite his sense that God had abandoned him, he refocused the group on Mo-deerf. He and Sekulovich pried up a board in their hut and found a way to lower themselves at night to the ground undiscovered. Subsequently they dug a hole under the perimeter fence for a man to get through and camouflaged it. Fortunately the guards did not patrol the perimeter of the fence carefully and the "rabbit hole," as they called it, remained undetected. SixBro was also unanimous about the need for water and that the breakout attempt had to wait for the monsoon. They also agreed that it was impossible to move in the jungle in the dark of night. Mo-deerf had to be a daylight operation.

Together they pieced together the practices and behavior patterns of their captors and the relative times that they spent engaged in their routines. The most significant observation was that the guards all gathered together for meals at the same time in the kitchen hut. Those on duty went to fetch their meal and return with it to their posts. Even more significantly, they left their weapons in their huts or at their posts during these times. So for about two and a half to three minutes there was an opportunity to escape. At other times, the guards randomly chose not to man the guard tower although generally the tower was manned during daylight hours.

Whether it was necessary to kill the guards or not remained undecided. Each man, except Sekulovich, had his reason be it morality, pragmatism, or a general distaste for having blood on one's hands. However, for Sekulovich, killing Stalin was a matter of justice, however, for the others, even the extreme sadism of the guards failed to offset their reluctance to plan to kill.

The matter of killing the guards was also a matter of international law which permitted executing prisoners who had killed a guard during an escape. Said another way, if their escape plan failed, the Thais, in particular, did not want to provide a cause for their own execution. But they were not unanimous on this point, and Sekulovich continued to feel vengeful and consistently identified Stalin for retribution while Campbell resisted the thought and posed pragmatic considerations. He allowed it may be necessary to shoot the guards if they resisted, moreover, he argued that the sounds of gunfire could bring irregulars or Laotian soldiers to the prison. He also emphasized that they needed to prevent any of the guards from escaping to the village.

So they planned to capture the guards and imprison them in the stocks and manacles, and search for weapons and food stocks, and hold the camp while trying to signal some of the aircraft that flew overhead. The back up plan was to make their way to the stream which they believe flowed into a river which they expected to be swollen by the monsoon rains and steal a boat or make a raft and follow the stream to Thailand or South Vietnam.

The following morning Sekulovich and Bundit got into an argument over the matter of shooting or not shooting the guards. They were loud and animated and Campbell became disturbed that the loose cohesion in the group brought about by Browne's murder was being ruptured, and although they argued in English, he was concerned that the argument would be a cause for suspicion and more oversight by the guards. Bundit refused to participate if the guards were to be shot, and Sekulovich was making a somewhat irrelevant point that if it became necessary to shoot them, they must do it, and if that happened, they deserved it. Campbell finally stepped between the two men and ended the argument.

"Slimy sonuvabitch is always fraternizing with the guards. Brownie allowed it. Thought it might be useful, but I never trusted the little bastard. Always seemed to have an inventory shrinkage problem when he was loading the airplane… Doesn't want us to kill Brownie's murderers. Give me a break!"

"We need him, Mike. We're now outnumbered seven to five. Let's keep the group together."

"Yeah, yeah. I know. You're right. I just don't trust the guy." They didn't speak for several minutes as they stood side by side watching the guards through a peep hole in the bamboo, stockade fence. Sekulovich broke the silence. "Bob, have you thought about the monsoon weather?" Pilots constantly think about weather, but other than to think of the monsoon as a source of essential water, Campbell had not.

"How so?"

"Well, the skies will be almost certainly overcast with low ceilings. Any low flier will have poor slant range visibility if they are on a search. There are breaks of sunshine, but they are hard to rely on. We need more than a signal mirror."

"Hmm. Damn, you're right. I was counting on finding something shiny in the kitchen hut to use as a mirror."

"Our chances of being seen are pretty slim. Might have to hold the compound for a long time. Manage the prisoners, et cetera."

"Are you suggesting that the back up plan, become the main plan?"

"Think so. Don't you?" Campbell did not answer. These were indeed factors that he had not considered. "Bob, another thing…"

"Yeah, Mike?"

"I think we have to be careful, what we share with the Asians, especially the little bastard, about our escape plan."

"You mean if they're captured?"

"Yes. Limit it to the break out. That's all."

"That all seems pretty reasonable. I guess you and Red had a lot of time to think about these issues."

"Yeah… and we failed once, and some of these problems are why we didn't want to try again. We thought the war would end by now."

"Not going to end soon enough for us, Mike." There was a long silence, and they both gave a thought to the chances of not dying even if they succeeded in breaking out of the prison.

Campbell and Sekulovich were beginning to build a close bond. Before, when Browne was alive, Campbell had always spoken to Browne who had been the pilot in command of the Air America crew. Now he planned and spoke directly with Sekulovich, and he was hearing things from Sekulovich that Browne might have passed along. These were legitimate planning issues that Browne had been silent about. He wondered if Browne's commitment had been full and complete. Maybe Sekulovich had been tentative, too, but Browne's death seemed to resolve any lingering doubts among the blood brothers of SixBro and the necessity of escape. Sooner or later they had come to believe they would all die if they remained prisoners, either from disease like Drang, or violently like Red Browne.

"Mike, we need to make a model of the compound and figure out how five men can get the jump on seven around mealtime. We need to know where all of the weapons are."

"Been thinking about that, too. From sticks and stones, small pebbles that we can brush away when the guards enter the hut." He stopped then he recalled another point that he wanted to make. "Bob, when the monsoon comes you have intermittent drenching downpours. Sometimes the cells have high velocity surface winds. Sound will not carry far through the jungle. It will be slippery and muddy, but our tracks will be washed away, too."

"IFR, all the way. Instrument flight rules. Mike wouldn't it be great to climb into a cockpit one more time. To be free and up in the air again. I pray to Jesus that it will happen."

"Amen."

"Okay, Mike, let's you and I have a prototype plan by tomorrow. Bundit and Thanawat know how to handle a weapon."

Cannon took the Star ferry over to Kowloon. The rain let up, and he walked the short distance on Salisbury Road to The Peninsula Hotel under an umbrella that he had picked up at his hotel lobby. During monsoon season there were ubiquitous umbrellas that one may borrow and leave from place to place throughout the Crown Colony.

The Peninsula was a large hotel of several stories built of gray stone and furnished in the British colonial style. He walked into a large cocktail lounge which could seat well over a hundred people at small tables. Across the back of the room, a bar ran the width of the room. Tens of people were gathered in the lounge, and the din of conversation was loud. The background noise made it difficult to overhear and record conversations and consequently made the lounge a preferable place for intelligence officers to meet.

He scanned the room and saw Mrs. Byrnes at a table along the wall. She waved discreetly towards him. Beebe Byrnes was a very attractive widow who was three to four years his senior. He had met with her on several occasions, but never personally, and she always wore a dark gray or blue suit with a white blouse and minimum make-up. As he approached her, she stood up and greeted him. Immediately he saw that she was different. Tanned, trimmer, her dirty blond hair highlighted, parted and pulled back behind one ear. She was wearing a florid, teal, silk print cheongsam with matching teal, silk heels, appointed with a gold necklace and matching gold bracelet and earrings. She was fully but tastefully made up—all very Asian in style. Neither the words 'attractive,' nor 'very attractive' applied to Beebe Byrnes tonight. Beautiful with a heavy dose of sex appeal were entirely accurate. All of it was reinforced with a hint of Shalimar from Givenchy that stimulated Robert Cannon's full range of senses.

"Hello, Beebe, so nice to see you again."

"Hello, Bobby." She picked the name up after Captain Pebbles had addressed him that way at their luncheon in Washington.

"Uh, uh. Its Robert or Bob…"

"Bobby, aren't we close friends by now… like Pebbles?" She was flirting.

"Beebe, you are always extracting something from me."

"I know, but Bobby seems like such a small price to pay for dinner in Hong Kong." She smiled teasingly at him.

"Never in front of a third party."

"Bobby, you have that so adorable mixture of youthful energy and a mature mind." She embarrassed him.

"Thank you, Beebe. I had forgotten that our professional relationship was always characterized by jaunty repartee. I can't help but notice that you are smashingly beautiful tonight."

"You have always noticed me, Bob. Even told me the second time we met that I needed to drop a few, and you noticed me again when I did, and said so."

"You have the memory of a Shakespearean actress, Beebe."

"All spooks do, Bobby. Especially when they are with a person of interest. It comes with the breed."

A Cantonese waiter arrived to take their order.

"Martini, please, Gordon's or Beefeater's with Noilly Prat vermouth, straight up."

"Yes, madam. And you, sir?"

"The same please, but on the rocks with three olives."

"Very good, sir."

Cannon changed the subject. Beebe was dangerously attractive to him, and he sensed that she knew it. The separated and widowed were lonely and vulnerable in Hong Kong. "What news do you have from Pebbles?"

"Yes. I saw him recently at a cocktail party. I told him I would see you, and he asked me to have you call him when you get back in September. He mentioned it twice."

"Hmm. What do you think his chances are for rear admiral?"

"Well, he has at least another year to go for early selection, but from what I hear, the CNO likes him a lot, and what the Chief of Naval Operations likes, he usually gets. Word around the agency is that the CNO has a kitchen cabinet of a handful of captains and admirals and Robert Pebbles is part of it. I'd bet on it. Maybe the whole farm."

"Hmm."

"You know, he's extremely fond of you, Bob. The man has three daughters, and you're his adopted son. You have to figure he'll make it to the three or four star level. If you played your cards professionally, he could bring you right up behind him. He's told me you are an unrecruitable talent. He's as much said that no one would have to compromise their standards to move you along...uh, that's provided you don't piss anybody off with that temper of yours."

The waiter brought the martinis to the table and carefully took them from the tray and placed them on the table after providing them with cocktail napkins. Beebe picked up her stemmed glass, looked into Robert Cannon's steel gray eyes, and said, "Here's mud in your eye, sailor."

"A votre sante," he responded, and the glasses clinked lightly. He took a sip of the ice cold martini and savored the slight sting of gin. "So, what's new with you, Beebe?"

"Oh, I'm glad you asked, Robert. I've been accepted into Georgetown's doctoral program for security studies. The agency has supported my application and will mostly fund it. We're working out a change of assignments. Less time in the field; more time at Langley; more analytical work."

"Excellent. As I recall you hold a master's in Russian from Penn. Will this build on that?

"Your memory isn't too bad either. Yes, it will. I'll be able to read Russian documents in the original. I'm interested in arms control. Specifically the control or mutual reduction of nuclear weapon stockpiles. I've been speaking with John Palfrey, former head of the Atomic Energy Commission. He's very thoughtful…nerdy, but very helpful and supportive." She sipped from her stemmed glass. "A little business, Bob?"

"Yes. Go ahead."

"We're interested in a one, Commander James Spencer-Davies, Royal Navy. Do you know him?"

"Not to my knowledge, should I?"

"He toured your ship the last day in Singapore."

"Yes?"

"Including CIC."

"Yes?"

"You were the Operations Department Duty Officer when he made his tour."

"Uh-oh. I'm going to be gigged here."

"Did anybody say anything about him to you?"

"Not to my knowledge. What's the reason for your interest?"

"You can use your imagination, but play along. Allow me to ask the questions."

"Sure. Go ahead."

"You're maturing, Bobby. Last year you would have given me a smart aleck remark."

"You're pressing your luck, beautiful." He surprised himself with how easily the last word slipped out.

"Beautiful? The gin must be getting to you, Bobby." She did not pursue the opening and stayed with business. "He's with British intelligence. He was formerly a junior naval officer. Today his cover is Commander, R.N., attached to the Royal Naval Base, Singapore."

"Yes."

"He invited three of your shipmates to a picnic on a Royal Navy yacht in the Straits of Jahore. On the yacht were four women."

"That's intriguing."

"Spencer-Davies' wife, two Caucasian ex-pats, and a Eurasian prostitute."

"Great first chapter. Possible double agent. Helluva a novel."

"What can you tell me about Messrs Chase, Smythe, and Reposa?"

"Uh-huh. Well, Smythe, I don't know him well. He's a J.O. in Communications. CR Division Officer, I believe—would know our gear well; would see a lot of traffic. Probably has cryptographic responsibilities. Had Anejo Goodies with him in the pool one afternoon in Cubi. Married, a kid on the way. Mid-westerners, both from Omaha. Engineering degree. Both went to the university in Lincoln. He's a little shy. Hasn't travelled the world much. Unsophisticated."

"Any reason to suspect his loyalty?"

"No."

"Can you affirm his loyalty?"

"No."

"Okay, what about Chase?"

"Chase and Reposa are on my watch team right now. Steamed up here from Cubi with them. Both excellent officers. I think I can affirm their loyalty."

"Good, okay then. So what if I told you, Chase and Reposa exchanged light conversation and pleasantries with the English women and returned to the ship that night."

"Uh-huh. Yes. Well, that would be a shame, wouldn't it?" Byrnes ignored his comment.

"And Smythe went home with the prostitute."

"Hmm."

"And remained shacked up with her for two more days."

"I guess Nebraskan corn makes for strong men."

"Surely. And it was all expenses prepaid."

"Now this plot is beginning to develop."

"Still don't recollect anything about Spencer-Davies?"

"I thought those hyphenated names were only for women who fawned over Prince Chuckie or British character actors."

"Very funny."

"Sorry, no."

"So the Officer of the Deck never called you, or sent his messenger after you and advised you that Commander Spencer-Davies was on the quarterdeck? Never advised you that the commander claimed to have been invited aboard by the Ops Duty Officer?"

"Not that I recollect."

"You're not in a courtroom. Yes, or no, do you remember being notified about Spencer-Davies?"

"No."

"Good. We don't think you were."

"What do you know?"

"Here's what I can tell you. This goes no further. Spencer-Davies pulled the same act on a comm officer off a DLG two months ago. Married. Two children. He pays the rent on the prostitute's apartment and has it bugged and wired for video cameras."

"Hmm." Cannon raised his eyebrow, took a final sip of his martini, rattled the ice cubes in his glass, and chewed on an olive.

"Now, there is nothing on your ship, a World War II, non-computerized, non-naval tactical data system ship that we haven't shared with the Royal Navy."

"True, except for state of the art communications—content and technology. The attack carriers are central to the Navy's responsibilities in SIOP."

"True, too…. The Geylang tootsie was given her target by name. And that name was the name of the in-port OOD that day, Lieutenant junior grade Smythe, United States Navy. Keep an eye on him for me, please."

"Aye, aye, ma'am." It was not an acquiescence. It was said with a sarcastic tone to blow off her request.

"Like to know if he's absent from the ship for long periods in port."

"C'mon, I'm not getting into this kind of crap."

"Go about your regular business. But, you know, if you're in the same officer boat coming back from the beach, engage him in conversation for me. That sort of thing." Cannon rolled his eyes.

Back at Langley, Byrnes' recorded interview transcripts with Cannon were always read with interest, and she was encouraged to maintain and develop the relationship for the intrinsic thoughts Cannon provided, but he was also seen as a comer and someone who might be relied upon in the future to befriend the agency through the periodic travails of Washington politics. Appropriately the current topic of interest was the wisdom and the necessity of the war, with the added twist of Cronkite's influence and LBJ's election withdrawal.

Cannon read the headline stories in the *South China Morning Post* and *Stars and Stripes*. He considered the latter a generally reliable source. It squared with what he subsequently read when *Time* and *Newsweek* arrived the following week. *Stars and Stripes* might be slightly more balanced on the military picture, although it was wanting on political news.

"Bob, what are your thoughts to end the war in Indo-China?" asked Byrnes.

"Beebe, let's not get started on a lot of theoretical speculation about Southeast Asia, Europe and containing the Soviet Union. It's all in my reading list somewhere. You don't need to waste tape on a junior naval officer."

"You sell yourself short, Bobby. Your thoughts are always well-considered and on, what I will call, the leading pragmatic edge of the debate. You're well-read and you are a naval officer of the line. Yes, we can collect and synthesize the thoughts of academia, but as the World War II generation leaves the scene, none of the replacement company of actors has gone to sea. None of them have the active-experiencing engagement with the military and the Soviets and their proxies on their curricula vitae."

"Thanks for the flattery."

"Bob, it's a genuine request. The agency has an interest in ending the war. If there is a preferred course of action, the agency needs to find the evidence or the most probable arguments to confirm or deny it. And keep yourself in perspective, dearie. In the case of a Soviet submarine collision with an American destroyer, we might have half a dozen people with a thoughtful point of view. In the case of the war in Southeast Asia, it's several thousand." She pulled from her evening purse what appeared to be a silver cigarette case and Zippo lighter. "Bob, do you mind?"

He shook his head, "No." Mrs. Byrnes initially wore a hidden microphone when they first met in Hamburg and on subsequent occasions, but by now they had come to an open and easy understanding that his words were being recorded.

"The cigarette case has a low-pick up mike; the Zippo is for added deception. It's real." She placed them next to his martini glass, and called the waiter over for another round of martinis.

"Very charming. I'd like a set for Christmas. Okay. I'll add to your sample size."

"Thank you, Bob."

"Do you know that I know one of your sharpest people in Southeast Asia? Knew him in college. Near brilliant intellect. Smarter than I. He's working these issues full time out of the embassy in Saigon. What's his perspective?"

"Yes, we figure you probably know him. We have his assessments. We need yours."

"Love to talk to him. Alright. Let's make this simple. There are two possible outcomes. We concede with some kind of artful fig leaf, or the North Vietnamese concede with a face-saving fig leaf."

Cannon continued, "It has belatedly occurred to me what it took to end the war in Germany and Japan. It was right there, being ignored, or perhaps, denied. Right there, staring me in the face. To make the North Vietnamese concede we need to be able to stand the sight of blood. That is to say, we need to turn up the level of violence to something like Hamburg and Dresden fire bomb levels, or raids over Tokyo, and take the criticism from Hanoi Jane, and Ramsey Clark... from Wayne Morse, Bill Fulbright, Gene McCarthy. You need to politically withstand the demonstrations in the streets. More lately, that means dealing with *The New York Times, The Washington Post*, and Walter Cronkite."

"Unh-huh."

"You need to salve your consciences that we are still fighting a justifiable war and that the death and destruction in North Vietnam would be within the limits of a just war. You need to be able to look yourself in the mirror when the casualty reports come in and believe that the ends justify the means. It's the Truman decision...Hiroshima, Nagasaki... without nuclear weapons."

"Yes...and the other option."

"That doesn't seem to interest you, Beebe. Maybe you can't stand the sight of blood, either."

"C'mon, Bobby. Be nice. What's the other option, please."

"Okay, you're buying the drinks."

"Be nice."

"Okay. Okay. Let's take a lesson from the Achaeans. After a ten year, futile, amphibious war on the beaches of Troy—sound familiar—they grew weary, withdrew, and sailed home. So basically, the other option is strategic withdrawal. We concede, pack up and go home. Of course, we will need a fig leaf for internal political consumption. We'll need to phase the withdrawal. The fig leaf may be an American assertion that certifies

the ARVN and the Republic of Vietnam are strong enough to carry on
without our assistance on the battlefield. Of course, our allies will not accept our assertion as credible, and those alliances will be damaged. But
sufficient fog and war-weariness at home, will, of course, gain acquiescence, and the hawks will sound tiresome and end up being ignored. Sort
of like Churchill."

"You're being cynical."

"But, of course…. This was a clever Soviet diversion. The second
Asian diversion. The real struggle for democracy, at this time in the world,
is in Europe, and the real struggle for economic freedom and vitality is
over the oil fields in the Middle East. Europe has no energy. He who controls the Middle East controls Europe…controls what Hitler
wanted…controls the markets and the economies of the world. We needed
to be in Vietnam, but we let it get way, way, out of hand. Mission creep.
Way, way out of proportion to its value. We entered the game without an
acceptable exit strategy. We did not need to win this war. We needed only
to prevent the communists from winning this war… like Korea. We
needed only to buy time for the Little Dragon economies on the Pacific
Rim to reach take off. But, of course, after World War II every American
politician is mandated to say that we must end every war with an *unconditional surrender*. Unconditional surrender, that's our hubris…our folly.
Here endeth the lesson. Done. The end."

"Sounds like you have tilted against the war since we met in Washington."

"Yes, you could say conceptually I have always been against war. It's
the last choice. The king establishes the military objectives; the fighting
knights carrying them out. I'm a junior knight doing my level best to
prosecute this war successfully. I'm in it. If I were a counselor to the king,
I'd advise the king it's time, if we can claw our way to a mutually equivalent negotiating position by degrading the enemy's position at acceptable
costs…it's time to negotiate."

"Every leading state in its day found itself perpetually at war until they
went virtually bankrupt—from Athens, Rome, to the British Empire.
Rome started out with the moderate ambition of defending its seven hills
until, greed, power, ambition expanded the empire until it was perpetually
at war." He paused here before adding, "Weakness invites aggression. I
want the biggest, the most reasonably affordable stick on the planet, and to
speak in a whisper. But I doubt that is sufficient to assure a Pax Ameri-
cana. America's infinite weakness, the future of democracy and the weak-

ness of the free world, is every weak and failed state on the globe. South Vietnam is a failed state. When and where to fight. That is the role of kingship. We are going to have to learn when and where not to fight." There, he picked up his martini, swirled the gin around the ice cubes, and finished the drink in a single swallow.

"Thank you." She reached over and picked up the recorder and shut it off and put it carefully in her evening bag, saying, "That's it. Finito. I'm off duty. Now Bobby, after those somber thoughts, let's you and I have a pleasant evening together. I need to go up and get my raincoat. Let me sign the bill."

When she got up to leave, Beebe Byrnes turned heads everywhere. She filled the silk cheongsam beautifully as it clung to her trim, firm body in all the right places. Tailored, tasteful, and immensely sexy. Cannon was not oblivious to her charm as a woman.

They were the only people in the lift as it made its way to her floor. Cannon watched the floor numbers as each one lit in sequence as the car rose to its destination.

"Bob, can I ask you a question?"

"You always ask the questions, Beebe."

"There. That's it. Our conversations. Is there something else going on between us, Bobby?" It was a safe leading question which allowed each party to safely back away if they chose. "Something beyond just kidding and professionalism?" The lift came to a stop and the door opened. She took him by the arm and led him to her room. Cannon knew what it meant when a woman touched him, placed her hands on him. No one was backing away, even though he was feeling conflicted. An old lyric went through his mind. Beebe turned the key in the lock and opened the door to an enormously large, colonial style, hotel room with a king size bed. The door closed solidly behind them.

"Ah...now, where were we?" asked Beebe.

"I believe, Beebe, that you were suggesting that something has always been going on between us while we conducted professional business." Beebe approached him and put her arms around his neck.

"We're two lonely people, Bobby. We're both lonely. Let me love you a little tonight." She looked into his eyes and kissed him gently on the chin. "Let's take care of each other tonight." She kissed him again, a lingering kiss, very gently on his lips, then firmly on the mouth. He remained indecisive for a last, few moments, and then he placed his hands under her buttocks and pulled her up into him and kissed her passionately.

They made love twice before falling asleep. She had her back to him as they lay side by side. In time, she awoke and turned over to face him, awakening him. "Thank you, darling. You were wonderful. I needed that," and kissed him gently.

"Lust," he said.

"Are you quite sure, Bobby?"

"If you can't love the one you want, love the one you're with."

"Really, Bobby? I'm not so sure.... No, I sense there is more going on than pure lust between us." Cannon lay back. Guilt was beginning to creep into his mind. Defining it as lust, and denying that there was something more between them appeared to be the safer explanation. He was definitely struggling with a sense of infidelity. "Darling, take a shower while I order room service. Then I'll join you." He demurred. "Go ahead, I'll be right with you," Beebe said.

Mrs. Byrnes had not been with a man since her husband died somewhere in Southeast Asia. A Marine Corps major, who headed up the military component of a classified CIA operation, she was never given the place nor the details of his death. His body was never returned. Cannon's mind and education caught her fancy a year earlier in Hamburg, Germany, when it was suggested that she interview him. Really smart men of action like John, her former husband, like Cannon, attracted her. True, his age bothered her. He was younger than she by three or four years, and she didn't like what she knew about his fiancée. In her mind, Laetitia Martin was rich, smart, had a pretty face and was skinny. She had life too easy and protested the war which annoyed Beebe Byrnes to no end. Several times she asked herself if it weren't simple jealousy operating. Tonight she had sought him out and seduced him. She wanted him, and she wasn't ready to let him go. In six months she knew if Pebbles could persuade him to stay in the navy, Pebbles would have him in Washington.

"I'm feeling god-awful guilty, Beebe." The statement struck her as irresponsible and was annoying to her.

"You took me and now you want absolution?" It was a statement-question, and the comment stung. Cannon might have argued the word "took," but he let it pass.

"Yes, that's about the size of it," he answered matter-of-factly. His glibness annoyed her and fueled her anger, which nevertheless, she hid from him.

"Bob, you have a problem. Two women want you. I wanted you ever since our meeting in Palermo, when I broke down in front of you. You were first a snotty twerp, then you were really kind and sensitive. It's a side of you that you hide. But I saw it, and I needed it. I need it now."

"Beebe, right now I'm very confused. You're a wonderful woman. Yes…it is more than lust. Just how much more, I don't know."

"You'll never know if you deny me. Deny us." There was a very long pause. "Of course," she resumed, "we could just agree that what happens in WestPac stays in WestPac, couldn't we? That's what you naval officers conveniently do, don't you?" she said derisively.

"No Beebe, that's just too easy."

"Take your shower, Bobby. You don't play Hamlet well."

She didn't join him in the shower, and sat on a couch in the room stewing until she became downright annoyed. The waiter arrived with the room service order and set up a table for two. She tipped him but continued to fume. She was annoyed at him, and annoyed with herself. *What did I expect? Was I in some fantasy world where I would seduce him, and he would love me ever after? Get hold of yourself woman.* She poked at the food with a chop stick—dim sum, and several Cantonese preparations with sauces for beef, chicken, and pork.

He emerged from the shower in a white, terry cloth robe provided by the hotel like the one she wrapped herself in, and took a seat in an upholstered chair next to where she was sitting.

"Beebe, I'm very fond of you. In another time and in another place I could be in love with you. I could be chasing you and contending with a dozen suitors. Half of Washington would want you. You are beautiful. You are very bright. You've got your head screwed on right. And frankly, you're sexy as hell."

"'Sexy as hell?' I always wanted to hear that from you, Cannon." She was still annoyed and scoffed at him.

"C'mon Beebe. You're making it hard on me. You know what I mean, and you very well know you intended to be sexy tonight, and you were every bit that. I was aroused from the moment that I laid eyes on you."

"Nice choice of words, Lieutenant."

"Beebe, please. Our relationship is difficult and complex."

"Yes, I'm sure it is."

"Beebe. Dammit. Less than a year ago, if I recollect, you were a grief-stricken widow. What makes you feel your emotions are so pure, your motives so authentic? What makes you so damn sure that you're not being driven by your own hormones, that your feelings can be trusted? Yes, we were lonely. Why can't we leave it at that?"

"I think I'll take my shower now."

"Good. Make it a cold one. Maybe that will cool you off."

"You're back to be being a wise-ass brat again!" She took her shower alone and thought about what had just gone wrong between them, and she thought about what it might have been like to have taken a shower with him after making love.

Lust? Loneliness in Hong Kong? So be it then. She got over her anger, stepped from the shower, dried off, dried her hair, put the terry cloth robe on, and prepared to accept whatever passed between them. She walked into the bedroom and saw him lying in the bed reading a magazine.

"Bobby, let's start this evening over," she said as she snuggled up next to him. She smelled very fresh and clean to him, and he kissed her softly on the forehead.

"You know, I'll have to report this to the agency. It will finish me as your case officer."

"That will be a relief," he laughed. "Now, tell me your life story." He held her tenderly through the night, and they made love again that night and again in the morning. Then he got dressed, returned to The Mandarin, checked out, and took the officer's boat back to the ship, and that's when he began to feel both sad and guilty all over again.

Chapter 19.

A very troubled Robert Cannon climbed the accommodation ladder to the quarterdeck and requested permission to come aboard. Ensign Reposa was the Officer of the Deck.

"Permission granted. Welcome aboard, Bob." Right away Reposa saw that Cannon was distraught.

"Good morning, Lou."

"Commander Fritz was here awhile ago. Left word that he wanted you to see him. Said he'd be down in the wardroom."

"Aw cripes. What have I done now?" He started for the ladder to the second deck, then stopped and turned around, "Lou, has O come aboard yet?

"Heard he would be back late tomorrow."

"Damn…well, okay. Thanks."

Cannon took the ladder down from the quarterdeck to the passageway on the second deck and entered the wardroom. "Good morning, Commander."

"Good morning, Bob. Why don't you grab a cup of coffee? I'd like to speak with you." Cannon poured himself a cup of black coffee, passed a salt shaker over the cup, and walked aft to join Fritz in the wardroom lounge.

"Didn't know if you were coming back aboard. But I'm glad to see you. Like to discuss an opportunity with you. Ken Wyman has left the ship, and he's going to a staff position with CruDesLant. He's been our GQ OOD. I recommended another OOD for the General Quarters watch bill, but after the *Fletcher* incident, the captain thought you would be a better choice. And I agreed with him. He asked me to discuss it with Dick Killinger and Frank Jeffreys. I've done that, and they have approved your choice." Cannon did not react, and Fritz was surprised at the lack of a reaction. Being selected for the General Quarters, Officer Of the Deck position was generally considered an honor. "The captain would like to have you as his GQ OOD. Said if we ever had to fight the ship, you were the best qualified. Your ASW plan was also cited."

"Uh, sir. This probably isn't hitting me at the right time. I appreciate the honor. Sir, I think you know that I stand 12 to 14 hours of watches a day. I'm pressed to get much sleep now, usually in three, maybe four hour, periods, sometimes six hours. I'm not keen to have to get up, dress, get ready to go to the bridge, or wait to be relieved on strike control, every time a fire alarm passes over the 1MC, two, three, four times a day."

"You have to do that anyway. You've got a GQ station, now, don't you?"

"Yes, sir." There was a long pause.

"Bob, frankly, I thought you would leap on this."

"Sir, yes, it is an honor. Thank you. Please thank the captain for me. Sir, uh, look uh, I've just come off the beach. I have some personal issues to work through. Nothing I can't handle. But this just catches me at a low moment. Thank you for assigning me to the bridge GQ bill. I won't let you or the captain down, sir.

"Anything, I can do to help, Bob?"

"No, sir. Female problems."

"Oh, sorry to hear that. You have my sympathies. Another casualty of a WestPac deployment?"

"Thank you, sir. Please excuse me, sir." Cannon left for his stateroom on the third deck. As usual only a fluorescent desk lamp was lit in the compartment. Lieutenant Soriano, one of the engineering officers, was racked out on the bunk beneath him. Cannon undressed quietly and crawled into his bunk and tried to go to sleep, but his conscience kept bothering him.

Ogilvy Osborne stepped from the officer boat to the accommodation ladder and climbed to the quarterdeck. He rendered a salute to the national ensign flying from the staff on the flight deck at the round down before he saluted the Officer of the Deck and requested permission to come aboard.

"Permission granted. Welcome back, O," said Ned Chase, returning the salute. "It's a delight to see you, sir.'" But Osborne was not his normal congenial self.

"Thank you, Ned. It's good to be back aboard *Tico*," responded Osborne perfunctorily.

"Chaplain, Captain Tarrant would like to see you, sir. He asked that you see him in his in-port cabin after you had a chance to settle in aboard, sir."

"Thank you, Ned. If you would be so kind, please call the captain and tell him I'll see him in 20 minutes." Chase thought he noted a profound sadness, a sorrow, in the chaplain's mien.

"I'd be delighted to call him, O. It's very good to have you back with us, sir."

"How 'bout a coke, O?"

"Thanks. I'll pass, Dick." Osborne and Tarrant were on a first name basis—a permission that Tarrant granted only in private to CAG, the XO, and Osborne.

"You're different, O. What happened?"

"Really? Is it so obvious?" Osborne spoke deliberately, monotonically. "I diagnose myself as clinically depressed. I probably have major depression disorder." There was a pause in the conversation as Captain Richard Tarrant tried to understand what Osborne was saying. Nobody readily admitted to a psychiatric disorder in the US Navy. Certainly, nobody did who wanted to continue to fly. "You know, Dick, I thought I could be helpful, but I lost this wonderful young, Catholic chaplain. Shea... Seamus Shea... Seamus Sean Shea... Say Hey Shea... Father Shea, Society of Jesus. Wonderful young priest. Everything a priest should be... Then there are those young marines. I've reached the limit, Skipper. I just can't see any more dead and wounded. There's a limit. I've reached that limit. I may have crossed it."

"O, what can I do?" Then he added, "Never should have agreed to letting you go to Khe Sanh. It was a mistake."

"Nobody should go to Khe Sanh, Dick. Nobody should go to war. It's so wonderful that they have to draft people against their will to go to war. Order them into boats to land on a hostile shore. Order them to live below ground and wait for an artillery shell to settle their fate. Order them...." He paused. A sense of futility pervaded Chaplain Osborne. Tarrant let him continue without interruption. "I'm jaded, Skipper. I've become a casualty of war. I'll get something from Doc Spath," the ship's medical officer. "I'll be okay, Skipper, but when we get back to the States. I'm getting out."

"Out.... Nobody will blame you for that, O. You sure you gonna be okay? I could get you home sooner."

Two days later, *Ticonderoga* and the six destroyers, including *USS Fletcher,* got underway for the two day trip back to Yankee Station.

By early May, the bombing halt had been in effect for two months with little progress towards peace. The infiltration of men and materiel into the South continued around the clock unimpeded by navy and air force air activity. In North Vietnam the damaged roads, docks, bridges, dams, rail yards, power plants and warehouses were diligently under reconstruction. New missile sites were being added to what was already the most heavily defended area in the history of military aviation. The President's staff asked the Joint Chiefs to consider a major strike as a way of signaling that American patience was not unlimited.

Operation Rolling Thunder was wearing into its fourth year of operation, and many pilots were increasingly questioning the risk and rewards of flying million dollar aircraft against five thousand dollar trucks. Stories went around Yankee Station about so and so refusing to fly armed reconnaissance interdiction missions, but he would gladly suit up for a mission over Hanoi or Haiphong. Such demonstrations of protest were greeted with dismay. Usually a pilot would be sympathetically talked out of his decision, but occasionally a pilot could not be dissuaded. In such cases the pilot was requested to turn in his wings. The message was clear. US Navy pilots could not choose their missions even if the choice were to accept the tough ones over the monotonous and low-value missions.

Aboard *Ticonderoga,* down in Strike Operations, the strike order was received cynically until they saw the target list that the Pentagon had made available to the navy and air force. All three Yankee Station carriers, *Ticonderoga, Enterprise,* and *Kitty Hawk* and an equivalent number of US Air Force planes from Thailand, were tasked for a strike. Nearly 200 strike aircraft and many additional support aircraft—tankers, electronic jammers, air control, reconnaissance aircraft and helicopters would be involved in a two-wave attack. The navy would strike first from the sea, and the air force, from bases in Thailand, would restrike the targets 15 minutes later.

The targets included the Thai Nguyen thermal power plant, the Kinh No railroad complex in the center of Hanoi, the Long Bien bridge between Hanoi and Haiphong, the Yen Vien and Ai Mo warehouse complexes, the Bac Giang trans-shipment point, and the Hanoi petroleum, oil, lubricant storage complex—targets which had been restored and left untouched since 1967.

The junior pilots groused publicly in the wardroom and in the ready rooms while the senior pilots and squadron commanders, reserved it for the privacy of their staterooms, but the message was the same. They had beaten down the air defenses over the previous year only to see them reconstituted during the bombing halt. Now they were being asked to risk their lives again.

Hanoi and Haiphong were the most heavily defended targets in the history of air warfare. There were over 7000 thousand anti-aircraft guns. These were made up primarily of 23mm and 37mm light guns which burst with white smoke, 57mm shells which burst with dark gray smoke, and

85mm and 100mm shells that burst with black smoke and might reach a ceiling of 5000 feet. Several thousand riflemen would fire their weapons in barrage style effectively reaching up to 3000 feet. About 500 surface to air missiles were available at 200 sites which could reach a ceiling of 60,000 feet and carry a war head with 350 pounds of high explosives. Several hundred MIG fighters were based around the two cities. The guns, gun directors, SAM directors, air control sites, and MIGs were manned by various combinations of North Vietnamese and Russian personnel with the Russians more likely to be found in the skill positions. Meanwhile the Russians operated "Gargles," the intelligence trawler on Yankee Station, to provide early warning information to their allies of impending air operations. It was proof once again that any target worth striking was one worth defending.

The US Navy countered this threat with radar jammers, radar deception techniques like reflective chaff, magnesium flares to deceive infra-red trackers, fighters fitted with cluster bombs to suppress AA fire, Iron Hand aircraft with Shrike missiles to home in on the radar guidance systems for surface-to-air missiles, and black box missile detection systems on board each aircraft. The latter were in such short supply that air wings returning to the States regularly transferred their componentry to relieving air wings. In addition, they flew various routes and altitudes on the way in and on the way out from the target. The whole strike was organized and coordinated so that no more than 120 seconds would be spent in the time over the target.

Off shore lay a modern frigate, call sign, Red Crown, with an advanced SPS-48 radar to check friendly aircraft in and out of North Vietnam and to call out MIG warnings when they scrambled to intercept the strike group. In addition, there were several special search and rescue, Big Mother helicopters, for rescuing downed pilots, air force rescue combat air patrol aircraft known by their call sign as Sandy, and two or three air force KC-135 tankers to augment the navy's tankers for refueling outbound aircraft. All of this was referred to neatly as the "package." The package was customized by type of aircraft and type of ordnance in accordance with the target. Mark 82, 500 pound, iron, gravity bombs were the usual navy weapon of choice against a target such as a power plant. The air force had similar capabilities and could mount a similar package from Thailand.

The alpha strike launch was scheduled for 1000 and *Ticonderoga's* own Commander Sam Hessmann, flying an A-4C, was selected as strike leader against the big thermal power plant just outside Hanoi. Hessmann had more than 325 missions over North Vietnam, and there was no better choice in a strike leader for either planning or executing a strike. Hessmann was tough-minded, extremely cool under pressure, and tolerated no carelessness nor irresponsibility. He was a military straight arrow without being officious. He was fair, firm, and friendly, but he was not your favorite guy to hit the beach with.

Cannon had read and heard stories about alpha strikes, but he had never experienced one, and his first experience would be as officer of the deck. The ship was already at flight quarters, and at 0930 *Ticonderoga* went to general quarters in an orderly fashion. Cannon, in long sleeved shirt, his pants tucked into his socks, with a steel helmet and Mae West life jacket, reported that he was ready to relieve the OOD on the bridge. Foxtrot was flying at the dip and Foxtrot Corpen was computed to be 295 degrees true. The Gearing class destroyer, *Francis J. Fielding*, was in *Ticonderoga's* wake as plane guard. Cannon said "I relieve you, sir," exchanged salutes and received the customary response, "I stand relieved." The just-relieved OOD had a GQ station himself to get to on the double. "Lieutenant J.G. Cannon has the deck and the conn."

'Bosun aye, Lieutenant J.G. Cannon has the deck and the conn." Everywhere men were in the process of relieving each other and running off to various battle stations. There was an air of calm excitement throughout the ship. Cannon could see the flight deck crews readying their aircraft.

Red shirt ordnance men were double-checking the ordnance and various pins and arming wires. Brown shirt plane captains were assisting pilots with their harnesses into their cockpits and giving the windshield a last wipe. The yellow shirt catapult crew was calling up the two EA-1s, radar and communications jamming aircraft, to the catapults for launch. The firefighters in their silver fireproof gear were ready with helmet in hand. Here and there an oxygen cart was being towed to a station near the island, and everywhere aircraft engines were being cranked up, and wings were being folded down. 32 aircraft would launch from *Ticonderoga* to be joined by similar numbers from *Enterprise* and *Kitty Hawk*. Across the sea Cannon could see the unique domed island structure of *Enterprise* with phased array radar and beyond the small, distant gray form of *Kitty Hawk*. "Left 20 degrees rudder. Change speed to 20 knots."

"Sir, my rudder is left 20 degrees. Speed 20 knots is indicated sir."

"Very well." Cannon stepped over to the 5MC, "Signals Bridge, close up Foxtrot."

"Signals, aye, sir."

Commander Fritz arranged for Ensign Reposa to take the JOOD slot and assigned Ensign Schweitzer as JOOW. Reposa and Cannon obviously worked well together and Schweitzer had stood watches previously with Reposa, but he had never served with Cannon. "Ease your rudder to left 10 degrees and steady up on new course two nine zero." Cannon could see the Russian trawler had cleverly positioned herself on Foxtrot Corpen to create a problem for the carrier's deck officers.

"Sir, my rudder is left 10 degrees. Steady up on new course two nine zero degrees, aye, sir."

Cannon looked at Reposa as if to ask are you ready for the conn? Reposa nodded. "Ensign Reposa has the conn."

"Bosun mate aye, Ensign Reposa has the conn, sir."

Cannon had been too busy to greet the captain in the rush to man up for battle stations, and he now saluted Captain Tarrant, "Good morning, sir."

"Good morning, Bob," returning the salute."

"Sir, I am steady on new course two nine zero," called out the helmsman. "

Very well," said Reposa. "Come right to new course three zero zero." Reposa did not quite have the wind down the flight deck, but when the helmsman steadied on 300, the wind was precisely 350 degrees relative at 30 knots down the deck.

Cannon had his binoculars trained right on Gargles. "Range to Gargles, Mr. Schweitzer?"

"1800 yards, sir, CBDR."

"What do you want me to do, Bob?" asked Reposa.

"Maintain course and speed for fox corpen."

"Trawler for a carrier, a pawn for a king. Poor exchange."

"Unless he's Crazy Ivan, with 43,000 tons at 20 knots coming at him, he'll move his ass." As Cannon said, Gargles slowly drifted off Foxtrot Corpen, registering her defiance, and passed down *Ticonderoga's* starboard side not more than 50 yards apart.

The plane guard helo lifted off, and the first EA-1 launched followed by the second EA-1 electronic countermeasures aircraft. The first of a dozen F-8s taxied towards the catapults. When the F-8s were on the catapult and popped into after burner the volume of noise already at extreme levels rose to incredible levels. The first four, F-8s headed north for Bar-Cap while the remaining eight would serve as flak suppressors and MIG-Cap.

In between launches, Cannon moved next to Reposa and asked him as inconspicuously as possible if Schweitzer was squared away and knew his stuff. Reposa nodded, "He's checked out on the basics, but I haven't seen him under pressure."

"Thanks." Cannon placed exceeding trust in Reposa's judgment of people and seamanship. Both Cannon and Reposa realized that people acted differently under stress, and they both had the ability to rise to the occasion while others fell apart or avoided the challenge of stress altogether. Reposa's seaman's eye in what was now referred to as The Fletcher Incident had been perfect. Cannon thought that Reposa was close to qualification as OOD, and in Cannon's mind he foresaw Reposa succeeding him as GQ OOD when Cannon left the ship.

Ensign Richard Schweitzer was obviously wary of the demanding Cannon, the more so after the Popplewell episode. However Schweitzer did note a degree of calmness even placidity as Cannon and Reposa managed the watch. Other watch standers could be very tight and anxious, "sweaters," as they were known in the navy, who often ran behind the power curve, but these two had excellent anticipation and were exceedingly cool and gave a sense throughout the bridge and the pilot house that they were confidently ready to handle whatever emergency might come their way. As anyone whoever stood a watch knew, a smooth watch was a gift of a sort, and it was intrinsically more desirable to stand a smoothly run watch even if the performance expectations were more demanding.

"Ever see anything like this before, Dick?" said Cannon to Schweitzer.

"No, sir."

"And I doubt you'll see many, if any, again," said Captain Tarrant.

"A hundred plane raid is quite an armada," said Cannon.

"Yes, it is," responded Tarrant, "Let's just hope the Maker will let us have them all back safe and sound." The import and solemnity of Captain Tarrant's words put a chill over further conversation. CAG arrived on the bridge to speak with Tarrant and briefed the captain on several final details of the attack plan.

"Keep an occasional eye on Gargles will you, please, Dick," referring to the radar scope.

"Aye, aye, sir."

The F-8s were followed by 16, A-4 bombers and two A-4 Iron Hand aircraft. One of the last to launch was side number 208, from VA-192. Pete Peterson's Iron Hand A-4 was armed with four Shrikes. Peterson, who became friends with Campbell, would have his SAM sites pre-identified by location based on intelligence, but the F-8 flak suppressors would use their judgment over the target and attack the most threatening guns.

Finally two KA-3 tankers, the Whales, launched and climbed to join the strike formation now assembling under radio silence high over *Ticonderoga*. Subsequently each carrier air wing would make up one large formation of three tightly bunched waves and fly ensemble until they broke apart for their respective targets with Sam Hessmann and Air Wing 19 in the lead. Meanwhile on the ship, things settled down to a period of edgy inactivity and relative quiet. An occasional yellow tractor moved across the deck, but compared to the normal rush of activity, it was like Sunday in New York.

The three bridge officers, the captain, and the navigator looked out over the flight deck, and out over the sea, and made themselves busy with trivial chores. A quiet tension was building everywhere.

Cannon was standing next to the captain who was seated in the captain's chair, which on a carrier, is located on the portside of the bridge to afford a full view of the flight deck. "Captain, may we speak, sir?" inquired Cannon.

"Sure, just as long as you know that we might have to break it off just like that," snapping his fingers. "What's on your mind?"

"Sir, for training purposes, could you give the three black shoes here a sense of what is going to happen?"

"I will if I can. Gather 'round boys as close as you can while tending to your duties so you can hear me over the noise." It wasn't Tarrant the captain now. It was Tarrant the archetypical father with his sons. And it was both an instructive and subconsciously sentimental several moments that the four officers shared together.

"Sam Hessmann will lead his chicks in over the beach at maybe angels 20 or 22. As he calls 'feet dry,' the young fellas will start to pick up the sounds of the long range air search radars in their earphones." Tarrant's Texas, whiskey-baritone voice was strong and had well-earned authority.

"Probably heavy caliber, but sporadic flak, will begin along the coast. When there is no flak, they should be looking for MIGs. And they need to be very careful that the MIG isn't just bait luring them into a flak trap. Mentally the pilots will be thinking about everything from their assigned target, to a strange or imaginary sound in their aircraft, to the best place to punch out if they get hit and need to eject, to making sure they don't fail to arm their weapons. They'll remind themselves of a hundred things including what could be the last letter that each of them wrote for home last night."

"On a raid this big, against this air defense system, anyone who says he isn't afraid is lying. Fear is a good thing to tune into. You can train yourself to manage it, but you never want to shut it out because fear keeps you alive... Sam will then begin a slow descent picking up speed for the target. He wants the strike force around 12 to 14 thousand feet ready for roll-in on the target. Do you follow me?" The captain used his two hands to demonstrate an imaginary roll-in.

Several, "Yes, sirs" followed as each officer strained to catch every word over the background noise.

"Just before beginning the let-down to 8,000 feet, the flak suppressors and Iron Hand birds will detach for their assigned targets. The Iron Hand birds are carrying all Shrikes today because we have enough of them to-day, and because we want to suppress them. We are not going back tomor-row so we want to primarily suppress them. We'll take any kills that we get. But we'll shoot Shrikes to keep them shut down today."

"You mean the missile control radars, the Fansongs, sir?"

"Correct, Bob. About this time everyone rechecks everything… par-ticularly their weapons arming switches. Now the pilots push the nose over into a 45 degree dive angle. At this point, you can be certain that all hell is breaking loose with flak in the air and SAMs lifting off. Some of the Fansongs can be jammed, but others will require a Shrike or two. Now the bombers are picking up speed, but they have a lot of parasite drag from the ordnance, and they feel mushy with the drag and the weight of the bombs. As soon as the SAMs fly up, you forget about radio silence, and the pilots start to identify the SAMs."

"How would they do that, Captain?" asked Reposa. The captain took the question as somewhat naïve until he recalled that Ensign Reposa was a Weapons department officer and how little exposure some of the purely black shoe functions of the ship had to the air war.

"Well, they might say something like, 'Two SAMs two o'clock, low. Break right. Break right.' As they dive and swerve around the SAMs, they are losing altitude and air speed. Speed is life. Speed is life, see. And they are approaching the range of the AA guns at 5000 feet." The captain paused before continuing, checking to see if the surface warfare officers were with him.

"Now the *Tico* attack will come from three different headings to split the defense. I believe the birds from the other carriers will do the same thing. The flak suppressors will be firing their Zuni rockets and dropping cluster bombs and, in some cases, using their guns on active AA gun sites. Through all of this, jinking and dodging, the attack pilots have to identify their target, correct for winds over the target, their airspeed and angle of dive and put in the proper correction in mils in their bombsight. Then they have to fly the aircraft to line up their pipper and drop their ordnance somewhere between 4500 to 3500 feet." Tarrant was patient and did his best to describe the air combat environment and the pilot's task load. "After that, it's get the hell out of there with your wing man as fast as you can, altering course and changing altitudes, trying to get feet wet and plug into a tanker." Again the captain paused.

"Now, this post-strike period of egress over the beach is a favorite time for MIGs to attack. The climax of the strike is over, adrenaline is down, vigilance naturally drops a bit, and the strike formation, by design, is widely dispersed including friendly fighters. It's kinda like everyman, and his wingman, for themselves at this point." The captain's phone rang. He picked it up and listened for a few seconds, "Boys, we have a hot one. F-8 with a nose cone fire," and hung up the phone.

"Bridge Combat, we have a Red Lightning with a 37 mike mike fire in his nose. He's feet wet, and taking a drink from a buddy tanker. Inbound to Panther."

"Bridge copy," responded Cannon. Captain Tarrant turned to Cannon, "Ask him how, where he got it?"

Combat answered over the 1MC. "Flak suppression. Took the 37 mike mike inbound to the target area." Cannon looked at Tarrant as if to ask if Tarrant was satisfied. Captain Tarrant shook his head slowly, grimaced and gave him a never-mind wave off.

Several minutes later the F-8 appeared coming down the port side of *Ticonderoga,* and making an easy left turn, she came aboard perfectly catching the third wire. As soon as the fighter rolled to a stop, white smoke emitted profusely from the nose. Within seconds, the firefighters were emptying their CO_2 fire extinguishers into the nose, but the fire stubbornly continued to burn with the Crusader in place fouling the deck. A yellow tractor with a tow bar pulled up and hooked onto the F-8, the pilot scrambled out of the cockpit, and the aircraft was towed to the bow of the flight deck clearing the arresting gear for other aircraft. The firefighters resumed using their extinguishers until they got the fire out several minutes later.

Bridge Combat, "Known battle damage follows: One Alpha-4 down in Haiphong harbor. Good chute, but ResCap are guns dry. One Alpha-4 down, feet dry, within a couple of miles of the beach. Good chute. Good radio. Over the CI net *Enterprise* reported they have an F-4 down 25 miles south of Haiphong near Route 1. Chippy leader also says that he has a couple other birds that may or may not make it back. Lawcase 303 is leaking fuel and is tanking at angels 20. The pilot wants to bingo to Danang. Chippy 512, also has multiple holes, control problems and has avionics from his RAT. Probably can make it to the ship but might not be able to come aboard. Chippy leader wants ResCap, sir."

Reposa whispered to Cannon, "Whatsa rat?'

"Ram air turbine. A fan that pops out to use air speed to drive a small electrical generator."

Captain Tarrant called PriFly and told them to get the Ready 5 ResCap on deck, and to have other sections of aircraft armed and ready to go every five minutes. Promptly, up the number two elevator came two F-8s from VF-191, call sign, Feedbag. Two sections of aircraft from VA-23 and VA-192, squadron mates of the two downed A-4s, came up right behind the F-8s armed with 20mm cannon and Zuni rockets. All of the remaining F-8's and A-4s were being readied on the hangar deck.

In another minute the first F-8s were off the deck under full military power bound for Haiphong harbor. Sampans with militia were attempting to earn the bounty for capturing or killing the pilot, and there was little time to waste. Commander Fritz advised the captain that the tide in Haiphong was flooding, and the current would be taking the pilot towards the harbor and captivity. In the meanwhile *Enterprise's* E-2C called for help from the air force Sandys, propeller driven A1-Hs, to search their F-4 Phantom and *Ticonderoga's* A-4 crash sites.

The job of *Ticonderoga's* ResCap was to either hold off potential captors until the Big Mother SAR helicopters could execute a rescue, or until the Sandys could arrive. However, after the launch of the remaining F-8s and A-4s, *Ticonderoga* did not have any aircraft available until the alpha strike aircraft could be recovered, rearmed, refueled, and relaunched. Time was of the essence. Captain Tarrant also ordered the last KA-3 Whale tanker put on Ready 5 Alert.

The Feedbag F-8s were briefed in the air by Hessmann and told to check in on the SAR (search and rescue) Common frequency with Jury 208, on scene SAR commander. It was Peterson. He advised them the downed A-4 was one of the Iron Hand birds. There was a chance that they could drive off the sampans before going guns dry, and allow the Big Mother, already bound for the SAR scene, to make a quick snatch.

Arriving on scene, the Feedbags saw Peterson's A-4 making a dangerous low pass dropping the only thing he had on board, magnesium flares meant to distract infra-red seeking weapons. The A-4 dove low over the sampans dropping a string of flares, made several barrel rolls, jinked and pulled up. The sampans, not sure what was being dropped upon them, briefly reversed course.

"Jury 208, Feedbag 101 is with you. Two Crusaders with Zunis and cannon."

"Roger, Feedbag 101, both Jury Skyhawks are guns dry and low fuel state. Big Mother 503 is inbound and up this frequency. ETA eight minutes. "Stick" is in the water with a good PRC (personal radio). Tidal current is taking Stick towards the sampans about a quarter mile to the west. We kept Charlie off Stick and we're guns dry. Nothing left for suppression when 503 is ready to snatch."

"Feedbag 1 copies all. Are your ready for relief, Jury?"

"Roger. You have command of the SAR. We need to find a drink to make it to the boat. Adios." Both Jury's switched to Panther Strike and requested a tanker join up.

"Feedbag 1 for 5."

"5 Roger"

"Let's set up a two-plane orbit at base angels minus 5." Feedbag 5 rogered with two clicks of his radio microphone.

"Big Mother 503?"

"503 copied your traffic. We have a tally on you. Give us 5 minutes." Feedbag 1, the leader, piloted by Bar Man, his nom de guerre, acknowledged with two clicks of his mike.

"1, do you see the two WBLCs to the southwest closing on Stick."

"Roger. Stay up here. I'll roll in with Zunis." Bar Man rolled in and squeezed off a volley of Zuni rockets for each sampan. One promptly began to sink while the second turned very slowly around heading for port and making black smoke. "I'm gonna strafe the others as long as I am down here." His wing man, Feedbag 5—Hasty was the pilot's name—clicked his mike twice.

The F-8 reversed direction and strafed several sampans with 20mm cannon fire. He walked his rounds across at least one WBLC and may have hit a second. The action was sufficient to force the WBLCs to back off. Bar Man climbed back to altitude. "

"503, we have ammo to suppress for three possibly four runs. Looks like they have small caliber stuff. Can you proceed?"

"Roger, we are approaching from the northeast and planning a westerly hover. Can Stick give us a smoke?"

"Stick, Feedbag 1. Can you give us a smoke now?"

"Stick, affirmative," came the voice in the water.

"503, Feedbag 1, we have a good smoke. Do you have a tally?"

"We're lookin'. " The F-8s could see the gray helo low against the muddy, brown water.

"503, the smoke is at your two o'clock." Bar Man watched the helo come right.

"Tally on the smoke."

"Roger, Feedbag 5 will strafe until dry."

"Feedbag 5, wilco."

"503 in position. Put their heads down, please."

"Feedbag 5, turning for first run... engaging with Zunis... First salvo away." There were long pauses between radio transmissions as the rescue operation was underway.

"503 has a swimmer in the water"...

...."Teeing up my second run"...

...."We have Stick... "Somebody is hammering us good"...

... "Second salvo away"...

... "That took care of the hammer."

"Feedbag 5 turning for final run with cannon." Then... "Guns dry."

"We have Stick and swimmer aboard. Turning port for heading 14 to clear the area....Wish they were all this easy."

Back on *Ticonderoga* the recovery was continuing routinely. Aircraft and pilots who could serve in a ResCap capacity were being hot-refueled, rearmed, and repositioned for launch. However, Chippy 512, the badly crippled aircraft, still courageously flying, was evaluated as too risky to recover. The plan was for the pilot to eject near the ship for pick up by one of *Ticonderoga's* plane guard helicopters. The aircraft with the fire, Lawcase 303, managed to get the fire out and diverted to the bingo field in Danang. From Tarrant's perspective things were encouraging at the Haiphong harbor SAR scene, but the situation remained ambiguous for the other *Ticonderoga* pilot down in North Vietnam.

The Sandy aircraft reported locating the A-4 wreckage and the chute, but they could not raise the pilot on either of his two personal radios. This was not a good sign. If he was captured the NVA would try to use the PRC to lure the Big Mother into an ambush. If the radios failed or were lost, the pilot's chances of recovery, already slim were slimmer.

Throughout all of this the bridge environment aboard *Ticonderoga* remained very calm. Cannon found it unreal. Everywhere on the flight deck crewmen acted with extreme urgency. If he were in CIC, the team would be feverishly working to collect, evaluate, and advise the bridge with accurate information as the SAR scenes developed. Aircraft were calling in information, and requesting tanker join ups. Helicopters were positioning themselves for picking up pilots. On the bridge, he had little to do but keep the ship steaming into the wind. He found it a little dull, and disliked the fact that he wasn't really in the action.

The A-4s bound for Haiphong harbor changed heading for the second *Ticonderoga* SAR scene and drew some AA fire as they went feet dry over the beach.

"Bridge, Combat. Feedbag 1 reports successful snatch by Big Mother 503. Big Mother is returning to Red Crown." Red Crown also served as a SAR helicopter platform with several corpsmen and an enhanced sickbay aboard, but they did not have surgeons and operating rooms like the carriers. It was a sign the pilot had no serious injuries.

A tension-relief cheer began and ended quickly on the bridge and in the pilot house. Captain Tarrant cupped his hands together and said, "One to go."

But nothing had been heard from the pilot, Chesty, for nearly two hours. When *Ticonderoga*'s A-4s arrived at the second SAR scene, the Sandys departed for the *Enterprise* F-4 scene further to the south. Gradually activity ratcheted down as the period of silence extended. The ship secured from general quarters and transitioned to 90 minute launch cycles for the ResCap until 1830 when *Ticonderoga* secured from flight quarters until 0600 the following day.

The air wing knew that only one in six pilots were recovered up North, and if they weren't picked up in the first 30 to 45 minutes, the odds dropped to one in twelve. Air Wing 19 awaited the bomb damage assessment from the subsequent photo-reconnaissance flights, but they were already glumly calculating their losses—at least three airplanes lost, several damaged and possibly one pilot. Reports from other Yankee Station assets, recruited spies and informants on the ground in North Vietnam, later that night indicated that over half of Hanoi was without lights. It was a small comfort.

Over the next day, *Ticonderoga's* aircraft routinely patrolled over Lawcase 310's last known position, but there was no trace of Chesty. Hopes aboard ship were fading. The air wing resumed interdiction missions but with decidedly less enthusiasm than the aggressiveness that they had displayed the day before.

Cannon felt the pall over the ship when he relieved Van Kirk at strike control for the 1330 launch. The launch went off smoothly as did the subsequent recovery of the 1200 cycle. At around 1450, Cannon suddenly received the following radio call.

"Panther Strike, Panther Strike, this is Restless 203, a flight of two Foxtrot-4 Foxtrots." It was unusual to have an aircraft from one of the other carriers call *Ticonderoga*.

"Panther Strike, go ahead Restless."

"Restless 203 believes that we saw mirror flashes on a hillside approximately 3 miles south of the Lawcase impact area. We went down for a second look but saw nothing else."

"Roger, unconfirmed mirror flashes 3 miles south of the impact area. Squawk Ident, please, Restless."

"Roger, squawking now."

Two rows of dashes distinguished the F-4 Phantom radar blip from several others on his scope. The SIF confirmed the side number as 203, the ship code was *Kitty Hawk*, and the mission was armed reconnaissance.

"Roger, I have you on Panther's two five zero radial at 95 nautical."

"Roger, we're working Route 1 for logistics."

"Panther Strike, roger on that. Thank you Restless, we'll check it out. Time is now 1453. Panther Strike, out."

Restless gave two clicks of his mike and was gone. Cannon rose quickly and called Lieutenant Commander Easley over to his station and gave him the information including confirming the side number and general location of Restless 203. Easley immediately called the bridge who in turn relayed the message to Primary Flight Control. PriFly would brief the VA-23 flight sitting on the deck preparing to launch. There was a flicker of hope, but just a flicker, since Chesty would normally have confirmed his location when *Kitty Hawk's* F-4s made a second pass. The mirror flash could have been mistaken for anything, perhaps a glaring truck windshield being repositioned for better camouflage, or it could be an aviator still on the move who felt it too risky to signal a second time.

For the remainder of the day, despite highly motivated searches around the pilot datum, there was neither confirmation of the Restless 203 possible mirror flash siting nor were there any other indications forthcoming from Chesty. Chesty was officially listed as missing in action.

On the last recovery of the day, which in May was a daylight recovery in the Gulf of Tonkin, Commander Repetto, the ship's executive officer, and Commander Gibson, VA-23's, CO, made their way to the bridge to speak with the captain. The XO carried two messages in his hand. One was green and the other was white. "Skipper, I have good news and unfortunately bad news. Which would you like first?"

"Well, you got Gibby here. I think I can guess." Tarrant pointed to the green confidential message.

Commander Repetto said flatly, "Lieutenant Commander Richard "Chesty" James is a confirmed POW at the Hanoi Hilton… It looks like he might have been trying to signal with his mirror, but he was passing in and out of consciousness due to severe injuries."

"Damn." The captain looked up sorrowfully and gazed for nearly a minute vacantly at the horizon as *Ticonderoga* headed for her next underway replenishment. Fatigue and years of experience cut deep wrinkles in his face.

"How you feelin', Gibby?"

"Hurts to lose a good man. He's my ops officer. First Campbell, now James."

"Yu-up, they're all my boys, too." Then Captain Tarrant turned towards Repetto and pointed to the unclassified message.

Repetto chuckled, "You're both gonna like this. Cubi Point Special Services has invited the ship's company and air wing officers to use the Cubi Point O Club… without restrictions. They sign it by saying 'please enjoy your visit.' "

Tarrant simply smiled and shrugged. "Get CAG up here. We'll tell him to read the riot act to the boys. I mean that!" shaking his finger, squinting his eyes and flashing a wry smile at Gibson. "Confine the antics to the Dilbert Dunker!" He paused for effect. "And let's have Sam order another 2500 Stingers."

Chapter 20.

Since leaving Hong Kong, Cannon felt guilty and generally miserable for bedding down with Beebe Byrnes and betraying his fiancée's trust and beat himself up pretty thoroughly over it. *I will not ever again be unfaithful to Tish Martin.* Cannon walked slowly aft down the second deck, starboard passageway towards the Chaplain's Office in the "C" section of the ship. He felt slightly anxious and uncertain about his appointment as he walked. He had in mind some vague sort of confession. Except for sampling the food in the crew's mess, he found it mildly amusing that he had never been in this section of *Ticonderoga*. It was vaguely familiar to him from his days in *Essex*. He stopped and stuck his head in an office and asked a seaman if he were near the Chaplain's Office.

"Yes, sir, just another 20 feet aft, to your left side, sir."

"Thank you, sailor." He walked slowly towards the office and stopped and lingered for a moment or two. *This will stay with me. O does not need to know. Nor Laetitia. It happened in WestPac.* He turned around and walked in the opposite direction. He retraced his steps and proceeded to the Operations office on the 02 level and phoned the Chaplain's office and cancelled his appointment and immersed himself reading through the latest messages and avoided his unwanted feelings of guilt and shame.

Across Laos a light rain began to fall. Campbell had never heard rain before on the roof of his hut, but in the early hours of the morning he could hear it and smell it. *Rain. Escape. Jesus, please be with us today.* Mike Sekulovich was awakened by the rain, too. "Today's the day," whispered Sekulovich.

"Affirmative. I have been mentally rechecking the plan."

"Me, too. Let's do it again when we can put the model back together after the morning walk-around."

Later, when they were all inside walking around the compound, word was passed that today was the day for Mo-deerf. But Bundit sought out Campbell and told him he and Thanawat did not want to go.

"Don't want to go. You kill guards. Pathet Lao track and kill all us."

"If we stay here, we die, too. Die like Drang and Brownie."

"Today not go."

"Each day we all get weaker. We must go."

"No. Not today."

"Bundit, you said the guards were running short of food and would kill us so they wouldn't have to feed us. They are starving us now. We must go." The argument continued throughout the noon-day break and into the early afternoon in whispers between the huts.

Sekulovich grew angry but stayed out of the argument, but he knew that only Bundit could speak more than pigeon Laotian. At times, he questioned Bundit's translations or interpretations as self-serving, and his fraternization with the guards led him to suspect the truthfulness of Bundit's information. Browne had also confided to Sekulovich that he was uncertain about Bundit's loyalty when the "chips were down." Finally Sekulovich lost patience. "Bundit, we're going with you or without you."

"No kill guard?"

"That's the plan. Hold the guards prisoners," replied Campbell.

"Okay. Guards not die. We go. Begin when guard go get dinner; leave weapon in hut and guard post."

"Affirmative. Mo-deerf goes down at dinner time." Sekulovich knew the Asians the longest and was unsure that the matter had been resolved and said so to Campbell.

"Ti, always remember the Asians are mercenaries...bought loyalty."

Intermittently rain showers, sometimes very heavy showers, lashed the prison compound making it hard to see and hear. Sekulovich inspected the prison model again for the nth time. He had the greatest distance to run to capture a .45 caliber submachine gun while Campbell got to the nearest hut and captured what they thought were all of the other guns.

Campbell lay awake without sleeping. It was like the night before a dangerous mission. The tension was rising for him and Sekulovich. He tried to meditate but thoughts kept entering his mind. One more time Sekulovich, who had never handled a Thompson sub-machine gun, asked Campbell how to operate the submachine gun, and Campbell patiently explained how the blow-back, .45 caliber, Thompson worked and stepped Sekulovich through the procedures again.

They took turns watching the guards through the interstices of the bamboo stockade from a peep hole in their hut. The Asians could see the kitchen hut, but the Asian hut blocked the view of the kitchen hut for the Americans, and they were reliant on the Asians to count the guards gathering to get their dinner portions. Finally the Asians gave the word.

"Two guard in kitchen hut... now free, four.... Now seben. Go!"

Campbell had already pulled up the floor boards and dropped below the hut onto the ground and was making his way through the rabbit hole.

Sekulovich was right behind, and he ran and unlocked the Asian hut before he ran back and crawled through the rabbit hole. The Asians followed him through the rabbit hole. They waited, hidden behind the stockade for Campbell to hand them the weapons. Campbell was up the front steps to the guard hut and found several weapons. An American Garand M1 rifle, and M1 carbine and four Kalashnikov AK-47s. He raced down the steps and waved the Asians on and handed three Kalashnikovs to Bundit with several bandoliers of ammo who passed the weapons to Thanawat and Dit. He also gave Bundit two grenades to booby trap the village trail.

Sekulovich made it to the far end of the compound and was breaking for the hut with the Thompson submachine gun. The heaviness of the Thompson surprised him, and he stumbled and hit the ground, and let off a burst of gunfire. Meanwhile Campbell and Thanawat approached the kitchen while Bundit moved swiftly up the trail to the village to booby trap the trail.

At the sound of gunfire, the guards sensed something was wrong and came streaming out of the hut.

"Yute! Yute!" Campbell pulled back the operating rod, chambered a round, raised the M1 carbine to his shoulder and eased off the safety. "Yute! Yute! A shot rang out from the kitchen. The prisoners miscounted the weapons, and where they were stored. There was obviously a weapon in the kitchen. At the sound of the shot, Thanawat and Dit took their weapons and ran for the stream. Campbell was now abandoned and alone. Another shot rang out from the kitchen hut. He aimed and let off two rounds hitting Fat Boy with the rifle. The force of the bullets drove Fat Boy backwards and spun him around in the hut.

Vicious now rushed Campbell with a machete. Campbell again stood his ground and fired three rounds in semi-automatic mode and dropped Vicious. Again the force of the .30 caliber bullets spun the victim to the ground. Campbell could see a large hole in Vicious' backside with blood flowing heavily from it.

Sekulovich had by now gotten to his feet and came running towards Campbell with the Thompson. One of the guards, Pawn One, bolted for the trail to the village. Again Campbell took aim and hit his target in the lower arm. Pawn One screamed. Campbell fired several more rounds, but Pawn One did not drop and was gone in the jungle. Bundit, after hearing the shots ring out, retraced his steps, and was surprised as Pawn One dashed by him with his bloody arm for the village. Bundit now became afraid and ran to the far side of the compound, out of the Americans' sight, and down the trail to the stream.

The Asians must have had a plan to take-off if there were any killing thought Campbell. Sekulovich moved menacingly towards Stalin. Stalin raised his machete, and Sekulovich let off several rounds ripping his torso in half. Campbell stared briefly at the bloody, raw human remains shredded and brutalized by the force of many .45 caliber rounds.

"Brutal bastard."

The three remaining guards, Nay, Pawn Two and Toad, were extremely frightened and surrendered. Sekulovich ran back to the huts and brought back several pairs of manacles while Campbell covered the guards. When Sekulovich returned, they shoved the three guards inside the stockade and manacled their ankles together and manacled their arms around the bench of the picnic table in the center of the compound.

Next they ran to the kitchen. They wolfed down all of the cooked rice and searched for uncooked rice. Sekulovich found a store of uncooked rice with green mold and maggots. Campbell ran back to the hut with the weapons and brought back two rucksacks. He then began looking for something to reflect light—a mirror, the lid of a bottle or can. What he found was even better—a stainless mirror from a GI shaving kit nailed to one of the hut's poles. He also found a box with about ten matches and placed everything in his rucksack. Again Campbell went back to the weapons hut with Sekulovich. They found their flight boots. Both pairs were covered with green mold, and they hastily put them on. Campbell grabbed two more bandoliers of carbine ammo and stuffed them in his rucksack.

They scrambled down the ladder steps of the hut right into the Kalashnikov sights of Bundit's weapon. He and Thanawat had doubled back. "Want rucksack." Campbell was shocked by the betrayal.

"Mike, do you believe this?" He was still reacting to the surprise of the betrayal. Sekulovich slowly raised the Thompson to firing position on his hip.

"Uh-hunh." Then Sekulovich said softly, "Ti, point your piece at the ten o'clock bogey," avoiding the use of Thanawat's name. "Wax him if he moves." Sekulovich was sure the Thais would be slow to follow slang that had not been used in front of them before.

"Want rucksack, now!" Campbell now studied Bundit's face very carefully and saw that he was nervous but insistent.

"Bundit, you would kill Mike and me for the rucksack?" Campbell was still in partial disbelief of what Bundit was saying.

"Yeah. Now!" He jabbed the AK-47 towards Campbell. Campbell now saw Bundit was determined and appeared willing to kill.

"Why?"

"You take all rice."

"So, why don't we share the rice?"

"No, not enough for four peoples." Bundit apparently thought that Dit had vanished.

"No."

"Why did you run away?"

"You break promise. You kill guards."

"We miscounted. Fat Boy had a weapon and shot at me and Thanawat."

"Bery bad. You kill guards."

"But you would kill us now, for rice?"

"Yeah. Gimme rucksack, now!" Several thoughts went through Campbell's head. First an M1 carbine was not the equal of an AK-47, and Bundit knew how to use it. He also considered Bundit's disloyalty and a caution that Red Browne said about what people would do to avoid more torture and another beating. He had genuinely offered to share the rice, but Sekulovich was becoming impatient and angry and saw that Bundit had adamantly refused. Bundit had gone from reluctant ally to an apparently treasonous foe who would easily sell them out if the Pathet Lao captured him.

Thanawat now spoke in Thai to Bundit, and Bundit responded with great animation. Thanawat answered him, and the two continued to speak back and forth in an apparent argument. Thanawat lowered his weapon, and then set it carefully upon the muddy ground. Finally, after more argument, Bundit shrugged his shoulders and faced Campbell.

"Okay. Share. You share rice."

"Alright, Bundit. Let's step out of the rain."

The four men climbed the stairs and entered the guards' hut and Campbell took the rice from his rucksack and showed Bundit the mold and maggots before he divided the rice. Bundit took his share, and Campbell placed his share back in the rucksack. The four men then climbed down from the hut, but when they had all gotten outside in the rain, Bundit appeared to have a change of mind.

"Not enough rice for four peoples."

"No, not enough for traveling 40 days, but enough to find more food." Again Bundit pointed his weapon at Campbell.

"Want all rice now."

Sekulovich raised the Thompson in response, but Thanawat did not cover him, and Sekulovich pointed it at Bundit. "Go to hell! Take your share, and get the hell out of here."

"You go to hell, shit man!" and Bundit swung the Kalashnikov from covering Campbell towards Sekulovich. Sekulovich pulled the trigger and on full automatic, the .45 caliber rounds virtually tore open Bundit's chest as he fell lifeless backwards. Then he swung his weapon on Thanawat. Thanawat raised his hands just as another heavy rain shower came through. Again Campbell was stunned by both the betrayal and by the violence of the shooting. Sekulovich had virtually executed two men in front of him, and it took several seconds for him to refocus on the situation.

"Mike, I'll get another set of manacles and secure Thanawat to the far piling of the hut."

"Selfish sonuvabitch, deserved it," said Sekulovich. "Brownie said, 'Never trust that guy,' but he cut him a lot of slack." He paused, "We didn't need this." He and Campbell were just astounded by what had taken place. "At least he won't be talking to anybody now."

"Never thought Bundit would turn on us like that."

"Never liked the guy. Things were never quite right when he was around."

Sekulovich became refocused and pushed the frightened and shocked Thanawat towards the piling, and Campbell secured his arms around the hut's piling, Campbell slipped on the rucksack and stepped over and looked at Bundit's bloody, lifeless body. "Judas," he said softly and vomited, viscerally reacting to Bundit's bloody corpse and the three men he personally had just killed. After vomiting until he was virtually empty, he said, "Forgive us, Lord Jesus, for we have just killed four men. May they rest in peace."

He caught as much of his vomit with his left hand and ate what he could of the undigested rice mush. He washed his hands and face in the rainwater run off of a banana tree leaf which had been stripped of all fruit. Then he drank, as a free man, from the leaf, the first, uninfested, pure water in nearly four months.

"Let's pull chocks." With that, the two American pilots set off down the path, past the latrine, towards the stream.

"Just a minute, Ti, I want to say good-bye to Brownie." They both prayed silently in the rain over Red Browne's grave. Tears rolled down Sekulovich's face, "Justice was served, Brownie…Sorry you aren't going with us. So long old friend."

They were weaker after an enormous expenditure of energy abetted with a big charge of adrenaline. Slowly, fatigued, they moved on through the rain, their clothing sopping wet, now operating under Plan B.

As they travelled along together Campbell's mind ruminated on Seku-lovich, and Bundit's killing, and on the two guards that he killed, and the third that he wounded. He wondered if they might have done things differently to avoid the killings. He particularly wondered if killing Bundit was necessary and justifiable, and if all of the killings were justifiable. He examined his conscience, and it appeared to him that the more that they were reduced to a survival level of existence, the easier it was to kill. The closer they were to subsistence, the more likely the issues appeared to be binary choices between living and dying, and the more acceptable it became to kill before they were killed. Turning the other cheek appeared more and more to be a negation of their own lives.

Was that it? To kill was a choice to live? To refuse to kill was a choice to die? Was that the rule, do it to them before they do it to you? The war of all against all? The Leviathan state? Was that what happened to Man without a sense of civilization, or without religious injunctions or a moral compass to nurture and support a basic sense of decency for all living things?

Civilization. Was my father right? Was that Man's collective effort to mitigate the hostile effects of Man's nature? Was civilization essential to protect man from his own worst instincts? And did civilization need a moral and just religion to give it a benign conscience?

The lives of Campbell and Sekulovich were now contending with different forces. It was, for the time being, no longer man against man; it was now man against nature.

They followed the stream in the direction of its flow until they saw what they thought were Dit's fresh, barefoot tracks in the mud along the stream and decided to cross to the other side hoping that the rains and the river crossing would make tracking them difficult. They were not used to the current which was now swifter with the monsoon rain, and they both slipped and fell crossing the swollen stream. When they got to the far side they were covered with leeches, and took time to pull them off each other and washed themselves as best they could to stop the blood flow.

The two escapees spent the night under a lean-to that they had made, but they were wet and chilled to the bone. Sekulovich wore a threadbare khaki flight suit, and Campbell wore the lightweight green utilities that he had changed into from his nomex flight suit the morning after his ejection. They snuggled next to each other, at times holding each, to keep warm. This was something they would do virtually every night together. At first light they pulled down the lean-to and dispersed the branches and leaves as best they could to disguise their trail from the Laotians who were expert trackers.

The both slept fitfully and Campbell lay awake, shivering and thinking about Bundit. Bundit's betrayal was shocking, but he was equally shocked by Sekulovich's rapid fire killing. *Was it self-defense or murder?* But he never spoke to Sekulovich about it.

At daybreak Sekulovich asked, "We need to rethink Plan B, Ti. Whad-dya think?"

"I concur. We are now prisoners of the jungle, and without sunlight to make a shadow, we have no sense of direction except I believe all the streams and rivers drain towards the Mekong River which separates Thailand from Laos and flows south."

"Step one is to put distance between us and the compound. The Pathet Lao will be looking for us."

"Yeah, I agree with that. Mike, I would like to stay near the streams and look for a river. Stay where we can signal aircraft and be seen from the air, while working our way south and west."

"That makes sense," replied Sekulovich. "But I'm weak; weaker than you are. I've been a captive longer. We need to find a boat or build a raft. I can't make Thailand 50 to 70 miles away on foot."

"We'll make it, Mike. We'll make it."

Two days later Sekulovich began another bout of yellow fever. The fever began about the time that they found a boat and a pole. Sekulovich had abandoned carrying the heavy Thompson submachine gun in the river the day before, but Cannon kept the lighter carbine, more, he hoped, for hunting purposes than for self-defense. They shot a lizard the day before and after skinning it, they ate it raw. With the rain, there also came a bloom of mosquitoes and flies, and they were both badly bitten.

Patches of occasional sunshine came through the cloud ceiling. The nights passed with showers and periods of clear weather, and they could hear aircraft passing overhead both day and night, but they did not have conditions where they could signal aircraft. Ironically, the bombing halt

brought more sorties below the 19th parallel and over Laos, over their position, than would have been the case if Operation Rolling Thunder were
being prosecuted as before.

Campbell examined Sekulovich. His skin and the whites of his eyes
were yellow, and he was extremely feverish and was perspiring profusely.
He complained of aches and pains as Campbell helped him into the middle
of the small wooden boat.

They were drifting down a wide, shallow stream, perhaps as wide as a
football field is long, along what was primarily an agricultural area. There
were trees and growth along the river, but the jungle was lacking. They
could make out huts of a small village, but they seemed to pass the village
safely without provoking curiosity. About a mile downstream, the water-
way began to narrow, and the current picked up speed. Sekulovich was
passing into and out of delirium and kept asking for water. Campbell
poled the boat to the side opposite from the last village, and gave Sekulovich some water to drink from a bamboo cup that they had brought with
them in Sekulovich's rucksack.

Sekulovich's hands were shaking, and Campbell had to hold his head
up with one hand and steady the cup with the other for Sekulovich to
drink. Sekulovich sipped about half a cup, not enough to replace the fluids
he was losing through perspiration, when he became delirious again.
Campbell waited a while for Sekulovich to sip some more water and managed to get a cup of water in him. He also wetted down Sekulovich's fray-
ing clothing with river water to cool him down and reduce the need for
perspiration. If they weren't so near the village, he would have brought
Sekulovich ashore and stopped for the day, but he thought it risky, so he
pressed on with Sekulovich in the boat intermittently thinking of Bundit.

The river narrowed further with a commensurate increase in current,
and Campbell was pleased with their rate of travel. However, Sekulovich's
condition worsened, and he vomited and began to cough mucus and blood
which distracted Campbell, and he did not heed an increasing rumbling,
roaring sound.

A torrent of rain swept over them, drenching them, and reducing visibility. The rain made a plinking sound and muffled other sounds as the
drops pelted the river water. Through the din Campbell heard a new sound
but could not identify it. Finally he recognized it as the roar of a cascade,
and he tried to get the boat ashore. But he lacked the strength to pole the
boat against the current. He only succeeded in making matters worse as
the boat turned broadside to the current. The roaring sound of the cascade

grew louder through the rain. Then the boat rolled over the cascade and sent the two men and the boat tumbling over the waterfall and into a deep pool below the falls.

The wooden boat inverted and quickly floated downstream. Campbell still had his rucksack and carbine on his back, and he held his breath and waited for the flow of the stream to carry him away from the falls and the deep pool at the foot of the falls. His lungs were bursting, and he realized he wasn't very buoyant with his loss of weight and the six or seven pounds of the carbine although the rucksack initially trapped air and helped bring him to the surface. His feet touched some boulders, and he was able to get a gulp of air. Working diagonally with the current, he was able to get ashore. He crawled up the side of the riverbank totally exhausted and sucking air heavily.

When Campbell recovered his breath, he sat up and began looking for Sekulovich. But there were no immediate signs of him. He stood up and removed the carbine and rucksack and searched the river rapids with his eyes. He saw that they were now in a canyon and the river was lined with stones and river run gravel, and, here and there, large boulders, and downstream the green jungle again crowded the riverbank. He saw the boat inverted about 60 yards downstream wedged between some rocks. Then he searched back upstream until he thought he saw Sekulovich in his khaki flight suit and with his rucksack, face down, his body caught up in the shallow rapids.

He picked up the carbine and the rucksack and carried them with one hand and made his way down the riverbank towards the boat and towards what he thought might be Sekulovich, but he saw no signs of movement. When he was abreast what, by now he was pretty sure, what he feared, he set down the carbine and rucksack and waded towards Sekulovich. When he got to Sekulovich, he managed to roll him over. It took all of his remaining strength to do so, and he looked into Sekulovich's yellow face, swollen by mosquito bites, and into his yellow eyes, and he felt for his carotid artery for a pulse.

Michael S. Sekulovich, Missoula, Montana, was dead. From what cause it did seem to matter—beatings, malnourishment, disease, drowning, exhaustion.

"Lord Jesus Christ, have mercy on Thy servant, Michael Sukulovich. May perpetual light shine upon him." Campbell repeated the prayer, and tears ran from his eyes as he tried to bring Sekulovich's body ashore, and again he used the current to help him move diagonally with the current. It took the rest of the day to get Sekulovich ashore and two body lengths up the riverbank. He took several breaks to regather his strength as he pulled the dead weight of Sekulovich's body, which was probably no more than 95 pounds soaking wet. Campbell then propped himself in the shade of some nearby boulders and with the stainless mirror in his hands, fell asleep from exhaustion. He remained there until dawn shivering throughout the night.

He slept through several passing rain showers, as exhaustion seemed more and more to overcome him, but at dawn the sun broke out, and the low sun angle awakened him, and it was shining directly at him. He wasn't sure that he was fully conscious, but he was conscious of his weakness. He had not recovered from pulling Sekulovich ashore which required great expenditure of energy and made him dizzy and badly weakened him even though that had occurred many hours ago. He thought he heard several aircraft and began reflecting the sunlight with the stainless mirror. He wasn't sure which direction, and he tried all reasonable points of the compass and angles. The aircraft seemed to be going east. He thought it might be an outbound strike from Thailand.

"I'm so alone, Jesus, Lord, help me." He got up and made his way to Sekulovich and said several prayers over him and concluded with the 23rd Psalm. It was the best that he could do for his friend. Partly out of hope and partly out of despair, he began searching for stones and rocks, and in six-foot letters he wrote out S-O-S in a space on the riverbank between where Sekulovich's corpse lay and the boulders where he sat. A section of jet aircraft were returning, and he could just make them out between the clouds. They were fairly high to conserve fuel, but he had a good chance to signal them. Again he reflected the sunlight in the general direction of the aircraft, which he thought were F-4 Phantoms, but they flew on towards the setting sun without any indication that they had seen him.

Once again an angry Campbell challenged God out loud. "How can I be made to die like this? I have tried to be righteous for the sake of being righteous. The notion, taught to me by my mother, was perversely suggested by the Adversary. Not righteousness for reward in heaven, but virtue for the sake of virtue. What kind of love is this? What kind of justice is this? To what purpose does our suffering," looking over at Sekulovich, "serve?"

He had killed to live, but now he was on the verge of complete exhaustion, a kind of death by exhaustion, and believing that he was unable to continue the struggle. He was too weak to go on alone, and he sensed that his last choice was dying here with Sekulovich or maybe a mile or two down the river and dying alone. In his solitary condition, he allowed a momentary sentiment and decided that they should not die alone.

Nevertheless, he looked into his rucksack and began to eat more of the remaining uncooked, moldy rice. The rice was rotting and had an unhealthy odor, and the maggots he considered a source of protein. It had been submerged at least three times since they escaped and bore a tinge of treated canvas flavoring. His state of exhaustion was extreme, nevertheless each kernel of rice seemed to offer a small, incremental extension of life, although the act of eating seemed to take all of his strength. He lapsed into sleep.

He awoke several times shivering in the night. It rained again, and then it cleared, and again he thought he heard airplanes overhead. But, he fell asleep exhausted and slept until the sun rose well-above the horizon. He got up slowly. His body ached everywhere and walked towards Sekulovich and saw that his body was bloating, and it was covered with worms, flies and insects. And the stench was heavy. Campbell wondered if he had the energy to cover Sekulovich with rocks from the riverbed, but he was very fatigued, and one or two bloating corpses on a Laotian riverbank didn't seem, under the circumstances, to matter to him.

Campbell believed that he was probably near the end of his life. He ruminated morbidly on the phrase from Job, *"The Lord giveth, and the Lord taketh away,"* but Campbell still continued to do what was necessary to live. He went down and bathed in the river and pulled three leeches from his legs. He was splashing water around when he thought he heard the sounds of an aircraft coming towards him. He stopped and listened. It was an aircraft—propeller driven, low. Campbell heard the sounds grow louder and now he could see the aircraft coming up the river, and he began weakly waving his arms. He could see the pilot as the plane, a Skyraider, passed down the opposite side of the river quite low, and he thought he saw the pilot's face. But the plane continued up the river towards the cascade. Campbell thought he could hear another propeller-driven plane up higher. *A wing man.* Now he could see the second Skyraider, and it appeared to climb for altitude and pull off to the west.

"Sandy 31, Sandy 25." The low flier was calling his wingman above. "Go ahead."

"I think I saw a guy in green fatigues waving at me. SOS was laid out in rocks on the riverbank. Maybe another man with him. Call Crown and let's check it out." Crown was a US Air Force C-130 Hercules aircraft configured specifically to command and control search and rescue missions. They worked with A-1H Sandy and with Jolly Green helicopters in a search and rescue team. Crown could also call in additional resources to effect a rescue.

"Roger, break, Crown, Sandy 31,"

"Go ahead, 31."

"Do we have anybody down around my current position?" Crown was holding Sandy 31 on his radar and could determine his location

"Wait out." After several minutes, Crown came back. "Sandy 31, negative. No air force, navy, or army aircraft down in your area for the last several months."

"Crown, we had a brief this morning of possible mirror flashes from two Fox-4s in this area."

"Sandy 31. Yeah, we have that report. Our intel guys think it is a set up for a trap."

"Roger, 31 copies, break, 25 did you copy?"

"Thought I heard, 'negative,' "

"Ay-firm. Intel thinks it may be a Pathet Lao trap."

"Roger. Just think I'll go back for another look." Sandy 25 reversed course and flew back down the middle of the river. The pilot could clearly see a man waving in green utilities, and the SOS in rocks and stones, the body of a second man, and upstream, the boat. He waved to Campbell as he flew by trying not to give away Campbell's location. Campbell saw the pilot wave and saw the Skyraider's US Air Force markings, external fuel tank and bomb racks loaded with olive green ordnance.

"Sandy 31, this is 25, can't tell if this guy is American or Asian, but I think we ought try and get this guy. Let's search the area for troops."

"Crown, Sandy 25 recommends that we try and recover two souls. 25 and 31 will search the area for troops."

Crown responded with two clicks of his microphone.

Several minutes later Campbell could hear the sounds of detonations in the distance to the southwest where the river seemed to meander, and then there was silence. "Jesus, Lord save me."

"Crown, this is 25. We engaged troops with Mark 81s, about a company, about four to six clicks south of our guy. They could be after our guy, over."

"Crown roger. Or the Papa Limas are part of the trap."

"Crown, this is Sandy 25. Pursue authorization all the way to Saigon if necessary. Advise them, pilot, Sandy 25, himself, personally and urgently requests recovery attempt." Sandy 25 was a lieutenant colonel and commander of 602nd Special Operations Squadron based at NKP.

"Roger, Sandy, Wilco, your personal and urgent request, break, interrogative your ordnance?"

"We're down to guns."

"Roger, we'll tee up some ResCap." The two Sandy A-1s remained in the area searching for troops but avoided passing over Campbell's position.

Down on the ground, Campbell's anxiety rose, and he feared he was being abandoned. He asked himself what more could he do. Campbell began to gather rocks again. He was getting dizzy. Every time he bent over to pick up rocks, when he stood up, he became progressively more dizzy. He had completed "VA" when he was returning with rocks, he became very dizzy and fell, striking his head on the rocks along the river. Campbell lay there breathing heavily with blood rushing from his temple.

"Sandy 25, Crown."

"Sandy 25."

"Negative your request. No pick up attempt."

Campbell struggled to his feet. He slowly made it up the riverbank and added a "2" and returned down the riverbank to get more rocks.

"Crown, Sandy 25, is going down for one more look."

"Sandy 25, roger, break, Panther is flying and is diverting two Alpha-4s configured for armed recce, call sign, Jury."

"Roger. Do we have an ETA?"

"10 to 12 minutes."

Sandy 25 responded with two clicks of his microphone and turned back to fly north towards the cascade.

"25, 31, we have troops running north. Couple, three squads. Saw them in a break in the trail before they got under the jungle canopy. At least 25 to 30 troops. Could be after our man."

"Roger, stay high. Let's not give this guy away." Sandy 25 flew north and dropped down as low as he could. As the flight leader and squadron commander, he preferred to take the risk of flying low. He banked sharply at a bend in the river and then leveled flying northward up the stream. Now he saw a figure bending over on the riverbank. Campbell stood up and began waving his arms madly until he got dizzy. "Jesus Lord, please save me, save me, save me, Lord, Jesus."

Sandy 25 flew up the stream and roared past Campbell, then he pulled up and banked to his left before reversing his course, performing a 90-270 degree turn and coming back the long way around to his reciprocal heading. He was higher now, and had a better angle of deflection. He also kept his right wing low as he continued his turn to better see the ground.

"Crown, 25."

"Go ahead, 25."

"Holy shit, our guy has just used more rocks to add victor alpha two three, VA- 23. That's navy isn't it for attack squadron. This guy is ours."

Tommie Jack Bolton was pilot in command of US Navy, Big Mother 507, an HH-3, combat search and rescue helicopter, sitting on the ground and monitoring the air force SAR frequency. Lieutenant Bolton came from the wrong side of the tracks in Youngstown, Ohio. He was cocky and determined to make a success of himself and persuaded an elderly congresswoman to appoint him to the US Naval Academy. He had the right mixture of aggressiveness, resourcefulness and instinct for survival learned in the schoolyards of a tough steel town to be a SAR pilot.

"Crown, this is Big Mother 507. We've heard enough. We're crankin' up and comin' in."

"Big Mother 507, we are not authorized to bring you in." Bolton climbed straight up from his location in southern Quang Tri province. At 3500 feet on the way to 4000 feet he called the air force C-130 command and control ship.

"Crown, 507 squawking ident, requesting vector," and Bolton started heading southwest with his co-pilot, gunner and corpsman. There was no answer. "Crown, juliet foxtrot bravo, give us a vector now!" Several tens of seconds later Crown came back.

"245 at 45."

"507, roger. What was so damn hard about that?"

"Sandy 25, Jury 208 and 202 are with you for about 30 minutes. Mark 82s and rockeyes."

"Roger, Jury 208. Interrogative, does Victor Alpha two three, mean anything to you?"

"Vee Ay two three, yeah, that's a sister squadron from Panther, break, Jury 202, didn't Cocktail go down in Laos, taken prisoner?"

"Ay-firm, Operation Igloo White."

"Sandy 25, he could be one of ours," added Jury 208. "Jury 202, call Panther Strike, and give 'em a sitrep."

"Click, click."

"Sandy 25, Sandy 31. I see another break in the canopy. I'm dropping to a lower orbit for guns."

"Sandy 25, Big Mother 507 will be on scene in 15 minutes."

"Roger, 507, call me when on scene."

"507, click, click."

Campbell could now hear the sounds of gunfire and see Sandy 31 engage the Pathet Lao troops with 20 millimeter guns downstream on the opposite side of the riverbank. He could also hear the pop, pop, pop, sporadic return fire from the ground at Sandy 31. He stepped back to the boulder where he left the carbine and the rucksack. He replaced his nearly spent magazine, fumbling in his weakness, with a fresh magazine containing 15 rounds.

"Sandy 25, 31 placed a white smoke north of the Papa Lima before engaging with 20 mike mike."

"Roger 31, have your smoke in view, break, Jury 208, I need you now."

"Jury 208."

"Head south down the axis of the river. 50 yards north of the smoke, give me a string of three mark 82s."

"208 on the way in."

"Roger 208, then reverse heading and drop three more about 100 yards south of the smoke."

"208, wilco." Jury 208 headed down the river in a shallow dive at 3500 feet AGL, saw the smoke, adjusted his course and pipper, and dropped three, 500 pound bombs in a string salvo. He then pulled off left and climbed before coming back around 270 degrees to rollout heading north. Again he adjusted his flight and bomb sight and dropped a second string of bombs south of the smoke.

"Sandy 25, Jury 202, is back with you and ready for a run. Break, Panther is sending four Alpha-4 Lawcases on the next launch, over."

"Jury 202, Sandy 25, roger that. Do you have a tally on the smoke?"

"Jury 202, roger."

"Single run, double salvo, string of three mark 82s. Salvo one on the smoke. Salvo two 50 yards south."

"Jury 202, is in.

"Sandy 25, Big Mother 507, where are you?"

"Standing by."

"Let's try and get you in now."

"Roger, what are the surface winds?"

"Sandy 25, Jury 202 is out. Heavy rain shower moving in."

"You copy the weather, 507?"

"Roger. Looks like winds are from the northwest until that cell comes through. We'll come in from the northeast and hover northwest."

Campbell could hear the chop, chop, chop of the helicopter. Then he saw the Big Mother coming in and turn starboard to face the northwest in a hover over him and also exposing a beam aspect towards the Pathet Lao troops. He could see the penetrator on the hoist coming down. The noise of the rotor blades was disorienting. The prop wash was blowing his matted hair around and kicking up debris and driving rain and wet sand into his eyes.

"Sandy 25, somebody is hammering us. We took several rounds. Light arms. We're aborting." Bolton broke his hover and pulled off to the right. "Think we saw a handful of troops in the tree line along the riverbank."

"Jury 208, 202. Need those rockeyes. I'll give you a smoke." Sandy 25 now dove low over Campbell's position and fired a rocket placing a smoke in the tree line on the opposite riverbank. Jury 208 approached from the west then banked to the right and dropped his cluster bombs on the second smoke.

"That should put their heads down."

"Roger 208, 507, let's give it another try. I'll be in trail behind you with guns and keep their heads down. 31 tee up for a run behind me."

"Click, click."

"507, we're on the way back in. We have a tally on you, 25." The helicopter was in the lead with the two Skyraiders spaced to his seven o'clock position in a loose echelon-left formation ready to suppress ground fire with their guns.

Campbell heard the helicopter approaching again. He was weak and dizzy but managed to move from the position of cover that he had taken behind the boulders. He could see the Big Mother approaching and settle into a hover over him. Again the debris, sand and driven rain swirled around him stinging his eyes and partially blinding him. And the sound of the engines and rotor blades again tended to disorient him. The penetrator came down. It seemed to take forever to descend to him. Driving rain came across the river, and just as he was about to grasp the penetrator, a strong gust of wind blew the penetrator on the hoist just out of reach. The penetrator was swinging around as Big Mother sat in her hover. Its oscillation would not be significant to a healthy man, but Campbell was dizzy and tried to grasp the penetrator several times in his weakened condition.

Finally he caught the cable to the heavy, wet penetrator as it bounced along the riverbank and managed to get a paddle down. His arms were extremely tired and heavy, and he was dizzy and gasping for breath with the flailing around and exertion. Rain lashed over his face, and blood flowed from his recent head wound, and the rain was whipped into a cyclone by the helicopter blades.

Both Sandy's rolled in with guns, first one, then the other, while Bolton kept 507 in a hover. "Sandy 25 is out; 31 come in. Jury 208, can you give us some suppression runs with guns?"

"Jury 208, wilco."

Campbell fell down on his knees in exhaustion. *You'll find dying is easy.* He was too weak to get on the penetrator. *Living is very hard.* Campbell was dizzy and unsteady, but, by force of will, he managed to rise again and get to his feet.

Lt. Bolton peered through the driving rain and could see Campbell struggling on the ground, and he brought the hoist up while he remained in the hover. "No, no! Do not forsake me!" cried Campbell. He sank to his knees in dismay as he saw the hoist take up the penetrator and pangs of anxiety from fear of abandonment passed through him.

Over the intercom, Bolton spoke to his corpsman. "Johnson, let's go down and get him."

"Aye, aye, sir." The corpsman took his position on the slippery, wet penetrator and was lowered to Campbell. When he got to Campbell, he slid off the two paddle seats that he had straddled with his legs and reached for Campbell. Campbell was unsteady on his feet, while Johnson held him up. He managed to get Campbell seated on one paddle in the driving rain, but Campbell slipped off the paddle and fell to the ground crying in frustration. Campbell was virtually dead weight as Johnson struggled to get Campbell to his feet and seated on two paddles. This time he placed Campbell's hands on the hoist, and Campbell held onto the hoist with a death grip.

Jury 202 roared by with both cannons firing in the vicinity of the smoke. Johnson ran over to Sekulovich, and saw from his condition that he had been dead for several days. He also saw the M1 carbine, grabbed it, cleared the weapon and put the safety on and slung it over his shoulder. Johnson pointed at Sekulovich and gave a thumbs-down signal to the co-pilot on the left side of the helicopter. When he reached the penetrator, he sat on the paddle behind Campbell and signaled to Bolton to take them up.

At the helicopter door, the gunner was shocked by the wet, emaciated, underweight appearance of a bearded man and pulled Campbell into the helicopter. Campbell smelled badly. His skin was red, scaly, and covered with sores. Blood flowed from the superficial scrape in his scalp. His beard was long and his hair thoroughly matted. It was virtually the skeleton of a human being who clung to the gunner's thigh, crying. "Oh, my God, I'm alive! I'm alive! Thank you, Lord Jesus, I'm alive!"

Epilogue

After ten and a half months *USS Ticonderoga* was delayed one more day
by fog in the San Clemente channel before returning to NAS North Island
in Coronado, CA on September 19, 1968. She remained for five days and
then proceeded to Long Beach Naval Shipyard for modifications to handle
the A-7 Corsair. In February 1969, she sortied for WestPac for another 10
month deployment.

Michael Sekulovich's body was recovered by a helicopter assault team
of US Army Rangers and was returned to his parents in Missoula, Montana, where he was properly buried. Red Browne's remains were never recovered.

Robert Cannon married Laetitia Martin, and they had two children. After business school, he joined an investment banking firm on Wall Street,
was a fund raiser for the Republican Party, and subsequently was appointed Under Secretary of the Navy during the time of Operation Desert
Storm. Based on his naval experience as a junior officer he firmly believes
that weakness invites aggression but counsels judicious application of
military power. He is a forceful advocate for the notion of a just war as
exemplified by the First Iraq War.

Laetitia Martin Cannon received her doctorate from Columbia University and joined the curator's staff at The Hispanic Society in New York
City and is an advisor to the National Gallery for 19th and 20th century
Spanish art. She continues to be a moral force and a champion for the un-
derdog with her husband.

The Rev. Ogilvy Osborne resigned from active duty in the US Naval
Reserve and returned to Manchester, MA, where he and Fiona lived until
he died several years later. He served on the Episcopal Diocesan staff, and
his ministry was dedicated to working with homeless veterans and fellow
sufferers of Major Depression Disorder and Post Traumatic Stress Disorder.

After a year of recovery from various parasites, diseases and surgeries
in naval hospitals, Lt. Augustine Campbell felt closer to God than ever
before and became what he had not been before, a scholar, and entered
Union Theological Seminary and earned a Doctor of Divinity. He and his
wife have two adopted Vietnamese children, and he is pastor of a large
Presbyterian church in Bryn Mawr, PA. The Reverend Doctor Campbell
came to believe that his suffering through two wars was God's way of call-

ing him to dedicate his life to world peace. Today he serves as a member of the Independent Monitoring Committee for peace in Northern Ireland.

Beebe Byrnes received her doctorate from Georgetown University and became an expert on nuclear disarmament and assisted in the Strategic Arms Limitation negotiations with the Soviet Union. She married a professor from Brown University and currently teaches at the US Naval War College, Newport, RI, and consults for the Central Intelligence Agency.

Robert Pebbles became a Vice Admiral and served as Commanding Officer of the US Sixth Fleet in the Mediterranean and as Commander in Chief, US Naval Forces, Europe, before retiring from active service. He and Robert Cannon remained friends, and he is god parent to Dr. Robert Cannon, Jr., who is a resident transplant surgeon at Baylor Methodist Hospital, Houston, TX.

Ned Chase went to Yale Law School and is a partner in a prestigious Boston law firm and serves on the boards of several charitable institutions. A widower, his wife died of breast cancer in her early 50s, together, they had two children. A son serves in the US Department of State and a daughter became head of a private girl's school.

Luis Reposa became a Rear Admiral and was the first non-aviator since Admiral Spruance to command a battle group. His flagship was the nuclear-powered, *USS Dwight D. Eisenhower* CVN-69. His son and daughter are both serving officers in the US Navy.

Colonel Charles Donigan, USMC (ret.) successfully raised funds to endow a prize at Boston College in memory of Father Seamus Sean Shea, S.J., awarded to that alumna/alumnus who most exemplifies selfless service under personally hazardous conditions.

Captain Tarrant and his wife retired to Austin, Texas, where he worked for a defense contractor and served as an elder in his church until he was killed in an auto accident by a drunk driver.

Professor John Meaney became Provost of Columbia University and played a key role in negotiating an end to the student riots and occupation of university buildings in 1968. He loyally served his alma mater and the country that he loved until he died in 1973 at the age of 70.

The end.

Afterword

I am often asked what parts of my novels are autobiographical, imagined, or based on true events. My style of journalistic fiction depends heavily on documented events and my personal experience, but that still allows plenty of opportunity to apply imagination and create fiction within the limits of verisimilitude.

When Herman Wouk finished *The Caine Mutiny*, he made a special effort to make it abundantly clear that there never was a ship called *USS Caine*, nor that there ever was a mutiny nor a court-martial related to the *Caine*. I think journalistic fiction mandates a similar declaration.

The opening paragraphs of *Down in Laos* are based on a true account of the Toktong Pass near the Chosin Reservoir. Two Medals of Honor were awarded to members of Fox Company—Pvt. Hector Cafferata, USMCR, and Captain William Barber, USMC, the company commander. This company of 220 men held off a Chinese Regiment, a force of 1400 men, for six days, killing over 1000 enemy soldiers.

The role of a military chaplain is fraught with many moral, ethical, and political conflicts, and this was never more true than during the Vietnam War when they were often savaged by protestors from their respective faiths back home. I chose a similar, non-political episode that occurred to at least one Roman Catholic army chaplain who was ordered not to go to the front line to illustrate these conflicts and the physical and moral courage that many chaplains demonstrated to serve the spiritual needs of Americans at war.

In Chapter 2, the conflict on *Essex* helm was wholly imaginary, but it is consistent with the emotional turmoil that people experience when going through divorce. An example of such, not included in *Down in Laos*, occurred when a lieutenant commander, pilot, on *Ticonderoga's* last day on Yankee Station, after six line periods and well-over a two hundred combat missions, failed to respond to a catapult shot and crashed in front of the ship and was killed. Six weeks earlier he received documents indicating that he was being sued for divorce. Whether it was accidental or deliberate could never be determined.

I regret to say the lack of courage to stay on the helm by a senior lieutenant occurred in fact, but the response by the Officer of the Deck was entirely professional. References to Captain Dixie Kiefer are all fact.

The incident based on the *USS Fletcher's* casualty while screening *Ticonderoga* in a serious thunderstorm while recovering aircraft is true.

Operation Formation Star, in response to the seizure of *Pueblo*, is fact. The preparation and ultimate cancellation of the strike as told here is the best of my recollection of the event. So, too, was my recollection of Operation Niagara, the aviation response to the Battle of Khe Sanh as stood up by the US Navy and the US Air Force.

The prisoner-of-war experience of my fictional character, Lt. Ti Campbell, was based on true stories, testimonies, investigations and reports of the treatment of American prisoners of war while held captive in Laos, and North and South Vietnam. The physical environments varied widely from individuals who were held in tiger cages, to small groups who were held in primitive POW camps, to relatively larger groups detained in prisons. However, the common denominator was always the same— continuous effort to obtain false confessions by means of beatings, torture, malnutrition, disease, isolation and exhaustion.

Many POWs perished in captivity from various causes under extreme conditions. However, it seems true that the prisoners of war who survived were religious and had experienced a period of very high stress in their prior lives. This is the theory behind SERE, a training program of extreme stress and abuse, and in some cases, questionable brutality, attended by all navy pilots. I reflected this notion quite deliberately when the reader can realistically presume that Ti Campbell was subjected to extreme stress as a young boy in Korea during the war. So, too, was he exposed to the many American military personnel and a natural familiarization with small arms during and after the war.

One of the worst POW cases which I encountered in my research, was the case of a flight surgeon who had been held captive for several years and had endured all of the above in the extreme to extract a false confession. At one time he was forbidden to practice medicine for months and was made to clean latrines. He withstood all of these efforts to obtain a confession, until, later, at another prison, he was permitted to practice medicine but was not given basic medicines to heal fellow Americans who were dying from diseases and infections. Finally, he was presented with a Hobbesian choice—barter his false confession for a meager supply of antibiotics to save the lives of others.

True stories like these need to told, even those that might be referred to as journalistic fiction.

The Indo-China Theater

About the Author

Francis J. Partel, Jr., better known as Frank, says he "was educated at Columbia University and in the Gulf of Tonkin with the United States Navy." Serving in *USS Ticonderoga*, Attack Carrier 14, as a junior officer, he simultaneously held down assignments as Office of the Deck, as a Combat Information Center Watch Officer, and as one of the ship's two Strike Controllers to gain a rich and unique perspective of aircraft carrier operations during the Vietnam War. His perspective spans from the surface ships that screen the formation, to the oilers, ammunition and stores ships which replenish the task group, to the squadrons which courageously flew the missions to deliver ordnance on the target. Given the specialization of skills and the complexity of carrier organization in the modern navy, and later as a civilian pilot, few writers of modern naval fiction have had the experience to write with Mr. Partel's authority and authenticity on the subject.

He received his commission as an Ensign after attending US Naval Officer's Candidate School, Newport, RI, and served in aircraft carriers on active duty from October 1965 until December 1968.

Prior to college, he graduated from Northfield Mount Hermon School, and after active duty he completed his MBA at Columbia University on the GI Bill. He grew up in Hoboken, NJ, and lived most of his adult life in lower Fairfield County, CT. He was a senior division and group executive with Citicorp, American Express, and Chase Manhattan Bank in New York City before retiring from US Bancorp in Minneapolis. For five years he taught as an Adjunct Associate Professor in the MBA program at Stern School of Business, New York University. Mr. Partel is also co-holder of US Patent 7,624,068. When he isn't writing he can be found fishing, sailing, or playing golf or tennis. He is married and resides in Vero Beach, FL, and summers on Chappaquiddick Island, Martha's Vineyard.

Mr. Partel integrates thorough research and historical accuracy with fictitious story-telling to create his own unique genre of literature which has been referred to as *journalistic fiction*.

His first work of fiction, *A Wound in the Mind, The Court-Martial of Lance Corporal Cachora, USMC*, was published in 2009. *The Chess Players, A Novel of the Cold War at Sea,* his first full-length novel, followed in 2011. *Down in Laos, Heroism and Inspiration during the Vietnam War* is his third novel.

CPSIA information can be obtained at www.ICGtesting.com
Printed in the USA
BVOW07*0034271214

379907BV00001B/1/P